Being close to her Jac and talking to him had seemed so natural. It had given her that extra bit of determination she needed to carry out the task of taking what was rightfully hers. Hopes of winning back his father, Jack, her ex-lover, hadn't been far from her mind when she first came up with her plan to return to Stepney. She might just be able to kill two birds with one stone.

It wasn't going to be easy, and Patsy wasn't so soft as to imagine otherwise. Almost four years had passed since she handed Jac over and the Armstrongs had not been slow in securing proper adoption papers. The courts would hardly reverse all of that just because Patsy's reason for giving up Jac had gone away. Tom – the traitor who had refused to take on someone else's bastard and then just a couple of years later had created one of his own with a young nurse.

She would deal with him later . . .

'She brings the East End to life' *Barbara Windsor*

'Unbridled passions run riot' *Daily Mail*

'A vivid evocation of a way of life' *East Anglian Daily Times*

*About the author*

Sally Worboyes was born and grew up in Stepney with four brothers and a sister. She now lives in Norfolk with her husband and three children. She has written several plays broadcast on Radio 4, and has adapted her own play and novel, WILD HOPS, as a musical, THE HOP-PICKERS. Already an established writer, Sally Worboyes continues her brilliant East End sagas to which she brings some of the raw history of her own family background.

SALLY WORBOYES

# The Dinner Lady

**CORONET BOOKS**
Hodder & Stoughton

First published in Great Britain in 1996 by Headline
This edition published in 2003 by Hodder and Stoughton
A division of Hodder Headline

A Coronet paperback

1 3 5 7 9 10 8 6 4 2

A CIP catalogue record for this title is available
from the British Library.

ISBN 0 340 81854 9

Printed and bound in Great Britain by
Mackays of Chatham Ltd, Chatham, Kent

Hodder and Stoughton
A division of Hodder Headline
338 Euston Road
London NW1 3BH

For my school teacher Kate Flenner and her husband
Ben, who helped so many of us when we were children
living in the East End.

# ACKNOWLEDGEMENTS

Although none of the characters in any of the books I have written so far are based on living persons, I would not have embarked upon *Wild Hops*, *Docker's Daughter*, or *The Dinner Lady* had I not been part of a world full of wonderful characters during my childhood and teens. I owe my thanks to those living in and around Stepney during my time there: 1946–1966. I shall never forget.

I would also like to thank the Bancroft Library who have not only helped by supplying me with vast amounts of information from their well-stocked research room, but also make me feel as though I still belong.

Discovering the publishing world has been a great new experience. Little did I know about the hard work that goes on behind the scenes. The team at Headline deserves much credit. Geraldine Cooke knows by instinct if a story is veering off course – her monolithic advice is always reassuring. My thanks also to: Kirsty Fowkes, Claire Scott and Jenny Page for their keen support.

Lastly, my family who are always there, slipping endless cups of coffee and plates of sandwiches through the small gap in the open doorway of my writing room. And my mother, sister, brothers and friends, who wait patiently for me to come up for air. Thanks again to Carol Butcher who helps to create the time for me to write.

# Chapter One

Patsy Hemmingway stepped off the train at King's Cross, and at once her breath was taken away by a surge of excitement that shot right through her. The buzz of London came flooding back. It was good to be in the city again. She had enjoyed the hustle and bustle of the capital and had been sorry to leave it behind when she returned to her home town, Leicester, seven years ago, in the autumn of 1959, when she was just pregnant with Jack Armstrong's son.

Sweeping her long ginger hair off her face, Patsy picked up her heavy suitcases and headed for the taxi rank. She knew exactly where she was going: to a furnished flat in Stepney, where she intended to keep her own company, distant from the world, until she had achieved the goal of winning back her six-year-old from his father, Jack – the spineless bastard she had failed to lure away from his family all those years ago.

Patsy pushed the face of Jack's attractive wife from her mind and went and stood in line with the commuters, waiting her turn for a black cab. Once again her old rival invaded her thoughts. The ever-increasing anger which she usually managed to suppress rose from the pit of her stomach. Not only had Laura Armstrong deprived Patsy of a life with the man she once loved, but she had also enjoyed the privilege, for the past four years, of acting as mother to Patsy's child. Handing little Jac over to that family was the worst deal she had ever made. Now it was Kay, Jack's seventeen-year-old daughter, who filled Patsy's mind: Kay, the freckle-faced natural blonde who had pleaded with her to let her parents adopt her half-brother. At least that was how Patsy recalled it.

Cursing herself for having allowed them all to bamboozle her, she willed the bitterness away and replaced it with a determination to see justice done. A smile spread across her face as she imagined the look of shock on the Armstrongs' faces when they would discover that little Jac had taken off with his real mother.

Suddenly aware of male attention, Patsy's face relaxed as she pushed her slim fingers through her wavy hair, thrilled that she could, at the age of thirty-two, catch the eye of younger men. She was wearing her emerald-green two-piece suit, navy shoes, and carried a matching handbag. Her long nails were painted flame red to match her lipstick. She knew she stood out in the crowd and loved it. Yes – it was good to be alive, Patsy told herself. Alive and well with everything to gain. Everything that was on offer she would grasp and squeeze until she had no further use for it. She would tip the balance for the unjust treatment she had received from the men in her life. Her latest lover had stood aloof when she brought up the subject of marriage, and had then slunk off into the night – never to be heard of again. She had something to thank him for though. It was because of him that Patsy Hemmingway was about to turn back the clock and begin all over again.

*The best lessons are learned through your failures* was something she had once been told and had never forgotten. Now Patsy had other things to look forward to. Other dreams to be made real.

'Stepney please, Jubilee Street. Do you know it?'

'Know it? I should say. I was born in Commercial Road, love. New to these parts, are yer?' The taxi driver checked his side-mirror and pulled out in front of an approaching car, defying it not to stop.

'I'm staying with a friend for a couple of weeks,' she lied offhandedly. Why should she tell the nosy bastard her business?

'I've bin trying to work out your accent. You're not from the North; and definitely not from Devon or Cornwall ... but you're not a Londoner either.' He looked at her through his rear mirror. 'Give us a clue then?'

'I'm the woman from nowhere.' She forced a smile and pulled out a paperback from her handbag. If the thick-skinned idiot still didn't realize that she had no intention of conversing with him, she would have to reduce herself to being rude, or honest, depending which way you looked at it.

'Traffic's a bit heavy in the City today, so I'll nip through the back-doubles. All right?'

Patsy raised an eyebrow. He was driving, not her. Why couldn't he just get on with it? She flicked through the pages of her book until she found where she had left off.

If she had caught the tone in the taxi driver's voice,

she would have known he was planning to take her for a ride.

But the fiery redhead wasn't as smart as she thought. The unfriendly bitch had put him down and for no reason. He had been trying to make her feel welcome. It was part of his daily routine. He would have enjoyed watching this one's expression through the mirror when he took the longest route with the heaviest traffic, but she seemed too wrapped up in her own thoughts to notice what was happening outside his cab.

Sighing, he did a quick left turn and decided to get her to her destination as soon as he could. He didn't want her in his motor. Didn't know why – but there it was. Instinct, some would say. He put it down to experience. He had had thousands of people in his taxi and had learned very quickly about the variety of the human race. This one was a cold-hearted bitch. Probably an only child who found that people outside her world didn't give a damn about her wants and needs.

Her presence reminded him of the time when his heater had packed up one bitterly cold winter. He felt a cold chill on the back of his neck.

Sitting on the bench under the shelter, watching the boys playing in the light rain, six-year-old Jac Armstrong shuddered as he recalled the day he first stepped into the playground of the Primary school. It had seemed more scary then. Like a castle where Dracula might have lived.

The smaller boy at the further end of the shelter, standing close to his mother and crying, caused Jac to

4

remember his own anxieties. It all came back to him, as fresh and clear as if it were happening all over again. Feeling safe and secure, now that he was no longer a new boy, Jac allowed the memory of his first morning at school to return. It would help pass the time while he waited for the bell to go.

Jac's first year in the Infants had been more fun than he expected. He thought that everyone had said he wouldn't have to work hard just to keep him quiet. But they had been right. Instead of having to spend the day doing sums, as he thought he would, the children were allowed to play with Plasticine, paint pictures and even learn how to knit on big silver-grey needles. His teacher, Mrs Way, told them a different story every day and he had loved learning to count with coloured wooden beads.

It wasn't until the third week that Jac had started to get bored. He needed to learn how to read so that he could choose his own story books from the library. Once Mrs Way had given in and set aside ten minutes each day to teach him, Jac was away. He had pestered his parents, Laura and Jack, and his sister Kay. He was constantly pointing out words and wanting to know what they meant and how to say them. It became apparent to all those around him that Jac had an inquiring mind and was quick to learn.

Christmas had been the best ever. It was like having it twice. At home *and* at school. His class, with the help of his teacher, had created their own nativity scene and the baby Jesus, which Jac had made from newspaper and paste, had been chosen from among five others.

Raising his eyes from the ground he stole another look at the new boy. He had stopped crying but was still hanging on to his mother's skirt.

This was the first time Jac had been left to wait for the bell. The rain had fallen quite heavily on the way to school and Laura's umbrella had blown inside out in the wind. She had had to return home to get another one. Her important position in Hammond's, in the fashion department, meant that she had to look smart and well groomed. All of this had been explained to her son, who now felt quite grown-up at being allowed to wait by himself.

Catching the eye of Patsy, who was sitting not far along on the bench, Jac smiled shyly back at her. She wasn't exactly a stranger. He had seen her before, he felt sure of it. So when Patsy Hemmingway moved up and sat next to him, he just thought she was being friendly. He expected she was someone's mother. Probably one of the boys playing football.

'Why do boys like to play in the rain?' she said, as if she wasn't really directing the question at Jac. He wasn't sure whether he was meant to answer. Feeling slightly uncomfortable, he pulled up his socks and feigned interest in a small hole which he had noticed that morning while getting dressed.

'They'll be soaked by the time the bell goes.' This time she smiled at him, admiring his mop of sandy-coloured hair.

'We're allowed to put our top clothes on the big radiator in the cloakrooms when it's raining.' He focused his eyes on some boys under the shelter who were flicking their bubble-gum cards up against the

6

wall. He glanced at her face when she wasn't looking. There was something about her voice that made him think he should know her. Maybe she lived in the flats too? On the top floor where he never went. That would account for him not seeing her very much. Just now and then perhaps, when she was coming down the stairs.

'I think you're very sensible staying under the shelter.' She was looking out now, the same as Jac, avoiding his eyes.

'My mum said I had to.'

'Ah.' Her tone conveyed her thoughts. She was suggesting he was a mummy's boy.

'I don't like football.' Jac scowled, setting the record straight. 'I'm not very good. And I don't like wet socks. We're not allowed to take them off and dry them on the radiator.' He didn't want anyone thinking he was wrapped in cotton wool, as his grandfather would say.

'I should think it would be a bit smelly if the boys were allowed to do that. All those sweaty feet.'

'Yes, it would.' Jac thought about it for a few seconds and started to giggle. Before very long they were both laughing. Then the bell went.

'In you go then.' Patsy spoke as if he were her charge.

Jac straightened his school cap. 'It's treacle sponge today,' he grinned, 'with custard.'

'Mind you wipe the corners of your mouth!' she called after him.

Stopping dead in his tracks, Jac stood with his back to her and then slowly turned. 'And the tip of my nose,' he recited.

'And the tip of your nose.'

As he ran up the steps, Jac wondered why he had said

that about his nose. He couldn't remember ever having said it before. But he felt sure he had heard it some-where – a very long time ago. A cold tingling sensation shot through his body and a song he couldn't quite grasp slipped in and out of his mind.

Watching Jac skip across the playground towards the entrance, Patsy's mind flashed back to the time when she had turned up unexpectedly with him at Jack and Laura's flat. For some reason she had imagined that her ex-lover and his small family were living in a high-rise block instead of a four-storey. Inside it was quite different from what she had pictured in her mind. Tasteful, comfortable, contemporary. She remembered it well. Black, grey and red patterned wallpaper against a white background, with a red carpet which almost fitted wall-to-wall.

Her passion would have been jealousy, had she not been besotted at the time by her lover Tom. He had persuaded her to take Jac away from the children's home where she had placed him and hand the boy over to the Armstrongs for adoption. It had been a perfect set-up until that exchange. Jac, at the age of two-and-a-half, had settled into Dr Barnardo's, which was a stone's throw from where she was living. It had satisfied Tom to have Jac out of the house, and meant that Patsy could pay him visits for a few hours on Sundays. But when Tom proposed marriage it came with a clause. She must break the tie with this other man's child. She didn't blame him. The last thing *she* would have wanted was the threat of being lumbered with another woman's offspring, had the situation been reversed.

What she hadn't envisaged at the time was that Tom

8

would welsh on her, change his mind about marriage. And then two years later leave her for someone else.

Once the playground was cleared of children and the last of the parents had gone, Patsy removed her damp headscarf and pushed it into her pocket. No need to hide her face and tell-tale red hair now: it was at least ten minutes since Laura Armstrong had walked out of the school gate and the chances of being seen by her were small. Opening her umbrella, Patsy made her way back to her new home, her rented flat in Jubilee Street.

Being close to her Jac and talking to him had seemed so natural. It had given her that extra bit of determination she needed to carry out the task of taking what was rightfully hers. Hopes of winning back his father, Jack, her ex-lover, hadn't been far from her mind when she first came up with her plan to return to Stepney. She just might be able to kill two birds with one stone.

It wasn't going to be easy, and Patsy wasn't so soft as to imagine otherwise. Almost four years had passed since she handed Jac over and the Armstrongs had not been slow in securing proper adoption papers. The courts would hardly reverse all of that just because Patsy's reason for giving up Jac had gone away. Tom – the traitor who had refused to take on someone else's bastard, and then just a couple of years later had created one of his own with a young nurse.

She would deal with him later on in life. He wouldn't get away scot-free. She would cut through his life when he was least expecting it.

Turning her key in the street door, she wondered which of the women she hated most. The attractive dark-haired Laura Armstrong, her rival from the past, or the blonde nurse who had stolen Tom away. Not that it mattered. She would relish disrupting *all* of their lives, the way they had fucked up hers. It would take time and careful planning, but time was something she had her fair share of. And as for planning, well, she couldn't really remember a time when she hadn't been doing that.

'Is that you, Patsy?' The nervous voice of her ageing landlady broke into her thoughts.

'Of course it's me!' Who else was there? 'I've got something to show you!' She hated raising her voice like that, but the old girl was nearly stone-deaf.

The varnished door to Mrs Simons's sitting room slowly opened and her deeply lined face showed that she was thankful for a bit of company. 'Something to show me? That's nice.'

Patsy pulled a magazine from her shoulder bag. 'I'm going to do it! I've made up my mind.'

Flicking through the glossy pages she found the feature on new hairstyles and began to read aloud. '"The new look for summer nineteen sixty-six! Short hair to match the short skirts."'

'Skirts are going to get *shorter*? Soon a handkerchief will do.' Esther Simons was enjoying the chance to talk to someone. 'They only just cover up their fannies.'

'What do you think then? Shall I go for the bob or the urchin?'

The last thing she was interested in was the old girl's opinion and had no intention of taking it, but Patsy needed to win her over, get her to believe that she had not only found a trustworthy tenant but a soul mate too.

'I think you should leave it be. It's lovely hair, you should be thankful.' Mrs Simons shrugged. 'But then again ... the urchin would suit your face, I think. But so would the bob.' She narrowed her eyes and studied her new tenant. 'Ha. You've such a pretty face ... I don't think it matters what you do to your hair. Have the bob.'

'Right. That settles it.' She was pleased to get that bit over with. She couldn't wait to get away. The smell of yesterday's fried fish was hanging in the air from the old woman's kitchen.

'It'll take me a couple of hours from start to finish, but I'll come and show you the results as soon as I've done.'

'*You're* going to cut it?' Her tired brown eyes widened. 'It's a joke?'

'Saving a few pounds is no joke.' Patsy knew that would impress the old hag. She was a Jew after all.

'I couldn't agree more, but all the same—'

'And what's more, I'm going to colour it myself too.' She grinned and winked at the bemused woman and stepped away from the doorway of the depressing front room.

'What colour?' she called up the stairs after her.

'Black!'

'I didn't hear!' She fiddled with her hearing aid. 'Say it again!'

'*Black!*' Patsy tried not to sound impatient. 'You'll love it!' She slammed her own flat door shut behind her, ending the conversation.

Leaning on the door, safe in her own world, Patsy clenched her fists, threw her head back and laughed out loud. At last the time was right for her to change her

11

appearance. A pair of glasses with plain lenses would be part of the finishing touches. After today, she would be able to move about in Stepney more freely, without the fear of being recognized by the Armstrongs, should their paths ever cross.

Standing in front of the green-tiled fireplace, Patsy admired her long red hair for the last time. She stroked her ginger eyebrows with a forefinger, and realized that transforming herself would take a little more effort than she had first imagined. She made a mental note to buy some black mascara. Every detail would have to be taken care of by the time she had secured the position of dinner lady at Jac's school. The appointment would suit her down to the ground. It would give her the opportunity to see her son daily and win him over, and would leave her afternoons and evenings free to continue her work as an usherette at the local cinema.

Patsy had her savings and was determined not to break into them, but gradually to increase the amount. She would need a substantial sum when the time came for her to take Jac away and settle comfortably in another part of the country – or the world for that matter. She would go on and on earning, stealing, saving, whatever it took, until she had enough to live on in the style she deserved. And she was, after all, still only in her early thirties, healthy and full of determination to end up with what she wanted. And God help anyone who tried to stop her! She was done with being the underdog. From now on, Patsy Hemmingway would reign supreme.

She had already decided to remain single and independent. Washing and ironing for a man was the last thing she wanted to do. She would have her relationships, but any man who came into her home would not sleep a night in her bed. Make love, yes. But never be there for breakfast. And her lovers would be carefully picked for their lack of intelligence and good financial status.

Jac, her only son and heir, would be groomed for a far better place than the East End. He would, one day, become a top man. Maybe a surgeon, or a lawyer? Or better still a man of the City, dealing in gold bullion and furs. He would be so thankful to his mother, his real mother, that all her needs and wants, when she was an old woman, would be taken care of. Once they were together again, they would never part. Of this she was certain.

With her hand mirror poised and the scissors ready, Patsy stepped back so that she was close to the looking-glass above the fireplace. Then with a steady hand she cut a straight line through her carrot-coloured hair, level with her small pointed chin.

As the thick locks dropped to the floor, she felt an overwhelming sense of well-being and optimism. A whole new world lay ahead, and the pure thrill of it was the best tonic she could have wished for. She felt as if she were shedding an old skin and a new Patsy Hemmingway was coming up for air.

As Jac tucked into his milk and biscuits, he stared into space and tried to remember where he had seen the woman under the shelter before. It puzzled him that she kept popping into his mind, and he didn't really know why he had painted a picture of her that day at school.

He hadn't remembered her face, just her ginger-biscuit eyes.

'I think I'm gonna have to lengthen these sleeves, Jac. Your arms looked as if they'd grown an inch longer when you put this blazer on this morning.' Laura brushed at a dried food stain.

Jac slowly nodded but he wasn't really listening, and Laura saw the familiar frown as his eyes glazed over.

'You look tired, love,' she said, hoping he would volunteer what was on his mind.

'Do gorillas eat people?' His thoughts were on to something else now.

'I don't think so. Why?'

'Grant Stock told me that his dad said they were using gorillas to fight in Vietnam.'

Managing to keep a straight face, Laura slipped his dark-green blazer on to a hanger. 'Guerrillas are not animals, love, they're men.' The words seemed to stick in her throat as she said them. How could she explain that gorillas were peaceful creatures, yet human beings called by a similar name were murdering each other?

'Sometimes soldiers are called guerrillas. It's spelt different from the furry kind Grant was referring to.' She hoped this would satisfy him and bring an end to his questions.

'Will Dad have to be a soldier and go there to get killed?'

'No. This country's not part of that war, thank God. Anyway, your dad's past all that. They want young strong men to fight their fights, not middle-aged oldies.' She managed a weak smile.

'Is Dad very old then?'

14

'Oh yeah. Forty-six. That's why he's going a bit thin on top.' She tousled Jac's hair. 'I can't see that happening to you. Your hair's as thick as wire.'

'So...' Jac was leaning back now, thinking hard again. 'If he does live till he's a hundred, like he says he will, he's not middle-aged, not yet. He's got to be fifty first.' A wide grin spread across his freckled face. He was pleased with himself for being able to work it out.

'All right, clever dick. Down you get. You'll miss the cartoons if you don't go and switch on.' Laura cupped his face, kissed the tip of his freckly nose and then hugged him.

Pulling away, Jac's eyes narrowed and his familiar frown appeared. 'Will you write a word down for me?'

'Depends what the word is.' She remembered when he requested the same from his aunt Liz. The word turned out to be vagina. When pressed as to why he wanted it, Jac had given lengthy muddled explanations about a project his class was doing on the Queen of England and that Sarah Brody had told him that the most important thing about the Queen was that she was the only person who had a vagina. And she *knew* it was true because her brother Gary had told her, and he was nearly eleven.

'It's nothing to do with the Queen's name this time. It's not rude or anything,' Jac said gravely.

'Go on then. What is it?'

'Gorilla.' His interest dissolved as the clock in the front room struck the hour. Darting out of the kitchen to watch his programmes, he left Laura free to laugh at him. When the serving hatch suddenly flew open and

Jac's face appeared, she just managed to compose herself, ready for whatever was coming next.

'Do I get food on my nose when I eat my dinner?'

'Not that I've noticed, love, no.' She bit her bottom lip.

'I didn't think I did.' He shut the small doors and went back to the television.

Laura shook her head in wonder. Whatever went on inside that boy's mind was beyond her. But one thing was for sure: every time another gem slipped from his lips she loved him even more.

The hatch door flew open again. 'Is Kay coming round tonight?'

'I don't think so. Why?'

'*She* might 'ave noticed that I get custard or whatever on my nose when I eat.' The doors slammed shut again.

'What *is* wrong with that boy?' Laura murmured to herself, wondering if something had been said during school dinners. Wondering whether to go in and ask him, she let it pass and poured herself another cup of tea. Maybe her little Jac had fallen in love and the girl in his life had said she hated boys who got food on their nose. No doubt it would be forgotten by the morning.

It did seem unusual for him to ask about his sister. Jac knew on exactly which days Kay paid a visit, and tonight wasn't one of them. Maybe he had worked it out for himself that once she was married, her thrice-weekly visits would probably dwindle. He was missing her before she'd even stopped coming. Trust Jac.

As if by instinct, Laura picked up the receiver and dialled Kay's work number. When she heard her daughter's voice she couldn't think of anything to say except 'Hello love, how are you?'

'What's happened?'

'Nothing. I just phoned to see how you are...' Laura searched her mind and then quickly added, 'How are the wedding arrangements coming along?' There was a pause but she heard a quiet sigh from her daughter.

'Why?' Kay sounded prickly. Something was going wrong with this phone call.

'I just wondered if you'd remembered to order the cake. I know it's months away, Kay, but these people get busy ... you have to get your order in—'

'Mum, what's wrong?'

'Nothing!' Now Laura's back was up. 'I just thought I would phone my only daughter, that's all!'

'And ask about the wedding? Right out of the blue? As if we don't discuss it when I'm round yours?'

There was another pause. 'OK. Your brother asked if you were coming over tonight, which is unusual for him, and I don't know ... it inspired me to call you. I wish I hadn't bothered now.'

'So you think Jac's upset about something? About my getting married? Is that what this is about?'

Laura started to laugh – it was all getting out of hand. 'Kay, please. I'm not one of your agony punters writing into your magazine for advice. I don't need analysing – believe me. Look, I'm gonna hang up now, OK? Everything is fine. There's nothing wrong. I'll see you on Friday, as usual, right?'

'No. I'll come round after work. Should be there about eight. Save me a bit of dinner.' There was a click followed by the dialling tone.

Open-mouthed and slightly irritated, Laura stared at the receiver. 'Oh, will you now?' She dialled the number again.

'I'd like to speak to Kay please. And before you say she's not there, I know she is. We spoke seconds ago. I'm sorry, Jenny, but I know Kay well enough to see what she's up to. She's got you to answer her phone. She knew it would be me. Well you just tell her—'

'She's just coming.' There was a dead moment as Jenny held her hand over the mouthpiece and told Kay what a mood her mother was in. Laura guessed this was happening and it did nothing to soften her.

'Mum, listen...'

'Kay? Oh for God's sake! You've been crying? I don't believe this. All I did was phone you—'

'It's not you, Mum. I've got something to tell you. Well at least I will have something to tell you – I think... I'll know for sure after I've seen Steve. I'm leaving work early to have a quick drink with him at the agency. We've got something to sort out, that's all...'

'And what's that?' Laura said, not liking the sound of it.

'Not on the phone. I'll be there before eight if I can. Try to get rid of Dad. Send him round the pub or to see Aunt Liz.'

'All right. I've got the gist of it. I'll do what I can. And Kay, no more tears, eh?'

'No. At least not until I get there.' Again, the click and the dialling tone.

The hatch door opened again and Jac's expressive face stopped Laura from sinking. 'Who was you phoning?'

'Kay. She's gonna pop in and see us later.'

'Why? It's not one of her days for coming over.'

'Oh, shut up, Jac, and watch your programme.'
Laura sat on a kitchen chair and put her feet up on
another.

'What time's she coming?'

'You'll be in bed, Jac. Fast asleep.' Laura yawned.

'What time?'

'Eight o'clock.'

'I can stay awake that long. Make her come in and see
me. She might have brought some chocolate buttons.
She forgot last time!'

'You're going to bed at seven, young man, and I don't
want to hear another word about it.'

'I never said I wasn't. I *said* I can stay awake that
long.'

'You reckon?' Laura knew that once Jac's head hit the
pillow his busy little mind would be sleeping within
minutes.

Once she was alone with her thoughts, Laura went
through all the possibilities of what might be the
matter with Kay. She had been very edgy when Laura
mentioned the wedding. Surely it wasn't going to be
called off? Kay and Steve splitting up? Impossible.
They had been inseparable from the time they met,
eighteen months ago. Her doubts about love at first
sight had certainly been challenged by those two.
They were meant for each other. She couldn't imagine
one without the other now. And there had been no
sign of a change in either of them. So what was
wrong?

'What do you think then? Looks nice, doesn't it?' Steve

said, referring to the way the small boardroom had been decorated. 'Smart but friendly.'

'It looks lovely.' Kay thought the last thing the room looked was friendly. Electric-blue carpet, white walls and a smoky-grey glass-topped table wasn't what she would have chosen – had she been asked.

'Would madam like a glass of sherry?' Steve teased, picking up the cut-glass decanter.

'You wouldn't be after seducing me, I hope.'

'Christen this room you mean? What a good idea.'

'I see there's a key in the door. I hope you don't have ulterior motives when it comes to a client,' she said flirtatiously.

'There's more than one way to win an account, I'll give you that.' He poured them both a drink.

'So long as you don't give anything you shouldn't to any of those beautiful art buyers. I have seen some of the women, don't forget.'

'Who needs an oil painting when I've got a water-colour to admire?' he grinned.

They clinked glasses, and she kissed him on the mouth. 'I'm going to take that as a compliment – whether it was meant to be or not.'

'Of course it was meant.' He swallowed his drink in one. 'You're all I think about – you know that.' He placed an arm around her shoulders and pulled her close. 'So – have you come round to facing practicalities yet?' He kissed the tip of her nose.

Knowing exactly what he meant, she lowered her head and sighed. 'I'm going to tell Mum and Dad tonight. Jac's gonna be disappointed. He was looking forward to being a page-boy.'

'Well, we mustn't upset your brother, must we?'

'There's no need for that, Steve.' She knew he was jealous of the bond between her and Jac, and as much as she tried she couldn't bring him to understand the love she had for her half-brother.

'I want as little fuss as possible, that's all. Us getting married is what counts.'

Kay kissed him on the neck. 'And you can't wait?'

'Exactly.' He pushed his hand through her hair. 'I'm marrying you – not your family. So long as you're happy with the new arrangements, that's all that matters.'

She looked into his soft green eyes. 'All I want is for us to be married. To wake up every morning and see your face on the pillow next to me.'

'And what about my body?'

'Yeah – I'll take that as well...'

'Steve—' The attractive Australian receptionist burst into the room. 'The art buyer from StaySafe has arrived. And he's in a hurry.' Raising an eyebrow at the sight of Kay on Steve's lap, she apologized faint-heartedly and left.

'She knew I was in here. Why couldn't she knock?' She suddenly felt like an intruder in his world.

'This place moves too fast for niceties, Kay. I'll phone you later. Around ten. See how you got on.' He was obviously in a hurry to see the back of her.

'Is this how it's always going to be?'

'Don't knock it. This is our livelihood.' He opened the door for her. 'Good luck with your parents – and Jac.'

As Kay soaked in her softened bathwater, Pamela, her

flatmate, was choosing one of her favourite albums, knowing full well that underneath Kay's jocularity she was really quite worried. They were childhood friends and had shared the same flat for nearly a year, often talking into the wee hours about things they wouldn't dream of telling anyone else.

'I don't know why you didn't go to your mother's straight from work! You'll get caught up in the West End traffic and you know how you love that!' Her voice drifted through the open doorway.

'I needed to come home and change into my casuals. I'll be there on time, stop nagging.'

'You can't get by without a bloody deadline, that's your trouble! I don't envy you, Kay. They're gonna go *potty*!'

'I know. But there's no going back now. I've been and gone and arranged it!' She leaned her head back and quietly sang along to the Kinks' *Tired of Waiting for You*.

'I still think Steve should be there when you tell 'em!'

'No. This is my battle.'

'I suppose you want me to wait up for you?'

'Of course.'

'Well, don't leave it too late, I'll be on my own. Simon's not coming over after all. They're behind schedule. Still got a studio scene to shoot.' She popped her head round the door and felt the bath towel on the wooden rack. 'This is *damp*, Kay!' She shook her head at Kay's careless ways. 'I'll get you a dry one from the airing cupboard. And don't stay in there too long or you'll go all wrinkly.'

Kay threw a wet flannel at her. 'Go and turn that record off. I need silence to work out what I'm gonna say.'

Sudden pangs of doubt pierced her. Maybe she had been a bit hasty, giving up her independence earlier than planned. Leaving the best flatmate and friend anyone could wish for. Then there was her dad. He would go berserk. She was risking a lot: it wouldn't surprise her if he didn't speak to her for months. She was about to cause so much trouble and disappointment. Why? Why had she set herself up like this?

Her thoughts turned to Steve and the doubts ebbed away. Why should she make him go through with something he would hate? No one but Kay knew about his shyness – he put up a good front. He had even gone so far as to buy himself a book, *Coping with Shyness*. He would have died if he knew she had spotted it hidden under his bed. It had come as a shock – she had had no idea about his hang-up before then.

'You *promised* me!' Jack's face was full of anger. 'After all that business of forging your passport form! You promised you would never do anything like that again!'

'Only because you made me say it! You put me on the spot!'

'Don't give me that! You were wrong and you knew it.' His hands were shaking with rage as he pulled the lid off his tobacco tin. 'You've got a short memory, Kay, that's all I can say.'

Willing herself not to break down, she took in a long deep breath. 'Anyway, I haven't forged anything. I'm twenty-one, I didn't need to.'

'You *went* behind my *back*. Arranged it without telling me! It's the same thing!'

'I had no choice! You would never have agreed. You *know* you wouldn't.'

'Too right. The bloody bans'll be read out in church soon. Who's gonna tell the vicar you've changed your plans, eh? Not me, that's for sure.'

'I can do that,' Laura murmured, keeping her eyes down.

'You will *not*.' He lit his roll-up. 'Won't be any need to – because that white wedding is going to take place.' His tone was intended to prevent any further discussion on the subject.

'I'm sorry, Dad, but it isn't. My mind's made up.' She looked pleadingly into his face. 'Try to accept it.'

'Nothing to accept. I'm gonna walk you down that aisle and that's an end to it.'

How Kay wished she was sitting closer to the kitchen door. To make an escape she would have to pass her dad and in his present mood he would stop her. Possibly lash out. 'You don't understand—'

'I'm not listening.' Jack shifted his chair as much as possible in the small space between the table and the wall. He was making it clear that he would rather have his back to her.

'Steve's not like you—'

'You can say that again. He lets you run rings round him.'

'No he doesn't!'

'Well why didn't he put a stop to all this? Bloody registry office! What was he thinking about, for Christ's sake?'

'It's what he wanted in the *first* place. I'm doing it for him! He hates ceremonies.'

Jack let out a short, hard burst of laughter. 'Some tough nut he's turned out to be.'

'He doesn't like church weddings! But you wouldn't understand that, would you? No. Not you. Not Jack Armstrong. The hardest man in the docks.'

'You're not too old for a right-hander, Kay.' His singsong tone was full of threat. 'You go ahead with this and you'll do so without me and your mother's presence.'

'Speak for yourself, Jack.' Laura twisted her handkerchief and glared into his face. 'If this is what she wants, then I'll stand by her.'

'Oh yeah? And I suppose you knew about this all along?'

'I wouldn't tell one without the other. You should know that.'

'Should I? I don't think so. Seems like I'm always kept in the dark around 'ere.'

'If you're not gonna get married in church, Kay, in September, what exactly are your plans?' As much as she tried, Laura couldn't keep the disappointment out of her voice.

'Stepney register office. With as few people as possible.'

'Fuck me!' Jack stood up and turned his back on them both.

'In September?' Laura asked.

'No. Sooner than that.'

'Oh, now I get the picture. He's put her in the family way. Couldn't stand up and tell us himself – he has to leave her to break the news.'

'I'm not pregnant.'

'How much sooner?' Laura wanted to get the worst of it over.

'A lot.'

Slamming his fist down on the kitchen table, Jack looked fit to burst. 'Stop pissing about! Your mother's asking you a straight question. Answer her!'

'*Saturday!*' Kay roared. There was a stony silence. 'This Saturday.' Having finally got it out, Kay let go. 'Eleven o'clock in the morning.'

For what seemed like an age, no one spoke. 'I'm sorry, but it seemed the only way. I knew you would never agree, so I wanted to get it done with as soon as possible. And anyway, we can't really afford a big wedding. Not now that Steve wants us to save up for a deposit on our own flat.'

Still neither Laura nor Jack could speak. All Kay could do was wait. Wait for one of them to break the atmosphere, one way or another.

'Good. I won't 'ave to be a page-boy after all.' Little Jac, in his striped winceyette pyjamas, looked appealing as he stood in the doorway rubbing his eyes.

'How long have you been in the passage?' Jack said, doing his best to use a softer tone.

'I heard you swear, Dad, but I won't tell my teacher or Aunt Liz.' Only Jac could change everyone's mood in an instant. Chuckles and quiet laughter escaped from all three adults.

'If any of my friends saw me in a white silk page-boy suit they'd laugh – and tell the girls.' He turned to Laura. 'Can I have a glass of milk, Mum?'

"Course you can.'

26

Peering into his dad's face, Jac's eyes narrowed as his familiar frown appeared. 'What's a registry office?'

Quick off the mark, Kay smiled at him. 'It's a lovely bright room with lots of flowers where people get married if they don't want a fussy church wedding.'

'Sounds all right. But it can't be this week. *Superman's* on at the Saturday morning pictures.' He took the glass of milk from Laura and went back to bed.

'I'll see if I can get it put back a month,' Kay said, hoping this might appease Jack.

Laura sighed with relief. 'That would help. We'll have to put our skates on, but we'll do it, between us.' She shot Jack a warning look. 'Your aunt Liz'll rise to the occasion. If she can't twist an arm, no one can. There'll be a cake and a proper wedding tea, and flowers.'

The three of them sat down again and lowered their heads, each one trying to hide their tears. 'I'm sorry,' Kay said, 'I didn't mean to upset you.'

She wished she could say what was really in her mind. That she was just as unhappy about it as they were – more so. It had come as a blow when Steve had first mentioned the idea. Of course she wanted to be a proper bride. It was something she had looked forward to all her life. She'd even tried on a few wedding dresses and veils. Yes, she did want a white wedding, of course she did. But how could she let on?

'It's the one thing a father looks forward to, walking his daughter down the aisle.' He looked at Kay and sighed. 'You can still 'ave a small wedding you know, even if it is in a church.'

'Oh come on, Dad, you know what would happen. We

wouldn't be able to ask one cousin without another six or seven ... Then there are the second cousins and the great aunts and uncles. It wouldn't work and you know it. Anyway, there is another reason.'

Jack narrowed his eyes and waited. 'Come on then – what?'

'Steve's an atheist.'

'Oh yeah? And what's that got to do with anything?'

Kay managed to stop herself laughing. 'Everything, I would have thought.'

It was obvious to Jack that there was no point in arguing with her. Kay had made up her mind, and she was too much like himself to go through with something if it went against the grain. He was disappointed. Gutted, in fact – but it was her life and he would have to go along with the little cow's wishes.

'Well if you do 'ave a change of heart, don't let your pride stop you from saying so.' He walked out of the kitchen, leaving them to it.

'We'll sit down together tomorrow night, Steve as well, and try to explain.'

'No need!' Jack called back from the living room. 'He shouldn't 'ave to answer to me. I'm only your *father*.'

Kay and Laura didn't dare look at each other. It wouldn't do for Jack to hear them sharing a joke at his expense. But the remark was so typical, and his little-boy-hurt act was beginning to wear a bit thin.

'Stop biting your lip, Kay. He'll get over it.' Laura filled the kettle ready to make a pot of tea. 'It's all right for you. I'm the one that's gonna have to put up with his moods until he does come round.'

'You know I wouldn't do this if it wasn't necessary.'

'I know. But you must understand that it's not easy for us. You being our only child.'

'*Mum!* How can you *say* a thing like that?'

'Jesus,' Laura murmured. 'That's the first time I have. I wasn't even thinking it. It just came out.' She sucked on her top lip and breathed in. 'May God forgive me. If our Jac had heard me—'

'Well he didn't – and neither did Dad, thankfully.'

In that split second, as they looked at each other, they realized how very easily it could come out. One of the neighbours ... one of the family. One day, someone might just say the wrong thing at the wrong time.

'Maybe we *should* tell Jac he's adopted? Before someone else does?'

'No. Not yet, anyway. Not until he's grown up a bit. Think of the effect it would have on him. And me. Once he knew I wasn't really his mum...'

Giving her a hug, Kay nuzzled Laura's shoulder. 'I love you.'

Laura kissed the top of her daughter's head and caught a whiff of the Silvikrin shampoo she still liked to use. 'What colour you gonna wear then?'

'Ivory and pale blue. I've seen a lovely outfit. In Peter Robinson's. Will you come with me—'

''Course I will. I'll have to get myself rigged out too. It'll make a nice change to buy something up West instead of from Hammond's.'

'I knew you'd be all right about this. I just knew.'

'Don't have much choice, do I? Anyway what does it count for? So long as you and Jac are healthy and...' Laura looked pensive. 'I still think of you both as my babies – daft really...'

'Speaking of Jac, I'd best go and tell him a story. Let him know I'm OK after the yelling session. You know what a worrier he is.'

'D'yer think they'll make me 'ave a white wedding when I grow up?' Jac asked, his face grave.

'No.' Kay chuckled and then sighed. 'It's always the same when it's the daughter. Now your girlfriend's parents might insist she gets married in white, in a church...'

'I'm not getting married anyway. You gonna tell me a story?'

'Yes.'

'Go on then. I'm s'posed to be asleep by now.'

'Oh well, in that case...'

'No, it's all right. I can get away wiv murder tonight – 'cos of the upset.'

'You crafty little sod. No flies on you, is there?'

'Nope. Go on then. A Marley story.'

'Please?' Kay tilted her head to one side and looked into his face.

'Yeah. That's what I was gonna say.' He grinned and then broke into a fit of the giggles. 'Do I get food on my nose when I eat?' He was laughing now.

'Yeah – all over it. Now shut up or go to sleep.'

He instantly fell back on to his pillow and never said another word.

# Chapter Two

Wheeling the large metal trolley from the kitchen to the dining hall, Patsy Hemmingway, with her dramatic new hairstyle, felt a wave of trepidation at the sight of the noisy children lining up to go in for lunch. She was tempted for a second to scan them for a sandy-headed boy but common sense prevailed. It wouldn't do to bring a passing teacher's attention to her interest in one particular child. She must appear impartial.

Making a turn in the corridor, she pushed the swing doors open with her back and pulled the laden trolley into the large hall.

'You should've got one of the others to help you with that, Hem', you'll end up with a weak spine.'

'I didn't realize how heavy it was, wheels or no wheels. I won't make the same mistake twice.' She grimaced at her work colleague and shuddered. 'Doesn't the food smell awful?'

'You'll get used to it. The main thing to remember is not to show your distaste in front of the kids. Otherwise some clever little snot'll refuse to eat it, and then tell the duty teacher that the dinner ladies think it's disgusting as well.'

Helping the woman to lift the stainless steel pots of

31

hot food on to the serving counter, Patsy wondered if this new acquaintance knew the Armstrong family. Any one of the kitchen staff could be a neighbour, relative or close friend.

'You have to have quick reflexes, I tell you that much.' The two women tipped steaming carrots into a large serving dish. 'Just as you go to dollop a spoonful of something they don't fancy on to their plates, the little darlings pull it away. Straight on the floor it goes, and then the next kid treads in it and the next in line slips arse over 'ead. And guess who gets the blame?'

'Us.'

'Dead right.'

Once all the food was in serving dishes the six kitchen staff, all dressed in green linen wrap-over style aprons with hats to match, stood behind the long row of tables and quietly waited. Within seconds the silent hall was filled with the sound of children stampeding over the polished parquet floor.

'Quiet!' A high-pitched whistle followed the command and a hush fell upon the room. 'Not *one* word! Is that clear?'

A chorus of 'Yes Miss Johnson' rang through the air. 'You will *walk* in a neat file and eat *everything* on your plate!'

The whistle went again and the sound of shuffling feet resumed.

'Bit strict, isn't she?' Patsy nudged another of the servers. 'Has anyone told her that this isn't the nine-teenth century?'

'You should keep your mouth shut if you value this

job.' The young peroxide blonde straightened her cap with no trace of a smile. 'They're not allowed to talk and neither are we.'

'Really? Well it's high time that little rule was changed.'

'Oh dear. A troublemaker. That's all we need.'

'I'm not a troublemaker, actually.' The tone in Patsy's voice gave her away – she wasn't the sort to take orders. 'You won't have to worry your pretty head about me causing trouble.'

'That's where you're wrong. I'm Gillian Cross. Your supervisor,' she grinned smugly.

The grubby faces of clammy children shuffling at a snail's pace peered pleadingly at Patsy when they arrived in front of her. They were silently begging her not to put too much swede on to their plates. But she had soon realized that she must appear to be following the behaviour of her supervisor, who deliberately piled on the sardines in tomato sauce, causing one little girl to retch.

'They don't know what's good for them,' she said quietly to her superior, trying to get on better terms with her. When she received a warning look, she hunched her shoulders submissively and mouthed an apology. That seemed to do the trick: the woman drank it in. She even spoke. Said that Hem' wasn't to worry and that she would soon get the hang of the system.

Privately commending herself, Patsy turned her attention to the solemn face peering up at her. Scowling with distaste, Jac did his best to get his message across. Casually spooning a tiny portion of swede on to his plate, she gave him a knowing wink and he responded likewise. She wasn't sure if he had recognized her as the lady under the shelter. Her hair was short and nearly black now, but then her head had been covered with a scarf that morning. But all of that was really immaterial. A very big step had just been taken. She had already created a secret that they would share. The first of many more to come.

As she walked through the playground on her way out of the school, Patsy resisted the urge to glance around at the noisy children to see if she could spot Jac. As she disappeared through the green gate she could have no idea that her boy had seen her coming out of the school building and had watched her leave.

Leaning on a brick wall, Jac withdrew his latest barter of five marbles from his trouser pocket. Examining them closely, he picked out a white glass with a pink and blue swirl running through it. Gazing back at the green gate, his eyes wandered to the shelter where he had first seen her. He instinctively wiped the tip of his nose with his thumb, just in case there was some food on it. Pushing the selected marble into the furthest corner of his top pocket, he decided that she should definitely have that one. He would slip it to her when no one was about. She deserved a present because of the swede.

Sitting on the edge of his grandfather's bed, Jac was making it clear that he wished he had never let Billy talk him into wearing a proper bow-tie. 'It's all right innit? No one'll notice if it's not straight.'

'Now then, that's enough of that. You don't wanna let

the side down. Think yourself lucky you got out of being a page-boy,' Billy said, wishing he hadn't suggested the idea in the first place. Popping a tie on elastic around his grandson's neck would have been far easier.

'You're not really gonna put that marge on my hair, are yer?'

''Course I am, sonny boy. We want you to look the part.' He gripped both sides of the bow-tie between his forefingers and thumbs and jerked the tie tight. 'That's it!' He leaned back and admired Jac. 'Cor, don't you look smashing!'

'Dad's got Brylcreem at 'ome. Can't I run round an' get some?'

'What – you wanna smell like a girl, do you? Brylcreem? Your dad's going soft in the 'ead.'

Jac looked across at the packet of margarine on the window-sill, melting in the sunshine. 'I dunno why we had to 'ave the wedding party 'ere anyway. Why couldn't we 'ave had it at our own flat? Where Kay used to live – with me?' Jac dug the toe of his polished shoe into a worn bit of the bedroom carpet, keeping his head down. The last thing he wanted was for his grandfather to see him cry.

'It's where your mother held hers, that's why. Family tradition. Anyway, Kay wouldn't want you lot round 'er while she gets ready.'

'Yes she would,' Jac said, holding back his tears. 'I don't *want* marge on my hair. It stinks and looks horrible and feels all gungy!'

'Oh yeah,' Billy started to laugh. 'And who d'yer think'll be looking that closely eh? You 'aven't invited a little sweetheart, 'ave yer?'

'No!' Jac pursed his lips and folded his arms. 'But I told my lady about it and she's coming to watch! She won't like me with my hair all stuck down flat! And it's hot outside. I'll 'ave marge dribbling down my neck!'

Billy slapped his leg and roared. 'And who the bloody hell's your lady when she's at 'ome?'

'My dinner lady!'

'Oh well then...' Billy splayed both hands, 'we must give 'er a good impression!'

'It's not funny.'

'No? Your face is though.' Billy wiped a tear from his eye. 'Now then – turn around and open Grandfather's medicine cupboard.'

'Why?' Still his arms were folded defiantly.

'See what's in there of course.'

'I know what's in there. Your medicine.'

'Suit yerself. If you don't want the present.'

'You couldn't get a present in a tiny cupboard like that.'

Billy raised his chin, sniffed and put on an air of nonchalance. 'I'll give it to the paper-boy when he comes – if you don't want it.'

'Oh all right then,' Jac sighed heavily and flopped his arms to his sides. 'If you're gonna sulk about it...' He reached out and turned the tiny key in the oak door. There was a silence as he stared into the small dark cupboard.

'Well?' Billy pretended to be more interested in something he could see through the window.

'It's a jar of Brylcreem,' Jac murmured, hopelessly trying to keep from grinning. 'A small one. A boy's size.'

'Oh yeah? I wonder who put that in there?'

'You did.'

'Did I?' Billy rubbed his chin. 'Well stone me, so I did. You'd best take that marge down then – before it really melts.'

'It was another one of your tricks.' Jac's face broke into a broad smile and he began to chuckle.

'As if I'd put marge on your 'air for your sister's wedding! And what with your dinner lady being there to watch you as well...'

Disappearing through the bedroom door with the soft margarine, Jac suddenly stopped in his tracks and turned to Billy.

'You remember when you told me about recarnations?'

Checking his appearance in the mirror, Billy shook his head slowly. 'Not that again, Jac. I'm sorry I bloody mentioned it now. And it's re*in*carnation.'

'Does it mean that I might 'ave lived before as I am now, only with a different mum and dad and grandfather?'

The humour drained from Billy and he felt himself go cold. 'Why d'yer ask that, son?'

'Does it?' There was an urgency in Jac's voice.

'No...' Billy's mind was full of questions. What had Jac overheard? Or had some nosy bastard been stirring things up? 'No son, no. You would 'ave been someone completely different. Probably a frog waiting to be turned into a prince.' Billy tried to make light of it.

'So I wouldn't 'ave been, then?'

'Been what – a frog or a prince?'

'Me! Me with a different mum! A mum who's alive

37

now as well. One who got recarnated at the same time as me!'

Billy reached out and pulled Jac close. 'What's this all about, Jac? Who's been putting daft ideas into your 'ead?'

'No one ... it's just that...'

'Yeah – go on then, what?'

'Well it's just that ... my dinner lady ... she feels a bit ... you know, a bit like a mum.'

Relieved that that was all there was to it, Billy squeezed Jac's arm and smiled. 'Every kid in your school probably thinks the same. Dinner ladies are like that. They're just like mums. And you know why? 'Cos they feed yer. Kids! Always thinking of your bellies!'

'Keep the ham covered in that cheesecloth till we're ready to cut it, Laura!' Liz's voice from below could be heard loud and clear. 'And put the sausages in the oven ready to turn on as soon as we get back from the registry office—'

'Liz, will you please *go*! Leave it much longer and you'll miss your appointment. It's nearly ten o'clock!'

'I've hung your outfit in my wardrobe! You'd best try it on in case I've taken a bit too much off the hem! I kept to the pins but you never know—'

'I've had a look – it's perfect!'

'Why're they shouting?' Jac said.

'Getting their knickers in a twist again.' Billy shrugged, making Jac laugh. 'Come on, let's go and sort 'em out before they wet 'emselves.'

Standing just outside the living-room doorway, Billy and Jac made a game of eavesdropping.

'I don't know about Billy's suit though, Laura. I still say he should have bought a new one.' Liz buttoned up her coat and grabbed her shopping bag and purse.

'I've only 'ad two wears out of that suit!' Billy told Jac as he stepped into the small living-room of his two-up two-down. Patting his best mate Liz on the shoulder he tried to calm her down. 'Go on, get going. Before I chuck you out.'

Once they heard the street door slam, Billy relaxed into a smile. 'Anyone'd think it was a royal wedding, the way she goes on.'

'She can't help it, Dad,' Laura said, massaging the back of her neck to ease the burning pain. 'You know how close Kay and her aunt Liz are.'

'You need a long soak in the bath, my girl. And then a bit of my rubbing-in ointment.'

'Yeah – that'd go well with my perfume. But you're right about the soak.' She rolled her shoulders and neck. 'I've had it. If I've forgotten anything we'll have to make do without.'

Billy peered at the trestles against the wall, which were covered with sparkling white sheets and decorated with a glorious centre-piece of fresh spring flowers. Stacked at one end were white china dinner and side plates, with dessert dishes to match; silver-plated cutlery, damask table napkins, and a large silver tray bearing wineglasses. All courtesy of Hammond's canteen where Liz worked. She had used her guile and persuaded the manageress to let her borrow the tableware which was only used for special functions. Only the very best for her niece's wedding.

'Where's the grub then?'

'Most of it's in the kitchen. Jack's fetching some more from home later on this morning and Milly's cajoled her Georgie to drop off the trifles and fruit tarts she's made.'

'Pickles?'

'In the kitchen.' Laura was enjoying her dad's role-playing.

'What time they fetching the jellied eels?'

'I don't know about you, Dad, but I could do with a cup of tea and a sandwich. What d'yer reckon?'

Billy looked sideways at his daughter. Nothing escaped him. She was sidetracking. 'Well?'

'It wasn't just Liz who thought eels were inappropriate. Jack was doubtful as well—'

'I might 'ave known! Turn my back for a minute and you all go against me.'

'Kay's in-laws won't be used to our customs—'

'It's our lot I'm thinking about. Making it all posh like this. They'll run a bloody mile!'

'Well, you worked into the wee hours polishing that silver.'

'That's different.'

'Is it?'

'What about this sandwich then? Won't get made by itself. Or is it beneath yer to butter a bit of bread now?'

Stifling her laughter, Laura sucked on her bottom lip. 'You 'aven't said anything about my new hairstyle.'

He drew his head back and studied Laura's dark chestnut curls. 'How much did they rob yer for that?'

'That's not the point. Do you *like* it?'

'You look like Shirley Temple.' Roaring with laughter

he went into the kitchen to check it over. 'How old are yer?' He called over his shoulder. 'Forty-four, innit?'

Laura glanced at herself in the wall mirror. Her dad had a point. She turned her face one way then the other. 'It looks like a bloody wig,' she grumbled.

Taking the stairs two at a time, she rushed into her old bedroom and grabbed a hairbrush from the dressing-table. A few good strokes and she looked more like herself. 'Much better.' She pushed and tweaked and pulled at the long strands until she was satisfied.

It seemed strange, standing in the bedroom that her sister-in-law Liz now occupied. It was good to see it being used though. And ever since Jack's sister had moved in with Laura's dad, Billy, the house had taken on a new lease of life. Similar to when Laura's mother was alive and well.

'What d'yer want in this sandwich then?' Billy called up the stairs.

'I don't mind, Dad. Cheese'll be fine.' Laura wondered why her spirits seemed to be flagging. At once her mind was full of Kay. This was her wedding day. Laura had been so busy during the past couple of weeks that she hadn't really taken it in. 'Make sure Jac eats something as well!'

It was ironical that Kay had chosen to hold the wedding tea at her grandfather's home. For some reason it had seemed quite natural when plans were being made. But here she was, sitting on the same bed she had sat on those twenty-six years ago, waiting to go to church to marry Jack.

'Don't you start blubbering yet. Save that for the

church.' Billy had crept in on her, knowing he shouldn't have laughed at her hair. His daughter was as sensitive as his wife had been.

'Oh, Dad...' Laura didn't care that her tears would make her eyelids swell up. 'Our little Kay. Getting married...'

'Now stop that! You wanna look all red and puffy-eyed when your in-laws arrive? I mean it, Laura. Stop it! Otherwise you'll start me off and that'll be it. I'll take to me bed and stay there!'

'All right, all right.' She took in a deep breath. 'You're right. I was letting go a bit too soon. Let's try to eat something.'

'Time's running on, you know. You wanna 'ave everything tiptop when people start to arrive. I told my neighbours and cronies to come in for a drink around two o'clock – *after* they've 'ad their dinner.'

Following him down the stairs, Laura began to feel relaxed and had to admit that a twinge of excitement had taken over from the blues.

'I hope Kay's all right back there. Little cow was adamant that I should be out of the way while she got ready. Jack'll be useless. I just hope he doesn't start drinking too early or he'll be drunk when he's taking her to the church.'

'Church?'

'Oh, you know...' Taking her sandwich from him, she sat upright in the old armchair and placed the plate on her knees. 'What's Jac doing down there?'

'Slapping Brylcreem on 'is hair. Good job Liz's gone out. She didn't want me to give it to 'im. Prefers 'is hair all fluffy, she said.'

'She's right as well. Still, if Jac's happy, Liz will be.
And while we're on the subject of you and Liz—'

'We're not.'

'How *is* it working out? I thought she'd 'ave moved
into your bed by now.' Laura enjoyed teasing *him* for a
change.

'She 'as once or twice. In the winter, when it was bitter
cold. Kept her stays on though. There was none of *that*.
Had a little cuddle to keep warm, that's all.' He began to
chuckle, enjoying a private joke.

The small congregation had already arrived and was
waiting inside the register office when Jack pulled up
outside with Kay and little Jac. As he guided his
daughter towards the steps, he was pleased to see that a
few friends and neighbours had turned out to wish his
daughter well.

'Good luck, Kay mate!' A woman's voice called from
the small crowd. Straining to see who the familiar voice
belonged to, Kay was surprised and choked to see Terry
Button's mum smiling at her. The face of Terry, her
childhood friend who had committed suicide four years
ago, filled her thoughts.

'Dad ... it's Mrs Button. I didn't think to ask her.'

'Don't go away Nell!' Jack called out. 'Come back for a
drink, OK?'

Nell gave him a thumbs-up sign and pointed to the
man standing by her side. 'Yeah – him as well!' Jack had
no idea who he was but the man looked OK as far as he
could tell. 'Must be her new boyfriend,' he whispered to
Kay.

Turning around to urge his six-year-old to get a move

on, Jack saw that he was waving to an attractive dark-haired woman who stood out in the crowd.

'Who's your friend?' he asked, giving Patsy the once-over.

'Our dinner lady.' Jac was full of pride.

'Looks more like a film star than a dinner lady. Come on, then, in we go. Let's get your sister married off.'

Standing in the small carpeted foyer, Jack gazed at Kay. 'You look lovely,' was all he could say. Her ivory silk dress and coat were trimmed with pale-blue satin to match her wide-brimmed hat, which had a small spray of fresh flowers hand-stitched to the front, matching her trailing freesia bouquet. He stroked her long silky blonde hair.

'But I still think a long dress covering your legs instead of showing your knees would 'ave—'

'Stop delaying the moment. Come on, they're all waiting.'

Taking a deep breath, arm in arm with his girl, Jack slowly walked her through the red-carpeted entrance hall and into the flower-decked register office. Moving in close he whispered in Kay's ear and made her giggle. They both began to laugh which started everyone off, including Laura. Whether it was from nerves or what Jack had said she had no idea, but it was enough to see her daughter looking so radiant and happy.

Poor Steve appeared to be having a bad time of it. Laura had never seen him look so uptight and miser-able. As her eyes wandered across to his family she was pleased to see they appeared relaxed and delighted. Maybe they would enjoy the jellied eels after all. As Laura had predicted to herself, Billy had slipped out once Liz was back from the hairdresser's and made a few arrangements of his own, adding cockles, mussels and whelks to the list.

As soon as the build-up to the marriage vows began, Laura realized that apart from the church, bridesmaids and choir, there really wasn't that much difference after all, and secretly felt pleased that Kay had opted for this small tasteful wedding. Had she known what Jack had whispered to Kay, she would have smiled. For he too had felt exactly the same and had said, 'Thank Christ we haven't got to walk the mile-aisle.'

Outside in the May sunshine, the well-wishers waited with the confetti, while Patsy Hemmingway walked slowly away, thrilled that she had not been recognized. Her new look had fooled the astute Jack, and that was everything she could have asked for. Everything, that is, except having her son by her side, instead of in that building with that family.

As Patsy turned into Jubilee Street, heading for home, she began to wonder just how she would get Jac past her landlady once she had managed to lure him back, when the day came. When she would tell him the truth. That she was his real mother.

Telling herself she would cross that hurdle when she came to it, she let herself in by the back door and slipped quietly up the stairs to avoid having to talk to Mrs Simons, should she appear.

With a glass of sherry in her hand, Patsy raised it to the photograph of Jack and his daughter Kay, taken in the hop fields nine years ago, when hers and Jack's affair was at boiling-point and she had been quite satisfied to be the other woman in his life.

She toasted the air. 'Congratulations, Kay. May you move a million miles away with your new hubby! And may my little Jac forget all about his half-sister!'

She was under no illusions about the bonds within that family. To get Jac away from his father was one thing. To stand up to a strong woman like Laura was another, but Kay? That was something else. After all, it had been her persuasion, as well as the bastard Tom, that had made Patsy give up Jac. Yes. It was Kay's fault as much as his. She was the one who had found out where Jac was, four years ago. She who had turned up at the children's home right out of the blue. She who had told Jac he had a sister. Yes – that innocent-looking bitch must get her comeuppance too.

There was a lot of manipulating to be done before Patsy could start a new life with her son. But then she had always liked a challenge – it was the spice of life as far as she was concerned.

The soft tapping on the door of her bedsit was the last thing she wanted to hear right then. Irritated with the intrusion, she pulled the door open and threw her landlady a black look.

'I hate to be a nuisance...' Esther Simons was obviously embarrassed. 'I was just about to go to the market...'

'Don't let me stop you,' Patsy smiled, knowing very well what her landlady wanted.

'A bit of rent money would help with the shopping,' the old woman looked pleadingly into the uncaring face. 'I didn't bother you with it last week when you forgot to—'

'I didn't forget. You did. I rely on you hovering by the

46

door on a Friday evening when I get home. When you weren't there last week, I thought you were feeling a bit flush. Didn't need the cash.'

'I wish.' The old woman smiled and shrugged.

'Actually, Mrs Simons ... I have been wondering about our arrangement and it puzzles me that you've never produced a rent book. Why is that?'

'A rent book?'

'You are meant to, you know, by law.'

'But we never have. There's never been any question of it before.'

Her pitiful response and her tone were like water off a duck's back to Patsy. She opened the door wide. 'Come in for a minute, Mrs Simons, take the weight off your legs.' She pulled up a chair for the old woman and smiled, then gently but firmly shoved her into it.

Patsy preferred to stand: she felt more intimidating with her arms folded and Simons looking up at her like that.

'Tell me something. Who was renting the flat before me? I'm intrigued.'

'A newly-married couple,' she said feebly. 'They were only here for six months, while they got on their feet. They took out a mortgage. Bought themselves a place in Leytonstone.' She lowered her voice to a whisper. 'Please God they continue to have work.'

'And before them?' Patsy could feel the blood pumping through her veins. Her killer instincts told her she was on to something.

'Before them?' Esther Simons shrugged. 'A young man, a schoolteacher. He was here for about a year. Got himself another teaching job – away from the East End.

Who can blame him? It's not like it used to be. So many different people here now.' She sighed and her voice faded away. 'Most of the old neighbours seem to be leaving...'

'And before him?' She was beginning to feel like a barrister.

'Ah, then it *was* different.' A faint smile broke across her face. 'Then it was more like the old days.' She touched her trembling fingers to her forehead and brushed a few strands of wiry hair from her eyes. Esther was happy to talk about the old days. To have someone who would listen.

'Poor Laurence,' she shook her head. 'Passed away in the Jewish. Always said he wanted to die in his own bed.' She shrugged and smiled. 'At least he went in his sleep. Thirty-five years he lived in the same house. When his wife passed away, ten years ago ... that's when he split the house into two flats and let me have the downstairs.'

Patsy couldn't believe her luck. She covered her excitement and sat down, trying her best to look sympathetic. 'So he owned the house then, did he?' she asked carefully.

'Owned it? Who can say? We didn't care about such things in those days. We had enough to worry about, making a decent living. He was a wonderful tailor. Could have worked in Savile Row.'

'So you don't actually know who owns it?'

The old woman looked puzzled. What did it matter who owned it? People came, people went – the house had been there a long time and was still sound. It was somewhere to mark time between this world and the next. 'I live here, so it's my house. If you stay long enough, it will be yours one day – with whoever you choose as a tenant.' She chuckled softly. 'I think maybe I have a few more years to go yet. Just a few, but enough.'

Patsy inhaled slowly and stood up, turning her back on the old woman. She smiled as she walked to the window and looked out. 'You do realize that you've been breaking the law? Taking money under false pretences?' She managed to sound grave.

'I hadn't thought of it like that.'

'So it appears. Well...' She turned to face her again. 'You've been very silly, but it's not too late to put it right. It's just as well I found out before the authorities caught up with you.'

Esther Simons's expression changed. Something was sinking in. The penny was dropping. This new tenant was not all she had made out to be. She had been cross-examining her and Esther had a feeling she knew why. 'What do you suggest I do?'

'Move out. And soon. As soon as possible.'

'*Leave?* Leave my home? It's a joke?'

'No, Mrs Simons. It's not. It's very serious. I'll stay on and do my best to sort things out. Smooth the way. Have a good story ready, should the authorities knock on the door.'

'I would have nowhere to go!' She started to wring her shaking hands. 'All my things are here. It's madness, and I'm not going to think about it. I'll face trouble when it arrives.'

'Oh but it *has* arrived. Now that I know. I would be seen as an accomplice. I could end up in court too.'

A silence filled the room as one woman schemed and

the other realized that she was trapped. This young lady was not one to mess with. Every expression on her face, every movement of her body, every gesture showed her to be a very cunning and dangerous woman.

'You once said you had a brother living just off the Whitechapel Road. I suggest you phone him. Get him to clear out some of that junk you told me he hoards. You'll be needing a room.'

The air was suddenly thick with hatred and tension as the two women eyed each other. 'You'd best be out of here by tomorrow.'

'You can't be serious?' Esther tried not to cry. 'This is my home. All my things are here. They would never fit into Maurice's flat.'

'Well then, you can store some of it here until I arrange for the council to collect it.' The tear hanging from the old lady's nose filled Patsy with revulsion. 'Just take what you need.'

Pulling herself to her feet, Esther Simons walked slowly towards the door. The expression in Patsy's eyes reminded her of something she'd always tried to push from her memory. She had seen that look many times before; before she was forced out of her homeland. When the Nazis had brainwashed people to hate the Jews.

It was a look she recognized from long ago. A look that never softened, no matter how much one might plead for one's life. And that icy stare had been in Patsy's eyes.

Esther could almost smell the Nazi soldiers, hear their marching feet, see them as they lurched forward threatening to strike out with the butts of their guns.

'This isn't a joke, is it? You really mean to do this evil thing.'

'I'm being Christian, Mrs Simons. I'm saving you from a fate worse than death. Prison will be much worse than a room with your brother.'

Esther spat at Patsy's feet. How dare she compare her brother's home to a prison?

'You will be full of remorse one day.' Esther spoke in a tired voice. 'And it will be too late. You will have to live with your guilt. And unlike people, guilt cannot be cast out. It will be a part of you. Like a second shadow.'

'On Monday I shall arrange for a private company to come in and fumigate your rooms. Make sure you take everything you need.'

She slammed the door in Esther's face and gradually began to relax as she heard the old woman shuffle down the stairs. Once she felt the vibrations from the door slamming below her, she shuddered and felt herself go cold.

Simons had looked like an old witch, standing there warning Patsy of her dark destiny. But she quickly saw the humorous side of it. She only wished she had someone to share it with. Her Jac would have laughed with her at the old hag. She imagined Jac standing next to her in the room, giggling and holding his nose against the 'old woman' smell which tainted the air.

'Mothballs and old clothes!' She looked at the space next to her where he should be standing, and laughed. 'If ever I get to smell like that, may someone turn on the gas.'

Her mind instantly filled with the vision of her son with that family. As she looked out of the window, she could feel the anger and bitterness twisting deep within her. She *would* get her boy back. Even if she had to kill to do it. The battle she had planned had now begun and she was exactly where she wanted to be – right in the thick of it.

The slamming of the front door could probably be heard all along Jubilee Street. 'There she goes – off to the Jewish market to buy some more bloody fish.' Patsy shook her head in disgust. 'I would rather be six foot under than live to be that old. Six foot under but up there with the angels!' She craned her neck to see that Simons had turned the corner and was out of the way.

Her heart thumping faster by the second, Patsy took a small palette knife from the cutlery drawer and made her way downstairs. She was thankful now for the time she had once left her keys inside her flat and Simons had shown her how to slide a blade between the lock and the door to get it open.

Once inside the ground-floor flat, she scanned the old-fashioned room until her eyes fell upon a cupboard which had been built into the wall next to the Victorian fireplace, where an electric two-bar fire stood. Why she felt drawn to it she had no idea, but as she eased down the tiny brass wing-latch, she somehow knew that this was exactly the sort of place where old house deeds might be kept, should there be any in existence.

The musty cupboard was like an Aladdin's cave. There were four shelves and they were jammed full of old biscuit tins and a variety of wooden boxes. Old newspapers and paperback books were piled up on the floor of the cupboard; some had turned yellow with age.

Ignoring the grotesque stuffed bird which stared down from the top shelf, Patsy's hand went to a square tin decorated with a faded Christmas scene. She pushed and pulled at the rust-bound lid, her excitement growing as she gradually eased the tin open. It was full of greetings cards which dated back to before the Second World War, and there was a distinct smell of lavender on a bundle of letters which were tied together with narrow pink ribbon.

She resisted the urge to read any of the cards and letters, closed the lid and carefully replaced the tin in its original place. Opening one box after another, she found a rich assortment of memorabilia, including a silver pocket-watch with a heavy ornate chain. There were bundles of family photographs, some in frames. One collection obviously belonged to Simons, for although she was younger in most of them, she was easily recognizable by her large brown eyes. There were some of her with her husband and a few portrait pictures of each of them. Patsy was surprised to see what a handsome pair they had been. She prayed that she wouldn't grow ugly with age too.

Unmoved by the sight of Mr Simons's sympathy card, edged with black, she continued with her search. Knowing how time slipped quickly by when she was enjoying herself, she kept an eye on her watch.

She was about to search the third shelf when a large grubby manila envelope caught her eye. Pulling it out from beneath some other papers, she used her long nails to untie the knotted string and free the package.

Much to her joy, the papers she withdrew were the deeds to the house and a neatly folded plan of each room. There was also a small key inside, which she hoped would be the one to the cellar door, which Simons said she had not seen since the day she moved in. What lay beneath the old floorboards was a mystery, and not one which the old woman had been interested in exploring. She slipped it into her dress pocket for another day.

With the envelope containing the deeds tucked under her arm, she closed the cupboard door, ready to investigate the contents of a dark oak carved dresser on the other side of the room.

'I hope you found what you were looking for.' Esther's voice was filled with repulsion.

Patsy felt her body jerk, as if she had just been struck by lightning. 'Fuck you!' she snapped as the envelope slipped from under her arm and fell to the floor. Snatching it up, she stepped closer to Esther and showed her the back of her hand. The gesture was full of threat.

'Yes. I believe you would. Old women and children would be your mark.' She couldn't possibly know how close to the bone her accusations were.

'You old hag. Creeping in like a spy!' Retrieving the deeds from the floor, she pushed the envelope up close to Mrs Simons's face. 'Here is the incriminating evidence that will put you behind bars! I've read who the owner was – and the name is nothing like yours. I should think the relatives of the deceased owner, Laurence Goldstein, won't be too happy when they see these! You've been cheating that family for ten years, ever since he died.'

'Get out of my flat.' The expression of disgust on Mrs Simons's face would have made most people feel ashamed, but not Patsy. She was as tough as old boots. 'If you ever step over my threshold again, I will put a knife through you.'

Pushing Esther aside, Patsy stormed past. 'While you're still hanging around I wouldn't want to come in. You turn my stomach over.'

Once Patsy had gone up the stairs, Esther pushed the door shut, leaned on the back of an old armchair and wished she were dead. The joy had been taken out of her life just before the Second World War. Why she had had to struggle on since then, she didn't know. God seemed to have forgotten His chosen people. And now, after years of getting by in that damp house, through cold winters, she was to be forced out by a cheat.

Laurence had said she could live there, rent-free, only minutes before he passed away. He had said nothing about who the house had been left to and as far as she had known, there were no living relatives. At least none that had ever paid him a visit. The only family he spoke about when they sat around his coal fire at night had been those he had lost.

It had never occurred to Esther to go through his papers looking for a will. No one had asked her to. His funeral had been a small affair, just herself and a handful of his old friends. There was no insurance claim – he hadn't believed in all that. All he had passed over to her was an envelope containing two hundred pounds to cover the cost of his burial.

And as far as taking rent from the tenants was concerned, she had seen nothing wrong in that. She was just carrying on as Laurence, her good friend and landlord, would have wished. But who would believe her? None of the people who mattered, she felt sure of that: the people who would have the right to lock her away. Was that the way she was meant to end her life –

in a prison? Her mind went to the nightmare. Back to the prison camp – back to the Nazis. Maybe God was judging her now, for escaping the fate so many others had suffered.

Trembling like a kitten, she opened the cupboard which Patsy had ransacked. Gazing trance-like at her personal belongings, which were now covered with that evil woman's fingerprints, Esther knew that tonight must be the last she would spend in this house. This was no longer her home. There was a strange dark feeling in the air and a chill she had not noticed before.

As the wall-clock in the narrow hallway struck midnight, Patsy lay in her bed wondering why she wasn't filled with pleasure. She had found a little gold-mine. Maybe it was only natural for her to feel edgy: after all, the old witch downstairs had threatened to take a knife to her.

Sitting up in bed, she stared at her door. The word *knife* had jarred. If the lock could be slipped so easily, what was to stop the old woman creeping up in the middle of the night?

Tiptoeing slowly across the room, Patsy lifted a dining-chair and wedged it under the door handle and then listened. She could hear her heart beating in the shadowy room. The silence was loud and closing in on her.

As she slipped between the sheets, Patsy knew that she would not be getting much sleep that night. Pulling the blankets and eiderdown up to her chin, she straightened her arms and legs so she was in a comfortable position, and then lay very still. She would not move a muscle; she must be able to hear every small movement, just in case Simons crept up on her. *I'll soon be away from this place,* she thought. *We'll soon be on our way. Just a few months, Jac, and we'll kiss the East End goodbye.* She smiled at the thought of it.

She eased one pillow from under her head and placed the two of them side by side. One for her and one for her son. 'Goodnight, Jac, don't let the bed bugs bite,' she whispered, and rested a hand where her boy should be lying, by her side.

Closing her eyes, wishing the night away, Patsy thought she heard shuffling from below. She held her breath and waited. Silence. Of course it was her imagination running wild. After all, if she could so easily imagine Jac in the room with her, a few bumps was nothing by comparison.

Just after midnight, once the champagne had been consumed, followed by spirits and beer, Kay's wedding guests were very much in a party mood. After all the work, she was determined to enjoy herself and to see that Steve's family weren't left out. She needn't have worried; the laughter filling the room was proof enough. Her eyes found Jac, who was attracting much attention from the adults and looked as proud as punch to be up so late.

Seeing everyone getting on so well, and hearing the excited buzz which had spread through her grandfather's cottage, Kay knew she had done the right thing. She couldn't imagine the same kind of atmosphere had they gone through with the original plan and booked a hall. She looked at Steve, who was chatting away to her aunt Liz. He looked more at ease now that the ceremony was behind him and he had a few drinks inside him.

Kay's mind flew back to the time when her life had been full of parties, theatre, cinema and restaurants. It made her fancy a reefer, but there was no chance of that now. Steve had been very strict about her not smoking pot. He had said that one thing could lead to another and she could end up being hooked on hard drugs. She thought it was funny at the time, still did, but he was worth stopping for. She had hardly been an addict, just enjoyed sharing a joint now and then.

Once the remains of the food had been cleared away and the tables pushed to the wall, Kay put on an LP, *Party Time at the Astor Club*, knowing it would go down well. Before long most of the guests were dancing and singing along – Billy's voice being the loudest.

As little Jac, with the remnants of chocolate cake around his face, danced with Steve's small sister, Kay watched the pair of them shrieking with laughter and her heart sank. Once again the Moors murders were on her mind. God knows what kind of people were still out there. Mental cases who had never been found out. She felt a cold chill run down her spine at the thought of her brother going off with someone. She would have to give him a little pep talk – and soon. Warn him about strangers. About not taking lifts from anyone he didn't know.

Shaking herself out of her sudden black mood, Kay could not understand why there should be a knot in her stomach. Why wouldn't the feeling of her brother being under some kind of threat go away?

Pouring herself a large port and lemon and hearing

Jac trying to sing along with the adults lightened her. After all, her brother was always in safe hands. Their doting mother hardly let him out of her sight.

She slipped one arm around Steve's waist and kissed his neck. 'Can you spare a few seconds for your wife?'

'You leave 'im be,' Liz said, the happier for drink. 'He's telling me all about the firm he's starting up. Gonna get me a job with one of his contacts – modelling corsets.'

'Don't even pretend to go along with her, Steve, or she'll turn up one day dressed up to the nines, ready for the photographer.' She put her arm through his and pretended to be jealous of the 'other woman' in his life. Dragging him out of the room, she led him through the kitchen and out into the back garden where they could be alone.

'You OK?' she asked, pushing her hand through his thick blond hair.

'Never felt better.'

'No regrets?'

'Of course not.'

'Well?'

'Well what?'

'Don't you have a strong desire to kiss the bride?'

'Yes, but it doesn't seem right leaving our guests.' He pushed her hands behind her back and gripped them. 'So stop teasing me.'

'I can't help it, you shouldn't be so handsome.' She nuzzled against his strong body and sucked on his neck. 'I wish we were on our own.'

'Plenty of time for that,' he said, pulling her closer. 'We've got the rest of our lives.'

'You needn't sound so happy about it.' She raised her face and looked into his eyes. 'You are happy, aren't you?'

'What do you think?'

'I'm not sure . . . sometimes, I don't know, you seem so preoccupied.'

'Don't be silly.' He slipped his hands down and squeezed her buttocks, pushing his hard body against her. 'I can't wait to have you to myself.'

Melting into a long passionate kiss, Kay was in her seventh heaven. 'I love you so much,' she murmured.

'And I love you.'

'Yeah, and *life* should mean just that!' With the Moors scandal on his mind too, Jack had got himself into a conversation with Kay's father-in-law, Hedley. 'Mind you, if they set the evil pair free now they'd be doing us all a favour. They wouldn't last two minutes outside. I know I wouldn't hold back if I caught sight of them.'

'Is prison the right place, that's the question. I should have thought Broadmoor.'

Arriving back in the packed living room, Kay slipped her arms through each of the fathers' and grinned. 'You two look very serious. Hope you're not still going on about the white wedding we should have had?'

'Your cheeks are glowing. What've you been drinking?' Jack didn't want to think about a white wedding. He was disappointed that Kay had got her way and only a few of his relations and friends were there. His sister Liz had put a brave face on it but he knew she was gutted too.

It was a family custom to have a big turnout with

everyone there. Babies, children, the whole lot of them. At least Billy's cottage was small and the place was crowded. The atmosphere was good – he had to admit that.

'So what were you discussing then?' Kay was beginning to feel tipsy.

'Your father and I were just saying that Brady and Hindley shouldn't ever see the light of day.'

'I might have known. That's all Dad's been talking about since the trial ended. Try to forget about it. This is supposed to be a celebration! It's not every day your daughter gets married.'

Jack raised his eyebrows sheepishly. 'I suppose she's got a point.'

'She has. Of course she has. All the same...'

'It's not right, is it?'

'They should have been hanged!' Steve's father was on the same wavelength as Jack. Like most parents they were finding it difficult to push the dreadful murders from their thoughts.

'Why they abolished 'anging, I'll never know.'

'When I think of what those children went through! What their parents are going through now. They'll never be able to live with it. Not without torturing themselves. Poor devils will end up insane, I shouldn't wonder.'

'D'you know what ... it's true what Kay said, I 'ave been going on about it but,' Jack swallowed hard, 'I'm *so* angry.' He clenched a fist until he could feel his nails digging into the palm of his hand. 'I'm boiling up inside ... I feel as if I wanna smash the prison walls down around them.'

'I've cried several times, you know. In private. Can't seem to stop myself.' Hedley looked as if he might shed a tear there and then. 'I've never *hated* so much.'

'The entire country hates the wicked bastards. The world, for that matter. They should have hanged them and be done with the scum.'

'Of course the trouble with the death sentence ... there was that dreadful case with that lad who had the mental age of a child—'

'Now *he* shouldn't have been—'

'What d'yer reckon then? On the jellied eels?' Billy pushed his head forward and grinned, doing his best not to sway from side to side.

'Oh er, yes, very nice. Tasty.'

'Good. I knew you'd enjoy 'em. Your missus wasn't keen though. Nearly chucked it up. Still, can't please everyone.' He leaned forward and roared with laughter. 'Should 'ave seen her face!'

# Chapter Three

It seemed fitting to Esther Simons that it should be drizzling that Sunday afternoon; the weather matched her grey mood. Had the May sunshine been out in full, it would have made her feel worse. As she pulled the old street door behind her for what she believed to be the last time, she felt herself shiver as if someone had walked over her grave.

Gripping the handle of her large battered suitcase with one hand, she bent down and lifted the two bulging carrier bags with the other. As she straightened she thanked God that the walk along Jubilee Street towards the Mile End Road wasn't that far. From there she would catch the 253 bus to Whitechapel, to her brother's ground-floor flat in Brady Dwellings.

With her brown coat collar up and her green wool headscarf knotted under her chin she walked slowly along the pavement, keeping her eyes down. She would tell any neighbours, should they happen to be out walking in the fine rain, that she was to spend a couple of weeks with a cousin in the country. A little holiday. What else could she say? How could she explain the real reason for her going?

By the time she had reached Mauri's flat, her arms felt as if they would snap off at the sockets.

As her brother opened the door to her she felt a surge of tears rush to the back of her eyes. 'Oh, Mauri – that it should come to this? What am I, the Wandering Jew?'

Guiding her slowly into his small sitting room, he sat her down by the electric fire. 'I'll fetch your things in.' He was too choked to say anything else, and she was too beaten to argue that the suitcase would be heavy for him.

When he didn't appear with her things, she stood up and walked into the passage, thinking he couldn't manage it. But the street door was shut. 'Mauri? Where are you?'

'In the bedroom, where else? You can unpack later. That I will not do.'

'You're giving me your bedroom?'

'No, Esther. I'm sharing it with you. My bed here – yours there. That way at least we can enjoy the sitting room.' He smiled and slowly shook his head. 'We spend a lot of time sitting, don't we?'

'Sure, but—'

'No buts. You're not here on a temporary basis. You're here for good. Accept that from the beginning and it will make life a lot easier – for both of us.'

He drew his sister to him and they clung to each other. 'What a cold-hearted woman your lovely new tenant turned out to be, eh?'

'I'm sorry to burden you like this—'

'Shush!' He pulled away from her and waved a hand. 'Don't start driving me mad with all that. Go and put the kettle on instead.'

'You know something?' Esther's eyes glazed over and she looked deep in thought. 'I had a strange feeling about her right from the start. Nothing I could put my finger on. She was polite, friendly, maybe a little too familiar at first ... And you know what she did? She cut and dyed her hair.'

'So?'

'I dunno. It was like she was hiding from someone, or running away from something.'

'Well, then, maybe you're better off out of there.'

'Maurice ... my home?' She slowly shook her head as the tears rolled down her lined face. 'It's my home, Mauri. How can I be better off out of it?'

'I've cleared the right-hand side of the wardrobe. Why don't you unpack and hang up your clothes? I'll make us a hot drink.' He left the room, unable to think of anything to say.

As Esther pulled open the lid of her suitcase, she felt a bitter cry escape from her throat, and there was nothing she could do to stop it. As the sound tailed off, so another started, and then another and another. All she could do was let go. Her body began to shake as the shock of yesterday's revelation made itself felt.

Her brother stood in the doorway holding a cup of tea, but he could see it would be impossible trying to get her to drink it while she was in that state. All he could do was wait until her pitifully thin body had rid itself of the bottled-up humiliation.

Walking from room to room in the small Victorian house, Patsy could hardly believe her good fortune. She had innocently ventured into an ordinary house and found herself a well-lined purse. Running a finger across the darkly painted window-sill, she decided to lighten every room. Paint over the varnished doors and window-frames – with brilliant white. She would let it to tenants with an offer that could not be refused. Six weeks rent-free, providing they paid six months in advance. And she would strike the deal with as many people as possible. Let them all turn up at once: she would be miles away by then. Screw the lot of them.

She would sell the furniture for a good price. Some of the pieces were just what antique buyers were snapping up. She would replace most of it with cheap new furniture on hire purchase, under a pseudonym. That way it would only cost her the first down payment.

Congratulating herself, Patsy settled down on her bed and with notepad and pen began to make a watertight plan, to be carried out over the following months. Soon she would be out of the pits and away from the low life and the smell of dirt.

Once school-dinner time was over and the children had rushed down into the playground to let off steam, Jac went into the boy's cloakroom and waited for Patsy to pass by. Hanging on to one of the black iron coat pegs, he lifted his feet off the ground and swung himself to and fro, keeping one eye on the entrance.

'Jac Armstrong? How many times have you been told not to do that?' Hilary Way, his class teacher, arrived through another doorway.

Dropping to the floor, Jac stood up straight and frowned. 'Sorry, Mrs Way. I forgot.'

'I'm sure. Well don't do it again, OK? I wouldn't mind

if these rules weren't made for your own good.' She tapped her stiletto heel on the concrete floor. 'Crack your head on that floor and you'd know it.'

'Yes miss.'

'All right, Jac.' She quietly laughed. 'You don't have to stand to attention. You're not in the army.'

'No miss.'

'Go on, out you go then. You've only got ten minutes' playtime left.' Still laughing at him, Hilary Way made her way towards the staff room, squeezing past Patsy as she manoeuvred the stainless steel three-tiered trolley which was loaded with dirty plates.

Taking Patsy by surprise, Jac stepped out and grinned. 'I've got something for you.' He held out his clenched fist and then opened it to reveal a sweaty palm on which lay one marble. 'It's my best one. Worth three greens.'

Patsy glanced around to make sure no one would see, and then tousled his sandy hair. 'This will have to be our second secret, you know. If I told the others you gave me this, they would want to know why. I could get into trouble over the swede.'

'All right. Two secrets.' He dropped the marble into her slim white hand. 'Oh and there's something else,' he closed one eye and screwed up his face, 'I hate cabbage as well.'

'I'll remember that. So – are you going to tell me your name, then?'

'It's Jac without a K.'

'That's different. Who thought of that, your mum or dad?' she asked, knowing full well it had been her idea to name him almost after his father. It was her way of reminding Jack that he hadn't finished what he had started.

Having thought about it, Jac shrugged. 'Not sure. Don't really care.'

'Well, Jac without a K, I'm Mrs Hem' and that's what you can tell any of your friends, should they ask. But my *best* friends, who I keep secrets with, call me Hem'.'

'See you then, Hem'.' Without looking back, Jac disappeared along the corridor and round a corner on his way to the boys' playground.

She had already worked out what he should call her. Hemmingway might just be picked up on at home, should he mention her, and she wasn't going to take any risks. And Hem' was as close-sounding to Mum as she was going to get – for now.

Pushing the trolley into the school kitchen and up to the large sinks, Patsy felt very pleased with herself. If things went along at the rate they were going, maybe she would be moving on sooner than she had imagined. Six months was what she had written in her diary. That's how long she thought it would take to get Jac into her confidence. She decided then and there, as she unloaded the plates on to a rack in the sink, that during the couple of hours between this job and her other part-time work at the cinema, she would do some shopping. She would buy some clothes for Jac to wear on his trip to Scotland.

'We've got a new dinner lady and she's really nice.' Jac pulled at Kay's wedding ring to see if it would come off. 'Where's your engagement ring?' He thought she had had to give it back when she got the gold band.

'It's hidden away in my secret drawer, safe and sound. I want the world to see this one, and only this one.' She proudly held out her hand and admired it.

'And where's Steve? He promised to fetch me some of 'is old comics.'

'Steve, you little scrap, is working.'

Jac got off the sofa where he had been lying next to Kay and studied the clock on the mantelshelf. 'The little hand's on the eight and the big one's on the five.'

'Well?' There was a pause. 'Come on, tin-head, you should know by now.'

'Nearly half past eight.' He couldn't be bothered working it out.

'Twenty-five minutes past!'

'Why's he working at night?'

'Because he has to.'

'Did his boss say so?'

'No. Steve's his own boss.'

'Well why's he doing it then?'

'Because he wants to be rich. Now stop your chatting and go and brush your teeth. It's bedtime.'

'You always let me stay up late when you're baby-sitting!'

'Well I have! Go on, or I'll have Mum after me.'

He jumped on Kay. 'She won't know, will she? It can be our secret.'

'No. Teeth!'

'What's wrong with secrets?'

Kay thought about that. 'I'm not keen. You shouldn't have to have them. Not really.'

'I've got some.'

'Oh, have you now?' Kay gripped his tiny neck with one hand. 'Tell me or I'll strangle you.'

'I can't, can I? Otherwise they wouldn't be secrets. But I will say who they're with.'

Kay tightened her grip. 'Talk or else.'

Giggling, Jac tried to escape. 'All right, I'll tell yer. My dinner lady. She only gives me tiny bits of what I don't like.'

'No! God, Jac, I'm really pleased you let me in on that one. I won't tell a soul!'

'Her name's Hem' to her friends and she's really nice.'

'You already told me that. Now then – bathroom.'

'Don't you wanna know about our new dinner lady then?'

'Not now, no.' Kay looked from her watch to the telephone. 'Go and get ready for bed, Jac. I want to phone Steve and then Pamela.'

'I am ready.' He held his arms out as if she hadn't noticed he had his pyjamas on.

'You know what I mean – now *go!*'

Grumbling under his breath, Jac slouched off leaving her in peace.

After phoning Steve and settling on a time when he would pick her up, Kay phoned her best friend. It was Lillian, Pamela's mother, who answered. She sounded pleased to hear Kay's voice, and wanted to know all about the wedding and why she had changed her mind about the church. Then she asked about hers and Steve's flat and when would they be buying a place of their own. And then, before she finally passed the receiver over to Pamela, she wished her luck and hoped she would be blessed with many children.

'I feel really bad that I didn't ask your parents—'

'Oh, don't start all that again. It's over and done with. So how's married life?' asked Pamela.

'It's good. Better than I thought. But listen to this. Steve reckons I'll be able to give up my job and be employed by him – he's making a bomb, and needs to offset some tax. All I'll have to do for my salary is go in once a week and fiddle the petty cash. Not bad, eh?'

'That doesn't sound like you.'

'Well maybe it's a new me. You saying I should carry on working long hours for low pay for a publishing company that turns over a million or two in a year, instead?'

'You'll turn into a cabbage. Your brain will shrink to the size of a pea. You'll end up a rich bored housewife who reads magazines all day instead of writing for them – hang on a sec.'

Once Pamela had kissed her aunt and said goodbye, she returned to the phone. 'Poor Auntie Esther—'

'She's not ill, is she?' Kay had been to Esther's house a couple of times with Pamela and she had really taken to the old girl.

'She's had to move in with my uncle Mauri.' Pamela lowered her voice and spoke right into the mouthpiece, 'Some fucking cow's thrown her out of her house.'

'She's *what*?'

'I'll tell you more when I see you. And speaking of seeing you, when will that be?'

'I'm babysitting Jac. Mum and Dad have gone to see *The Spy Who Came In from the Cold*. It's Dad's birthday.'

'I suppose I could come round . . .'

71

'Yeah, go on then. Steve won't be here till gone nine, probably later. Come on, you know you want to ask me all about married life.'

'And Steve'll drop me off?'

''Course he will.'

'See you in half an hour.' There was a click and then the dialling tone.

'I wanna wait up to see Pamela.' Jac folded his arms, showing his determination. He had crept back in while she was talking.

'I'll send her in when she gets here – promise.' Kay took him by the shoulders and marched him into his room.

Once she had tucked him in and switched on his night-light, she sat on the edge of the bed and ran her fingers through his hair. 'Funny old freckle-face,' she smiled and kissed him.

'You gonna read to me, or tell me a story out of your head?'

'Neither, Jac. It's late. Mum would kill me if she knew you were still awake, let alone me reading to you.'

'Five minutes of Mr Marley, that's all!'

'Oh, I can't just come up with a story like that! I need a bit of time to think about it.'

'Make it up as you go along.'

She couldn't help smiling at him. What did he think she did? 'All right, but a short one carried on from the last time, right?'

'Yep. Mr Marley had locked Justine and Duncan in the maintenance room on the roof of the block of flats where he kept all the things he'd stolen from the people's flats.'

'Nothing wrong with your memory, is there?'

'Nope.' Jac made himself comfortable, hands behind his head, eyes closed, sheet up to his chin, and waited.

'Come on then, Kay. Before I fall asleep.' He opened one eye. 'You're not tricking me, are you? Just sitting there 'cos you know I can't stay awake long?'

'No, I'm not tricking you.' She inhaled slowly, brought the characters into her mind and began to do what she loved best. Create a fantasy world for her Jac.


Pamela was, as expected, half an hour late, but it didn't take long for the best friends to settle down to a good chin-wag. They did finally get round to the problem of Auntie Esther, but by then the drama seemed to have gone out of it.

'Mum thinks it's for the best in any case. Her and Uncle Mauri will be company for each other – and they can share the bills.'

'But your uncle's flat is only a one-bedroom!'

'I know, but they don't seem to mind sharing. And they'll be warmer. Auntie Esther's house did get damp in the winter. She's always had trouble with her chest.'

'Well if it was my aunt I'd be straight round there to sort this cow out. Who is she anyway? Did she buy the house or what?'

'Don't know. Esther didn't want to elaborate.'

'I can't believe your apathy.'

'My auntie is seventy-six, you know. Her mind's not as sharp as it was. Maybe she got it wrong.' There was a pause. 'I can't believe anyone would be that bad.'

While the girls were discussing Patsy, whom Kay

believed to be a stranger, Patsy herself was enjoying a glass of whisky and writing a letter to her mother. She felt like she was dreaming. The house was very quiet. No more booming from the radio below, filling the place with fictitious people who talked too much.

Before she signed off, Patsy read the letter aloud:

I've been extra busy helping my lovely landlady have a good spring clean. She's been so good, cooking my evening meals and refusing to let me pay, save for a few extra shillings to help with the shopping.

Things are going so well for me down here – but then, Stepney was my home for a few years, wasn't it?

I had to put you off coming to see me because my sweet old landlady has a thing about her tenants having visitors. And we don't want to tip the apple-cart, do we? So please don't make any surprise visits. It could ruin things for me. And if Father won't accept this, tell him to take care, or he might cause a rift between you and your only child.

Your ever-loving daughter.

The letter was a pack of lies, but as long as it stopped her parents coming down and messing up her plans she couldn't have cared less.

As she signed her name, Patsy was suddenly filled with mischief. It was a nice evening and it seemed right that she should take a stroll on her night off from the cinema. She was bound to find a postbox somewhere near the Armstrongs' flats, and there would be no fear of meeting Jac out playing at that time of night. She might be courting danger, but the chances of bumping into any of that family seemed very slim. And there was even less chance that they would recognize her.

Arriving at the block of flats, she decided not to walk through the tarmacked grounds but took the route along the back of the four-storey building.

When she arrived beneath Jack and Laura's back balcony, she crossed the narrow road and sat on a low wall. And as the shadow of Jac moved behind the curtains, with the light behind him, Patsy was confident that should he look out of the window, he wouldn't be able to see her as she sat watching him in the dark, away from the lamp-posts.

'You little tyke,' she laughed, watching him as he jumped up and down on his bed, using it like a trampoline. 'I bet they think you're tucked up in bed fast asleep.'

The small step of her being close but unseen created a feeling of power within Patsy. She would, from now on, take the same stroll on her evenings off. Another secret could be added to the list. She would tell Jac that she just happened to look up and had seen him at that window. A chance in a million, she would tell him. And she would be sure to drop a hint that she would be passing by at that time every Thursday night – should he be awake and want to wave to her.

As she popped her letter into the postbox, Patsy wondered if fate destined the way, or whether people really did, subconsciously or not, make things happen. Either way she didn't care. Life was going too well for her to question why.

* * *

'Thanks for telling Pamela I would give her a lift. That's all I need at the end of a long day.' Steve looked and sounded very tired. 'Isn't it enough that I have to come and pick *you* up?'

'Well what was I supposed to do at this time of night? Walk? It's ten past twelve!'

'You could have got a train a bit earlier. I've got to be up at six.'

Kay felt suddenly ashamed. Steve was right. She had been thinking of herself and not him. 'I'm sorry. It's just that I haven't seen Pam since the wedding. She is my best friend, you know.'

Braking suddenly at the traffic lights, he sighed. 'You were complaining yesterday that you hardly saw me. The one day when I could have been home by nine and you decide to go out.'

'You didn't get to Mum's until gone eleven! Someone twisted your arm to go to the pub, I suppose?'

'I decided to make the most of my bit of free time. Babysitting's not at the top of *my* list.'

'It's Dad's birthday, for Christ's sake! What did you expect me to do? Leave Jac by himself because I must be a good little wife and have your dinner ready?'

'Something like that, yes.'

'Well, when Mum asked me I didn't know you would be home before midnight for a change. It was arranged over a week ago.'

'It's not easy, starting up a business. I need all the support I can get.'

As he drew up in the parking space behind their flat

above the Westminster Bank in Stroud Green, Steve casually announced that he had been thinking about buying a car for Kay. A Volkswagen.

'A *Beetle*?' She couldn't keep the excitement out of her voice even though she felt guilty at having sulked for most of the journey home.

'You won't have to rely on me so much then.'

She laughed inwardly at his remark. It was just like him to dampen the good news. 'Steve . . .' She grabbed his arm before he got out of the car. 'I'm sorry.' She hoped for a smile, but his expression remained dour. He was still angry at arriving home so late when they could have had a couple of hours together, enjoying a drink at the end of the day.

Slipping in bed beside her new husband, Kay snuggled up close and gazed at his handsome face. She wondered how long it would be before he responded to some of the very attractive girls in the advertising world who weren't averse to flirting with him in front of her. She had felt jealous several times when they had been to the pub or to one of the many agency parties. Advertising seemed to be one continuous round of company entertaining.

No matter how many times Steve told her that he wasn't interested in anyone else, she was still full of doubt.

'Are you asleep?' She eased her leg over Steve's, stroking his foot with her big toe, and brushed a kiss across his cheek. The only sound from her husband was a low sleepy groan.

'Steve . . . ?'

'Mmmmmm?'

'Shall I leave you alone?' She drew her hand along his leg.

'Mmmm.' He sighed and turned over, too far into sleep to rouse himself.

Snuggling up and fitting her body against his broad back, she kissed his shoulders and whispered goodnight into his ear, hoping he might just stir himself.

Pulling herself out of her passionate mood, Kay turned her back on Steve and curled up. The sighs, grunts and low mumblings coming from him made her smile. She carefully turned over again, hoping to catch what he was saying in his sleep. As he stirred and turned to face her his voice became clearer. 'Put the phone down, she might want to ring me.'

'Who might?' she quietly asked, doing her best not to laugh.

'Mmmmmm?' Steve slightly opened his heavy eyelids. 'What?'

'Nothing. Go back to sleep,' she chuckled.

'You smell nice,' he murmured, sweeping one hand down her spine. 'Why are you wearing knickers?'

'I'm not. These are my new baby-doll pyjamas.' She ignored his soft laughter.

'They feel like knickers to me,' he said, pushing his hand under the soft cotton gingham.

'I thought you were tired?'

'I was. But you were determined to wake me up.' His voice was still full of sleep. Slowly lifting his head as if it were a dead weight, he kissed her gently on the mouth. 'You're so sexy in the mornings,' he drawled.

'It's not the morning.' She wasn't laughing any more. Longing had taken over from amusement as she found his mouth again and kissed him. All doubts and fears gone, Kay resolved not to be suspicious or jealous again. She must learn to trust that her husband's pensive moods were due to the pressure of work, and not another woman.

'I can't 'elp worrying about Kay, Lizzie. And it's *not* because she's my only granddaughter.'

Liz eased off her shoes and flopped back in the armchair. She wasn't going to show Billy that she too was a little concerned. Not after a busy shift in the canteen at Hammond's. She was ready for her afternoon doze.

'I could understand it if she'd married a lazy good-for-nothing so-and-so.' She closed her eyes and relaxed.

'But she 'ardly sees anything of 'im! Working all bloody hours – and for what?' asked Billy.

'For a shilling! That's what! Now shut up and leave me in peace.'

'And she spends too much time on 'er own as well. It's all wrong if you ask me.'

'Well I'm not. No one is.'

'On 'er own all day . . .'

'Billy – she fills every hour! Decorating and furnishing that little flat of theirs. She loves it.' She adjusted the small cushion behind her head and snuggled into it. 'You're bored, that's your trouble. Go out for a walk. Go and put a bet on or something.'

'And what if he does make a rich woman of 'er? What then, eh? She'll get too high and mighty to come and see her own grandfather.'

'And that's what's really bugging yer. You've got to

learn to let her go. If she ends up living in a bloody mansion – so what?'

'Anyway, I've already put my bet on,' Billy said sulkily.

'No you haven't. It's on the sideboard, waiting to go to the bookmaker's.' Liz could feel herself floating off to sleep.

'I'm telling you I've put it on. Why don't you listen?' He lifted himself from his armchair and strode to the sideboard. Seeing his bet written out but no book-maker's receipt baffled him.

'But I remember going...' His voice gave him away and caused Liz to open her eyes.

'You're getting mixed up with yesterday,' she said carefully.

'Yeah? Maybe you're right. But I could 'ave sworn...' Screwing up the piece of paper in his hands, he turned away. 'Think I'll go and 'ave a lie-down.'

'I'll give you a shout in an hour. We'll 'ave a nice cup of tea.' Once again, Billy had added to the nagging doubt in her mind. He had always been a bit forgetful but lately he'd been worse. She had put it down to his age at first. In his seventies – it was to be expected. But she knew deep down that it was more than that. Poor old Billy was in the early stages of senile dementia. The signs all pointed to it. She had looked it up in her *Family Medical Guide*.

Settling down again for her nap, Liz felt sure that this was something she must keep to herself, making light of his errors. Neither Billy nor the family must get to know – it would be too much of a blow for him. She would go on covering up his forgetfulness until it became obvious to Laura and Jack. At least that way Billy could maintain his dignity for as long as possible.

In the four years of living under the same roof she had come to love the silly sod. Not in a sexy kind of way. She had no time for that, although she had to admit, when they did cuddle up now and then, when it was freezing cold, she had felt something stir. Maybe the next time they did it she would leave her corsets off and see what happened. It would do Billy good to have a bit of the other.

'So you think that Kay's done the right thing, then, Liz? Marrying above 'erself?' He was back in the doorway again.

'She 'asn't married above herself! Steve's family are from Edmonton – that's hardly posh, you dozy sod!'

'He seemed all right, I s'pose ... Wassisname? Hedley, weren't it? Steve's old man. The mother was a bit of a snob, mind.'

It was obvious to Liz that she wasn't going to be left in peace unless she came up with something drastic to get rid of him. She looked up, keeping a dead straight face. 'You're not after a bit of nooky, are yer?'

Caught off guard, Billy wasn't his usual quick self. There was no humorous retort for a change. 'You can be bloody crude at times, you know that?' With the blood rushing to his cheeks he stormed out of the room.

Closing her eyes again, Liz leaned back and smiled. That had taken the wind out of his sails. Silly old goat.

'Why? Are you?' His shadow fell across her.

Grabbing a cushion she took aim and threw it at him. 'Get off, Billy!'

Again he left the room, only this time he was laughing. He had called her bluff and was enjoying it. There was nothing he liked more than to score a point. And no doubt, once he had had a doze and more time to think about her offer, he would be back with another quip.

Her only real worry was Jac. Billy often met him from school when Laura was on lates at Hammond's. What if Billy forgot to collect him one day? Even if Jac made his way safely back to the cottage, she and Billy could so easily be out shopping.

She quietly cursed, for what had been a niggling concern had now grown into something worse.

Pulling herself out of the armchair, she silently blamed the evil woman who had been in the headlines for several months now. How could children be trusted out by themselves when you couldn't even trust a woman to leave them alone? Myra Hindley was one of nature's rare bad eggs, it was true, but who was to say there might not be another insane bitch out there somewhere?

As she pulled her little blue snuff tin from her cardigan pocket, Liz decided that she would somehow get Billy to use the diary she had bought for him. If he became angry and stubborn over it, she would mention the bet he was so *sure* he had put on.

If he still refused, she would have no choice but to insist. She would have to tell him the reason why it was important that he made a note of everything he was meant to do. Especially when it came to collecting his grandson from school.

\* \* \*

Laura pushed her bare feet into a big cushion at the end of the settee, feeling her stomach rumbling. 'I don't suppose you wanna go out and get fish and chips, do you?'

Jack didn't look up from his paperback. 'No.'

'I could really fancy piping-hot chips and crispy battered fish. A nice piece of cod ... or maybe rock eel? Washed down with a long glass of cool beer. And then an early night.' She stretched her arms and pulled her long wavy hair into a french pleat and pushed in two pins to hold it. 'After a nice soak in the bath with my favourite Blue Grass bath oil...'

'Yeah, all right – I've got the point, crafty cow.'

'I don't know what you're talking about,' Laura grinned and winked at him. 'I was really rushed off my feet today. Bloody sales are a nightmare. You'd think some of those women had never seen a new dress before. And you know which ones go first? Those that 'ave been specially bought in for the sale.'

'What's wrong with that?' Jack closed his book and looked at her.

'Well when I go to the sales, I make a grab for the good labels. They're usually the real bargains.'

'Yeah. But still dearer than the ones they buy in.'

'Can't help it if I've got good taste, can I?' She blew him a kiss. 'You're gonna go then?' She slipped into her sexy voice which she knew he couldn't resist.

'Only because I'm 'ungry – no other reason.' He pulled his shoes from under the coffee table. 'And when I get back I've got a proposition to put to you.'

'Oh yeah?' She raised an eyebrow, wondering if he was going to ask if he could get in the bath with her. It would be the first time. They hadn't gone in for that kind of thing. It had never occurred to Laura, until Kay told her quite casually, in passing, that she and Steve often bathed together. She was a bit shocked at first, but when she thought about it, the idea rather appealed to her. She had thrown a few hints Jack's way – that very evening in fact.

With his jacket on, standing by the living-room door, Jack nodded thoughtfully. 'Yeah. I'm seriously thinking of taking redundancy if it's offered.'

'I thought that was only a rumour?'

'It is. But containerization's already arrived. It won't be long now before they start putting us off. Anyway, I've had enough. The docks are not the same any more. The colour's gone out of the job.'

'You've a long while till you retire, Jack. What will you do in the meanwhile?'

'That's what I want to talk to you about. What d'yer want then, cod or rock?'

'Cod.' Laura didn't push for an answer to her question. She had a feeling it couldn't be answered in one sentence.

'Shall I get a bag of chips for the Jac?'

'No! He's had his tea and should be asleep by the time you get back, providing you don't go in there and tell him where you're going.'

'Won't hurt, surely. Just this once?'

'You say that every time – but this time I'm putting my foot down. I love him dearly, Jack, but enough is enough. Three and a half hours of Jac's non-stop questions is as much as I can take. And anyway, he needs his sleep. Give that brain of his a rest.'

'All right, but if he smells them when I get back, don't blame me.'

'If he's still awake, and *if* he gets up, I'll give him a few of my chips.'

Rolling his eyes, Jack pulled on his cap and left her to think about his taking redundancy money and getting out of the docks.

She imagined Jack with his own little fruit shop, flirting with all the women, winning them over with his blue eyes. Little Jac by his side, mimicking his father – serving the customers.

There was a time when she would have been jealous of the attention Jack received, and gave. But Laura had seen a change in Jack over the past six or seven years. He had settled down to be the loyal husband she knew before all of their troubles had started up, way back, when Patsy Hemmingway had come on the scene.

It seemed strange that she should think of Patsy. It was almost four years since she had left Jac in Laura's care. And for that she would be eternally grateful. It had crossed her mind from time to time to write to her, but somewhere deep inside a voice had told her to leave things alone and to put the past behind her. Laura dreaded the day when she would have to sit Jac down and tell him that she wasn't his natural mother. If she had her way, she would never tell him.

If Jack was going to come out of the docks and use his money to buy a fruit shop, Laura decided there and then that it would have to be on one condition. That they moved out of London to somewhere in the country where no one knew them. She hadn't been able to forget that careless slip of the tongue, when she had said to Kay *You're our only child*.

Kay had been right, it only needed one spiteful person to mention he was adopted when Jac was within earshot and their world would fall apart.

'So what's this proposition, then?' Laura sprinkled some salt on to her fish and chips.

'I fancy moving out and getting a little country pub.'

'Oh yeah? And where would the money come from for that? Your redundancy would never cover it.'

'I don't mean buy one, you silly cow. We'd be tenants. Until we had saved enough to put a down payment on a free house.'

She could tell by his tone that he had been thinking about this for a while, and had practically settled himself to it. 'What do we know about running a pub, Jack? Talk sense.'

'I'd 'ave to go on a training course.' He was being very matter-of-fact about the whole thing.

'Sounds to me like you've made up your mind.'

'Mine, yeah. Now it's up to you. We've both got to want it, Laura. Really want it.' He blew on his steaming crispy battered fish.

'I suppose I am allowed to have some time to take this in?'

''Course you are. There's no rush. I was thinking of the future, not straight away. In about four or five years, something like that.'

'Five years? Jac'll be eleven by then.'

'So? What's that got to do with anything?'

'If we're gonna go, maybe it should be sooner, while he's still little.'

'We'll see.'

They sat in silence, enjoying their fish supper, each wrapped in their own thoughts. Laura was visualizing life in a small village in Dorset, where they had taken Jac for a holiday the previous summer.

'Kent would be the place.' Jack couldn't resist throwing in another little teaser. He reckoned Laura would love to be surrounded by orchards and hop fields. 'Somewhere close to where we used to pick.'

The face of her ex-lover, Richard, the rich landowner, crossed her mind. She tried to imagine how she would feel if they were to bump into each other. If he were to appear at the very bar where she was serving. A warm sensation engulfed her, and she could feel her heartbeat become rapid. It took her by surprise. Surely she wasn't still carrying a torch for him after all this time?

'I wonder how Richard Wright's getting on with his picking machines?' Jack said.

'I wonder.' Laura screwed up her toes, something she did when she was irritated. Jack could be a tormenting bastard. There was no way he would have forgotten the man he could have lost Laura to. She toyed with the idea of mentioning his woman of the time, Patsy. The one who had probably been the cause of her straying in the first place. The one who had tricked Jack into getting her pregnant. The mother of that little boy who was in the end bedroom, sound asleep.

'I'd enjoy pulling a pint for him,' Jack grinned.

'Yeah, and I would enjoy serving him his favourite

drink, gin and tonic.' She wouldn't look up to catch Jack's eye, as he wanted. She could feel him looking mischievously at her. 'It would be nice to see him again,' she added, winding him up for a change.

There was no need for her to say anything else. He had his head bent now, over his fish and chips, eating as if he hadn't taken in her barbed retort.

'At least you like the idea then?' he said. 'Or is your mind somewhere else?'

'As it happens, yes. Patsy flashed through my head. Strange really. That she hasn't bothered to get in touch. You'd think she'd want to know how her son is.'

'Out of sight, out of mind. Nothing that woman did surprised me. I could never tell which way she would blow.' He stared up at the ceiling and narrowed his eyes. 'I think she was a bit of a schizo.' He shook his head. 'Something wasn't quite right, up top.'

'Just as well Jac's in our spare bedroom then, and not hers.'

'You're telling me.'

By the end of the summer term, Patsy had made quite a bit of progress. She and Jac now shared many secrets, and she had managed to win him over more than she had dreamed possible and in such a short time. They had even shared a cuddle one day, when he gave her a second marble and a necklace he had made at school from different coloured wooden beads.

With excitement reaching fever pitch, Jac's teacher had given up trying to keep her class in order. Once her charges had parcelled up their used exercise books and left them in neat piles on their desks, she summoned a monitor to collect them and take them to the store cupboard.

Looking at her wristwatch, with just thirty minutes to go before the end of the longest term of the year, Hilary Way brought the class to attention.

'Now if any of you want to stay in class to collect your paintings from off the walls, that's fine. But for those of you who don't have anything on display, or do but don't want to take them home, you may go into the playground until home-time bell.'

A cheer went up as the sound of banging chairs and desks filled the room. The noise was horrendous. 'I'm not letting any of you leave the classroom unless you line up *quietly*!' Her voice was drowned by the din which was still at full volume.

As a last resort, Hilary blew her whistle. That almost did the trick. The second and final blow brought a degree of calm. 'That's better. Now then: whoever is up the front, I want you to open the door and lead everyone *quietly* along the corridor.

'When you arrive at your staircase, I want the boys to stand very still while the girls make another line and file into the girls' playground. And then the boys will walk very quietly and—'

'Yes, miss!' came the excited voice of a little girl, who had her hand on the door handle. Before Hilary Way could finish her sentence the door was open and the sound of running feet could be heard from the corridor.

Apart from one or two children who were carefully removing their works of art from the walls, the only other child, still rummaging through his desk, was Jac.

Dropping into her chair, Hilary stretched out her

legs, leaned back and closed her eyes. At last it had arrived. End of term, seven weeks without the sound of her own voice. Without the look of expectant eyes gazing up at her, waiting for a jewel to drop from her lips, a jewel which they hoped would solve the mystery of sums in one sentence.

'You can have this one, Miss Way.' The quiet, shy voice drifted across her thoughts. Opening her eyes to Jac, she was moved to see his freckled face smiling up at her. 'It's the painting you said you'd be proud to 'ang up in your 'ouse.'

'Oh, Jac, that's so nice of you. Thank you. I would love to have it.' She held it out admiringly. 'I know just the place for it.'

'I'll probably share the others out between my sister, my Aunt Liz and my mum and dad.' He closed one eye and looked at her. 'D'yer think they'd like 'em?'

'Oh, definitely.' She felt like hugging him, but there was a line that had to be kept drawn between pupils and staff. 'There's something I've been meaning to ask you . . .' She placed the painting on her desk and leaned towards him. 'Why do you close one eye sometimes, Jac? Does the left one hurt or feel more tired than the other?'

'No. I didn't know I did that. Have you got a mirror?'

Hilary smiled at him. 'No, I haven't, not on me. Anyway, don't worry about it – I'm sure no one else has noticed.'

'Can I go now?' He made a point of opening both eyes as wide as they would go.

'Of course. And thank you again for my present.'

As his thin grubby legs disappeared through the door, she was reminded again of her longing to have a baby.

Standing by the window, watching the girls in the playground with their skipping ropes, she thought that she might do something positive during the summer break. She would ask if she could see a specialist. Enough time had been wasted taking her temperature and filling in her monthly cycle chart.

Hilary wondered why little Jac Armstrong had caused her to think about her personal life. She had always followed her principle of not dragging her problems into school, and vice versa. She supposed it was his cheeky face and blue eyes that did it. Jac was a very special little boy who could bring out her maternal instincts without even trying.

Instead of joining the others in the playground, Jac made for the school kitchen, but everything had been packed away and the stainless steel sinks were dry and shiny. Stretching himself up on tiptoe, he bent his head forward and peered at his reflection in the large silver-grey draining surface. As he studied his face, with one eye closed, another image appeared. It was Patsy.

Spinning around, he grinned up at her. 'I thought you'd all gone.'

'The others have but I stayed on to say goodbye.'

Jac felt his heart sink. 'You're not leaving, are yer?'

'No, silly. I meant for the summer break. Seven weeks. That's a long time not to see your chums.' She hoped that her leading statement would have good results.

'I could come and see yer. My grandfather and my aunt Liz look after me in the holidays. I could ask 'em if it was all right.'

'I don't think so, Jac. You know what worriers old people are. I suppose you could...' She pretended to be thinking about something.

'What?' Jac was his usual impatient self. 'I could what?'

'Well... you *could* pop round to see me and not say... But no, that would be like telling fibs.'

'No it wouldn't! I just wouldn't say where I was going. Not telling the truth's not the same as telling a lie, is it?'

'That's one way of looking at it. I'll tell you what. Take this.' She pulled a small hand-drawn map from her pocket and showed it to him. 'This shows where I live and how to get there.' She pointed out the Mile End Road and then drew her finger across to Jubilee Street.

'I know where that is. Everyone knows where that is. My mum gets my school shoes down there. I could cut through Assembly Passage.' He screwed up his nose. 'It really stinks down there. Of fish or somefing.'

Laughing, she told him it was where they smoked salmon and cured other fish. 'But you're right, you could go that way.'

'When?'

'When what?' She knew exactly what he meant, but she was doing her best not to sound too enthusiastic.

'When shall I come?' There was a touch of irritation in his voice. She liked that. Every so often Jac reminded Patsy of herself.

'Oh, I don't know. In say... three weeks?'

'Two?'

'Done.'

Turning on her heel, she gave a short wave. 'Enjoy your break from school!'

92

'What *time?*' Jac called to her.

With a finger on her lips she looked crossly back at him. 'Shhh.'

He held out his arms and spread his hands, keeping his voice to a whisper. 'What time?'

She checked to see that no one was around to hear or see them. 'Three in the afternoon.'

As she crossed over the Mile End Road, Patsy commended herself. Everything was going according to plan. She had no less than nine people begging to rent the house, and five of them had already offered to give six months' rent in advance. The receipts she would sign and hand out would prove to be worthless bits of paper. She would sign each one with a different name and use a different style of handwriting.

Although she had given her real name when she applied for the job at Jac's school, Patsy had never actually filled in the address, using the excuse at the time that she wasn't quite sure where she would be living once she left Leicester for London.

In two weeks' time she and Jac would be on a train heading for Scotland, where she had already found employment as a kitchen hand at the Infant school Jac would be attending from then on.

Pleased to be back in the house, which was filled with the smell of fresh paint and wallpaper, Patsy dropped into an armchair and kicked off her stiletto-heeled shoes. With the sun streaming in through the window, she felt a touch of regret at having to leave the house after she had spent so much of her time improving it. The white paintwork and walls had transformed the place. Even the old-fashioned furniture had taken on a new life.

She had been surprised to see the difference in the wood once she had been at it with some good polish. And once she had got rid of the bits of junk, added some scatter cushions and cheap bright curtains, the shadowy presence of Mrs Simons had soon faded away.

Now that the end of term had finally arrived, she admitted to herself that she was tired. It had been hard, keeping two jobs going and decorating the house. There had been times when she had only managed to get a few hours' sleep at night. Feeling more relaxed, with the sun shining in on her face, she closed her eyes and made a mental note to write to her mother. She would tell her not to send any more mail as she would be moving out in just a few days' time. There seemed little point in risking a letter arriving for her once she had cleared away every trace of her having been there.

Of course, the neighbours would remember seeing her come and go and they would no doubt pass on information about Mrs Simons who had lived there and disappeared overnight. But the description they would give of Patsy would be of a young woman with black hair, cut in a dramatic, Cleopatra-style bob. The Patsy who would be travelling to Scotland with her little boy would sport her natural carrot-coloured tresses – which would be short and curly. She would give herself a perm on the evening before she and Jac set off.

# Chapter Four

Returning from the biggest shopping spree of her life Kay dumped her bags on the bed, desperate for a coffee and a cigarette. She would put her feet up for ten minutes before unpacking her new clothes. Instead of feeling guilty about spending so much money on herself, she decided to be thankful. Between herself and Steve, they had more than enough in their joint account to cover the cost. And besides, he had reassured her enough times that he was happy for her to buy new clothes if that's what she wanted, although he adored her even when she was wearing old jeans and a sweater – and she knew he meant it.

Sipping her coffee, Kay lay back on the sofa and couldn't stop herself from smiling. She couldn't wait to wear her new pink and navy-blue suit. She would pay Steve a surprise visit at work the next day around lunch-time. She wanted him to be proud of her. She would wash and brush her long hair until it shone. She wished now that she had bought the pair of pink patent-leather shoes to go with the outfit.

Just as she was beginning to drift off into a light sleep she was brought sharply awake by the ringing of the telephone. Quickly getting to her feet, she tried to sound alert. It wouldn't do to be caught napping at that time of the day.

'This is Jac. I'm bored. Can I come and stay with you?'

Taken by surprise, she found herself laughing at him. 'And who showed you how to use the phone?'

'Mum dialled the number for me. Well? Can I?' He hadn't time for chit-chat.

'Of course you can. When?' She picked up on his rhythm of speech.

'Tomorrow. You can come and get me.'

'Oh, Jac, I can't. I'm going into the agency. I promised Steve I would go to lunch with him.' She hated lying to her brother, but she really had set her heart on going into town to surprise Steve.

'I'll come with you.'

'No, Jac. Listen – what about next week?'

'I can't come next week.'

'Oh really? Your diary's full, is it?'

'What about the day after tomorrow then?'

Kay gritted her teeth. 'We've been invited out to dinner.' This time it was the truth. 'Trust you to pick the wrong week, Jac. We've got some friends coming over for dinner on Friday so—'

She heard the dialling tone. 'You little sod!' She quickly dialled her mum's number and was pleased that Jac picked up the phone.

'Now listen, you. It's very, very rude to put the phone down on someone – even your sister!' There was a pause. 'You can come over for a few days next week. You can stay the whole week if you want—'

'I told you I can't!'

'Well, the week after then!'

'But I'm bored *now*. I might not be then.'

'Well, I'm very sorry, but that's life. Anyway, what's happening next week?'

'I'm going somewhere.' Jac's voice had a different tone to it now – as if he were trying to tell her something but unsure whether he should.

'What d'you mean, going somewhere? Where exactly and with whom?' She really wasn't in the mood for guessing-games.

'It's meant to be a secret.'

'Oh, for Christ's sake, Jac! I've just got in from a big shopping trip and I'm tired!'

There was another pause. 'I'm gonna help my mate to clear out his mum's coal cupboard. We're gonna sweep it and paint the walls white. It's gonna be our den. I'm going now. My programme's on telly.' There was a moment's silence. 'I'm gonna put the phone down now. Is that all right?'

'Yeah, of course it is. I'll see you at the weekend.' She felt really moved by his sincerity. At least her chastise-ment had gone in. He didn't really want to hang up on her.

As she wandered into the bedroom to unpack her shopping, she felt a pang of guilt. She had put her brother off for no real reason and felt bad about it.

Picking up the telephone, her eyes moved to the bed, to the pink and navy-blue suit. She put the phone down again. Jac would just have to learn to be patient. Learn that she couldn't just drop everything like that. He could come and stay once he had got bored with the impossibility of trying to turn a coal cupboard into a den.

Lifting her legs on to the sofa again, Kay ran her and Jac's conversation through her mind. Something wasn't quite right but she couldn't put her finger on it. Nothing that he'd said – more the way he'd said it.

Sighing, she closed her eyes and put it down to her brother trying to get his way. He had always managed to wind her round his little finger in the past, and now that she was married and had other commitments, maybe Jac was simply trying a different tack. Maybe he was feeling left out of her life? She would make it up to him in a couple of weeks' time. Take him out for the day, to the zoo maybe. Jac and chimpanzees: that would be something to look forward to.

Jac had surprised himself making up that story on the spot. Kay had believed him too. He was pleased with himself that he hadn't told her where he was really going the next Monday at three o'clock. Hem' had told him not to say anything.

The fib he had told about the coal cupboard started him thinking. His mum and dad had electric fires. Maybe they would let him turn their coal cupboard into a den. There would be room for his small armchair and he could have a candle in there too.

He suddenly felt excited and wondered why he had been bored. He opened the hatch door into the kitchen. 'Can I paint the coal cupboard white, Mum?'

Putting away the dishes she had just dried, Laura shook her head. 'Say that again?'

'Turn it into a camp.'

'Your dad'll be in soon. Ask him.' The last thing Laura needed on her afternoon off was to get into an hour-long discussion with Jac. 'What did Kay have to say then? About you going over there?'

He was still preoccupied with his new idea. 'She's going out for lunch and having parties and fings...'

'Oh, well, never mind. I expect—'

'D'yer think dad'll let me do it?'

'I don't know, Jac! You'll have to ask him. I'm going to make the beds. Try to settle down, yeah? Do some colouring in or something.'

'I've been colouring in all morning. I did a picture for Aunt Liz. Grandfather's put it up on the wall. Wasn't that good?' Jac had his sulky look on again. 'I s'pose I could make a sign to go on the coal-cupboard door...'

'Good idea.' Laura left him to it, hoping he wouldn't follow her from room to room telling her all about it.

'Or I could draw a picture...' He checked that she had left the kitchen and then murmured, 'for my dinner lady.' He looked at the calendar again and checked how many days it was before he was due to visit Hem'. Six. Nearly a week. He thought about Kay again and how much he hated her for not saying she would come and get him. At least being somewhere else would have made the time go by.

'I was gonna take some of the biscuits I made with me. Aunt Liz said they're the best she's tasted.' He grumbled away to himself until something on the television caught his attention. *Popeye* – his favourite programme. He needed to go to the lavatory, but he could wait. He didn't want to miss any of it. His favourite programmes always seemed to come on at the wrong time.

\* \* \*

When Monday finally came around, Jac sat in Billy's front room pretending to read a comic while his grandfather and Aunt Liz relaxed in their armchairs. It was a hot July day and Jac was hoping that the heat would cause both adults to slip a little earlier into their usual afternoon doze.

With his eyes flashing from his comic to their faces every other minute, he was beginning to get worried. It was nearly half past two and even though they had their eyes closed, neither of them was breathing the way they did when they were properly asleep.

Trying his best not to make a rustling sound, he carefully turned a page, just in case they were listening for it. In case they had guessed he was going to nip out once they were asleep. In case they were suspicious that he wasn't really interested in his comic.

It wasn't until ten minutes to three that Jac felt confident enough to creep out of the cottage, closing the door very quietly behind him.

Once he was out of the tiny cul-de-sac, with the green gate between him and his wards, he ran along the pavement, weaving in and out of passers-by, hoping that he wouldn't bump into anyone who knew him. He would have to lie about where he was going.

Paying special attention to the instructions which had been drummed into him about road safety, he waited patiently while the traffic lights changed, and once he was across the busy Mile End Road, he felt less anxious. It was plain sailing from then on.

Holding his nose while he skipped along the cobblestones in Assembly Passage, or Smelly Alley as he and his friends called it, Jac wondered if his dinner lady, Hem', had remembered that he was going to visit her that day. If she had forgotten and gone out shopping it wouldn't matter – he could sit on her doorstep and wait. He hoped he wouldn't smell of fish.

'Where you off to, cock?' A large woman wearing a green overall was leaning on a gate smoking a cigarette. 'Gonna get your 'air cut, are yer?'

Jac stopped in his tracks and pulled his socks up. 'No.' His hand flew to his neck and up the back of his head. He had only had it cut two weeks ago.

'You wanna look like a Beatle, do yer?' she laughed.

'No.' The woman reminded him of his aunt Liz. 'Why would I wanna look like a beetle?'

'You wouldn't mind their money, I bet.' She drew on her cigarette.

'Beetles don't have money!' Jac wondered if she was a nutter. He had often heard his dad say that the world was full of them. This was the first time he had actually talked to one.

'Get yerself a guitar and you'll be well away!' She threw her head back and roared with laughter.

'What d'yer do in there?' Jac nodded towards the open doorway that led into a dark place.

'What do we do?' She sniffed. 'Can't you smell them 'errings? We stuff 'em into jars.'

Jac moved closer to her and smelt her overall. 'Urggh, that's horrible! You stink.' He retched and backed off. 'Wouldn't catch me eating fish out of a jar!' he said, and ran off. Her laughter echoing down the alley seemed too close for comfort. He thought she was coming after him

101

so he ran faster, praying that Hem' would be in and save him from the nutter.

Patsy had made sure that nothing that could link her up with the house had been overlooked. It was as clean as a whistle, and the door leading into Mrs Simons's old flat had been fitted with an extra padlock. The delay between the various would-be tenants realizing they had been conned and calling the police to force the inner door open, would give her a little more time to be out of England before they rummaged around and found something which would lead them to Mrs Simons.

With a tray set with chocolate cake and lemonade, Patsy couldn't think of anything else she needed to do. Her suitcases were packed and she had laid out the new clothes she had bought for Jac to travel in. The Meccano set she had bought as a present was in a carrier bag by the door and a box of sweets was on the table next to the tea tray.

Unable to ignore the butterflies inside her, she pulled back the net curtain and looked down at the pavement. Soon he would be coming along the road. Her little sandy-haired boy was about to learn the truth. That he wouldn't have to call her Hem' any more, but *Mum*. Her heart beating rapidly, she closed her eyes and prayed that Laura Armstrong hadn't found out about Jac's visit and stopped him.

When she opened her eyes again, a smile spread across her face. Rushing along the street was Jac, peering at the door numbers as he flew past each house.

Forcing herself not to open the window and wave for fear of drawing a passing neighbour's attention, she took a deep breath and went downstairs to wait in the passage – ready to let him in.

As Jac stood staring at the black iron knocker on Patsy's door, he thought about Kay and what she would have said to him if he had told her on the phone where he was really going. He took a step backwards. Kay would have told him not to go by himself. She would have said that he should get Grandfather or Aunt Liz to walk him round there. Why hadn't he? He took another step back and wondered if he should go back to the cottage and start again. But then he would be late and Miss Hem' would be cross.

Ignoring the worried feeling inside, he pushed Kay's scolding face from his mind and reached up and gave three loud knocks.


Pressing her finger on Mrs Button's doorbell, Kay wondered why she should be thinking about her brother. Jac's face kept coming and going from her mind and she had a strange feeling in the pit of her stomach.

'Oh, hello, Kay. I'd forgotten you were coming today.'

'Just on my way to Mum's—'

'Tch. Don't you look the part, all done up to the nines? All dressed up and nowhere better to go, eh?'

It seemed wrong somehow, sitting in Mrs Button's living room, drinking a cup of tea with her as if they were equals. It really didn't seem so long ago that she was just a kid and looked up to her elders. No one could have been more surprised when Mrs Button turned up at the register office to wish Kay good luck on her wedding day. If only her son Terry could have been there too.

Kay could so easily picture Terry, her childhood friend with whom she had spent her happiest days back in the fifties scrumping apples, climbing haystacks, swimming in the river – before it all came to an end. Even picking hops had been fun, so long as she and Terry were competing with each other to see who could pick the most bushels in a day.

'You could 'ave knocked me down with a feather when Terry's dad turned up at the funeral.' Mrs Button shook her head and sighed. 'Why he had to leave it till one of us was dead . . .'

'I didn't realize he was at the funeral.' Kay swallowed hard, forcing back tears. 'But then, I don't think I really knew *what* day it was.'

'No, I know. It must 'ave been just as 'ard for you as it was for me. Still – my Terry's all right now. Up there with the angels.' She became pensive, lost in thought. 'In a way, my boy was an angel, wasn't he? Wouldn't harm a fly. A lot of good it did 'im.'

Desperate to turn the conversation around, Kay admired the room. 'It looks so different now. You've made a really lovely job of the decorating.'

'Not me, love. Terry's dad. Couldn't do enough to make amends. He walked out on us when his son was no more than two years old. Some old tart in Forest Gate 'ad got her hooks in.' Mrs Button sipped her tea. 'He never sent us a penny, you know.'

'I guessed not.' Kay clearly remembered when she had first paid a visit to the house, when Terry was in hospital recovering after some flash boys had kicked his head in for being homosexual. She had been shocked to see the way he and his mother were living. Hardly any furniture, just the bare essentials; worn mats on thin lino and curtains which, once drawn, weren't wide enough to meet in the middle.

'I always had that fear, y'know, that my Terry would do something silly. He didn't like being the way he was, not really. He loved children. And he would have made a smashing dad.'

'Yeah – he would have.' Kay regretted having promised Terry's mum that she would drop in on her – it was proving too much.

'I s'pose you'll be starting a family soon?' There was a hint of envy in her voice.

'I've only been married eight weeks, Mrs Button,' Kay laughed, trying to lighten the mood.

'When I 'eard that your mother 'ad adopted your dad's bastard—'

'Please don't call Jac that.' Kay placed her cup back on the saucer. Mrs Button hadn't changed from when she knew her at hop-picking. 'He's just a little boy—'

'Can't blame 'er, I s'pose. It was one way to hang on to your father.'

That was it. Kay stood up, wished the woman well and got out of the house as soon as possible. This wasn't how she had expected it to be. She thought they would have talked about Terry. About the happy times when he was a rosy-cheeked youngster and Kay was his best friend.

Walking along Globe Road towards the flats where she had grown up, Kay arrived at the familiar sweetshop. How things had changed. She recalled the times when she had looked at the half-pound bars of Cadbury's chocolate and wished she had enough pocket money to buy one. Now that she could easily afford it the desire had gone. At least she could buy a box of Black Magic for her mum, some tobacco for her dad and an assortment of sweets for Jac.

Taking the long way round to her parents' flat, Kay made for the small stables opposite St Peter's Church, where she had often bought a half-hundredweight of coal and dragged it home in a pushchair. It hadn't been just the sixpence she earned that had made her willing to lift more than her own weight, but the rag-and-bone man's old cart-horse in the stable. She remembered being allowed to feed it with lump sugar.

Thinking back, she remembered the smell of the horse's sweaty body and the sight of steaming manure in the cold winters as it dropped from the animal's enormous behind. It was so easy to bring that place to mind, the cobbled yard, the hay and straw piled up in one corner of the shelter, the coal in another; the blackened face and hands of the coalman in his oily soot-covered overalls and cap. She could almost see the two tired workmen as they sat round the glowing red and orange coal brazier sipping tea from enamel mugs. The coalman and the rag-and-bone man – enjoying a few minutes together after their rounds. Jac would have been in his element here – and no doubt he would have found his way up on to the back of the old mare.

It was no great shock to see that the place was no longer used as a stable. Cart-horses had had their day. Apart from a few bits hanging up on nails, all trace of the horse and cart had gone.

'You're a sight for sore eyes.' Laura was pleased to see her rosy-cheeked daughter. 'Been sunbathing, I see.'

'Too right. That little balcony of ours gets the sun for most of the day. Where's the sprat?'

'At Grandfather's. Liz's gonna fetch him home for me. He wanted to stop for egg and chips. And you know they have to have tea on the dot of five, not a minute sooner.'

Kay glanced at her gold wrist-watch. 'God, is that the time, ten to five? I can't believe that.'

'I've only just got in myself. Ten minutes ago and you would have had to wait on the doorstep.'

'Oh yeah?' Kay pulled her key on a string from her pocket. 'Don't you believe it.'

'I was forgetting you've still got your key.'

'You can have it back if you want.' Kay feigned a hurt look.

'Oh shut up.' Laura smiled, filling the kettle. 'Your room'll always be here for you.'

'Let's hope I won't need to come running home.'

'I should hope not. Now then, I'd best phone Jac and let him know that you're here. You never know – he might even forgo his Aunt Liz's special chips. I wouldn't be surprised if the three of them don't come marching round once they know you're here.'

'I thought Jac was going to his friend's house today – to turn a coal cupboard into a den?'

'I don't think so. You're getting mixed up. He wants to turn our coal cupboard into a den.' Laura laughed at the thought of him sitting in that tiny dark place with a torch.

'No. He definitely said he was going to his friend's today. Monday. He turned down coming to me – so he must have meant it.' Kay suddenly felt uneasy.

107

'I don't know what you're looking so worried about. D'yer want tea or coffee?' Laura asked.

'I've got this peculiar feeling in my stomach.'

'Like what?'

'I don't know. As if something has happened...' She pushed a hand through her hair. 'Something's not right, Mum,' she murmured. 'I'll phone Aunt Liz.'

Dialling the number, Kay couldn't understand why she should be trembling. Tension instantly filled the tiny kitchen as Kay reacted to the sound of her aunt's heavy voice. 'It's Kay, Aunt Liz – are you OK?

'Well you can stop worrying, Aunt Liz. Jac told me last week that he was going to a friend's house today—'

'What's wrong?' Laura demanded.

'Jac's not there. When they woke up from their nap, he'd gone.'

'Gimme that phone!' Laura snatched it from Kay.

'Liz, what is this? What's going on?'

Liz's voice, full of self-reproach, could be heard as she cried down the telephone line.

'I'm going round there.' Kay grabbed her handbag.

'Wait for me!' Laura snapped. 'Liz, did he say anything about going to a friend's house?'

The look on her mother's face told Kay that Jac hadn't gone to the friend's house, and the unease which had crept into her mind earlier was growing into something far more serious.

'They're coming round,' Liz said quietly as she replaced the receiver, 'Kay and Laura.' She put her hands up to her face and was pleased to feel Billy's hand on her shoulder.

'You're letting your imagination run away with you, Lizzie. The boy's gone out to play, that's all. Can't blame the poor little sod. Anyway, I might have 'im back 'ere before they arrive.'

'You're gonna go out and look for 'im?' she said, slipping a pill under her tongue. She might have known that the shock of Jac not being there when she woke up would bring on a pain. Angina was like that, always there, ready to strike when you least wanted it to.

"Course I'm gonna look for the little bleeder.' Billy slapped his cap on. 'I know where he'll be – over the park. I bet you a pound to a penny.'

A half-hearted smile lifted Liz's face. 'Yeah, you're right. I just feel so, I don't know—'

'There's nothing wrong with taking a nap. Stop blaming yerself.' He gave her a wink and left, feeling a lot heavier inside than he was letting on.

As he walked along Cambridge Heath Road, it occurred to Billy that his grandson might have gone to the waste-paper factory with the bag of newspapers he had been saving. He cursed himself then for not checking first to see if it was still in the corner of the kitchen.

He couldn't help smiling as he remembered Jac's face when he'd told him he could be paid sixpence if he took a month's supply of *Daily Mirror*s to the paper factory. When he reached the turning which led to the site he stopped and wondered where to go first. He decided on the park, and was surprised at how many children were in the paddling pond, splashing each other and screaming with laughter.

Sheltering his eyes from the sun with one hand, Billy studied the boys – keeping a sharp lookout for Jac's sandy-coloured hair.

'I 'ope you don't make a habit of that.' A young mother's voice came right out of the blue.

Billy turned to the two women sitting on a low wall. He had got the gist of the remark but shelved it. 'I'm looking for my grandson.'

'Oh yeah? That's what they all say.' The dark-haired woman looked knowingly at her blonde companion. 'I'd like a shilling for every dirty old sod who says that.'

Controlling his temper and emotions, Billy walked away from them, heading for the enclosed playground where there were swings and roundabouts.

'A habit is it?' the woman called after him. 'Staring at little boys and girls in the paddling pool?'

Feeling ashamed when he knew he had no reason to, Billy stepped up his pace.

His concern for Jac deepened. A boy of six shouldn't be out wandering the streets alone. It was a different world now. Very different. When he was a kid abduction was unheard-of. For all that had been said about the old East End, it had always been a safe place for the natives. There had been fights between grown men and brawls between women after a good drinking session, but no more than that. And as for Jack the Ripper, it was obvious to those who lived in that part of London that the maniac had come from another class. An outsider, rich enough at the time to have a horse-drawn carriage to taxi him around the London slums.

Cars were a nightmare, as far as Billy was concerned. Over the past ten years, since 1956, the amount of traffic had doubled. More cash flow meant more luxuries. More cars. More movement of people from one part of the country to another. Strangers could come and go as they pleased and grab a kid if it took their fancy.

He walked through the double gates into the playground and went directly to the small wooden shed where the attendant sat, keeping a watchful eye out for boisterous children who deliberately misused the park equipment.

'D'yer mind if I take a look to see if my grandson's around?' Billy hoped she wouldn't think the worst of him.

"Course not, love. What's 'is name?"

'Jac.' Billy found that saying his name brought a lump to his throat.

'Nipped out when you wasn't looking I s'pose?' The woman's throaty chuckle lightened him.

Looking from the swings to the brightly painted see-saw, umbrella and roundabout, Billy felt his heart sink. No sign of Jac.

'How long's he bin missing?' the grey-haired woman asked, with just a slight hint of concern.

'About an hour and a half – maybe two.' Billy turned to face her. 'What d'yer reckon I should do? Stroll up to the police station?'

'No, love. It could be more trouble than it's worth. What if he's sitting there enjoying a glass of lemonade, when you get back?'

'Yeah, that's a point. I'll wait till I see my daughter. It's up to her really, what she wants to do. It's her son we're talking about, after all.'

Billy was saying all the right things but the words

didn't match what he was feeling. He wanted to go to Bethnal Green Police Station more than anything in the world. He wanted the bobbies on the beat to be looking out for his grandson.

'You tell me what he looks like and I'll keep an eye out. And I'll have a word with the park-keepers. How's that?'

'That'd help. Tch, kids eh?' Billy pursed his lips and swallowed hard. He couldn't believe this was happening. It was him searching for his Jac. He always thought that this kind of thing only happened to other people. Parents who let their kids roam the streets.

Pushing open the green gate in Delamar Place, Laura swiftly changed from a worried mother into an angry one. 'If Jac's slipped out to go over the balmy park, I'll kill him!'

Waiting in the doorway of the cottage, Liz was close to tears. 'I only meant to doze for ten minutes, Laura...'

'And?'

She looked sheepishly at her. 'Neither of us woke up till half past four.'

'And what time did you go off to sleep?'

'Just before three ... I think.' Liz wished Billy was back. She needed a bit of moral support. 'Our Jac was as happy as a sandboy, reading 'is comics.'

'Did he say anything about going to his mate's house to paint a coal cupboard?'

'No, Laura! I told that to Kay!' Liz remembered Billy's face when she had asked him the same question. His puzzled expression at the time had sent a wave of fear through her.

112

'He would have written it down in the diary...' Her voice trailed off. Surely Billy hadn't forgotten to tell her something as important as that?

Laura turned to Kay. 'Can you remember his friend's name?'

'He just said he would be at his mate's house. He didn't mention any names and I didn't think it was necessary to ask. It was just ... something he said, the way Jac does.'

Laura shrugged and sat down. 'Well, I suppose that's where he is then. No doubt the little sod'll turn up in a minute and wonder what all the fuss is about. You'd best start frying his chips, Liz.'

Half-heartedly she agreed and tried to set her mind to it. 'It's all this bloody publicity about the Moors—'

'Liz, please!'

'All right, all right. I'm sorry I said it.' Her voice and her face were full of regret.

'Don't upset yourself. He'll be all right, you'll see.' Kay placed an arm around her aunt's shoulder. 'He's just done what all little boys like to do. He's gone out to play.'

After all Patsy's careful planning and with everything going so smoothly, she could hardly believe how difficult she had found it to turn the conversation around to her and Jac. He had drunk his lemonade, eaten his chocolate cake, watched a cartoon on the television – and now he was saying it was time for him to go home. He had been there for nearly two hours and she was no further forward.

'I forgot to say I was going round my friend's house.

113

My aunt Liz will be worried.' Jac pulled his socks up and grinned at Patsy. 'They always slip down like this. My grandfather says it's 'cos my legs are too skinny.'

'Jac . . . there's something I want to talk to you about.' Patsy stood up and turned her back to him. 'It's something quite important.'

Looking up at her, Jac wondered why she had curled her hair and dyed it ginger. It looked silly. He thought he had come to the wrong house when she first opened the door.

'You must have wondered why I look different.' She turned to face him and Jac felt himself blush.

'It's very nice like that.' He rapidly reeled out the words. 'Lots of people dye their hair a different colour. My aunt Liz does sometimes as well – and she's *old*!'

'It's not dyed, Jac. This is natural. The colour is, anyway, but not the curls. I gave myself a perm.' She sat down on the armchair next to him and reached for his hand. 'I coloured my hair nearly black and cut it short just before I applied for the job in your school, as a dinner lady.'

'Was it very long then?'

'Yes, it was. Very long and ginger. Just a bit lighter than it is now.'

Jac felt uncomfortable at the way she was looking at him and stroking his hand. 'I fink I'd better go now.' He didn't want her to think he had only come for the lemonade and cake, but something told him it was time to leave.

'You see, I had to change my appearance so no one would recognize me. Not that I've done anything wrong. I wasn't hiding from the police or anything.'

114

'Why d'yer do it then?' Jac started to clench his toes – he really did want to go home.

'I'm going to show you some photographs of me, when I used to live in Leicester, with my little boy.'

'I didn't know you had a boy.' He relaxed again, wondering how old her boy might be.

'Not *had* Jac. Still have.' She smiled and reached out for the envelope on the side-table. 'Now I'm going to show you these, and let's see if you recognize anyone, shall we?'

He pulled himself back into his armchair. He didn't like the way Hem' was talking to him. Her voice sounded different. Talking to him as if he was a baby. 'Then I'll go,' he murmured, trying not to sound worried. She might think he didn't like her any more.

She handed him a photograph of herself taken a week before she handed Jac over. 'Does that ring a bell?'

He stared at it. 'I know it's you, but...' There was something familiar about the photograph but he couldn't say what it was.

'And here's another.' She carefully held the photograph out.

'Is that your boy?'

'Yes, Jac. That's my son when he was two and a half years old. It was taken the day before I had to give him away. What do you think of him?'

He shrugged, unsure of what he was supposed to say. 'Who did you give him to?'

'Hold the photograph up close. Take a good look at that freckly face.'

Jac did as he was told and felt himself go icy. A strange cold, yet burning sensation spread down the back of his neck. He had seen similar pictures of the boy. Not with Patsy; by himself. There was one on the mantelshelf in his aunt Liz's bedroom. His eyes wandered from the photograph to Patsy's smiling face. He wondered why tears were trickling down her face.

'How would you like to go on a train all the way to Scotland, Jac?'

'Sounds all right,' he said warily, shifting in his chair.

'You could play with the new Meccano set I bought for you—'

'When?' He quite liked the sound of a holiday but he wasn't too sure what his mum and dad would make of it.

'Today.' She smiled into his face.

Jac felt his body jerk and then begin to fizz as if he were a glass of lemonade, just like the time when the school nurse stuck a needle in his arm. 'I'm not your boy, am I? He just looks like me.' The words tumbled out as strange things happened inside his head – as if a hand were sweeping across his thoughts. His school classroom came to mind, his teacher, when she drew the dust-pad over the blackboard, wiping away the words. He didn't feel like himself. Maybe he did have a secret button just like the robot he got for Christmas? Maybe Miss Hem' had pressed it? He felt like his tin robot. The one that flashed red and green lights when you pushed a switch.

'Oh but you are my boy, Jac.' She wiped her tears away with the back of her hand and began to laugh softly. 'And I came all the way down from Leicester to take you home. I'm your mum, Jac. Don't you remember anything? Try to think back – when I used to sing to you.' She pushed her face closer to his and sang:

Time to close your eyes now, put your toys away,
Little man you've had a busy day...

'It went something like that,' she smiled. 'Your grandad used to sing it to me when I was small, just before he turned off the light.' She pushed her hand lovingly through Jac's hair. 'I had to give you away ... I didn't want to.'

Words were swimming through his mind as he looked into her face. A stream of words all saying the same thing, over and over and over. *Run Jac, run.*

'My grandfather'll be looking for me. He'll be worried. He might have gone to the police station.' He tried to block out the voice but it wouldn't stop. Red lights were flashing, bigger than the ones on his robot. New words followed the others: *Get out of there, Jac! Get out!*

'You've got another grandfather, you know that? One you didn't even know you had.' Patsy was still smiling as she carefully withdrew his birth certificate and a crisp new five-pound note from an envelope. 'This money is for you to spend when we get there.'

Jac stared at the note. Five pounds was a lot of money. She wouldn't really give it to him? Surely not?

Patsy pointed to a name on the birth certificate. Jac Hemmingway. Then she pointed to a date of birth. *His* date of birth.

'I don't understand,' Jac's bottom lip curled under as he swallowed hard, trying his best to be as grown-up as Hem' wanted, and not cry.

117

'You will. In time. I'll explain everything on the train.'

Jac was finding it difficult to speak. He swallowed once, then twice, and finally managed to say 'What train?'

'The one which will take us all the way to Scotland to start our new life together.' She reached out and pulled him to her. 'I should never have given you up. I should have left you in the children's home. It was a stone's throw from where I lived.' She was talking more to herself than to Jac. 'I did it for Kay, really. Yes. I thought you should have been with your sister. That's why I did it. For Kay.' Patsy was even beginning to lie to herself, and to believe the new version of what had really happened.

Hearing his sister's name made Jac cry now. 'I want to go home,' he sobbed, trying to smile.

'I didn't want to give you away, Jac.' She held him by the shoulders and pushed her face up close. 'Kay's mummy made me do it.' She would try another tack. 'She said they would give you a better life than I could.' Patsy was a convincing liar, but Jac wasn't listening.

He pulled away from her, stood up and spoke very quickly. 'I'll go home and talk to them about it. I'll ask them if you can have me back. They'll say yes. I know they will. But not if you take me to Scotland. That would make my dad really, really mad.' He walked around the back of the armchair, inching his way to the door.

Reaching one arm out and quietly laughing at him, Patsy grabbed the back of his trousers.

'I've bought the tickets, Jac. I've given up my job. I've put your name down at a new school. And, tomorrow, other people will be coming here to live in my flat, so you see—'

'No!' Jac's anger was taking over from his fear. 'I'm not going to Scotland!' He punched Patsy's arm away and ran out of the room. Fast behind him she grabbed him on the landing at the top of the stairs.

'Now stop it, Jac! You're acting like a spoilt brat! I'm your mother and I've got every right—'

'I don't care if you are! I want to go!' Sinking his teeth into her arm he felt her other hand come up to slap his face.

'You see what they've done! Allowing you to grow up wild! It'll be different in Scotland,' she said, changing her tone, 'we'll be in the middle of the countryside!'

Again he kicked out and managed to free himself, but she grabbed him by the leg and brought him down, kicking for all he was worth as she held him by his shirt collar.

'Just try to calm *down*!' She pushed the five-pound note in front of his face. 'Just think what you could buy with this. We could go on an outing once we're settled. We'll use this five pounds for a trip to Loch Ness. You'd like that, wouldn't you, Jac?'

Pulling his head back for all he was worth, Jac turned it sideways, anything not to have to look into Hem's eyes. They were different. Bigger. Staring out like big brown marbles. He hit out again and then rapidly punched her chest. 'You're not gonna kidnap me,' he sobbed, 'you're *not*!'

'You're my son!' She grabbed him by the shoulders

119

and gave him a good shaking. Pulling away and ducking down Jac pushed himself through the gap between her legs and the banister. In a flurry of anger, she turned sharply and lost her balance. With her arms flailing wildly she screamed as she lost her footing and fell backwards. Down the long flight of stairs she went, banging against each side of the banisters, rolling over and over to land with an almighty crash at the bottom.

With his small hands pressed against his face, Jac sat on the top stair and waited for her to come and get him, to start shouting again, but the silence remained. Other than the distant sound of traffic on the main road outside, he could hear nothing. It was as if he was in a bubble, separated from the world around him.

Slowly uncovering his face, Jac looked down at the twisted body and the blood seeping out of Patsy's head on to the white skirting board. Her eyes were closed and she wasn't moving.

'You shouldn't 'ave tried to take me away, Hem'.' His voice sounded strange to his own ears. Almost as if another little boy was talking through him. Another Jac. The one who had killed Hem'.

'I have to go home to my mum and dad...' he cried quietly, 'they'll be worried about me.' The stairs leading down to the body seemed to go on for ever, but that was Jac's only way out of the house. He would have to step over Hem's dead body. But what if she suddenly moved? What if she was only pretending? What if she grabbed his legs again and put a hanky over his mouth so he couldn't scream? What if she tied him up and put him in a cardboard box and had him delivered to Scotland?

He would have to wait. He would have to wait for a long time, to see if she moved. He would sit dead still, on the top stair, to make certain that she wasn't breathing. He put his hand to his cheeks: they felt so hot, burning like fire, and his heart was thumping as if it was trying to get out of his body.

If it got too quiet, he would sing to keep himself company, like his grandfather had told him. Before he could decide which song he would sing, the lyrics of one ran through his brain. *Little man you've had a busy day*...

Staring back down at Patsy, Jac noticed the five-pound note beside her head – drops of blood were soaking into it. He thought about the Loch Ness monster coming up from the water, creating a foam in its wake. He wished there was a lot of foam at the bottom of the stairs to cover up Miss Hem'.

'It's half past six, Laura! Surely to God the boy's mother would have fetched him back by now?' The worry in Jack's voice matched the way Laura felt. But one of them had to stay calm. Liz was in tears, and her dad had gone to his room.

Laura moved her mouth closer to the mouthpiece of the telephone. 'Try to be sensible, Jack, please! I've got enough to cope with here. Just stay in the flat in case he's taken straight back there instead of here. And half past six isn't *late*. The little sod's probably told her he doesn't have to be home until seven!'

'But we don't even know if he *has* gone to his friend's house!'

'Of course he has! He told Kay that's what he would be

doing but forget to tell us or Liz. He probably remembered it once Liz and Dad had gone off to sleep and didn't want to wake them up.'

There was a heavy sigh from Jack. 'Yeah, I suppose you're right. I dunno, kids eh?'

'Make yourself a strong cup of tea and be patient. He'll be back soon. I'm sure of—' The sudden loud banging on the front door of the cottage stopped Laura in her tracks. 'Hang on, Jack! There's someone at the door!' Rushing out of the room she shot Liz a reassuring look. 'I'll kill him for this.'

Pulling herself out of the armchair, Liz wasn't so sure. Jac never knocked on the door like that. Never. And neither would the boy's parent. There was urgency in that banging, and she knew it.

Bracing herself for the worst, Liz kept her eyes on the door and prayed that Jac would walk through it with Laura. When she heard Laura shouting in the passage she knew that her wish had been granted.

'I forgot to say where I was going,' Jac said laconically. He had obviously been running, Liz could tell by his breathing, yet he was as white as a sheet.

'You wait till your father gets hold of you.' Laura picked up the telephone and waved the receiver at him. 'Just you wait.' Turning her back to him she spoke to Jack. 'He's just come in. I'll have a cup of tea and a cigarette and we'll make our way home. You'd best tell Kay he's home safe and sound.'

'She already knows. I just told her.' Jack sounded as if he was about to cry with relief. 'We'll see you soon.'

'Have you had your tea, Jac?' Liz asked, studying his face. 'Jac? Do you want something to eat?'

'I want Kay.' As he gazed out at nothing, Jac's small body began to tremble.

'Kay was here, but she's gone home to keep your dad company.'

'Where's Grandfather?' Still he stared past them.

'In his room. He'll be down soon I expect. Now he knows you're safe and sound.' Laura knelt down and held Jac by his arms. 'Aunt Liz asked if you've had your tea, love?'

'I didn't.' Still there was no expression on his face or in his voice.

Laura and Liz instinctively looked at each other and then back to Jac. 'I'll make a pot of tea,' Liz murmured.

Dropping down on to the settee, Laura held out her hand. 'Come on – don't look so scared. We're only too pleased to see you, you little stinker.'

Instead of falling into her arms as she expected, Jac chose to sit down on the edge of an armchair as the slight trembling rapidly grew into a fit of shaking.

'*Liz!*' Laura's high-pitched scream seemed to go above Jac's head.

As Laura held him tight and willed the shaking to stop, Liz could only stand there and cry at the heart-breaking sight. It seemed to take an age before his body became still again.

Kneeling in front of the sorry sandy-haired Jac, Laura and Liz could not bring themselves to say a word. They just looked into his face. A face that spoke a million words. Jac wasn't there. His laughing blue eyes had glazed over and the sparkle had gone.

Sitting in the doctor's waiting room, with Jac curled up

on Laura's lap, Kay tried to push away the horrid thoughts which kept sweeping through her mind. Jac hadn't said another word since he had had the small shaking fit and had avoided looking into anyone's face.

'D'yer wanna drop of lemonade, Jac?' She leaned to one side and tried to catch her brother's eye, but he just nuzzled into Laura's chest.

'Leave him, Kay. He'll talk to us when he wants to,' Laura murmured. 'You know our Jac can't keep quiet for long.' She kissed the top of his head and stroked his ear.

As the door leading into the doctor's surgery opened, Jack stood up and spoke to the patients who were waiting to go in. 'Look – I know you were all here before us,' there was a crack in his voice, 'but our little boy has just had a fit and—'

'Bring Jac in, Mr Armstrong.' The family doctor turned to his other patients. 'I'm sure you won't mind?'

A chorus of voices agreeing with the doctor was too much for Kay. She waved her parents away, signalling for them to go in without her, that she would remain in the waiting room.

Once they had gone inside, Kay buried her face in her hands and began to cry.

'Poor little soul,' said the woman opposite Kay. 'What happened to set it off, love?'

Kay shrugged and shook her head. 'I don't know.' But deep inside Kay had a feeling she should know. She remembered Jac phoning her, saying he was going somewhere secret, and she hadn't been bothered to pick up on it. If she had, maybe he wouldn't have been through whatever it was that had caused him to have the fit. She would never forgive herself if there was a connection. Never.

'Could be the beginnings of epilepsy,' said another woman.

'One of my neighbour's boys gets that. It's a terrible sight to watch.'

And so the conversation went. On and on, one exaggerated story after another. So much so that Kay could actually see the funny side of it, which helped. Giving her nose a really good blow, she took a deep breath and felt a little better. She even managed a faint smile.

'Feeling better, love?' The tone in which it was said set Kay off again.

'Kay – would you come in, please?' The doctor was in the doorway again. 'Your brother's asking for you.'

Once inside the small room, which smelt of disinfectant, Kay put her arms out to Jac, but he turned away and buried his face into Laura again.

The doctor waved Kay towards a chair in the corner and sat down in his own chair. 'I've given Jac the once-over, and as I've just told your parents, there's no indication whatsoever that he has been harmed in any way.' He swivelled in his chair and turned to Jack.

'It's possible that your son has seen something which has brought on shock. I'm sure that in a day or two he'll be able to tell you about it. But until then, I suggest you resist the temptation to question him. The nervous system has a mind of its own. At the moment it's telling Jac to be quiet.'

'That makes sense.' Jack nodded slowly. 'Thanks for seeing him, Doctor. You've put my mind at rest.'

'I'm going to give you a prescription for a very mild

sedative. Keep him in bed for a day and I think you should see an improvement within twenty-four hours.'

Handing the prescription over to Laura, he tousled Jac's hair. 'If you have a repeat of the shaking meanwhile, give me a call and I'll come out.'

Laura thanked the doctor and followed Jack out of the surgery. She wished she felt as relieved as her husband, but she had been in to see this family doctor many times over the past years, with Kay and Jac. She knew him quite well and there was no doubt in her mind that he was using the gentle touch. As far as she could tell, he half expected them to be on the phone that night.

'Mum, I think I'll go straight to the station from here,' Kay said, bending down and giving Jac a kiss on the cheek. 'I've got Steve's dinner to cook and a couple of shirts to iron.'

'OK, babe. Thanks for coming with us to the doctor's.'

'Wild horses wouldn't have stopped me.'

As she walked towards Bethnal Green Underground, Kay couldn't get Jac's face out of her mind. He seemed like a different boy. She hoped that a good night's sleep would have him back to his old self.

# Chapter Five

The residents and shopkeepers in Jubilee Street had never seen anything quite like it. The first of the hopeful tenants had arrived in a dark-green van just after nine in the morning. By ten-thirty, there was an assortment of vehicles and angry, bewildered people, who had turned up ready to move into their newly rented accommodation. Speculation that there had been a dreadful murder was rife.

The flashing blue lights of the police cars and ambulance created a scene worthy of a James Bond film. Everyone, it seemed, was out and the stories, rumours and assumptions were flying around like wildfire.

Those who had been there when Patsy's body was seen through the letter-box were having a field-day as newspaper reporters ferreted from one to the other for any snippets of information they could get.

'Terrible sight – shocking.' A young Jewish woman relayed what the poor man had seen when he pushed open the black iron letterbox. 'Blood everywhere! A pool of it on the floor – and who knows how much splashed on the walls and furniture? Shocking. Jack the Ripper all over again. A woman isn't safe—'

'Is that gentleman still here?' The young spotty-faced

journalist from the local paper was flushed with excitement. 'I need to get a quote. Do you know who he is?'

The Jewish woman shrugged and waved a hand. 'It could be any one of that lot.' She looked across at the confusion as the police tried to sort onlookers from fraud victims and take statements.

'So you didn't actually speak to the gentleman?'

'I was told by a neighbour – isn't that enough?' She rolled her eyes. 'If you want more, go and see Hymie, the old boy wearing the black trilby. Nothing gets past him. He'll back my story.'

'They say there're a dozen more bodies in there,' another woman chimed in. 'Each room is padlocked. I dread to think!'

'We're lucky to be standing here,' said another, clutching her shopping bag. 'I was out walking last night, went to post a letter.' She tugged at her headscarf and stroked her neck melodramatically, 'I could have had my throat slit.'

'Was *her* throat slit, Becky?'

'So I heard. I could only see her face above that red blanket, white as a ghost it was. I wouldn't be surprised if he hadn't dismembered her parts. The shape under that hospital blanket didn't look right to me. And I saw one of the plain-clothes policemen bring out two suitcases. I swear it was blood I saw oozing through the seams.'

That was enough for the inexperienced journalist. He walked away from the small group of women, willing himself not to be sick.

Once the scene of the accident had been cleared by the

police, the onlookers wasted no time in splitting up and scurrying away to spread the word. Each one couldn't wait to be the first with the news. Into the shops they went, down the Jewish market, along the Whitechapel Waste, even stopping people as they strolled along the street, warning them not to be out after dark if they valued their lives.

'Believe me, Liz, this is the mark of a madman. And to think he's probably been luring women into that house for months on end. Poor devils. They say he's a very handsome man.'

'You mean they caught 'im red-handed?' Liz was used to the gossips: having worked in Hammond's canteen for the past four years, she had hands on experience. She knew how to get to the truth.

'Caught him? Who said they had caught him? The man's gone into hiding! For all we know it could be one of our own. Maybe he's got another house somewhere – with more dead bodies.'

'If they haven't caught him, Becky, how do they know he's handsome?' Liz couldn't help smiling.

'Stands to reason. Would *you* go back to an ugly man's house for a drink?'

As she handed the woman her cup of tea, Liz caught Laura's eye as she entered the canteen. 'Do me a favour, Becky, will yer? Go and ask Rose if she'll come and take over for me. I wanna 'ave a word with our Laura.'

'But she's having her tea break.' Becky was looking forward to joining Rose and another woman at the small table and telling her all about it.

'She's already had twenty minutes. You can guess what they're talking about.'

'I thought you were taking a couple of days off, Laura, to sit with Jac?' There was a tone of chastisement in Liz's voice.

'I am. I only popped in to let Mr Lyons know and sort out a couple of complaints from yesterday. Kay just turned up so I asked her to sit with Jac for me.' Laura sipped her tea. 'Anyway, what's all this about mass murder? The place is buzzing with it.'

'Gawd knows. A woman was found dead in a house in Jubilee Street. That's more or less the gist of it, as far as I can tell.'

'Murdered?' Laura could hardly believe it.

'So they reckon, but you know what people are like. She could have had an accident—'

'No. Has to be more than that, Liz. No smoke without fire and all that.'

'We'll see. How's Jac this morning?'

'Very quiet. Can't get a word out of 'im. It's not easy, I tell you, taking the doctor's advice. About not quizzing him.' Laura looked thoughtful. 'You don't think there's any connection, Liz, do you?'

'With what?'

'Well, you know ... with what they're all talking about.'

'Don't talk daft! How could there be?'

Laura inhaled slowly and shook her head. 'I don't know. It just seems a bit of a coincidence, that's all. The doctor said that Jac had probably seen something to make him go into shock. And Jubilee Street's only a stone's throw. Maybe he saw something on his way back from his mate's house.'

'Oh, so he did go there then?'

Laura leaned back in her chair and shrugged. 'Where else?'

The two of them sat pondering for a while until Liz finally spoke. 'No. It's too far-fetched. You know what I think? I think he was so bloody scared of getting into a row for not telling us where he was going, and that's why he shook like a leaf.'

'And we assumed the worst?'

'Overreacted, the lot of us.' Liz stood up ready to go back to her duties. 'Anyway, Jac will come out with it in his own time – *if* he's got a problem.'

'Yeah ... of course he will,' Laura chuckled at the thought of the little chatterbox going on and on. 'I had best get back to him anyway. Just in case he is going down with something.'

Lying in his silent bedroom, staring up at the ceiling, Jac wondered if he would ever have the chance of growing up now that he was a killer. He had always wanted to be an astronaut. Once a policeman came for him he could ask if, instead of going to prison, they could use him as a guinea-pig. His dad sometimes said they might one day. He could be the first boy in space and it wouldn't matter if he never came back – if he just kept going round and round the world.

If he went to prison Jac knew he would be murdered. He'd heard his dad say that child-killers would be done in if the other prisoners got hold of them.

Hem's face slipped back into his mind again. Not the dead face. The alive one with the big smile and ginger-biscuit-coloured eyes. He thought about her carrot-coloured hair, when it was long, like in the photo. She didn't look like a kidnapper with long hair, but she did once it was all short and curly. He thought she looked a *bit* like one when her hair was black and straight.

He remembered the blood seeping out of Hem's head on to the five-pound note and wondered if it could be used with blood on it. He had stopped worrying about her lying there because he had remembered when he woke up that Hem' had said someone was moving in the next day. Well they would find her. And if she wasn't really dead, she would tell them that he pushed her and they would come for him. If she was dead they might not come. They might not find out he had been there.

The sudden tapping on his bedroom door drove Jac under the bedclothes, where it was dark and private.

'That's funny, I could have sworn my little brother was in bed. Oh, well, I'll just have to go home without saying goodnight.' Kay was playing a game, and no matter how much Jac wanted to pull back the covers and make her jump, he couldn't.

'Right then – I had better be off. I've a train to catch.' The sound of her turning the door handle threw him into a panic.

'I don't want you to go!'

'Come on, Jac, you know I have to. I'll be back tomorrow.'

'I don't care if you don't!' Sitting up, he wiped a tear from the corner of his eye, determined not to let her upset him. When she sat down on the edge of his bed, he disappeared under the covers again. 'It's hot under here!'

'Well come out then – don't be silly.'

'No!'

'Please ... just for two seconds, to give me a hug.'

'I'm suffocating!'

'I'm sure you are. You'd best come up for air. You don't have to kiss me goodnight if you don't want to.'

'I can't breathe!'

Much to his relief, Kay took charge of the situation and pulled the bedclothes back in one swift movement. 'Oh, thank goodness you're still alive.' She grinned broadly at him. 'What would I do without you to make me laugh, eh?'

With his chin stuck out defiantly, Jac sat cross-legged on the bed and folded his arms, his perspiration-damp hair sticking to his forehead.

'You could stay one more night.' He studied one of the racing cars on the wallpaper so he wouldn't have to look at Kay.

'There's no need for me to stay. You're not ill. And I've got a husband to feed.'

'I didn't eat any of my tea!'

'Now don't fib. You left a sausage, that was all.' She cupped his chin and pulled his face until he had no choice but to look at her. 'What is this all about, Jac?'

He pulled his face away and sulked. 'What's what about?'

'You know what I mean. All this business of staying in your room and not talking to anyone.' Her voice had that big-sister tone to it.

'You're worrying Mum and Dad, you know. Not to mention Grandfather and Aunt Liz.'

'They never told me that.'

'Well they wouldn't, would they!' Now she was getting

cross with him. 'It's enough now, Jac. You're acting like a spoilt brat.'

'I had to go to the doctor's yesterday. I was ill!'

'I know. I was there. But you're OK now, so stop playing up. Tell them where you went yesterday. They won't kill you.'

'I didn't go anywhere. I stayed at Grandfather's all day – till Mum came to fetch me.' The word *kill* brought the picture back into his mind again, the picture of Hem' and the bloody five-pound note. Drawing away from his sister, he moved to the furthest part of the bed, drew his knees closer to his chest and closed his eyes. He filled his mind with lots of sheep and began to count them under his breath. This had worked in the night when he had woken in a sweat, with that staircase on his mind.

Once he had counted the sheep up to ten, he would let them out into the field and shut the gate. Then he would sit in his corner of the pen, close his eyes and not see anything.

'Jac?' Kay's worried voice drifted into his counting but he carried on. He was up to five. But when he felt Kay pull him on to her lap and rock him, all the sheep vanished and he started to cry.

'It's all right, babe. It's all right. We'll forget about yesterday. About you being a bit naughty. I'll tell Mum and Dad not to ask you any more questions, OK?'

Jac nodded, wiped his face with the back of his hand and cried more loudly. Not because he was sad but because he was pleased that his sister hadn't gone. Maybe she would stay the night if he kept crying. He knew he wouldn't be able to stop it now. He was having one of his proper outbursts.

'We'll just forget all about it.' Kay's voice sounded strange, as though she were talking through a bubble. But it didn't matter, she was still rocking him and patting his back and saying good things. He knew she was telling the truth and that from now on, they wouldn't ask him about that day. They would forget all about it. He crossed his fingers and made a wish: *please God let me forget it too.*

'I've got to ask you this one last thing though, Jac. For my benefit as much as yours. OK?' There was a silence while he waited to hear what was coming. 'You told me on the phone that you were going somewhere secret. Is that where—'

'No. I was fibbing!'

The definitive tone told Kay to stop right there. She knew now that there was a connection and with time, she might get to the bottom of it.

'Fair enough Jac. I needed to know, that was all.'

By the time Kay reached the phone box, just around the corner from her parents' flat, it was almost seven-thirty. She was sure that Steve would still be at work – his normal time for coming home was between ten and eleven, sometimes not until midnight. The agency seemed to be expanding by the week. He had taken on two extra staff and still they couldn't keep up with the commissioned work. Advertising seemed to be at a peak, and clients didn't seem to mind how much they spent on promoting the public's interest in their products. Especially in the car and cosmetics trades.

'Steve, it's me. I'm not interrupting a meeting, am I?' She had learned from experience to check that out first.

'No, but I am sharing a glass of wine with a client,' he said quietly.

The tell-tale note in his voice was all Kay needed to know. Steve was letting her know that he was entertaining someone very important.

'I won't go on then, but listen ... Jac's still not up to much, so I said I would stay overnight. Is that OK?' There was a pause.

'I suppose it'll have to be.' He was obviously put out.

'I'm worried about him – and you'd be too if you saw him.'

'He's a good little actor, Kay, don't forget that. He's managed to wind you all around his little finger and not get a good hiding, which he knows he deserves.'

'You think I should go home then – is that what you're saying?'

'No. Do what you think's best. I'll be here until late. I've got some work to get ready for tomorrow morning.'

'What about your dinner?' Kay was feeling guiltier by the minute.

'We had a late lunch. Greek.'

'Lucky you. I'll see you tomorrow then.'

'OK.' He wasn't letting her off the hook too easily; the tone of his voice was flat. 'I should be home earlier. About nine. Bye.' The sound of the dialling tone seemed louder than usual.

As she walked slowly back to the flats, Kay wondered why she had bothered to phone him from a call box. The conversation was hardly intimate. In fact it had left her feeling low. The image of Steve and a small happy crowd in a Greek restaurant made her feel lonely. She wondered whether to call Pamela and arrange to go out for a drink.

Surprising herself, she did an about-turn and headed back to the warm light of the red phone box, a smile on her face. She wouldn't phone Pam – she would phone Zacchi. It would be good to hear his deep voice, and with a bit of luck he might not have some gorgeous bird with him. Maybe he would pick her up and take her to the pub where they used to drink.

'Hello, Zac.' Kay felt lighter just calling him by name.

'Kay! I was just thinking about you.'

'I'm sure. Fancy going out for a drink?'

'That's a bit off, isn't it? Not been married five minutes...'

'Yes or no?'

'Where are you?'

'I'm calling from a phone box near Mum's. I'm stopping overnight.'

'Are you OK?' His concern brought back familiar waves of warmth. No matter what happened between her and Zacchi – long spaces of time when they didn't see each other, disagreements, new relationships – none of it made any difference once they were together. It seemed as if nothing and no one could break the special bond between them.

'I'm all right. Can you come over then?'

'I'll have to make a couple of phone calls first and see someone for ten minutes or so ... but I can be there by nine.'

'Thanks, Zac.' There was a pause. 'There's nothing wrong ... well, you know ... it's just...' She drew a breath and tried to control her emotions. Why on earth should the sound of his voice make her want to cry?

'I know, I know. Bye.'

With watery eyes Kay gazed at the black receiver in her hand and wondered what she was doing. Phoning someone she used to love? What would Steve think? Replacing the receiver, she could see no harm in not telling him. They were only going for a drink after all.

'You can't do a thing like that! You're married for Christ's sake!' Jack was on his soapbox again.

'He's a friend, Dad. Not a lover.'

'Tch. Things she comes out with!' He directed his anger at Laura, hoping she would back him. But Laura just shrugged it off.

'You can have friends of the opposite sex y'know, Jack. *You* should know.'

'You reckon?' He stormed out of the kitchen before Laura had the chance to go on about the women he enjoyed a joke with when he was in the pub.

Using her small handbag mirror, Kay put on her favourite pale-apricot lipstick. 'He's so old-fashioned, Mum. I thought you would have changed him by now.'

'When pigs grow wings I might.' She eyed her daughter with a look of suspicion. 'Tell me something. Would you make your face up if it was Pamela you were going out with?'

Brushing mascara on to her lashes, Kay sighed. 'If we were going out for a drink – yes. And so would you, if you needed to. You're lucky to have dark eyelashes and not fair, like mine.'

'And what if Zacchi was coming round and you weren't going out?' Laura was beginning to enjoy her interrogation.

'I would still put it on, yes. There again – so would you. We behave differently when we're in male company and you know it.' She pulled a grin at Laura, knowing she had won that round. 'I've seen you at parties, Mum. You flirt with the men a bit, you know.'

'Saucy cow.'

'It's where I get it from.' She dropped her small cosmetics case into her handbag. 'If men find us attractive, what's wrong with that?'

'Just be careful, Kay, that's all I'm saying. You and Zacchi were more than just friends at one time, don't forget.'

'Oh, come on. Our relationship fizzled out ages ago. I would no more dream of kissing Zacchi than I would Pamela.' Having to defend her intentions was beginning to anger Kay. 'And if you dare say *Me thinks she does protest too much* ...'

'Wouldn't dream of it. But it's a good one. I'll keep that on the back burner.' Smiling with tongue in cheek, Laura left Kay to herself and joined Jack in the living room.

'I 'ope you've given 'er a good talking to? She's not been married five minutes and—'

'You should have a bit of respect for your daughter. She's not a tart.'

'No, but Zacchi's a bloke and I know the way our minds work.'

'The way *your* mind works, you mean.' She shot him a look to kill.

He stuck his nose in the air and sniffed deliberately. 'Don't know what you're talking about.'

'No, I'm sure.' Laura was pleased to have put him in his place. It made up for losing ground with Kay.

'It's good to see you again, Kay.' Zacchi eased himself on to a chair behind their table for two in the Prospect of Whitby, and handed her her drink. 'Why are you staying at your mum's?'

'Jac's not very well and Steve's working till midnight again.' She shrugged. 'So why not?'

He looked at Kay over the top of his pint. 'You must be missing your workmates.'

'I am, Zacchi, yeah. But I also like not having to get up in the mornings and set off with the rat race. Swings and roundabouts.'

'What do you *do* all day?'

'Fuck the milkman and then the window-cleaner.'

'Very funny.' He tried to keep a straight face but couldn't stop himself smiling at her. 'How *do* you fill your time?'

She leaned back in her chair and thought about it. 'I might have known you'd cotton on.' She leaned towards him. 'Yes – I do get bored and fed up with my own company.'

'You were weaving a rug last time we spoke.'

'I got bored with it.'

'You'll be turning into a sad little rich girl if you're not careful.'

'Rather that than a sad poor one.'

140

'You might think so.' He emptied his glass. 'Another drink?'

'I'll get them.'

He stood up before she could. 'I'm not one of your trendy friends.'

'Still playing the proud Romany?'

'You don't have to drink with me.'

'Oh, shut up and get it in.'

'You know your trouble?'

'What?' Her expression would have been enough to make a flower wilt. But Zacchi was no flower – her play-acting just aroused his desire to rekindle the fire.

Gazing into her forget-me-not eyes, he felt a strong urge to make love to her. The passion he had known in the past was back again. 'You're prouder than I am.' He smiled and turned away.

Finishing her gin and tonic while he was at the bar, Kay quietly admired him. Six foot tall, broad as ever and as for his face, well, that could hardly be more hand-some. She remembered when she first looked into those dark-blue eyes. And for all his good looks, he wasn't vain. At least she didn't think so.

Checking the girls grouped together in a corner of the pub, it was evident that they were discussing her handsome escort. Admiring his body. Kay's eyes wan-dered back to Zacchi leaning on the bar. He was smiling back at the girls and his pose had changed. He was lapping it up.

Unable to stop herself smiling at his flirting, Kay realized that he dressed much the same now as he had seven years ago in the hop fields. Baggy black T-shirt tucked into tight jeans, worn leather belt and boots. His

141

footwear was the only small change. He was wearing Chelsea boots instead of the strong black leather ones that most of the gypsies had worn.

'When's your book coming out?' Kay soon forgot about his good looks once he was back at the table and they were in conversation. They were just two old friends enjoying a drink together, their history back in the past where it belonged.

'Last week.'

'Oh, Zac, I'm sorry, I didn't realize. I would have sent you a card or something.'

'I don't go in for all that – as you well know. Anyway, a travel book is hardly on your reading list.'

'Not normally, no. But I would read yours. It's autobiographical, isn't it?'

'So they tell me. It's about the history of travellers as well as modern-day gypsies, so I suppose I am in there somewhere.'

'How's it selling?'

'Very well, apparently.' He was obviously pleased, but being Zacchi, he wasn't going to let on.

'You'll have to give up journalism soon. I bet they'll want another book. Next thing we know you'll have a film company wanting to buy the rights.'

'I'm working on a novel.' His face broke into a smile. 'Now when that comes out I will scream from the rooftops. And you'll get a signed advance copy. Mother Rose says hello, by the way.'

'That's nice. She still remembers me.'

'What would you expect? You were very nearly her daughter-in-law.'

'I don't remember you proposing.'

'No? And I thought you had a good memory.'

Kay knew he was referring to when she was fifteen, when things had got a bit out of hand on a haystack, during the hop-picking. Their words came flooding back: *We can wait, can't we Zac? We can do it ... I promise I won't try again, Kay. I promise. We'll wait until we've jumped the broomstick.*

'We were just a pair of kids.'

'You might have been. I was seventeen and knew what I was saying.'

'Well you never asked me again, did you? And you had four years to, before we split up.'

'I shouldn't have had to ask again.' He finished his second pint.

'What is this?' Kay shook her head and laughed at him. 'When we parted company, it was by mutual agreement.' She finished her drink and pointed a finger at him. 'It was you who said there was nothing left for us to discover about each other.'

'And you agreed.'

'Because it was true.'

'Everything had got too familiar – your words, not mine.'

'You knew what I was thinking before I had said it.'

'Or so I thought.'

'Or so you thought.'

'Another drink?'

'And then we'll go back to your flat?' She pushed her fingers through her long hair, enjoying the harmless flirtation.

Smiling to himself, Zacchi looked away and then back into her face. It wasn't until the record on the jukebox finished that they lowered their eyes. 'I Can't Help Falling in Love with You' had been playing.

'When you think about it,' Zacchi said, gazing into her face, 'the only difference between our relationship and yours and Steve's is that he signed a piece of paper.'

'Ah,' she smiled teasingly, 'but *you* wouldn't do that, would you?'

'Ah but,' he smiled, flashing his even white teeth, 'that's not the Romany way.' He reached for her hand, lifted it to his mouth, kissed her fingers and raised his eyes to meet hers. 'It's still there, Kay, you can't ignore it.'

Kay leaned forward until their faces almost met. 'Drink up or leave it.' She kissed him lightly on the mouth.

'You *were* joking about going back to my flat?'

'No. I was testing the ground.' She kissed him again, 'Ready?'

'You want to?'

'Don't you?'

'What do you think?'

As Zacchi pulled into Station Road in Leyton, Kay felt her stomach turn. She suddenly felt cheap and tacky. The short ride from Stepney had passed very quickly; she had hardly had time to think about her behaviour. They had not stopped talking. Him telling her about his trip to Europe, and Kay filling him in on her new life of leisure and open cheque-book.

Drawing up outside his basement flat, Zacchi picked up on Kay's silence. 'Changing your mind?'

'Maybe the drink has worn off.' She bit her lower lip and looked apologetically at him.

'Come on, you idiot. We don't have to make love. I'll dig out a copy of my book while you make the coffee.'

Following him inside, she felt bad for starting something she hadn't the nerve to carry through.

'You don't mind then?'

'It's not the be-all and end-all, Kay. I'm not desperate.'

'Point taken.' He was still good at sticking pins in. She felt her hackles rise, but knowing it was from vanity she kept her mouth shut.

'Fancy an omelette, Kay?' he called from the kitchen.

'Oh, *do* I? With cheese?'

'Why don't you put a record on!'

She stood in the kitchen doorway and saluted. 'Yes *sar*!'

'Stop acting, Kay – it's not you.' He broke an egg into the Pyrex basin.

Irritated by his know-all tone, she left him to his cooking. 'Which would you prefer ... the Stones, the Beatles, or ... the Kinks?

'Kinks! "All Day and All of the Night"!'

'Good choice.' Having found the track, she placed the needle and turned up the volume.

Settling herself on his small sofa, she lay back and enjoyed the song. She knew what Zacchi was up to – and it was working. The delicious smell of sizzling cheese omelette, the moody lighting and those terrific lyrics were causing her to slip back into the mood she had been in earlier.

'Here.' Zacchi stood above her holding a glass of red wine. 'It's only Bull's Blood but it'll have to do.'

Taking it from him, Kay couldn't help smiling. His

seduction might not have been all that original but it was working.

'What?'

'Nothing. I was just thinking about our Jac and some of the things he comes out with.' She regretted those words as soon as they were out. Not wishing to bring domesticity into the atmosphere she quickly added, 'I love this flat. It's so relaxing.'

The sound of Kay singing along to the Kinks made him smile. She had a terrible voice and could hardly sing a note in tune.

'The only time I feel all right, is by your side...' Kay was singing at the top of her voice. Someone really should tell her she's tone-deaf, he thought. So long as it's not me.

By the time they had eaten their omelettes and cleared away the plates, a Beatles record was on the turntable: 'You've Got to Hide Your Love Away'.

With his head back and his legs stretched out in front of the sofa, Zacchi stroked Kay's feet as they rested in his lap. He was humming along to the record, singing a line here and there, knowing that Kay was watching him, waiting for him to look back at her. Waiting for him to ask with his eyes if he could make love to her. Well – she would have a long wait. It was up to her now.

'Zac...'

'Yep?' Still he wouldn't look at her. 'What?'

'No, don't stop singing – I love to hear your voice. Just listen while you sing.'

'No – I've lost it now.' With practised nonchalance, he

casually drew his fingers across her foot and gently massaged her ankle, knowing how she loved to have her feet caressed.

She pushed her toes into his hand. 'Come and lie next to me.'

'You know what will happen if I do.' He lay his head back on a cushion.

'Please...'

'And then you'll change your mind again.' His heart was beating rapidly but he was determined to remain cool.

'No I won't.'

This time he did look at her, straight into those Love me eyes. 'Are you sure?'

Her smile conveyed everything – she could be very seductive when she wanted.

Keeping his eyes on her face, Zacchi brushed the back of his fingers across her foot and up her leg until he reached her short skirt. He checked again to see if she was happy to go on. She didn't have to say a word – her expression spoke volumes.

Pushing his hand under the soft material he found the top of her stocking and squeezed the soft flesh, his hands always on the move, inside her knickers, squeezing and stroking, until touching wasn't enough – he wanted to *see* her again. Easing her skirt above her waist, he lowered his head, kissing and licking her thighs until his teeth found her silky briefs and then the tiny join at the side. With one good tug he ripped the few stitches and then tore them off her.

With his hands pressing down on each thigh he began gently to push and squeeze, his thumbs caressing the hollow parts either side of her fleshy crevice. Working up a steady rhythm, he massaged until she was slowly twisting and turning beneath his grasp. Her heavy breathing and soft moaning urged him on as he made her smooth thighs and stomach wet with his kisses and then filled his fiery mouth with her firm, erect breasts.

'Don't, Zac ... don't. I won't last ten seconds.'

As her body rocked to and fro and her moaning gradually built up in time with his urgent desire to draw liquid from her body, Zacchi knew that she was fulfilling his wishes, and it took every bit of his willpower to control his own juices from flowing too soon.

As Kay lay beside Zacchi in his double bed watching the sun come up, she wished that time could stand still. Being there beside him felt right, and she wondered why they had split up in the first place.

Their lovemaking had always been good, but this night of love had surpassed even her wildest dreams. Each time they had reached the heights and collapsed, spent, either she or Zacchi had begun to caress the other and the deep sharing of bodies started all over again.

The unexpected first call of a blackbird piercing the quietness triggered off a feeling of lament in Kay. The birdsong marked the beginning of a new day and very possibly the end of her and Zacchi. Their past relationship, which had changed from being lovers to close friends, could never be the same now that they had repeated history. A liaison like this would be wrong; unfair on Steve. If she started to weave a web of deceit and arrange secret meetings with Zacchi, it would cheapen everything.

She looked into Zacchi's face as he gazed at the

ceiling, smoking a cigarette. He was just as pensive as she was. She wondered if a thought transference had been taking place between them – the way it often had in the past.

Knowing there was little point in discussing their future, she tried to engineer a conversation which would lead them back to being soul mates again instead of lovers.

'What's your novel about, Zac?' she asked quietly.

He turned his head slightly and gave her a knowing look which confirmed they were on the same wavelength; even at that precise moment, he had seen through her ploy.

'It's a highly political, sensational, intellectual, crime, sex and horror story with strong moral themes.' He blew a smoke ring towards the ceiling.

'That should sell well then.' She kept a straight face and spoke in a serious tone. 'So long as it's a science fiction novel.'

'Didn't I mention that? Oh and it's autobiographical as well. I name names. Only famous ones, naturally. How about a mug of tea?'

'What about the journalism then? Will you give it up to write more books?'

'No.' He turned on his back again. 'I was tempted to rush over to Stepney yesterday, as it happens. Until I heard how overblown the story had got.'

'What story?'

'The woman who was found at the bottom of her stairs in a critical condition. Don't tell me you hadn't heard about it? It was on your parents' doorstep. Almost made the nationals.'

'Why would something like that make the nationals?'

He turned over and squashed his cigarette into an ashtray on the bedside table. 'It was a good lesson for trainee journalists who thought they could get good copy from gossip!'

'Are we talking about Stepney?' She studied his expression to see if he was winding her up.

'Jubilee Street.' He plumped his pillow.

'You *are* serious.'

'Of course I am. What's so sensational about something happening in Stepney?' He pushed his hands behind his head and grinned. 'Of course, I was forgetting, the poor little rich girl, Kay Whatsername, came from those parts, didn't she? The journo's missed out on that little scoop.'

Pulling the pillow from under his head, she pushed it down on his face and held it there. 'The poor rich murderess would make better headlines.'

Enjoying a rough-and-tumble, their laughter filled the room, in time with the dawn chorus which had been building up outside.

'Now the *real* story, the one I'll follow up, *is* interesting,' Zacchi said, falling on to his propped-up pillows. 'Ingenious little plan from the mind of one woman I *would* like to interview.' His eyes glazed over as his imagination took hold. Kay had seen that look before.

'Come on, Zac, don't be mean. Half a story's worse than nothing. You know that.' She hoped he wasn't going to do his silent act to torment her.

'You move into a rented house.' Zacchi narrowed his eyes, reporting the facts and working out the plot at the same time. 'Do it up – cheaply, no doubt. What does a tin of paint cost?' He paused while concentrating. 'Then you advertise it to let. You promise a fantastic deal which can hardly be refused in return for six months' rent in advance.

'You agree to let it to six interested parties, more if you can get them, take their money – and run.' He chuckled softly. 'Brilliant.'

'You're forgetting one thing. She met with an accident. Maybe someone found out that they were about to be cheated.'

'Maybe. But all the signs point to it being an accident. Her bags were packed and ready to go. They found two train tickets to Scotland.'

'So there was a partner. Maybe he finished her off.'

'I doubt it. One was half-fare. She must have been planning to take a kid with her.' He looked pensive again. 'No . . . our little crook obviously went one step too fast – at the top of a staircase.'

'Sorry. Too far-fetched. I don't believe it.' Kay's imagination was firing now. 'Someone who could plan something like that would be more careful. I don't suppose you got her name?'

'Of course I did. Shouldn't have done – but it's not what you know—'

'Yeah, all right. What was her name?'

'Can't remember. It's in my notes.'

'Here or at work?'

Zacchi narrowed his eyes. 'Why?'

'It's important, Zacchi.'

'Oh yeah?' She was arousing his inquisitive mind.

'Pam's aunt was squeezed out of her home by some bitch of a woman, in Jubilee Street. It could be her.'

Zacchi roared with laughter. 'Now you *are* being melodramatic!'

'She lived in Jubilee Street!'

Pulling himself up he looked sideways at Kay. 'You're sure about that, are you?'

'Zacchi – I'm talking about my best friend's aunt! I used to go with Pam to visit her. This woman, whoever she is, turned up out of the blue and threw an old woman out of her home.'

Jumping out of bed, Zacchi pulled on his underpants and raced into the living room, leaving Kay with a strange tingling sensation filling her veins.

Once he had returned with his briefcase and dropped it on the bed, Zacchi got into his jeans. 'Don't!' He glared at Kay, daring her to look through his papers.

'Sorry.' She pulled her hand away and waited. 'I was getting carried away.'

'That's OK.' His voice took on a gentler tone. 'That briefcase is like my private diary.'

'You don't have to explain, I should have known.' She admired his tanned body and tight jeans.

Searching through his notes, Zacchi found what he was looking for and Kay had to force herself to get back on track. They could make love again later.

'Right – here it is ... would you recognize the name?'

'No. Pam never mentioned it.'

'Terrific. Why didn't you say?'

'You didn't ask.'

He slammed his notebook down. 'You do it on purpose, don't you?'

'Come on, you're getting a bit carried away—'

'I thought I was on to something.'

'Well you are! Just because I don't know her name...'
Kay sighed and shook her head. 'What's the woman's
name, anyway?'

'Hemmingway.'

Kay felt the blood drain from her face. 'Say that
again.'

'Hemmingway.'

'First name?' she demanded.

Zacchi looked at his notes. 'Patricia.'

Kay's entire body felt empty and light. Her eyes
widened as she stared back at him. She could feel her
heart racing. 'It can't be. It's not possible.' She pushed
her hand through her hair. 'Coincidence, that's what it
is. A fluke chance...'

'Kay?' Zacchi watched as she wrapped his towelling
robe around her naked body and paced the floor,
repeating over and over that it couldn't be possible.

Quick to his feet, Zacchi reached out and guided her to
the sofa, alarmed at the way her body was trembling.
'It's all right, Kay, it's all right.' He kissed her forehead
lightly. 'Calm down and then tell me.'

Sipping hot sweet tea, comforted in Zacchi's bathrobe,
Kay asked him to read out some more of his scribbled
notes before she tried to explain why she was so
disturbed by the story.

'A set of child's clothing was laid out on an armchair—'

'That's enough, Zac.' Her contorted face reddened as
the blood rushed to her cheeks. She stared in front of her
as if she were in another world. Trying to string the
words together, she made an effort to explain, but was

unable to finish a sentence. Nothing she said made sense.

'I can't help you if I don't know.' Zacchi inhaled slowly, wondering what to do next. 'Drink the tea, Kay. Drink it right down. It's not too hot.'

Obeying his instructions, her hands shaking, she raised the mug to her lips and swallowed until the cup was empty.

'Good. Now I'm going to get you a drop of brandy, OK?'

'No. Keep on holding me, Zacchi. Don't let me go.' She looked pleadingly at him. 'Please don't ever, ever go away and leave me again.'

Taken aback by her unexpected plea, he got a grip on himself and tried not to think about what she had just said. This wasn't the time for him to question his past behaviour, when he had left her to go on a six-month trip abroad. When he had thought her a selfish cow who hadn't shown any sign of regret at his leaving.

'You've got to stop this, Kay.' He forced himself to control his own emotions.

'Get me the brandy,' she said, trying to compose herself. 'A very large one.' She clasped her hands together, willing them to be still.

Warming her body, the alcohol soon produced a relaxing effect. 'That's better.' She took a few deep breaths, inhaling slowly. 'Right. Ready?'

He nodded, hoping he was.

'Jac. My Jac. My brother.' She stopped to control her breathing again. 'Patsy Hemmingway is his mother. His real mother.'

Zacchi loosened the grip on Kay's hand, too stunned to speak.

'She gave him up to Mum and Dad four years ago, when he was two and a half.'

'I remember.'

Kay gazed into his face. 'Oh, yeah, of course you do.'

'But I never knew who his mother was.'

'No. That's right. Well – now you know.' She sat upright, composed herself again. 'Patsy Hemmingway. She must have come back with the intention of taking Jac.'

'Oh come on, Kay...'

'I told you that he wasn't right yesterday!' she cut in. 'Or the day before, rather. Anyway – he'd gone missing. Something he never does. Never. I thought...' She pushed her lips together and swallowed against the lump in her throat, forcing back the tears. 'I should have listened to him on the phone ... when he was trying to tell me something.

'I knew there was something wrong when I saw him – once he got back from wherever he'd been. He was so white. And his thin little body was trembling. And his eyes, Zacchi, his eyes...' She started to cry again. 'It was as if Jac had slipped out of his body – escaped. Well, we all feel like that sometimes, don't we?

'If he did go to that house – if by some sinister manipulation she had managed to lure him there – what happened? What did my brother go through?'

'Stop tormenting yourself. I'll check it out.'

Seeing her standing there like that, a pathetic child inside, he was filled with the longing to look after her for ever. It was becoming very clear to him that their relationship was going to have to be brought to a head. She belonged with him and no one else.

The one thing he wasn't prepared to do was have an affair with her. It would have to be all or nothing. They did love each other and always had. Misunderstandings had pushed them apart.

Driving Kay home, Zacchi felt uncomfortable with the silence. It was unlike her to be so quiet. 'You'll have to wait, you know, Kay. Before telling your parents any of this. It may be that they've already had it thrust under their noses, but—'

'I don't intend to tell them anything. No one must know, Zacchi. No one. Just in case.' She turned her head away and stared out of the window of his car. 'If Jac *was* there when she fell; if he *did* push her . . .'

As he drew up outside the block of flats, Kay looked to him for support. 'I wish you could come up with me, but—'

'I know.' He glanced briefly at her. 'Stop treating me as if I'm no more than a friend you've confided in, Kay. I know what your dad's like.'

'Sorry.' She stroked the side of his face. 'We'll talk later. I'll call you.'

'Oh, so you've decided to show your face then?' Jack was furious with Kay. 'Jac was crying for you in the night. Asked if you might have been murdered. What d'yer think you're playing at?'

'I should have phoned you but it got too late. We did a pub-crawl and ended up near Leyton, so we went back to Zacchi's for coffee. We got talking and—'

'Yeah? And what d'yer reckon your husband's gonna say about that?'

'He won't say anything! He knows Zacchi. We've all been out for a drink together – more than once. They're friends.'

Jack shook his head. 'No. Sorry. It's not on.' He pointed a finger in Kay's face. 'It's not on, Kay. Right? No more Zacchi!' His voice was getting angrier with each word.

'You can't just go out for a drink – oh no! Not you! You 'ave to stay out all bloody night! I never did trust 'im. Bloody gypsy.'

'You hypocrite,' she said, keeping her voice down. The last thing she wanted was to wake Jac and give him something else to fret over. 'How can you stand there judging Zacchi, with your past record?' Pushing her face up close to his she spoke in a low, tight voice. 'I'm gonna close the door so Mum doesn't come in, right? I want a private word with you. Your pigeon's come home to roost again. Patsy.'

Closing the door for her, Jack clenched his teeth and narrowed his eyes. 'What about Patsy?'

'I'm not even thinking that you might have known she was back...' Kay hoped he wouldn't say otherwise.

'What d'yer mean – she's back?'

'Been living in Jubilee Street. You'd best sit down. I don't know the full story. Zacchi's gonna find out all he can today. But you're in for a bit of a shock.'

The sound of the telephone took them both by surprise. 'Who's that at this time of the morning?' Jack looked at his watch. 'It's only ten to eight.'

He picked up the receiver, a deadpan expression on

his face. He asked whoever it was to hold on and then whispered to Kay, 'Make sure your mother's still in the bathroom! And if she asks who's on the phone tell her it's a bit of trouble at the docks.'

'Why do I 'ave to check she's in the bathroom...?'

'Do it!'

Keeping the phone call short, Jack slammed the receiver down and cursed, swearing at himself for being a mug and getting mixed up with Patsy in the first place.

'Mum's only just getting out of the bath. Who was that on the phone?'

'I'm gonna 'ave to go to work, Kay. I'm late as it is. I'll tell you about it later. And no – I didn't know she was back. All right? You've got my word on that.'

Pulling his cap on, he again asked Kay to tell her mother that there was trouble at the docks and that he'd probably be late home.

'Dad! Please – who was on the phone?'

'Patsy's mum.' Desperate to get out of the flat, he marched along the passage calling cheerio to Laura as he went.

'Trouble at the *docks*?' Laura raised an eyebrow. As if they weren't loaded with trouble at home. 'Go and see if Jac's awake will you, Kay? I don't want him getting up but just check he's not still worrying about you – or fretting about yesterday.' She rubbed her eyes and sighed. 'If he's awake he would have heard you and Dad shouting at each other.'

'He'll be all right, don't worry. I'll spoil him rotten today. You get ready for work. Leave Jac to me.'

'I wasn't gonna go in—'

'Please, Mum. Let me have him to myself today. I think if we're on our own and quiet he might say a bit more about what happened yesterday. If anything happened, that is.'

'If you're sure. We are busy. And Kay ... you were out of order you know. What did you think your dad would do – spending the night with Zacchi? What were you thinking of? I told you a long time ago that once you were married—'

'I remember, Mum. And I said that I could see no harm in having male friends so long as that's all they were – friends.'

'And?'

'And what?'

'You and Zacchi?'

Kay felt herself blush as she lowered her eyes. 'I still love him.'

'Oh, terrific.'

Instead of making his way to the bus-stop, Jack decided he would walk to work. He had a lot to think about. The phone call from Patsy's mum had cut him to the quick. He needed a clear head to work out whether or not to go up to Leicester to see Patsy's family. See if her mother really meant what she said – that she wanted to see her grandson, Jac.

He hadn't taken it in. Not really. It had been like something out of a film. Patsy on death's doorstep? He couldn't believe it. The fact that she had actually been living in Stepney for the past few months was enough to cope with. He couldn't understand why she would want to move back down from Leicester. If she had wanted to be near her son, surely she would have written and said so. Questions flew through his mind, one after another, and for the life of him he couldn't come up with an answer. She had never been slow in coming forward. Not Patsy. Maybe something had happened to change her.

Going over every word her mother had said on the phone, it soon dawned on Jack that Tom, the man he thought she was going marry, must have left, or hadn't turned out to be right for Patsy after all. Whatever the case, Jack was still perplexed as to what he should do for the best. After all, little Jac's grandparents had every right to insist that the boy be taken to see his dying mother.

Arriving at the gates of the docks, it was now clear in his mind that he and Laura were going to have to tell Jac that he was adopted. And they would have to do that soon, before the authorities poked their noses in. He had no doubts that they would advise that Jac be told, and the last thing he wanted was that it should come from someone else. A stranger. A stranger who didn't know his six-year-old the way he did.

No matter how much he tried to push it out of his mind during the day, Jack was fully preoccupied with it. Talking to the other dockers only when he had to, to stop them wondering what was wrong, he probably unloaded more crates of tomatoes in a morning than he would usually do in a day.

Choosing a quiet pub just off East India Dock Road, Jack found himself a small table in a corner where he could enjoy a pint and a couple of cheese and tomato rolls. With his newspaper spread on the table, he feigned interest in the crossword puzzle. If he kept his head down, that would stop any of the other blokes in there starting up a conversation. He had to work things out in his mind before he returned to the flat at the end of the afternoon. Laura should have been told who had actually made the phone call that morning.

Before he had eaten one of his rolls, he realized that he had drunk his pint and was ready for another. Breaking his rule of never having more than one during his lunch-break, he ordered a half. When that was finished, he got another pint in. Sod it, he wouldn't go back. He would phone and leave a message that he had the gut-ache. He would hardly be lying.

With the beer inside him, Jack felt his mood rising and began to make plans. He would go to Leicester and talk to Patsy's mum. Try to persuade her not to make any waves, that her grandson would only suffer if he saw his mother in a coma. He would promise her everything. Promise to set things straight all round once their daughter was off the danger list. He had no reason to believe she wouldn't pull through. Patsy was a fighter, always had been.

Resolute that he wasn't going to shilly-shally any longer, he found a phone box outside the pub and looked up the number of Hammond's store. Once he was through to Laura's department, he took a long deep breath and prepared himself. The last thing he wanted was for Laura to note that he was a bit tipsy.

'There's a little bit of discontent among the men, Laura. I'll tell you all about it later. I just wanted to let you know that I won't be in for dinner. The meeting'll probably go on till the pub shuts. You know what—'

'Jack, I'll have to go. I've got a bloody bus-load of bargain hunters in.'

'A what?' Jack couldn't believe that day-trippers went shopping in Hammond's.

'You know what I mean. I'll keep your dinner warm, all right?'

'Yeah. Sounds good. See yer later. Oh – how was Jac when you left?'

'Fine. Pleased to have his sister back again. Look I'm gonna have to go, Jack...'

'Yeah, all right. Go and make a killing.' He hung up and smiled to himself. *Should have been an actor, Jack boy*, he thought, pleased with his performance.

Pulling the wrinkled piece of paper from his pocket, he could only just make out the number he had scribbled down in haste earlier on.

'Hello! Mrs Hemmingway, it's Jack. I'm in a call box and I don't have much change.'

'Why couldn't you phone from home? Still trying to keep my Patsy under wraps, are you?' It was obvious that the woman had been crying.

'I'm at King's Cross station,' he lied. 'I thought I'd pop up to see you.'

'Don't bother. It's my daughter you should be visiting, not me.'

'I thought we should have a talk.' Jack should have expected a rebuff – Mrs Hemmingway had never liked him.

'She's in the London Hospital. We plan to go tomorrow. Maybe we'll visit our grandson while we're down there.'

'No!'

'And why not? We haven't seen him for over four years,' Eileen Hemmingway said, 'thanks to you!'

'Come on, be fair. We all agreed it would be best for Jac to make a clean break. You weren't too bothered at the time, according to Patsy.'

'Well I'm bothered now!' She slammed the receiver down before Jack had a chance to persuade her away from turning up on his doorstep.

'Fuck it.' Jack fumed as he stormed out of the telephone kiosk. 'Like mother like daughter!'

Unsure as to what he should do next, Jack found himself running to catch a bus. One which would take him to the hospital. He would keep a low profile once there, just go in to see how bad she was. If she had come out of the coma by then he would ask her why she had decided to move back to Stepney. Maybe she planned to stay for good. If so, what was on her mind? Surely she wasn't going to try to get her son back after all this time? No one could be that selfish. But then, thinking back to the time when she did her best to get him to leave Laura, he realized that Patsy was capable of anything.

Arriving at the inquiry desk he glanced around the waiting room, hoping that no one he knew would be there. His wish was granted: the gloomy faces of patients waiting to be attended to were none that he recognized.

'Can I help you?' a young nurse asked.

Spinning round to face her, he asked which ward Patsy Hemmingway was in. Checking her entry book she found the name and told Jack where to go.

'Visiting isn't for another hour,' she warned, 'but if

you speak to the ward sister, she may let you see her. She's in a side-ward.'

Jack peered at her, his face full of questions. 'Side-ward?'

'Solitary.' She threw him a sympathetic look. 'You do realize it's a head injury?'

''Course I do.' He took a deep breath and exhaled slowly. 'Thanks for your help.'

As he neared the ward, Jack's legs began to feel strange, almost like pins and needles. *Needles without the pins*, he thought as he glanced in through a small window of one of the side-wards. He stopped in his tracks. Whether or not it was Patsy lying on the bed he couldn't tell. The patient's head was completely covered by bandages to just above her eyes and there were wires and tubes everywhere.

'Are you looking for someone?' the ward sister asked.

'Miss Hemmingway,' Jack said, his fingers crossed, hoping that the poor devil he had been looking at through the window wasn't Patsy.

'Are you a newspaper reporter?'

'No.' Jack found that amusing. 'I'm a docker. Is that her in there?'

'Yes. Are you related to the patient?'

'You could say that.' He cocked his head to one side and narrowed his eyes. 'Confidentially?' he asked.

'Of course.'

'She's the mother of my son.' He felt as if he were a Catholic at confession.

'And you can prove that?'

'No.' He almost added that he didn't have Jac in his pocket, but thought better of it.

164

'I'll have to check. Get permission. And even so ...'

'Yeah, what?'

'You'll only be allowed to look at her through the window. She still hasn't come round.' The nurse smiled sympathetically at him.

'What's wrong with her?'

'I'm sorry,' she shrugged, 'I'm not allowed to give out any information. You would have to speak to the doctor, and he's on his rounds at the moment.'

'Off the record then ...?' Jack looked pleadingly at her, hoping he could win her round.

'I'm sorry. Even if I could answer the questions you're about to throw at me, I wouldn't be allowed to tell you. It's a strict rule.'

'What are her chances?' Jack could feel his temper rising. One bloody answer, that's all he wanted.

'I'm sorry.' She shook her head. 'I must ask you to wait in the room at the end of the corridor. Matron should be here in twenty minutes or so. She can advise you better than I can.'

'You mean she'll tell me to make an appointment to see the doctor?'

'Something like that, yes.'

'And he might not tell me anything because I'm not family.'

'It's not for me to say.' The nurse was beginning to lose her patience with him.

'She must have had an X-ray by now. Surely you can tell me the outcome of that?'

'Absolutely not.' She checked the time on the watch pinned to her uniform. 'Now I really must ask you to leave.'

Jack turned away and glanced at the small window again. 'A fifty-fifty chance?'

'Please. You're making it very difficult for me.'

'Fair enough.' He backed off. 'I take it I am allowed an opinion?'

She rolled her eyes and sighed. 'I can't really stop you, can I?'

'Fractured skull? Brain damage?'

'The doctor's the only one who can confirm your opinions,' she said without committing herself, but her expression showed that he could be right. Her face relaxed and she half-smiled. 'This can't be easy for you.'

'No, it's not. I would hate to see Patsy in a wheelchair.' Jack hoped his leading statement would get a result.

'They're improving them all the time, you know.' She looked straight into his eyes. 'Wheelchairs, that is.'

Jack felt himself sink. She had just answered his question. He glanced at the window and back to the nurse. 'Poor cow,' he murmured, and walked slowly away, his eyes cast to the floor.

'I thought the meeting was after work?' Laura couldn't believe her own eyes. Jack meeting her from work! It was unheard-of.

'It was no more than a flash in the pan,' he said, holding open the staff side-entrance door for Laura. 'All sorted now.'

Slipping her arm into Jack's, Laura felt sorry for him as they walked silently along Cleveland Way. She wondered which of the two upsets was eating away at him at that very moment. Kay spending the night with Zacchi, or little Jac's strange mood. Whichever it was, there was nothing she could think of to say that might make him feel better. She wasn't feeling that light-hearted herself. She remembered her mother's favourite saying, that trouble always came in threes. Well she was right there. Liz had finally said what had been bothering her. She had told Laura over lunch about Billy's confused state of mind, which seemed to be worsening.

When Liz mentioned senile dementia, Laura's heart had sunk. Her own grandfather had suffered with the same thing and she remembered the way it had affected her grandmother's life. She had had to watch him very closely, and no responsibility could be left to his sole attention. Any paperwork or bill-paying, which he had always insisted on doing, had to be constantly checked for mistakes. He would put things away in safe places and forget all about them. Important papers, insurance policies, birth certificates; even his will.

The saddest bit should have been the funniest. Liz had found Billy's dinner untouched, on a shelf in the sideboard. When she asked him about it, he swore blind that he'd put it in the fridge.

'Remember when we used to go dancing, Laura – they were good times, weren't they? The old Ilford Palais...' Jack chuckled quietly and squeezed her hand. 'Snogging outside that old green gate...'

He slipped his arm around her small waist and tucked a finger under the waistband of her skirt. 'See – if I hadn't have bunked into Charrington's Christmas party we might not be together now. We might never 'ave got together again, and you would 'ave married that dozy git you was going out with.'

'Yeah – and I'd be living in a nice big house in Chingford.'

'Money's not everything though, is it?'

'No?' She raised an eyebrow.

"Course it's not. What would you do differently, eh? If we came into a fortune?'

'Oh well, where shall I start? A new wardrobe . . .'

'I've been meaning to talk to you about your clothes, as it happens. Your skirts are getting a bit too short. It's bad enough that Kay walks about showing her bloody knickers off—'

'Well, well, well,' Laura laughed quietly. 'Look who's coming. And just look at her hemline, if you think mine's short!'

'Hello, Laura, Jack. How's tricks?'

Milly the bubbly blonde never seemed to age. Her hair had been cut into an urchin and bleached a bit lighter than Laura remembered and she had put on a bit of weight – mostly to her breasts, of which she was obviously still proud. She was wearing a pink mini-skirt, purple silk blouse and four-inch white stiletto heels.

They chatted to Milly for a while and Laura noticed that Jack was having difficulty taking his eyes off her cleavage. 'I've just come from work,' she giggled. 'I do a bit of cleaning at the umbrella factory. Cushy little number – push a bleeding vacuum cleaner around the place and that's about it. Can't be bad, eh?'

They watched her wiggle her arse as she walked away in a world of her own where the sun always shone.

'Jac's having a little sleep on the settee,' Kay said as her parents arrived in the kitchen. 'He doesn't have a temperature any more and he says his headache's gone.'

'That's something, I s'pose. The gypsy's not 'ere then?' Jack said, avoiding his daughter's eyes.

'Zacchi left after he dropped me off this morning, if you remember rightly.'

'I know that. I just thought he might 'ave crept back, once we were out of the way.' The sudden noise from the television distracted Jack from his plans of advising his daughter not to make a similar mistake to those he had made in the past. But Jac had obviously woken from his nap and his needs were greater than Kay's.

'You'll have to have a word with him, you know,' Kay said, once her dad was out of earshot. 'He's overstepping the mark.'

As she poured herself a glass of cooled water from the fridge, Laura shrugged at Kay's anger. 'Nothing I say will stop him, you should know that. He'll soon get bored with it.'

'He'd better. I'm beginning to loathe him.' She pulled her white leather jacket from the back of a chair and slipped it over her black and white dress.

'Don't say things like that. You don't mean it.'

'The way he insults Zacchi, never mind me!'

Leaning against the kitchen sink, Laura admired Kay's outfit. She had expensive tastes. 'You should wear black and white more often, it suits you.'

'It was in a sale,' Kay said quietly, the colour still rising in her cheeks from Jack's remarks.

Laura tossed back her long wavy hair and laughed. Her daughter was much like herself: embarrassed at the price she paid for her clothes. Of course it would have been in a sale, but it was a Mary Quant after all. 'What are you gonna tell Steve? About last night?' she said light-heartedly, hoping Kay would pick up on her tone and treat it with a bit of humour. 'I don't want your dad or me to put our foot in it should Steve phone and—'

'I'll tell him what I told you. We got talking, it was late, so I slept on Zacchi's put-u-up!'

'OK, OK. Keep your hair on.'

Kissing her mother on the cheek, Kay relaxed. 'You don't have to worry about me and Steve.' She picked up her handbag and went into the front room to say goodbye to Jac and her dad.

'Why can't you stop another night?' Jac said as he climbed back into his bedding on the sofa.

'Because I've got a wonderful hubby to go home to.' She looked sideways at her dad. 'And I miss him.' She gave her brother a big hug and kissed his warm cheeks. 'Be a good boy and don't go wandering off again.'

'You said you wouldn't talk about that any more!' Jac snapped.

'Sorry. I forgot.' She winked at him. 'See you in a few days.'

Feeling Jack's hand on her shoulder, Kay turned around and gave him a warm hug. 'Stop worrying about me, Dad,' she said quietly. 'There's no need. I'm a big girl now.'

Jack patted her back as if she were still a baby, a habit he would probably never grow out of. 'We'll talk about you-know-who as soon as we get a chance, eh? I don't know how much you know, that's the trouble. And I'd rather your mum didn't—'

'Don't worry. I don't want her to know either. Not yet. Phone me when she's out, OK?'

'All right babe. And you don't think I should have a word with Steve?'

Kay stopped short and looked into his face. 'About what?'

'Leaving you on your own all the time.'

'No, Dad. It's not his fault. They're really busy and there's no one else that can do his job.' She lifted her hair off her shoulders. 'He's very good at what he does, you know,' she smiled proudly.

'I'm sure he is. But I don't like to think of you in that flat—'

'He phones me on the hour when he's working late to make sure I'm OK.' Kay wondered how long she would have to go on making excuses and telling white lies to cover up for her workaholic husband. 'Another few months and we'll be able to spend our evenings together.'

Jac's small voice drifted across the room. 'Will you be getting babies now that you sleep in a bed with Steve?'

'Um ... not necessarily ... I'll tell you what, Jac.' Kay was stuck for words. 'Why not let Dad explain the birds and the bees to you?' She turned to Jack and grinned. 'Tell it like a story, Dad.'

On her way towards the Underground station, passing by Bethnal Green park, Kay was reminded of the summer of '62. She and Zacchi had sat on the low wall by the paddling pond and she had risked losing him over a confession about a springtime holiday romance in Spain.

171

She remembered their blissful reunion, and felt like turning back the clock, just for a brief spell, so she could relive the experience of those sunny days when they had been so carefree. She wondered how she would have got through the nightmare when her best friend Terry committed suicide, if she hadn't had Zacchi to lean on.

Slipping further back into the past, she pictured them together in Kent, hop-picking. They had wanted to spend every minute of those times together. She couldn't help smiling as her dad's angry face came to mind. He was as much against Zacchi then as he was today. The time in between had been OK, when Zacchi had turned up out of the blue and they had been together for eighteen months or so. He and Jack had got on really well.

As she passed a telephone kiosk, Kay suddenly remembered that she had promised faithfully to phone Zacchi. Not that she had anything to report. She had spent the whole day trying to wheedle something out of Jac, to no avail. She had tried coaxing him, getting cross, demanding the truth, everything she could think of, but her small brother would just purse his lips and shrug, saying he'd never been in Jubilee Street by himself.

Leaning on the park railings, waiting for the phone box to come free, Kay scanned her surroundings. It was rush hour, and Cambridge Heath Road was choked with traffic. She was thankful that she didn't have to be part of that scene any more. She'd had her fill of relying on buses when she worked for Thompson's. She counted five of them, one behind the other, like a red train, crawling along in the congestion.

But London Transport apart, she still loved the buzz of the East End. Probably because it was her home ground and she knew every little patch. She looked across the main road at a new building which seemed to have sprung up overnight. It had been built on the piece of wasteland where she used to spend hours as a kid, collecting different caterpillars which she carried home in a jam jar.

'All yours, love!' The red-faced man held open the door of the phone booth and beamed at her. 'It's a boy!'

He clenched a fist and punched the air as he walked away. 'I've got a son!' he yelled to the commuters as they streamed out of the Underground station. 'At last! A son!'

'Hello, Zac, it's me.' Kay did her best to sound casual when her heart was pounding. She had no idea why it should be.

'Me? Now let's see. Is it ... Karen, or Mandy, or Sandy, or Jane ... ?'

'It's Kay, as you well know. Did you find out anything yet?'

'Don't assume you're the only woman in my life, and no, I've not had a minute. But I will, don't worry. Where are you?'

'At Bethnal Green Underground. I'm on my way home.'

'Husband home early tonight, then?'

'No. Well, you know ... around nine, maybe half past. Why?'

'It's only six o'clock. We could go for a drink. You can tell me how you got on with Jac.'

'No ... we'd best not.' Her dad's face came into her

mind. 'We have to take it slowly, Zac,' she said, not knowing how to end the conversation. 'Listen – I'm gonna have to go. I'll phone you next week, shall I?'

'What do you mean, next week? Monday, Tuesday, Wednesday—'

'I don't know.'

'I'm not making it easy, am I?'

'No. You're not.'

'Good.' A click and the dialling tone followed. Zacchi was gone and the distance between them suddenly seemed like a thousand miles.

Replacing the receiver, Kay made up her mind there and then that she mustn't keep phoning him. She loved Steve, and didn't want to risk the chance of losing him.

As she sat on the train, homeward-bound, she was filled with guilt. What would Steve do if he ever found out? How would he feel? How would she feel if it had been him making love to another woman? She knew – she would hate it.

# Chapter Six

'Come on, Jac, cheer up.' Laura straightened his tie and brushed some fluff off his shoulder. 'You look really smart. Kay'll be proud of you.'

Jac hung his head. 'I've changed my mind. I don't want to go,' he grumbled.

Pulling him on to her lap, Laura squeezed him tight. 'You wait till you see that shop. Not that I've ever been there, but I've heard about it. Shopping in Hamley's — whatever next, eh?'

'I still don't want to go.' Jac's voice sounded quiet and dull compared to the way he used to be. Laura kissed the top of his head and tried not to think about it. Not right then. Not until he had gone with Kay to the West End.

She was eager to see him go out for more reasons than one. He needed the fresh air and a change, and Laura was desperate to thrash out with Jack what it might be that was wrong with their son. Every time she tried to broach the subject, Jack had stopped her, saying that Jac might hear. He was right of course. Ever since Monday, when he had gone missing, Jac hadn't moved from Laura's side when they were together. Liz and Billy had said the same thing when Laura picked him up after work on Friday. It seemed as if he had to be close to one of them, as if he wanted to be in their shadows.

'Kay's gonna take you to a restaurant as well, you know.' Laura couldn't believe that she had to coax her son to speak. It had always been the other way round. Now it would be like a gift from God if he would only start talking again. She would never tell him to shut up again, the way she had before.

'I'll only eat chips.' Jac kept his head lowered, making it difficult to hear what he was saying.

'I'm sorry, love, I must be going a bit deaf. What was that?'

'Nothing,' he murmured, and clamped his lips together.

Laura could have kicked herself. If she hadn't been preoccupied with wishing that Jac would speak, she might just have picked up what he had actually said.

'Blimey, you look the part all right!' Jack stood in the doorway, beaming proudly at his boy. 'You'll 'ave all them little rich girls hanging round you, dressed like that.'

Laura closed her eyes and quietly cursed him. Jack could be so tactless. She sighed and looked at Jac, expecting him to rip the red tie from his neck. Instead of which she thought she saw a hint of a smile. Maybe Jack was right to treat the boy's mood lightly. Maybe she had been getting steamed up over nothing.

Checking his watch, Jack shook his head. 'Kay's late. Said she would be 'ere by eleven. Half the day's gone now.'

'Speak of the devil,' Laura said as she saw Kay fly past the kitchen window to the front door. 'You watch, she'll be like a bloody whirlwind!' She kissed Jac on the cheek. 'Have a lovely time.'

'Here's ten bob. Spend it all at once.' He pushed the note in Jac's top pocket and ruffled his hair.

'I don't want it.' He pulled the ten-shilling note from his pocket and dropped it on the kitchen table.

'That's all right,' Jack said. 'We'll save it for next time. Once you've seen the things you can buy in that shop, you'll soon change your mind.'

'Come on then!' Kay shouted through the letter-box. 'Half the day'll be gone by the time you open this door!'

Once Jac was safely out of the way, Laura insisted that Jack sit down and talk about their problem. He had tried to brush it off but she was determined. If nothing else, at least she would have the chance to talk about her worries.

'It's driving me mad. I can't think straight when I'm at work, I'm all over him when I'm here.' She covered her face with her hands. 'I keep thinking back. Did I do something that day to upset him? Had I promised something and then forgot?' She looked into Jack's grave face. 'He's not right. Something is very, very wrong with our boy.'

'I know, I know.' Jack bit his bottom lip. 'I suppose I'm gonna 'ave to tell yer.'

'Tell me what?'

'I kept pushing it out of my mind. Not wanting to believe it. It didn't seem possible that there would be a connection. Something like that going on without us knowing...'

Leaning back in the armchair, he gazed up at the ceiling. 'I might still be wrong. I'm just surmising, that's all.'

Laura swallowed hard and braced herself. 'Go on then, spit it out.'

'You haven't read this week's *Advertiser*, 'ave you?'

'Should I have done?'

'Nope. Neither should I. But there you are, I did.' He leaned forward and clasped his hands. 'The Jubilee Street murder—'

'It wasn't a murder for Christ's sake!'

'I *know*! Just listen, will yer?'

Laura drew back as far into her armchair as she could. She pulled up her knees and hugged them, her eyes fixed on Jack's face.

'It made the papers not because she fell down the stairs but because she had conned five or six people out of their money. Rent money. Anyway, that's not the point. The woman's in a coma. She might not pull through. If she does live she'll likely be brain-damaged; stuck in a wheelchair.'

He looked up at the ceiling and stuck his chin out. 'Who the 'ell knows?' He clenched his fists and shut his eyes tightly.

'That phone call I 'ad on Tuesday wasn't about the docks, Laura. There wasn't a meeting. It was Patsy's mother. It was Patsy who fell down the stairs. It's Patsy who's in a coma. She's in the London. Hanging on for dear life.'

Laura stared blankly at him. His face was hidden now, behind his hands. She couldn't see if he was crying but had a feeling he might be. Crying for Patsy. Patsy, who had been living spitting distance away. Patsy whom he had made pregnant. Patsy whom he had loved. Patsy whom Laura thought he was over.

'How long?' was all she had the heart to say.

He looked up at her. There were no tears. 'Since the accident. Since Monday.' He thought she was referring to the hospital.

'How long, Jack?'

'I just told yer!'

'Jack, *how long*?'

'What the fuck's wrong with you Laura? I told yer. Since Monday!'

'How long—' she began again but he cut her off.

'Does it matter?' he yelled. 'What's the difference?'

She avoided his glaring eyes. 'One year? Two?'

Jack shook his head. She had lost him this time. 'I'm sorry, Laura mate, but,' he shrugged, 'I don't know what you're on about.'

'How long has that cow been living in Stepney?' She stamped her foot. 'And don't lie to me!'

Jack seized the meaning of it. 'Jesus!' He felt like laughing. 'You surely don't mean to tell me that you think I've been seeing her?'

Trembling inside, Laura managed to control her voice. The last thing she wanted was for him to think she cared. 'You can't afford to play games this time, Jack. Our marriage is on the line,' she warned.

Jack fell back in his armchair and rubbed his eyes. 'Sit down for Christ's sake,' he murmured, too tired to react to her accusations. 'Sit down and listen to me. It concerns our Jac. And he's *all* I'm concerned about right now.' He raised his eyes to meet hers. 'OK?'

179

'One question before I sit down.' She pulled her shoulders back and raised her chin. 'How long have you known that she's been living on our doorstep?'

'Since her mother phoned. On Tuesday morning.' He looked straight into her eyes. 'Now sit down and let's try to work out what the 'ell Patsy's been up to.'

Instantly ashamed of her suspicious mind, Laura did as she was asked. 'I'm sorry.'

'That's all right. I can see what it must 'ave looked like. But I did think you would be able to trust me by now.'

'I do. It came as a bit of a shock, that's all.'

'Yeah, well, I don't think the shocking part of this is over yet.'

Laura lit a cigarette and leaned back. 'Go on then. I'm all ears.'

Leaning forward, Jack placed his hand on Laura's. 'She's been living in a flat in Jubilee Street. And according to the papers she was about to do a midnight when the accident 'appened. Her suitcases were packed. I don't know how long she'd been living there, it didn't say. But it did say that she'd conned six couples out of six months' rent in advance for a flat they had all been promised. If she hadn't fell down the stairs, she would be away now, and laughing.'

'That sounds like her. But I don't see why you're concerned about Jac. Where does he come into it?'

'I'm only guessing at this, Laura, so don't go berserk till we've talked it through, will yer? It's not that easy for me to 'andle.'

'Bloody hell! I think I know what you're gonna say.' Now it was her turn to cover her face. 'The same thought

180

flashed through my mind when all the rumours were flying.'

'Apart from Patsy's suitcases, there were some ... some kids' clothes there. New clothes. An outfit. That would fit a boy of about six or seven.'

'And Monday was the day that Jac supposedly went out to 'is friend's house and came back looking as if he'd seen a ghost...'

'Exactly.' Jack sighed quietly, relieved that she was with him on this one.

'You think he was there, in that house, when she fell?'

Jack shrugged. 'I don't know what to think.'

'She must have lured him there – but how? When would she 'ave made contact? And where?'

He rubbed his chin thoughtfully. 'If we're guessing right, you know what this means, don't yer?'

Laura turned her head away and pressed her hand against her mouth, desperate to stop herself crying. 'He knows,' she said, wiping away her tears, 'he knows.'

'Not necessarily. She might not have got round to it.'

'Why else would he go there, Jack? Maybe he's known for ages!'

'Don't treat it like it's a foregone conclusion!'

'Why not? That's what it is! It's obvious. Big letters spelling it out! And we should have picked up on it before now! He knows I'm not his mum!' She twisted her body and buried her head in the armchair cushions. She wanted to hide from the world and its curses. Her little Jac had found out from someone else! From Patsy of all people. What must he have been through? She pounded the arm of the chair with her fist until she felt Jack's strong arms lift her up.

He settled himself on the settee and held her tight, as she curled up like a baby. 'I knew she was a bitch, but to do something like this...'

'It's my fault. I should have told Jac before now.'

'Don't be silly. You can't live your life doing things just in case a one in a million chance comes up.' He pulled his clean handkerchief from his pocket and dried her eyes.

They lay there for a while in silence, the sun streaming through the net curtains, the sound of children playing in the street below drifting in through the open window. 'We're gonna 'ave to face it. He might have been there when she fell. The poor little sod must 'ave been shocked out of 'is life.'

'I can't believe our Jac would have gone off with her. He wouldn't leave without...' She covered her face to hide the hurt.

'It's all right.' He stroked her long chestnut hair. 'It's all right.' Jack said this knowing full well that it wasn't all right. Far from it. It had crossed his mind that if Jac hadn't wanted to go away with Patsy, which was more likely than not, he would have fought against it.

Patsy was a cute woman, always had been – she might easily have got him to that flat under false pretences. Nothing would surprise him. After all, she had pulled a fast one on him years ago, when she had removed the packet of three from his pocket, letting him believe he'd forgotten to buy any that week. And knowing full well it was exactly the right time of the month for her to conceive. He should have known then that something was up, the way she had practically poured the Scotch down him.

And if Jac had struggled with Patsy, it was possible that, in his defence, he pushed her down the stairs.

'Perhaps he just thought they were going to go on a little holiday. He's only a kid. It would 'ave seemed like an adventure. She probably told him he could phone as soon as he got to wherever they were going. Leicester, no doubt.'

'Yeah. That's probably it.' Jack withheld the other bit of information he had read, about the tickets to Scotland. Laura had enough to cope with.

'Maybe she'd already fallen before he got there. He could have looked through the letter-box, seen her on the floor, panicked and run away.'

'Yeah, that sounds more like it.'

'And I'm sure that if she had told him previously that, you know, who she really was, we would 'ave picked something up. No one could keep something like that to themselves – especially not a six-year-old – and especially not our Jac.' A faint smile flicked across her face. 'He would have been firing questions at me one after the other. Like bullets from a machine gun.'

Jack chuckled quietly. 'You're not kidding.'

'I suppose we let our imaginations go off at a tangent?'

'Yep. Easy done.' He tried to sound convincing.

'So we can stop worrying then?'

'I reckon so.'

'Try to forget about it. And not say anything to Jac.'

'Definitely not. No point.'

'He'll probably be a different kid when he gets back. After a day out with our Kay.'

'Back to his old self.'

Laura snuggled into Jack's chest. 'Yeah. Driving us mad again with his questions.' Laura yawned and closed her eyes. 'Why do I feel tired at this time of the day?'

'It's your first Saturday off in ages. Your brain's telling you to make the most of it. You needn't 'ave got up at the crack of dawn, you know.'

'Habit,' she murmured and pulled her knees up under her, settling in for a catnap.

Staring up at the ceiling, Jack tried once again to fathom what might have happened that day. He kept as still as he could. Laura was drifting off. His next problem was deciding whether or not to tell her that Patsy's parents' wanted to see Jac. Tell him who they were.

'Ja-ack...?' Laura's voice was soft and husky.

'Mmmm?'

'Patsy's in a bad way then?'

'Looks like it, yeah.' Jack didn't want to think about that.

'I'm sorry. It can't be easy for you.'

'No. None of it is. Talk about the sins of the father.'

While Billy was making the most of the sunny weather outside in the small garden, forking over the dark soil, Liz busied herself in the kitchen. Standing in front of the yellow-and-green-painted kitchen cabinet, she stared forlornly at the way he had stacked the plates. All sizes, one on top of the other, precariously placed on the wrong shelf.

It was quite different from when she had first moved

in. His crockery had been arranged in neat piles, in strict order. Keeping one eye on the window which looked out on to the back garden, she lifted the piles of plates and set them down on the small scrubbed pine table. Billy was a lovely old boy and she thought the world of him, but he would interfere whenever she tried to organize anything in his cottage. She could only hope he would be so absorbed with his gardening that he wouldn't keep popping in and out.

Sorting the blue-edged plates into separate piles, she wondered why one or two were missing. It had been a full set and she couldn't remember Billy mentioning that he had broken any. Using her thumb to wipe away a small mark from one of them, Liz's thoughts were filled with the memory of Laura's mother, Beatrice. A dark-haired, nicely rounded woman, who had been set in her Victorian-style ways. A churchgoer who, as far as Liz could remember, would never miss a Sunday service.

Beatrice had always believed that her daughter Laura had married beneath herself and, try as she might, she had never really taken to Liz's family. Drinking in a pub was not her scene. But underneath it all Liz had always thought she had a heart of gold. Moving to the East End, having been brought up in a strict Christian family in Dagenham, must have been a bit of a shock.

'Ah well . . .' Liz murmured to herself, 'at least she was lucky enough to get this cottage.' Many young families would have given their right arms for it at the time. Still would. It was a world apart from the hustle and bustle of Whitechapel. A haven with just a green gate in a brick wall to separate the tenants, who could at least imagine they lived in the country.

The small front gardens of the terraced cottages were a picture in the summer. Full of pink and blue hydrangea bushes, flaming orange, red, and white roses, trailing blue lobelia, marigolds and an abundance of dahlias and chrysanthemums. Liz thanked her lucky stars to have had the opportunity of moving in with Billy when Bert had died four years previously.

'I 'ad a lovely cock once,' Billy said thoughtfully, as he stood in the kitchen doorway. 'That chicken-run is still in bloody good nick, you know, Liz.' He rubbed his bristly chin. 'I'm thinking about having some poultry again. What d'yer reckon?'

Liz hadn't quite got over the statement about his cock. The first vision he conjured up was better than the one he was replacing it with. Her body started to shake as laughter escaped. 'You say some things at times, Billy.'

'What's funny about keeping chickens? I always used to.'

'Oh yeah? Why did yer get rid of 'em then?' She was still chuckling.

'Laura's mother got fed up with the smell of potato peel boiling on the stove. Plus the cock I 'ad then was too bloody sure of itself. Noisy? It used to crow in the middle of the night and start off all the others in the alley.'

Keeping her back to the plates on the table in an attempt to hide what she had been up to, sorting out his cupboard, she realized that he was too preoccupied with his latest madcap idea to notice. Edging round the table as he passed to get himself a glass of water from the kitchen tap, she knocked over an empty blue and white milk jug. Quick to stand it up again, she looked into Billy's face and waited. He was poised to say something.

'We all kept fowl in them days. Rabbits an' all.' He drank his water in one go. 'You like rabbit stew, don't yer? We could 'ave some bunnies out there as well. Wouldn't take five minutes to knock up a rabbit 'utch.'

Filling a kettle, Liz wondered how to handle Billy. It was 1966 after all, not postwar. People didn't keep chickens in their backyards any more. The neighbours would go mad. But then, on the other hand, it would give Billy something to do. A hobby that would keep him from under her feet. Torn between the devil and the deep blue sea, she decided to leave it, not offer any advice. Knowing him, he would forget about it within no time and be dreaming about something else.

'I could sell the eggs we don't eat. Young Martin would take some off my 'ands.'

'Who?' She had never heard him mention that name before.

'Young Martin. Old Martin's son. He's got a stall down the Waste. Sells light-bulbs, batteries ... old wirelesses, any old toot he can get 'is hands on.'

'What makes you think he'd sell eggs then?' Liz wondered which of the two of them was in a more confused state.

'Who?'

'Young Martin.'

'What, the one who sells electrical bits?'

'That's the one.' Liz stopped herself from laughing – it wasn't easy. He looked so comical standing there with his shirt tucked into his long johns, which were showing above his old baggy trousers.

'No...' Billy said emphatically. 'He don't sell eggs. His old man would though. Took a few trays off me in the past. Got a fruit and veg stall down the Waste.'

'Fancy a cup of tea, Billy?' Liz said, trying to bring a degree of normality into the conversation.

'Yes please, dear. I'll have it outside though. I've got a lot to arrange in the yard.' He walked out of the kitchen with a lighter spring in his footsteps, feeling ten years younger.

'I don't think I'll bother with rabbits. Chickens'll do me.' He hovered in the doorway. 'You'll come down the Lane with me in the morning, won't yer? Down the animal market. Cheap Charlie's bound to have a nice cock.'

'I promised Milly I would pop round for half an hour,' she said, amused by his bizarre train of thought.

'I should think a dozen chicks'll be enough.'

Sensing that he wasn't going to forget this idea, Liz realized it was time for her to try and make him see sense. 'But you know 'ow noisy a cockerel is, Billy. The neighbours would start to complain and that would be a shame. You've always got on so well.'

Billy threw his shoulders back and roared with laughter. 'You can't keep chickens without a cock, they wouldn't be 'appy! They wouldn't lay as well!' He pulled his sparkling white handkerchief from his pocket and wiped away a lone tear. 'Things you say. Chickens ain't no different from women, you know. They like a bit of the other as well.'

Now they were both laughing. 'You'll be the death of me, Billy, I swear it.' She poured boiling water into the teapot.

'What d'yer reckon about that outside lav? Shall I pull it down, or what?'

'The outside lav?' She could hardly keep up with him.

'Yeah. Make a bit of space for the ducks.'

'The what?'

'You like a bit of roast duck, don't yer?'

Inhaling slowly, she raised her eyes to meet his. 'Don't knock down the lavatory.'

'Why's that?'

'Well...' she had to think fast. The last thing she wanted was for him to start using the sledgehammer. 'You never know when you might get taken short out there. And anyway,' she put on her mock-posh voice, 'I'm accustomed to having two toilets. And I must live in the style—'

'I'm just imagining our Jac's face when he sees them chicks.' Billy looked really pleased with himself. 'He'll love feeding 'em ... collecting the eggs once they're bigger.'

'Yeah.' Liz felt exhausted and he had only been in the room for five minutes. 'Go on then. I'll fetch the tea once it's stood.'

'So I'll keep the outside lav then?'

'Good idea, Billy. You do that.' She hoped that would end it.

'But no ducks. There wouldn't be the space.'

'Oh all right. I'll get over it,' Liz said, letting him think it was his idea not to have them.

'You can't 'ave everything, Lizzie!' he called over his shoulder, on his way out into the backyard.

'No.' Lizzie grinned to herself. 'You're dead right there, Billy-boy.' She instantly thought about her nephew, Jac. If he could be brought back to his old cheerful self again, that *would* be everything.

She watched Billy through the window again. He was pulling at some chicken-wire, checking it for rust. 'You just might be wiser than we all think,' she murmured. If little chicks didn't put a smile on Jac's face, she couldn't think what else might. It would be good for him to have something to do when she and Billy looked after him. And it would be good for Billy as well. Two birds killed with one stone. And all from the mind of someone whom she had been so worried about? Billy knew exactly what he was doing, even if he did get a bit muddled at times.

She relaxed in her favourite kitchen chair and sipped her tea. It had to brew a bit longer to come up to Billy's liking. If he couldn't stand his spoon up in it, then there was no point in drinking it. Besides, she needed a couple of minutes to allow her brain to slow down again. She felt as if a whirlwind had just swept through it.

It was just after four when Kay and Jac returned from their trip to the West End. There had been a minor success. The assistant in Hamley's had managed, in the end, to persuade Jac to allow his sister to buy him the small drum set they knew he wanted.

'Couldn't you have got him something else, Kay? Anything else? I mean, Jac and a drum set? Once he's back to his old self he'll drive me insane,' Laura said, hoping to raise a smile on the six-year-old's face.

'I said I didn't want it.' Jac walked slowly out of the kitchen to his bedroom at the end of the passage and slammed the door shut behind him.

'He's been like that all day.'

'No one can say you didn't try, love. I don't know what else we can do to—'

The sound of the telephone ringing stopped Laura mid-sentence while Kay answered it. It was Steve.

'Oh, that's good.' Kay sounded sincere. 'I've bought some fillet steak—'

She narrowed her eyes and looked angry. 'Say that again?'

'Nine o'clock? You said *early*, Steve. Nine o'clock on a Saturday night is hardly early to get home from work!'

Laura leaned her head back and sighed. She wished she could turn the clock back a few months, to the time before Kay was married and everything was calm. A bit on the boring side – but calm.

'I'd better get going.'

'Bear with 'im, Kay. He's doing his best. It can't be easy starting your own business, especially at his age. He's had no experience of that kind of responsibility.'

'I know. But sometimes...' She swallowed hard and pressed her lips together. 'Tomorrow's Sunday, right? A day when we could be together. But you know where Steve's going? To play golf with a client.'

'Well, that's probably what he has to do. Don't knock it. Look at the way he's free with his money. You've got all you can spend.'

'I *know*. I was just saying—'

Jac suddenly appeared in the doorway. 'Can I come 'ome with yer?'

Kay looked from Jac to Laura – torn between saying no to the sorry-looking face or taking the risk of making Steve angry.

191

'Please?'

''Course you can.' She tousled his hair. 'Go and pack your pyjamas and a clean sloppy joe.'

# Chapter Seven

Once Jac had eaten his favourite meal of egg and chips and had a bubble bath, he was more than happy to snuggle down under his bedding on the sofa and watch television while Kay busied herself. She wanted to make a special effort in case Steve was put out over Jac being there. After all, her tone when he delivered the news that he would be spending Sunday with his golfing friends had been frosty to say the least. He might think she was trying to get back at him by spoiling their evening which they had meant to spend together.

After selecting a few flowers from the vase standing on the stripped pine Welsh dresser, and creating a decoration for the centre of their small round dining-table, Kay stood back and admired her delicate work of art.

'What d'yer reckon, Jac – red napkins or white?'

'Napkins? Steve's not bringing a baby home, is he?'

Laughing at him she decided on red, which was more striking against the polished wood. Turning her attention to candles, she chose white which enhanced the hand-painted candlesticks.

Next was the wine. She uncorked a bottle of red

Beaujolais and stood it on the brass fender by the small tiled fireplace. Steve had taught her how much better the wine tasted if was just above room temperature. She carefully tonged a few more pieces of smokeless fuel on to the glowing embers, not wanting to build up the fire too much. She had lit it more for effect than warmth. At eight-thirty the setting sun was still shining through the French doors which opened on to their small balcony.

With the mixed salad ready in a beautiful handmade pottery bowl, the crispy French bread on a board and the prawn cocktails in the fridge, all that was left for Kay was to grill the fillet steak and sauté the potatoes when Steve came home. She had added the final touch by making an apple crumble – his favourite dessert.

There was still plenty of time for her to change out of her jeans and white cotton skinny-rib and put on a summer dress. Opening the doors of their mahogany wardrobe she wondered which suited her mood best.

As her hand brushed across her clothes, Kay picked up a faint waft of perfume. Not one she recognized. Not one that *she* had ever worn. Moving closer she realized that the scent was coming from one of Steve's suits.

With her head practically in the cupboard, she sniffed at each jacket until she found the one. The collar smelled distinctly, and Kay wondered why she hadn't noticed it before. She took out the suit and hung it on the open door. Her instincts dictated that she put it back, not to check any further, but her heart was saying something else.

Slipping her hand into each pocket she found nothing other than a fresh handkerchief and a crumpled receipt. Feeling ashamed at behaving like a spy, she pushed them both back into the deep side pocket. Her inner voice spoke again. *Take out the receipt, you silly cow, and check it*.

Smoothing out the small piece of white paper she could only just make out the faint print. *Single red rose, 1*. Peering at the date, she was shocked to see *14 February 1966*. Valentine's Day. Five months ago. Her mind flashed back to that time. She and Steve had been making plans for the white wedding that he eventually said he didn't want.

In a daze, Kay sat on the edge of their bed and stared at nothing. A single rose on Valentine's Day? How thrilled she would have been to receive one. Steve had given her a card. She remembered it. Remembered the verse. Knew it off by heart. *If I could I surely would give all the world to you*.

She looked at the date again, hoping it might be a very old receipt, but not so. Replacing it and hanging Steve's suit back in the wardrobe, devastated at the implications, Kay pulled out her peacock-blue minidress, not bothering to choose or select as she had originally planned.

'Steve comes 'ome late, don't he?' Jac said sleepily. 'I might not be able to stay awake.'

'That's all right. You doze off. I'll nudge you when he gets in,' Kay said, hoping he would fall into a deep sleep and not wake up until the morning. If Steve did react to him being there at least Jac wouldn't hear or see the other side of him. The side she had come to know since they had been married. It had crossed her mind more than once that it might have been a good idea if they had lived together for a short time before they had made the pledge. Kay thought she knew Steve inside out, but not so. She found his silent moods difficult to cope with. He seemed to withdraw into his own private world. Especially once he had bought the new stereo. She sometimes wondered if he deliberately listened to his music – to shut her out.

Maybe he regretted marrying her; had met so many other interesting, attractive career women that she now appeared dull in comparison. Or maybe there was a connection with the perfume and the rose. Had he fallen in love with someone else so soon after their marriage?

By ten minutes to nine, Jac was fast asleep and Kay was ready and waiting. There really was nothing else to do but sit tight, while Aretha Franklin's love songs quietly filled the room. Opening the cupboard next to the fireplace where they kept the drinks, Kay took out a bottle of medium-dry sherry and poured herself a large drink.

At nine forty-five the key turned in the lock.

'That looks nice,' Steve said, admiring the dinner table. 'Sorry I'm a bit late.' It was a tired token phrase. Glancing down at the sofa he sighed. 'What's Jac doing here?'

'He asked to come back with me. I don't know why but he's been a bit clingy. I expect it's because of his trauma...' Kay gazed up at him, wondering if the suit he was wearing also smelled of someone else's perfume.

'I'll put the steak under the grill,' she murmured and went into the kitchen.

'Bloody clients! They think they own my time!' Steve went into the bedroom to change into his casuals.

Leaning against the white kitchen units, Kay managed to control her breathing. Why was she so scared? Why did she suddenly feel as if *she* was in the wrong? One question was all it would take. One question. *Who was the red rose for?* But she was too frightened to ask. Why? Steve was the quiet, placid type. So why was she scared of him?

'Don't give me too much, will you?' He kissed her lightly on the cheek. 'I had a late lunch.'

Smelling drink on his breath she turned her face away. 'Do you mean you're not hungry?'

'Not madly, but I'll manage. That steak smells good already.' He removed the Aretha Franklin LP and replaced it with the Rolling Stones.

Keeping her thoughts to herself at his changing the record, which he often did, she stood in the kitchen doorway and sipped her drink. 'There was a strange smell in our wardrobe. It was coming from one of your suits.'

'Oh, yeah?' He narrowed his eyes and flopped down into an armchair. 'What, a musky, dusty smell from the old wood, you mean?'

'No. It wasn't from the wardrobe. It was perfume. Someone else's, not mine.'

He stood up and poured himself a whisky. 'So?'

'Whose is it?'

'You're asking me? Kay – do you realize how many

female clients I see in a day? And they don't skimp on the old smellies. It's usually expensive and heavy.'

'What about the red rose you sent on Valentine's Day?'

'What red rose?'

'I know you sent one, Steve, so don't lie to me. Just tell me who it was for and why you sent it.' The flames from the grill were causing the steak to smoke at the edges. Kay turned both pieces over without a hint of enthusiasm.

Steve lowered his tone in case he woke Jac. 'Not that it's really any of your concern, but it was for Dotty, the cleaner. She'd been pouring her heart out. Her husband ran off with another woman and her daughter, her single daughter, is pregnant. She felt like shit. So I picked up the phone and called a florist. I thought it would cheer her up.'

'And the perfume which just so happened to be on the collar of the suit where I found the receipt . . . I suppose you've got another lie lined up ready?'

'Keep your voice down, for Christ's sake.' He sat down again wearily, sipped at his drink and began to read the newspaper. The silent act, then? This was all she was going to get.

She served the steak on to the plates. 'I didn't bother with sauté potatoes after all. Since you're not hungry.' She sat down at the table and waited for him to join her.

'Any salad dressing?' he said, unfolding his napkin.

'No. I forgot to make some.' She was about to stand up when he told her not to bother.

'I don't believe you about the rose.' She tried to make light of it. 'I think you've got a secret lover.'

He reached out, pulled his *Evening Standard* from the arm of his chair and placed it next to him so that he could read while he picked at the salad.

'Have you?'

He flicked a page over and ignored her, but the flush of colour rising in his cheeks gave him away.

'What's her name?' Kay was beginning to feel better now that she was getting it off her chest. 'Is she one of your *clients*?'

Steve pretended to be absorbed in his reading.

'How long have you been having an affair? Ever since I've known you? *If* I know you.'

He looked into her face. 'Can I at least eat in peace? I've had a long day.'

'Who is she?'

Back to the newspaper. 'A long, tiring day. How was your shopping spree? Little Jac get what he wanted? Toys, toys and more toys?'

'Just tell me and then I'll shut up.' Kay couldn't believe that the pain she felt earlier had almost gone. The pain in her heart that pills couldn't ease. Maybe some unseen force was at work, making her feel as if a dark heavy cloud was drifting away.

'Is he over his play-acting yet?'

'Play-acting? Mmmm ... Maybe he *would* make an actor. You should give him some lessons. You'd have to brush up on your art of lying first—'

The sudden crash as Steve brought his fist down on to the table stopped her. His face was full of anger. 'Have you quite finished?'

'*No!*' She glanced at Jac who was still sound asleep. 'I'm not.' Moving quickly from the table she knocked over her chair. 'I wasn't born yesterday. You're *lying*.'

'And you're so innocent? We're not married five minutes and you spend the night with Zacchi!'

'That was different! He's a friend!'

'Well, so is Cathy!' He threw his napkin on to the table and stormed into the bedroom.

Kay sat down again, her mind spinning. Cathy? Cathy? Cathy who? He had never mentioned that name before. She would have remembered. She knew the names of most of the women he mixed with at work. Now *and* before he left Slater & Jones. A Cathy had never been mentioned.

She turned off the record-player and flopped into an armchair, hardly able to believe what was happening. He had virtually admitted that there was someone else. Fighting back the tears, she went into the bedroom.

'Steve?' She stood over him as he sat on the edge of the bed, head in his hands. 'I'm sorry. I shouldn't have gone on and on ... All over a silly rose. Me and my jealousy.' She stroked his hair but he pushed her hand away.

'I shouldn't have married you,' he said.

'Don't be silly. It's not that serious. We just had one of many rows to come, that's all. It's normal. All married couples argue. Wouldn't be natural if they didn't.'

'I've known her for over a year. She's an artist.'

Kay sat beside him. 'Why haven't you mentioned her?'

'Oh, grow up, Kay. Why do you think?'

She inhaled slowly. 'You mean – you've been having

200

an affair for over a year? Is that it?'

'If that's what you want to call it.'

'I was gonna ask if you'd been shagging her for over a year but I thought that was a bit crude. Closer to the truth, but crude.' She could feel herself getting angry. Anger was taking over from shock. 'So why did you marry me then?'

'Cathy thought it was only right. She couldn't bear the thought of what it might do to you. And she's very shy. She wouldn't have been able to handle it if you went for her. And ... she felt sorry for you.'

'She *what*?'

He sighed and lowered his head. 'She didn't think I should let you down.'

'Let me down? We're talking a lifetime here, not a one-off date!'

'Anyway, she was married then.' He sniffed and looked into her face. 'And now she's not. Her divorce came through last week.'

'Oh. Right. That explains it then.' She remembered the book she had found under his bed before they were married.

'Explains what?'

'The book on shyness I found in your room. I was dumb enough to think you'd bought it for yourself.' She suddenly felt very stupid. Naïve. Throwing her shoulders back, she did her best to act as if she didn't care. As if her heart wasn't breaking. 'And you helped her to cope with her shyness, did you?'

'Yes. She seems to have overcome it – almost.' He looked into Kay's face. 'Anyway, you've got Zacchi. And don't lie. You've been sleeping with him. You reeked of his aftershave. Your hair, your clothes – all I could smell was that gypsy.'

'Yes I did. But only once. I'm not seeing him again. It's over.'

'I haven't touched Cathy since our wedding. I stopped all that for your sake. And what did I get in return?'

'That night wasn't planned, you know. I phoned him after I'd phoned you and, well ... the rest is history.' Kay glanced at him, hoping to read something from his face. 'How come I smelled perfume on your jacket then? It would have worn off by now – if you haven't seen her since our wedding.'

'I said I haven't *touched* her since then. Or to put it the way you might, I haven't screwed her since then. We've been out for a couple of meals...'

'When you were supposedly working late?'

'Yes.'

'While I sat here night after night feeling lonely?'

'Oh dear – what's this, the guilt trip?'

'Perhaps you never did love me.' The possibility seemed more real by the second. 'Not love as I see it. And those times when you said you were exhausted – I believed you. No sooner were you in bed than you were asleep. Was I really that boring? That unattractive? Were you missing her that much?'

Kay stared down at him and slowly shook her head as it all began to fit into place. 'You pushed me towards Zacchi. You did it on purpose, leaving me on my own for hours on end. You knew how close we were.' With tears flowing she turned away.

'He was bound to be the one I would phone that

night, after I spoke to you. Whether you meant to or not, you bloody well planned it!'

'I wish I was that clever.' He grinned sardonically at her.

'Oh, you are, Steve, you are. You can stop lying now. It's all water under the bridge.'

'What's that supposed to mean?' There was a hint of hope in his eyes that he hadn't quite managed to cover up.

'Exactly what you want it to. Our marriage is finished. There, I've been the one to say it. So you can still be the good guy. You can hide behind Zacchi. Blame him. That's what you want, isn't it?'

'I don't know what you're talking about.'

'I can't believe that I'm seeing you for the first time. You're such a liar. A lousy liar. Your face gives you away.' She leaned forward and pushed her tear-stained face up close to his, not caring that she would have black-ringed eyes from the smudged mascara. 'You can stop it now. You don't have to squirm or lie—'

The sudden flash of his hand against her cheek-bone knocked her sideways; the succession of face-slapping as he gripped her by the collar sent her sprawling across the room; and the fist which struck her jaw sent Kay spinning out of consciousness until she felt a sharp pain to her head as it hit the floor.

With half-open eyes, she could just make out the shape of Steve's body as he towered above her.

'Why did you do that?' Jac stood in the doorway. 'Why did you hit Kay?'

'I'm OK, Jac. Go back on the sofa. There's a good boy.

We argued – that's all.' A dreadful nausea swept through her body.

'Are you all right?' His small frightened voice seemed to come to her through a tunnel.

'Yes.' She flinched as Steve's hand reached out for her. 'Don't, Steve...' she murmured as her body began to shake.

Feeling him ease her up from the floor and carry her to the bed, her thoughts were on Jac and what he must be feeling.

She could hear Jac crying softly. 'Why can't she walk?'

'She'll be all right,' Steve snapped. 'Go back to bed.' He practically dropped Kay on to the bed. 'I'm going out for a drink.'

She couldn't believe her ears. 'You're not gonna leave me like this?'

'I'm not made of stone, Kay. This has upset me. I need to get out of here for half an hour. I'll pour you a glass of water before—'

'Steve, please ... not yet ... wait ten minutes ... please?'

He sat on the edge of the bed, still angry. 'You goaded me into that. I've never hit a woman in my life!'

Relaxing back into her pillow, Kay asked if Jac was still there. She wanted to comfort him instead of having to listen to the man she loved become more like a stranger every minute.

'A bruise will probably be out by the morning. Christ knows what your dad'll have to say about this.'

'Do you honestly think I would tell him?' Kay cupped her hand, tipped some water from the glass into
it and splashed it on to her throbbing face. 'He'd kill
you.'

'You won't have to tell him – Jac'll do that.'

'No he won't. I'll talk to him. And I'm not moving out
of this flat until my face is back to normal.' She hated
Steve for thinking only of himself. 'Don't worry, you
won't be found out.'

He hung his head and Kay thought she saw a look of
shame on his face, which filled her with remorse. 'I'm
sorry, Steve.'

'I'm the one who should be sorry.'

'Well, why don't you say it then?'

'I'll percolate some coffee.' He stood up. 'Do you want
a brandy?' He was full of self-pity.

'Please. And a wet flannel for my face.' She watched
him walk from the bedroom. He looked so miserable.
'Did you really knock me out?'

He kept his back to her. 'I hit you in the face.'

'It was my fault. I made you lose your temper.'

Still he wouldn't look at her. 'I'll get the brandy.'

Lying on the bed nursing her sore face, Kay suddenly saw the irony of it. Her husband had knocked her
out and all because of one red rose. One red rose. One
lover. One year of deceit. One broken marriage.

'The coffee shouldn't take long.' He handed her a
brandy and then swallowed most of his own. 'So what
now?' he said.

'I don't know. It's not really up to mé, is it? I'm not
the one torn between two women. You are.' She sipped
her drink. 'I still love you. I don't want us to split up.'

'Oh, please! Don't do this.'

'Do what?' She lay back and covered her face with the flannel. 'I only said—'

'How do you think it makes me feel? I've just given you a hiding and you plead with me not to leave you. Don't use those tactics, Kay. It's cheap.'

Pleased that the damp cloth was covering her face, Kay allowed herself the privilege of tears. The cold truth was hitting home and it hurt more than the swelling on the side of her face. Steve had already made up his mind to leave her. He had been making plans with this other woman. Maybe even that night, before he came home.

'Are you saying you want us to get divorced?' She surprised herself at the way she delivered the line. Cool as a cucumber, with tears soaking into the flannel.

'A separation more like. Don't be dramatic.'

'And then a divorce?'

'Not necessarily. We might want to get back together again.'

'You mean it might not work out for you. You want me as a safety net.'

'Christ, you can be a cold-hearted bitch at times.' He stood up. 'I'll get the coffee.'

As soon as he left the room, Kay was on her feet. Grabbing the end of the headboard, she waited for the sudden dizziness to pass. Then making her way slowly towards the wardrobe, she opened it, took out one suit after another and laid them on the bed.

'Now what?' Steve stood in the doorway.

'You can go tonight. I don't want you in my bed.' She

couldn't shake off the touch of fear, but something else was overcoming it. A kind of inner strength. She looked straight into his face. 'I mean it. If you don't go I'll throw this lot out of the window. If I had the strength I would pack your bags for you.'

'Fair enough. You've made your point.' He pulled his suitcase down from the top of the wardrobe and threw in his clothes.

Watching him from where she sat on the bed, Kay knew that giving him a way out like this was exactly what he wanted. Apart from hitting her, showing his weakness, he had achieved his goal.

'I'll come back for the rest of my things later in the week.'

They looked at each other with misery in their eyes. 'Are you sure this is what you want?' Kay said, trying to get a grip on herself.

'It was your idea...'

'You know what I mean!' she yelled. 'Is this what you *want*?'

He swallowed hard. 'Yes.'

Once he had gone, Kay buried her head in her pillow and cried, hardly recognizing herself. Her body heaved as she sobbed uncontrollably. Jac crawled in beside her and cuddled up close.

Pulling herself together for the sake of her little brother, she hugged him tight and told him not to be upset. All marriages went through bad patches. It was just a lovers' tiff.

She dried her face on the sheet, got up and made her way to the balcony to see if Steve's car was still parked outside. Maybe he had changed his mind and just gone for a drink at their local instead. Looking down, she felt her heart sink. Their parking space was empty.

Wandering around the flat, she was desperate to talk to someone, to tell them what had happened. She daren't phone Pamela, she would go mad and make her feel worse. And her parents were definitely out of the question. They would be round like a shot, and she needed time by herself.

She picked up the receiver and dialled Zacchi's number. There was no answer.

She poured herself another brandy and hoped it would make her sleep through the night.

'This is how Aunt Liz must have felt when Uncle Bert died,' she murmured as she curled up in bed next to the sleeping Jac. Thinking of her uncle made her cry again. If only she were at home with her mum and dad.

After just a few hours of sleep, Kay awoke in the middle of a nightmare. She was soaked with perspiration and her face was throbbing.

Dragging herself out of bed without disturbing Jac, she went into the bathroom and peered into the small mirror above the sink, shocked at what she saw. It was as if a stranger were staring back at her. Someone with the same long blonde hair but with a different face. A red face which was badly swollen on one side, making her right eyelid look like the seam in a fat cushion.

It hurt Kay to smile, but she couldn't help it. She looked like something out of a horror film.

Splashing water on to her face, she flinched with pain and cursed Steve for doing this to her. Not only would she have to suffer the aches and pains but she would be a prisoner too. How could she go out and let people see what her own husband had done to her? It was out of the question. She would have to make excuses and lock herself away from the outside world until her face was back to normal.

After a long soak in the bath, Kay began to feel better. *The devil you know is better than the devil you don't know*, she thought determinedly as she wrapped a soft bath towel around her, trying to reap some small comfort from her trauma. At least now she knew exactly where she stood.

Kay curled up on the sofa, snug in her towelling dressing-gown. She prepared herself to phone Zacchi, knowing she must choose her words carefully. The last thing she wanted was for him to storm enraged into Steve's agency and give him a thrashing.

Knowing that Zacchi was an early riser, she hoped to time it right, catching him between getting up and going to see his family at the gypsy site, something he regularly did on Sunday mornings. She dialled his number and thanked her lucky stars that she had him for a friend.

'Hello?' The chirpy voice of an elderly woman caught her off guard. Kay checked she had rung the right number.

'Yes, dear, that's right. I suppose you want the lad?'

'You mean Zacchi?' Kay smiled – he was hardly a lad.

'He's not here, dear. And I don't have a forwarding address. He's travelling the world!' Her high-pitched laughter rang through the earpiece. 'I'm his daily. Or should I say his weekly? I'm going right through the place – windows an' all. Making it nice for when the young couple move in. You're not Kay, are you?'

'Yes, I—'

'Oh right. I've got a message for yer. 'Ang on. It's 'ere somewhere.' There was the sound of rustling paper. 'Ah. Here it is. Are you there dear?'

'Yes I am. What does it say?'

'"If Kay rings, tell her I've gone away for six months."'

Kay waited for more. 'Is that it?'

'Yes, dear. Why? Should there be more?'

'Well ... it would be nice to know where he's gone ...'

'Abroad, dear. Travelling, you know ... stopping here, stopping there. Gonna write another book. What it must be to be clever, eh?'

'If he gets in touch with you, will you ask him to ring me?'

'Oh I shan't hear from him now, luv. No. He's gone. Back in six months, he said. He paid me up front to come in weekly. I thought that was very trusting. But I shall do a good job for 'im. I shan't cheat the lad.'

'Well if he does phone ... please give him the message.'

''Course I will. Good-looking boy, isn't he?' The woman laughed and replaced the receiver.

'Thanks, Zacchi. Thanks a lot. And thank you, Steve. Two in one, not bad.' Kay talked to herself while she rubbed furiously at the grill pan with a Brillo pad. 'Talk about love 'em and leave 'em!' She picked up a vegetable knife and pushed the pointed end into a stubborn burnt-on mark.

'I'm starving, Kay. What's for breakfast?' Jac rubbed an eye with one hand and scratched his bottom with the other.

Seeing him standing there half asleep in his crumpled winceyette pyjamas lit Kay up. 'What would I do without you, eh?'

'Who's gonna take me home today?' Jac had obviously heard most of the heated argument, the night before.

'Pam'll come an' get you in her new Mini,' Kay said, tipping cornflakes into a bowl. 'She was coming over in any case. I'm lending her some of my LPs,' Kay lied, hoping that Pamela would be able to take Jac home for her.

'You won't say anything, will you? About ... you know?'

''Course I won't. Steve didn't mean to bash you. He got wild, that's all. When's he coming back?'

'Later on today. When he's cooled off.'

'Right. Well, make sure Pam takes me before he gets back, eh?'

'If you want.' Kay inhaled slowly. Six years old and as sharp as an adult. Jac knew he was best out of the way. And he was making a good job of trying not to let on that he knew.

Dialling her best friend's number, Kay winced as the pain shot through her swollen eye. 'Pam, it's Kay. Listen, I want to keep this brief, OK?'

'Go on.' Pamela picked up the urgency in her voice.

'I've got Jac here and he needs to be taken home this morning. I don't want to go out. You'll see why when you arrive. Will you act as taxi driver for me?'

'You OK?'

'Coping. I have to. Steve and I had a fight. I came off worse.'

There was a pause. 'He hit you.'

'Afraid so.'

'Well, you know what they say. The quiet ones are the worst.'

'I'd rather we didn't go into it while Jac's here, Pam. He's been through enough already. Try to smile your way through it, yeah?'

'Come on, Kay. This isn't a stranger you're talking to, it's me. I'm just as good an actress as you. But one thing: once I've delivered him to your mum's, I'm gonna phone you for a full report, right?'

'I'd be very disappointed if you didn't. And Pam...'

'Go on.'

'Thanks.'

'That's not what you meant to say.'

Kay quietly laughed. 'No. I meant to say I love you – you're a wonderful friend. My best and closest friend.'

'I know – and I love you too, best friend. Don't forget we're blood sisters. I've still got the scar on my thumb to prove it.'

'See you soon then.' Kay swallowed hard and replaced the receiver.

Leaving Jac to enjoy his playtime in the bath while she waited for Pamela, Kay thought about all that Steve had said and the gravity of the situation. He was going to leave her for someone else and she must rethink her future. Or maybe try to talk to him. Surely there was still some love there? Maybe this other woman could be weathered and got over? She was someone he wanted because she was unavailable. He wanted what he couldn't have. But now that she was free...

Her mind flashed up one thought after another. What, for instance, would Steve do now about her monthly cheque – if he really had left her for good? Would he continue to put it into their account or was she to earn her own living again? And would she be able to go back to Waterman's Publishing and get her old job back on *Female Weekly*? She flopped into an armchair, knowing that in the publishing world once you were out it was not so easy to get back in again.

Fighting back her tears, Kay silently longed for yesterday, for a rerun. With hindsight, she would never have brought things to a head like that. She would have kept quiet and been extra loving to Steve, to try and *win* his love.

Making a snap decision, she went back to the phone and dialled his mother's number, hoping he would be there. When she heard his voice she lost her own. 'Kay? Is that you?'

'What's going to happen about my salary? I can't live on air.'

'It'll be posted to you. Are you OK?'

'I'm fine, thank you. It's not enough. I want you to double the amount.' There was a pause. 'I'm not asking for half of your wealth. Just twice as much salary, so I can pay the bills and live.'

'I was going to do that anyway,' he said quietly.

'I'm sure.'

'How's your face?'

'How's your tart?'

There was a pause. 'I'll have the cheque sent earlier.

You can use our joint account until I get it changed, probably at the end of next week.'

'I should hope so. I'm not going to live on nothing while you dine on caviare!' She slammed the phone down and wished she felt better for it.

She picked up the phone and dialled again. 'And what about my car? You promised me a Beetle.'

'I can't buy another one through the company just yet. You'll have to wait.'

'Another one?' Surely the bastard hadn't treated himself already?

'I've ordered the Morgan I was after.'

'The expensive green one?'

'Yes. And it's not expensive-green, it's racing-green,' he said drily.

'Well, I'll use your old one then. Until you get my Beetle.'

'Sorry, but I need that for work.'

'You shit!' She slammed the receiver down again, but for some strange reason felt better this time. If he could afford to be a two-car man he could afford to give her more. Much more. She would have to think about it long and hard. Catch him now while he still felt guilty. While he still owed her.

Gazing at nothing in particular, her attention focused on a framed water-colour on the wall of a young man looking out to sea. She had always thought there was something familiar about the shape of the lean body and broad shoulders. Taking a closer look she noticed for the first time that it was signed. *Cathy Brown*. Her mind flashed back to when Steve had told her about his mistress. *Cathy ... she's an artist.*

With a feeling of dread she examined the picture. It had to be Steve. The hair was a little darker but it was him all right. She even recognized the checked shirt collar which lay over the dark-blue sweater. *The bastard.* How could he hang his lover's painting of him in their home? Had he subconsciously been trying to tell her about his affair? And when had it been painted? Again she thought back to the night he left. *I've known her for ages.* Had they had a day out at the seaside during hers and Steve's own courtship?

She tried to think back, to remember anything that would have given him away at the time. But there was nothing. No indication that he was seeing anyone else. How could something like that have been going on without her having the slightest idea? Was she really that blind?

The sound of a car drawing into the courtyard below pulled her out of her melancholy. She must pull herself together.

Checking that Jac was happy to continue playing with his bath toys, she added a little more hot water and told him she would get him out in ten minutes.

Before going down to let Pamela in, Kay's eyes scanned the room to make sure it was tidy. It did look nice. Cosy. Red carpet, white walls, lots of old pine furniture, bits of gleaming old brass ornaments here and there, red and black patterned curtains with cushions to match on the ivory-coloured sofa. Only one thing was missing: Steve.

'Do you want to talk about it or not?' Pamela kicked off her shoes and dropped on to the sofa.

'There's not much to say. It's an old story. He's been

having an affair and wants to live with the bitch.' Seeing the look of pity on her friend's face broke her brave act. She could do nothing to stop her face screwing up and the tears flowing. She pointed to the painting. 'She painted that while we were courting. She painted it and he had the nerve to hang it on our wall!

'How could he do that to me, Pam? I don't understand...'

'It proves what I've always said. There are only two kinds of men – boring and bastards.' She smiled drily. 'Steve, of course, is both.'

Rinsing her face with cold water, Kay resolved to be strong. No more self-pity. She dabbed her neck with a soft towel, lifted her eyes and looked miserably at her reflection in the mirror above the kitchen sink. She thanked her lucky stars that she had Pamela. She dried her hands and walked back into the living room. She looked again at the painting of Steve.

'I just can't believe he would hang it up there...' Before Kay could stop herself she started to wonder what he was thinking at that precise moment. Surely he couldn't sweep aside their marriage without feeling something? *Why did you hang it up there, Steve? Why?* She covered her face, trying to block it out of her mind, and then began to cry again. Before long she was hysterical, calling his name, asking all kinds of questions. She sat down, she stood up, she paced the floor, going over the same thoughts. 'I thought he *loved* me!' she shouted.

'Before we go any further...' Pam said, examining her fingernails to avoid looking at Kay's sad puffy face, 'you've got to take that down.' She nodded towards the painting.

'No. I want it to be a constant reminder of the traitor I married.'

'That's feeble and you know it. If you don't remove it from the wall, I will.'

'And what am I supposed to do with it?'

'Put it face up on the floor and I'll show you,' she grinned.

Dropping the damp towel on a chair, Kay reached out for the picture. 'It must have taken her ages to paint it.'

'Shut up and unhook it.'

'Give me time, for Christ's sake! I want one last look.'

'You've got thirty seconds.' Pamela held out her arm and watched the second hand. 'Twenty seconds. Ten seconds. Five, four, three, two, one.'

There was a sudden crash as Kay dropped it to the floor, face up, as her friend had instructed. 'Now what?'

Pamela kicked her stiletto-heeled shoes at Kay's feet. 'Put those on and stand on the bastard. Dig your heels in.'

'I can't.'

'Yes you can.'

'No Pam. It's Steve.'

'Do it!'

Carefully placing one foot on the glass, avoiding his head, she paused. 'What if I cut myself?'

'It'll heal. Go on. Give it one good whack with the heel. Aim for the balls.'

Shaking her head at her friend, Kay began to chuckle. 'You're a cold-hearted cow at times.'

217

'Then go for the heart.'

Laughing, Kay drew back her foot. 'This is silly.'

'I bet that's him gazing down from the sand dune where they had just made mad passionate love. I bet it's meant to be symbolic of the freedom he really wanted, staring out to sea like that.'

The sound of glass cracking under her heels suddenly sparked Kay's anger. As she drove the steel tip into the picture her vigour intensified. She stamped on his face, his neck, his chest, until the glass became a white mass and the figure of Steve could hardly be seen. Not satisfied with that, she grabbed the frame, tipped the crushed glass on to the floor and proceeded to smash the gold-painted frame itself to bits. She could hear Pamela laughing as she cursed and swore.

'Here, drink this.' Pam held out a small glass of brandy she'd poured from the drinks cupboard.

'Thank you.' Kay raised the glass, and saw that a flying shard had caught her finger and a drop of blood was trickling down the side of the brandy glass. She held her hand poised and waited for the blood to drop on to the mess, on to the ruined picture of Steve. She hoped it would hit the mark, his heart, but the splash of blood found his face instead.

'I want more than this,' Kay said, deliberately dropping the empty glass into the debris. 'Much more.'

Opening the drinks cupboard she turned coolly to Pamela and asked what she would like.

'I'm driving, but you go for it. Get totally pissed.'

'Out of my brains,' Kay said.

'Out of your brains.'

Placing the bottle of whisky on the floor beside the

sofa, Kay looked at the smashed painting and smiled.
'What am I gonna do with that now?'

'Have you got a strong cardboard box?'

'Probably.' She thought about it. 'Yeah – one that his
new stereo came in.'

'Good. We'll parcel that lot up and send it to him.
Have you got her address?'

Kay raised an eyebrow. 'What do you think?'

'No. Right, well, nothing for it but to send it to the
agency.'

Tossing back her long blonde hair, Kay laughed. 'No,
I couldn't do that. What would people think when he
opened it?'

'Fuck what they think.'

Worried, she looked at Pamela. 'It'll mean the end of
my marriage.'

'What marriage?'

'Yeah – what marriage?' she sighed.

'Now then. I've got some incredible news. Sit back
and listen to *this*! Remember Auntie Esther getting
thrown out of her house in Jubilee Street? Well the old
boy, my auntie's friend Laurence, who died some years
ago, owned the property and left it to her. He made out
a will. My auntie Esther owns the property! She's in
her seventh heaven. I've never seen her so happy. The
police found the will amongst the house deeds.

'And – you wait till I tell you what that bloody bitch,
Patsy Hemmingway, had been up to—'

'I already know. I read the local paper,' Kay said,
hoping to end it.

'You never said.'

'No, I've had other things on my mind.'

'Anyway, my auntie was at the house one day and who should knock on the door, but Hemmingway's mum and dad. She said they're really nice people. Wanted to see the place where their daughter fell. She's got brain damage.'

'I think she already had that before—'

'She let them move into the upstairs flat for a couple of weeks, so they could visit the hospital every day and—'

'That was nice of her.' Kay's mind was on Jac again, the old doubts and questions beginning to surface.

'Once the Hemmingway woman's parents have gone back to Leicester, Auntie Esther's going to move back in. She said I could live in the top flat – rent free.'

'What a turn of events. You know who that bitch Patsy Hemmingway is, don't you?'

'Some nutcase from Leicester,' Pam said.

'Yeah – Jac's real mother.'

'Come again?'

'It's a long story. But I've got to get Jac out of the bath, so I'll fill you in later – when you phone me.'

'Can't wait. I won't be moving into the flat, not for a couple of years anyway. I've got other plans. You can be part of them if you like. I'm going to the Caribbean. To the Bahamas, Nassau. They're desperate for English secretaries out there, and the pay is brilliant. Stuff grey England!'

'I'm in! Just let me know when.' She raised her glass. 'Here's to sun, sand and Jamaican rum!'

'In the winter,' Pam grinned.

'In the winter.' Kay began to sing ... 'Summertime ... and the living is ea-sy...'

'Your husband's rich ... and your mama's good-looking ... So hush little baby ... do-o-on't you cry-yyyyy ...'

'I'll ta-ake his mon-ey ...'

'And we'll have a good ti-iiime ...'

Screaming with laughter, the girls slipped back to where they had left off a few years ago, before lovers came along and drew them apart. Just two old mates – together again, ready and willing to take on the world.

'It's time you stopped being a goody-goody and got on with a more exciting life. Christ knows why you had to get married so young.'

'You never did like Steve, did you?'

'No. He's a jerk. At least he's proved me right. What kind of a wally would put a picture of himself on the wall? And one that had been painted by his *lover*? Do me a favour.'

'You're a tough old boot, aren't you?'

'Yes. Let's hope some of it rubs off on you.'

# *Chapter Eight*

Once Jac had been dropped off home, he was bombarded with questions from his mum and dad. Jack wanted to know why he hadn't stopped the whole day, while Laura was wondering why Pam had brought him home and not Steve.

Unable to think fast enough to cover for his brother-in-law, Jac slipped into a long silence after explaining that Steve had previously arranged for Kay and himself to go and visit some friends.

'Well, what about the golf then? We were under the impression that Kay took you home because she didn't want to be on 'er own all day. And how come Pamela was visiting so early on a Sunday morning?'

'I don't know!' Jac was on his feet ready to escape to the privacy of his bedroom when there was a sudden rat-a-tat-tat on the window. It was Billy.

'Now what's he doing round this early?' Laura turned to Jac. 'Go and open the door for your grandfather, there's a good boy.'

Jac narrowed his eyes and looked up at the ceiling thoughtfully. 'Is he my grandfather...?'

''Course he bloody well is! What's up with you?' Jack snapped.

'Can't I call 'im Billy? Kay does sometimes. I've heard her.'

Laura shook her head and left the kitchen, mildly amused by her son and some of the things he came out with.

'Call 'im Grandad, if you don't like Grandfather. I don't know where your mother gets her ideas from sometimes. Grandfather! Bit on the posh side if you ask me.'

'He's not my grandad.'

'Eh?' Jack sounded far from pleased. Surely he didn't actually mean what he had just said?

'He's my *grandfather*,' Jac quickly added, covering himself. He daren't let them know he had found out about his real mum. That would lead to all sorts of trouble.

"Course I mean it, Laura!' Billy's hearty laugh echoed along the passage. 'I might even give one to Jac to fetch up!'

'What's the old devil on about now? Bloody nutcase.' Jack tapped his temple with one finger and managed to induce a smile from his son.

'Get your coat on, sonny boy! I'm taking you down the animal market,' Billy said, full of the joys of spring.

Jumping up from his chair, Jac beamed. 'You gonna buy me a dog, Grandad?' It was the first sign of life his parents had seen from him in the past week or so.

'Grandad? You 'ear that, Laura? He called me Grandad!' Billy seemed pleased. He rubbed his chin. 'Yeah ... like that ... sounds more ... I dunno, more cosy.'

'That's what I'll call you then. That or Billy.' Jac was back into his old ways within seconds.

224

'Grandad'll do, son.'

'Are you gonna buy me a *dog*?' Jac asked.

'We can't keep a dog! How many more times do I 'ave to tell yer?' Jack said. 'Not that everyone abides by the rules.'

'No son, not a dog. Chicks.'

'Chicks?' Jac wondered what he meant.

'That's right. Little yellow balls of fluff that'll grow into chickens and lay some eggs for our breakfast.'

'Dad! We can't keep chickens!'

'No, Laura, but I can. In my backyard. Like I used to. Jac can 'elp me look after 'em.'

'Sounds all right . . .' Jac said, disappointed about the dog.

Holding Jac's hand tightly, Billy walked him along Three Colts Lane. 'What's all this about Grandad then? Don't you like Grandfather any more?'

'Grandad's not as posh.'

'And what's all this about you not eating up your dinners?'

'I don't eat anything,' Jac said, puzzled that Billy should only be concerned about dinners.

'And what's this about you sulking all the time?'

'I don't sulk. I just don't talk.'

'And why's that?' Billy pulled him past a large yard where much wheeling and dealing was taking place. Where anything could be bought, from old worn-out bikes to rare antiques. He didn't want Jac to spot the second-hand toy stall, where he'd be lucky if he found anything intact. 'I'm surprised you've stopped talking so much. You always liked to rabbit.'

Jac was thoughtful. 'Do they sell rabbits down the market?'

'Sell every bloody thing!' Billy laughed. 'Probably get a parrot with two heads if you asked the right man.'

'Can you get dogs with two heads?'

'Gawd 'elp us,' Billy roared, 'things you say.' He stopped in his tracks. 'I'll tell you what we'll 'ave, Jac.' He looked down at his grandson and beamed. 'We'll 'ave a nice hot salt-beef sandwich. You won't turn your nose up at that, will yer?'

'I'll try not to.' Jac blinked at him, wondering why grown-ups always talked about food.

'Right,' Billy said, 'here we go. Now then, from here it gets more crowded, so you hang on to the tail of Grandad's jacket, right?'

'Why?' Jac's voice was filled with dread. 'Will someone try to kidnap me?'

Billy chuckled. 'What? You think they trade in kids an' all, do yer? 'Course no one's gonna nab you. Not while I'm around.'

'Why do I have to hang on to you then?'

'You'll see.' He gave Jac's hand a tug. 'Come on, Cough Drop.'

Jack dug his heels in. 'I want to go home!'

'Don't be a baby, you'll be all right. Just hang on to me when we get into the crowd.'

'No! I want to go back!' Jac yanked his hand from Billy's. 'I might get lost!'

Concerned by the sudden change in Jac, Billy kneeled down and looked into his grandson's tearful face. 'What it is son, eh? You can tell me. What yer scared of?'

'Nothing. I just want to go home.'

Cupping Jac's face in his hand, Billy swallowed. The boy looked petrified. 'I'll tell you what. We won't bother going all the way to Petticoat Lane. We'll go as far as the animal market and call it a day. It's not so crowded in that part. Fair enough?'

Jac narrowed his eyes. 'Will I still have to hang on to your jacket?'

'No. Grab Grandad's hand, that'll be enough. OK, soldier?'

Jac swallowed and nodded, even managed a smile. He would always remember their little repertoire. It never failed to please him. He wiped his arm across his runny nose and sniffed.

'Let's march on, lad!' Billy winked at Jac, keeping up their little game.

'After you, Sarge,' Jac managed to say.

'Come on you little darling.' Billy grabbed Jac by the waist and pulled him up. 'I'll carry you for a little while.'

'Why? I'm big enough to walk.'

'I know that. I just wanted a cuddle.' Billy's eyes watered as Jac's thin little arms went around his neck and hugged him tight.

'Don't bloody strangle me then,' he chuckled and walked on. He would eventually get to the bottom of what was really bothering his grandson. The boy was deeply troubled about something, and it would take time to draw it out of him.

'I wish I could have a dog, Grandad,' Jac whispered in his ear.

'No, son. Not a dog. Not allowed in the flats. But we might 'ave a look at some kittens as well as chicks.'

'We could let the dog live in your cottage...'

'A cat would be more useful. It'd chase the mice away,' Billy said.

'And it would chase the chicks. Have you thought about that?'

Billy couldn't help smiling at his grandson. He had a quick brain all right. A bit like himself really. 'We'll have a look at the puppies, but I'm not promising anything. Now then, down you get. I'm getting a bit winded.'

As soon as Jac was on his feet he grabbed Billy's hand and clenched it tight, looking up at him with wide eyes. 'Why is everyone shouting?'

'That's the market boys, son. Letting everyone know what they've got on offer.'

Jac tightened his grip. 'I won't let go,' he promised.

'Good boy,' Billy said, leading him over to the long makeshift kennels where dogs and puppies of all shapes and sizes were waiting to be given a loving home.

As the yapping and low whining filled their ears, Jac pulled Billy towards a tea chest on a stall. It was placed sideways-on, with wire mesh stapled to the front. Lying down, with its head in its paws and looking very sad, was a six-month-old puppy.

'Why ain't it barking like the others?' Jac narrowed his eyes and peered through the mesh.

'Probably on its last legs,' Billy shook his head slowly. 'Poor devil.'

Turning from the puppy, Jac looked up at his grandfather. 'What d'yer mean?'

'Dying, sonny Jim. Be lucky if it sees the week out.'

Jac pressed his face up to the wire. 'Where's your

mum then, eh?' he asked, as if the world surrounding them had drifted away and he and the white puppy with brown-tipped ears were the only ones there.

'Not so close, Jac. He might snap at your nose.'

'Little thoroughbred that one!' The pet seller seemed to appear from nowhere. 'A lovely smooth-haired terrier, waiting for a little boy to take 'im 'ome!' He smiled at Jac.

Billy threw his shoulders back and laughed loudly. 'I'm bloody sure! There's a bit of terrier in the mongrel – I'll give you that. Bit of Jack Russell.'

'He looked at me!' Jac shrieked. 'Only with one eye but he did, Grandad! He looked at me!'

'What's up with it then?' Billy looked the man straight in the eye.

'Bit neglected, that's all. A few square meals and it'll be as fit as a fiddle. Look at that coat.'

Billy already had and had noted the sheen. 'What's the damage?'

'A tenner to you.'

'What – you gonna pay me to take it away and bring it back to life, are yer?' Billy threw him a knowing look.

'Wants a bit of loving, that's all.' The man wiped his lips and thought about it. 'Eight pounds.'

'Come on, Jac. We'll wander down to the kittens.' He reached for Jac's hand, and before the boy could plead with him he gave him a sly wink.

'All right. Seeing as you're a pensioner – a fiver.'

'Three quid,' Billy said resolutely.

'Four.' The man raised an eyebrow. 'And that's the bottom line.'

'Nar. Can't afford that. Come on, Jac.'

'Three pounds ten then. Go on, rob me. Everyone else does.'

Seeing that the man's attention was on a young couple looking at a golden retriever, Billy pulled three grubby pound notes out of his wallet and then two half-crowns from his trouser pocket. 'Here. Three pounds five shillings. You've cleaned me out.'

'I'm bloody sure!' He eyed his potential customers. 'Be with you in a minute, sir!' he called out, while prising the staples from the wire mesh. Then, reaching in, he carefully pulled the pup from the tea chest. 'Come on then, Conker – we've found you a new master.' He looked down at Jac. 'What's your name, son?'

'Jac.'

'We've found you a Master Jac!' The man gave the puppy a squeeze and placed him in Jac's waiting arms.

Slipping the money into the front zip pocket of his apron, he spoke in a voice loud enough for the other customers to hear. 'It might be a cross-breed, sir, but that's the best fifteen pounds you've spent!'

Thrusting his arm forward, Billy shook the man's hand. 'Best buy I've 'ad in a while!' he replied, just as loudly. The couple watching them looked as if they had a few bob to spare. 'Good doing business with yer! You're a fair man!'

Both men enjoyed the play-acting. 'Here.' The animal seller bent down and grabbed a bag of dog biscuits from under his stall. 'A present for the boy's birthday!'

'It's not my birthday,' Jac said in a quiet voice.

Billy gave him a nudge. 'It is now,' he whispered.

'You're looking at a prize-winning bitch there, sir!' The man's attention was immediately on the couple.

'Couldn't accept a penny less than fifty! And let's face it – if I can get fifteen for a mongrel...?'

As Laura basted sizzling fat over their Sunday joint of lamb, there was a ring on the door bell. 'Get that will you, Jack! My hands are full!'

She had a feeling it might be Liz come for a chat about Jac. She would have to try and get it across to her that she didn't want to make any waves for the boy. Make her see that it was best to leave him to come out of his strange mood by himself. If she could convince Liz, then maybe she would in turn persuade Jack to let it ride.

'We've got company, Laura,' Jack said quietly. 'Come in the front room once you've put that back in the oven.' He closed the kitchen door behind him and Laura heard the sound of muffled voices.

'I'm sorry to barge in on you like this but I thought you might like to know how Patsy is.' Laura had never met the woman who sat down in her armchair as if she owned it, but she knew exactly who she was. Patsy Hemmingway's mother. She looked from her to the short thin man who accompanied her.

'I would like to know,' Laura said. 'We've been worried about her.'

'Shall I go and put the kettle on?' Jack asked sheepishly, looking uncomfortable.

'I think a glass of beer might be more suitable,' Laura said, trying to ease the tension.

'Thank you, that would be very nice,' said Patsy's dad.

'Yes. Thank you.' Patsy's mother nodded. 'It's close today,' she said, unbuttoning her cardigan.

Sitting on the edge of an armchair, Laura clasped her hands together and looked from one to the other. 'It must have come as a shock...'

'Yes it did. My name's Eileen by the way. And this is Albert.'

'Oh ... right. I'm er ... I'm pleased to meet you.' She managed a smile. 'You are Jac's grandparents, after all's said and done.'

'Where is Jac?' Eileen asked with a touch of a plea in her voice. She obviously wanted to see the boy.

'He's gone down the lane with his grandfather.' Laura inhaled slowly, preparing herself for battle. 'I really would rather you didn't see him. Not just yet anyway.'

'Oh? And why's that?' Eileen stuck out her chin defiantly.

'Because we haven't told him yet. Who his real mother is.' The woman opened her mouth to speak but Laura put up her hand. 'Let me finish, please.

'We decided to leave it until he was a bit older because we felt – feel – that a boy of his age wouldn't be able to handle the truth. That he was dumped into a children's home before he was given away by his own mother.' She looked directly into Mrs Hemmingway's eyes. 'Jac is *our* son legally and – as far as his father, Jack, is concerned – blood-related too. So *I* will say what is the best for him, OK?'

Patsy's father nodded. 'You're right.' He glanced at his wife. 'I told you. I said we shouldn't have come. It's not right. I apologize, Mrs Armstrong. For barging in like this.'

'As it turns out, it's OK. But if Jac had been at home it

could have caused a lot of problems. And frankly, we've got enough just getting on with life at the moment.'

'Put like that, there's not much I *can* say, is there?'

'As far as Jac's concerned, no. It would make you feel good, I'm sure, if he were to walk in now – but it would be bad for my son. And no one, and I do mean no one, is going to hurt him.'

'He's our grandson! Hurt him? We love the boy!'

'Well you should have thought of that when you allowed your daughter to put him away. And that is the end of it. Now you can stay and tell us how Patsy is and enjoy a beer, or you can leave right now. It's up to you.'

'We'll stay for ten minutes, if that's OK,' Albert Hemmingway said agreeably.

Jack arrived, carrying a tray with four glasses of beer. 'Everyone all right then?' he asked hopefully.

'Yes, Jack, we're fine. Eileen and Albert are leaving before Jac comes in. I've explained our plans to tell him about Patsy when he's older and that they're welcome to visit whenever they like after that.'

'Good, that's good. That's that settled.' He handed out the beers and sat next to Albert. 'So, how is Patsy? She didn't look too good when I dropped by.'

'You've been in?' Eileen's voice changed instantly. She was pleased that Patsy had had a visitor.

''Course I 'ave. The day you phoned me. They wouldn't tell me nothing though.' He drank some beer. 'I'm not next of kin.'

Laura glared at him. 'You said that as if you wish you were.'

'Don't start, Laura. This is hard enough as it is. I feel like the nut between the crackers.'

'Yeah well, you would, wouldn't you, Jack?' She smiled wryly at him. He would never change. Always turning it around, hoping to get some sympathy.

'We were told this morning that when Patsy knocked her head, she damaged a blood vessel in the brain.' The man bowed his head and took them all by surprise. He burst into tears, completely broken. He had been keeping it inside until that moment. None of them could say a word. They just sat there in silence, watching his grief, unable to do anything for him.

'It's called a haematoma,' he finally managed to say in between sobs. 'She may have lost her speech.' He pushed his hands through his hair and took a deep breath. 'And the use of her legs. She could be in a wheelchair for the rest of her life. She could be a cabbage—'

'She will not! Don't listen to him. Yes, there is a bleeding vessel in her brain and yes she might be in a wheelchair for a while, and *yes* she may have to learn how to speak and walk again. But she *will* do it! She will *not* be a vegetable! Not my Patsy!' Now it was Eileen's turn to cry.

'Oh my God....' Jack looked up at the ceiling. 'Someone tell me this isn't happening. Someone tell me this is a nightmare!' He looked to Laura for strength, but she too was struggling with her emotions.

'She'll be all right, Eileen,' Laura said. 'Your Patsy'll get up fighting. You know she will.'

'But how long will it take, Laura?' Albert cried. 'How long will it take, Jack?' He buried his face in Jack's shoulder. 'Hold me, mate, please hold me. I can't take this.'

Jack sucked hard on his bottom lip, doing his utmost not to show what he was feeling, how miserable he felt. It would only upset Laura.

'It's all right, Albert. You have a good cry, mate. It's the best thing for yer.' He pressed his lips together and caught Laura's eye.

'You all right?' she asked, feeling sorry for him.

'Yeah. I'm fine. Fine.'

'I'll fetch some more beer in. Sod it, we might as well finish the bottles off.' She turned to Patsy's mother. 'But if our Jac...'

'Of course. If he comes in, we'll go without saying a word. You can tell him we're Jehovah's Witnesses.' She sniffed and then burst out laughing. 'Tell him that we went on so much about the end of the world coming that we all got upset!'

Suddenly their crying turned to laughter and then to a mixture of both. It was doing all of them good and for different reasons.

'What a life eh?' Albert said, blowing his nose.

'Yeah ... but we all cling on to it though, don't we?' Jack added. 'So it can't be that bad, can it?'

'No,' Eileen said, 'but if we could have Christmas twice a year it would be nice.'

'Two birthdays an' all,' he chuckled.

'Two birthdays?' Eileen became pensive as she stared down at the floor. 'Two births. It'll be a bit like that for our Patsy, won't it? She'll have to learn all over again. How to talk, how to walk. How to live.'

'She's in a good place. The best. London Hospital? They come from all over the country to see our specialists.'

The four of them sat in silence, wrapped in their own thoughts. 'I had better check our roast...' Laura couldn't take any more. It was a bit much, seeing the way it was affecting Jack.

'Would you like a hot meat sandwich—'

Albert put up his hand, a gesture to show that they had already outstayed their welcome. 'I'm taking Eileen to Bloom's restaurant. We've heard enough about it so we thought we'd give it a try. But thank you anyway.'

'Yes, time we went.' Eileen stood up and sighed. 'Let's hope things will look a lot different in a year from now.' She raised her eyes from the floor to meet Laura's. 'I'm not sure what we should do about Jac. Maybe we ought to wait until Patsy's back on her feet before we introduce ourselves.'

Laura's back went up. 'We'll let you know in good time, once we've explained everything at this end ... maybe in a year or two. We'll make arrangements for him to meet you.'

'I think that's fair.' Albert shot his wife a look of warning.

'Well I don't, but there. You're holding the trump cards at the moment, aren't you? If my Patsy wasn't where she is we might well go to the adoption society and insist you tell the boy the truth.'

'And risk damaging a six-year-old?'

'I think that's a small risk compared to the one you're taking. If you put if off for too long it might well affect him worse later on in life. Living a lie is a dreadful thing. Once he's told, it'll alter everything he's believed in. Certain relatives will bear no relation to him. His grandparents will suddenly be—'

'I think I've got the picture! We've not exactly buried our heads in the sand – we do discuss these things.'

'Thank you for your hospitality, Jack.' The men shook hands. 'I'm sorry things couldn't have worked out differently.'

'You what?' Laura glared at Albert. 'I hope you're not saying what I think you're saying?'

'Albert always got on well with Jack in the past.' Eileen buttoned her chunky-knit cardigan. 'Way back. When he and Patsy practically lived together. When she had the opportunity of becoming a successful career woman, but got pregnant instead of—'

'Yes all right! Thank you for the historic running commentary!' Laura showed them to the door in silence, leaving Jack to make conversation. He seemed to be quite at ease with them. Very familiar.

As she plunged the sprouts into boiling water, Laura continued to fume over Patsy's mother. 'The silly bitch. If *she* hasn't got a split personality . . . ! One minute she's as nice as pie and the next, she's in with the knife, right in the back. And what did you do? Sweet FA!'

'And what was I supposed to say?' Jack folded his Sunday newspaper. 'That I was glad I 'adn't lumbered myself with their daughter?'

'Put a bit more politely than that, yes! You could have showed some small sign that you were pleased our marriage hadn't been blown apart!'

'You're being too 'ard on 'em. Try to imagine what they're going through.' He stood up ready to leave the kitchen. 'They don't know which way to turn.'

'I don't want you going near Patsy. Hospital or no hospital.' Laura stared him out.

'Well that's too bad, because I am gonna go! And if there's anything I can do to help her back on her feet I will!'

'Oh right. So Patsy's back in our lives! It's come round full circle. We're right back to where we were seven years ago.'

'If we move into that little pub in Kent, near to your ex-lover, it will 'ave, yeah.' He stormed out of the kitchen.

Slamming the oven door shut, Laura was filled with hate. 'The bastard,' she murmured. 'The two-faced bastard.'

'Mum! Quick! Open the door. I've got something to show you!' Jac urgently called through the kitchen window.

'Oh Jesus,' Laura sighed. 'He's bought him a puppy, I know he has.'

Seeing Jack make his way along the passage to open the street door in answer to the loud banging, she flopped on to a kitchen chair and waited.

'His name's Conker!' Jac beamed, cuddling the puppy close to him. 'Look at 'is face,' he chuckled, 'he looks all worried in case you say we can't keep him.'

'We can't, Jac...' Laura felt exhausted. She couldn't face more cross words.

'The trouble is, Jac, he won't always be that small and he won't always be that quiet.' Jack was taking over and Laura was thankful for that.

'Where's the grandfather?' she asked suspiciously.

'Gone 'ome.' Jack half smiled. 'Left this pair at the door and ran.'

'So he bloody well should. I'll kill 'im for this.'

'Grandad said if you don't want 'im here, he'll look after him for me.' Jac buried his face in Conker's soft coat.

Laura looked at Jack and shrugged. Not one word needed to pass between them. Each felt the same. If the council found out, Laura reasoned to herself, then Billy would have to look after the dog, but meanwhile they may as well try. They wouldn't be the first on the estate to keep a dog. Mr McCarthy the caretaker was a dog lover. He had three himself, even though his cottage garden was small. Maybe he would turn a blind eye.

'All right, Jac. You can keep the puppy but you're responsible for taking it for walks, right?'

Jac's eyes filled with tears. 'Yes, Dad.'

'And I don't care if he needs to go out in the middle of your favourite cartoon—'

'Poor little thing looks terrified.' Laura held out her arms and took the soft white bundle from Jac. 'Not your fault, is it? Chucked out to fend for yourself. Dumped in a dog's home no doubt. Your mum was a bit of a tramp, was she?'

Jack knew exactly what Laura was up to, using the dog to mirror their circumstances. But what he didn't know was that his son was taking it all in too.

'I think he loves you, Mum,' Jac said quietly, stroking Conker. *And so do I*, he thought. *We're the same ... both adopted by my mum*. 'I think he must want some dinner.' Jac looked into Laura's face. 'I'll share mine with 'im.'

'Oh, so you're gonna eat something, then?' Laura smiled.

'Yeah. We've gotta keep our strength up. Grandad said so.'

'Yeah, he would.' Laura would deal with her dad later. 'So – we're gonna need a dog basket, a lead, a bowl for his food, a bowl for his water, a name-tag, dog food...'

'I'll go and see 'ow much is in my money box.' Jac was out of the kitchen in a flash.

'You don't mind then?' Jack said, using the topic as a way of patching things up with Laura.

'Look at the difference in Jac. How could I mind?' She stroked the brown patch on Conker's head. 'Anyway ... how could anyone not fall in love with this little scrap?' Conker lifted his head and looked into Laura's face, his light-brown eyes begging for affection.

'So you don't think I should go and see Patsy then?'

'Do what you want. I don't care.' She scratched the puppy's ear and couldn't help smiling when he reacted by pushing his other ear into her hand.

'No. If you don't think I should—' The sound of the telephone stopped him. 'I bet that's your dad, testing the ground,' Jack laughed.

'Yes, Billy?' He did his best to sound angry. 'Whoops, sorry. I was expecting a call.' Jack's expression changed from jovial to serious and back to happy within seconds. 'Well, that's good news and I would love to be able to pass it on, but they left about twenty minutes ago.'

Pushing her fingers through the puppy's short coat, Laura fixed her eyes on Jack's face wondering what the good news might be. And wondering how the caller got their number. It was obviously a message for Patsy's parents.

'You'll never guess what, Laura? She opened her eyes ten minutes ago. She's out of the coma.'

'Why did they ring us?'

'Albert left this number as well as theirs in Leicester. Next of kin.' He shrugged. 'In case Patsy died I s'pose.'

'Oh right.' Laura sighed.

'They wouldn't tell me any more than that, only that she had come round. I wish Eileen and Albert had been here when that call came. Would 'ave made their day.'

'Phone Bloom's. Leave a message for when they get there,' Laura said.

'No need. They're going back to the hospital after they've had their dinner.'

'Phone and leave our number. Then you can take Conker and sort out an old dish we can use for his drink.'

'I don't know the number.'

'Well look it up! You know you want to. Leave our number and ask if they can call as soon as they get there.'

'And you don't mind?'

'Just get on with it, Jack. I'm gonna see how much Jac's managed to prise out of his money box. I think we should let him pay for a dog's collar.' She stood by the door, paused and then turned to Jack. 'I'll say this just the once – and then it's up to you what you do. I don't want you visiting Patsy unless I'm with you.'

''Course not. I wouldn't do that. Not now I know you don't want me to.'

'Yeah well. Make sure you don't forget. Or you'll be out on your ear. And I'm not joking.'

'All right, you've made your point.' He thumbed his way through the telephone directory. 'It's good to see you're still jealous, Laura,' he grinned.

# Chapter Nine

Lulled by the quiet, seductive voice of the neurosurgeon explaining in simple language that she had had a fall and hit her head, Patsy was content to lie back and let his voice drift across her mind.

'We've carried out some tests while you've been sleeping. And I'm pleased with the results. Of course there will have to be more tests, but we're almost a hundred per cent sure that surgery won't be necessary. The fact that you've come round this soon indicates that the bleeding from the torn blood vessel around the brain has stopped. Of course we shall be keeping a very close eye on you.

'The best thing for you now is peace and quiet. In a day or two you'll be checked by my colleagues to see if there has been any short-term damage to that part of the brain which deals with the processing and storage of language. In other words, Patsy, is all I'm saying to you making sense? And if it is, are you able to answer me?' He smiled warmly and patted her hand.

'I'm not looking for answers from you. I'm just explaining so that you won't panic if things are not quite as you remember. You might find that your speech has gone a little awry. You may not be able to say what you are thinking, for instance, but that's the worst that could happen. I have a feeling that all your brain is going to need is rest. And that's fine. Please don't feel pressured to talk to anyone just yet.'

Pulling himself to his feet, he smiled down at her. 'Once the team of therapists arrive, then you'll know it.' He turned away and spoke quietly to the house doctor and matron.

There were questions floating around Patsy's mind, but there seemed to be a space between her thoughts and her speech. The journey from one to the other seemed very long, with no signposts to help her. But it was quiet everywhere – quite and clean. The scent of sweet-smelling sheets filled her being and she was happy to close her eyes and drift away, safe in the feeling that her life was the responsibility of others now. She would do as the man had suggested, rest until she was ready to test herself. And she couldn't think of a better place to do just that.

She fought against the desire to close her eyes, which were beginning to feel heavy. She knew they were keeping her sedated and that had been fine, but now she was feeling trapped. But this man might say things she didn't want to miss. Using all her will-power she forced herself to be alert.

Turning back to Patsy the specialist spoke again. 'Either a colleague or I will pop in most days to see how you're coming along. And you'll soon get used to the nursing staff, who you might think are over-fussing at times, but positioning you correctly in bed, as well as giving you passive exercise, will help prevent muscle weakness and spasms.

'Now the area of your brain which sends messages to your arms is not affected by the bleeding, so you'll be able to press this button here should you need assistance, but it will be a matter of time before you begin to feel sensation in your legs. But it will happen, I promise.'

Forcing her lids open she met his eyes. *It's my promise – not yours. My legs ... my body ...*

The doctor stood in the doorway and smiled at her. 'I've studied your medical records.' He chuckled softly. 'I have a feeling you'll surprise everyone around you. You're a strong woman who fights back.'

She felt a familiar sense of determination sweep through her. *Except that I won't surprise but shock you. Once I put my mind to it ...*

'See you tomorrow. I was delighted to see the colour of your eyes – now I look forward to seeing your smile.'

Gazing up at the ceiling, ignoring the nurse who was listening intently to the doctor as he spoke to her in a low voice, Patsy decided there and then that she would not allow the loneliness of her situation to get her down. She would use every bit of her resolve to help the staff help her. Help her get back to her old self. A staff nurse had taken the trouble to explain her accident, how and where she was found. She needn't have bothered. Patsy could remember it, right up to when she and Jac struggled at the top of the stairs. She could even remember falling. The rest would be obvious to a moron. But what of Jac? Had he fled, believing she was dead?

'I'm going to lift your head very slightly, Patricia.'

Patsy caught the faint aroma of the nurse's cologne. It

was nice, fresh. It reminded her of a spring day in the garden.

'Sip this slowly. It'll keep the aches and pains at bay. Not a very nice taste but we'll soon get rid of the bitterness with some squash.

'After this,' the nurse said, bringing the small glass to Patsy's lips, 'I'm going to give you another gentle massage.'

*Good. But please try to do it without prattling on.*

'Then it will be visiting-time. I expect your parents will be in again. They told me they're staying in your flat for a couple of weeks. That'll be nice for you. You'll be able to see more of them.'

She had seen enough of them already. Two visits a day for five days.

As the nurse folded back the bedclothes to expose her legs, ready for massage, Patsy allowed her mind to go blank.

Just as she was drifting into a comfortable slumber, something brought her back sharply to the small hospital room. A tingling sensation similar to pins and needles. In both her legs. Along her shin-bone and through her muscles – and yet the nurse was massaging her feet. Rubbing and pushing her thumbs in and around the fleshy parts of her soles. And she could feel something.

As the blood surged through her legs the rest of her body seemed to come to life. It was as if she was warming herself by a roaring fire having been out in freezing cold weather.

Resisting the urge to try lifting one leg, she smiled inwardly. Slowly dragging her arm, which felt like lead, she touched her lips. They were straight. Not turned up as they should be. She was smiling but her lips were still. That was good. She liked that. It gave her a sense of power.

'Good girl, Patricia. Excellent. The more you use your arms the better.' The nurse brushed a few strands of hair from Patsy's face. 'I don't really know if you can understand me but if you can, I want you to know that I'm rooting for you. I lit a candle for you on Sunday. I'm a devout Catholic. And say what they will about us, our faith is just as strong as medicine. I say a prayer for my patients every night. And then I watch them slowly but surely get better.'

Rolling Patsy's left leg to and fro as if it were a piece of dough she was kneading, the nurse looked into her face and smiled. 'I can feel the heat in my hands. I wonder if you can too? Some of my patients say I've got healing hands.

'I read the bit in the local paper about you.' She chuckled softly and shook her head. 'About the people you were supposed to have conned. I couldn't stop myself laughing. What a nerve. I would love to have seen their faces when they all turned up at the same time. Of course I'm not saying that what you did was right ... but it was clever – and funny.'

Patsy looked up at the ceiling. *Not that clever in the end.* She felt water building up in her eyes as she pictured Jac. She should have realized he wouldn't have wanted to go away with her. He needed time to get over the shock that she was his mother. Maybe fate was working for her. He would have had time by now, and would be so relieved that she was still alive. She imagined him throwing his arms around her neck and pleading with her to take him away from that family.

The more the nurse pushed and pulled at Patsy's legs, the faster the blood seemed to flow through her entire body, and her mind, which was alert with new questions. Why, for instance, had her parents been allowed to stay in Jubilee Street? Had the old witch Simons returned there once the gossip had reached her ears? And would she let her parents stay there out of the goodness of her heart? Surely not. No one would do that, no one. It was a rat race out there. A sewer full of rats. Rat eat rat.

'I think that's enough for now. We don't want to tire you, do we? I thought you had fallen asleep as soon as I started on your feet.' She pulled the bedding down and tucked it in neatly at the bottom. 'There. Let's hope that wasn't a waste of time.'

*Oh please ...* All Patsy wanted was for her to go away so she could try out her legs.

'Well now, medicine next, then I'll read you a passage from the book I've just started. It's a romance.'

Tempted to try out her voice, Patsy willed herself not to. If she could speak too the last thing she wanted was for anyone else to know – for the time being. She closed her eyes and feigned sleep. Maybe that would do the trick.

'Just a couple of pages before Matron does her rounds. She wouldn't see the benefit of reading to a patient like I do. She's a bit old-fashioned.'

*Please let her turn up early.*

'I'm just slipping out for half a mo to collect your medication.' When she reached the doorway she looked back and caught Patsy with her eyes open. 'One of these days you'll answer me and I'll be the one who's struck dumb.'

Patsy stretched the palm of her hand and slowly splayed her fingers. She tried the toes on both feet first, pushing them forwards and then straightening them again. With that small success she found the courage to try one leg. Gradually inching her heel up the bed, she began to bend her knee. Pausing for a rest, she repeated the motion slowly with her other leg. Pulling up both knees, she felt as if she were smiling again. And with good reason. Patsy Hemmingway would not be confined to a wheelchair. She would sit in one, though. She would keep this glorious discovery to herself. Let them believe she still hadn't any feeling in her legs. It was a brilliant stroke of luck. Once she felt strong enough, she would devise a foolproof plan and walk out of that hospital, when the time was right, walk boldly into the Armstrongs' flat and demand they give her Jac.

Slipping back into the position in which the nurse had left her, she slowly dragged both hands across the bedclothes in an effort to smooth them down again.

'I've got some good news for you!' The nurse's voice pierced Patsy's thoughts. 'Your rehabilitation programme starts as from now. You are allowed to sit up!'

Patsy sighed and focused on the ceiling.

'It's no good you rolling your eyes at me. I've just read the doctor's notes. You're allowed to sit up for ten minutes before medication.' She sat on a chair close to the bed and smiled. 'We're going to remove the foam wedge from under your head and shoulders, OK? Staff

Nurse will be here in a half a mo to assist me. We're going to put up the sloping backrest and position the pillows just right so you'll be supported.'

It felt strange, the nurse picking up her hand and squeezing it like that. She looked as if she really cared. Cared about a stranger. *She must be missing something in life*, Patsy told herself.

'We'll both have to sit with you, Patricia, to see that you don't slide down the bed into a poorly supported position. OK? You're going to get a view of the wall instead of the ceiling.'

Staff Nurse Lisbon arrived suddenly in a flurry of activity. Her starched uniform seemed to rustle more than those of the other nurses. She was bright and cheerful. Too cheerful. 'We'll soon have you back into a routine.

'What time is the physio coming tomorrow?' She was talking to the nurse now.

'Eleven-thirty, just after Speech.'

'Occupational?'

'She's dropping by somewhere between five and six, before tea-time in any case.'

'Good. We don't want to slow her recovery with too much sympathy, do we?' She raised her eyebrows at her blushing inferior.

*Sympathy?* Patsy felt like digging her nails in.

Sliding one arm carefully but firmly under Patsy's breasts and pushing the other behind her back, Lisbon instructed the nurse to support Patsy's neck. Once they had eased her into a sitting position, with a quick, efficient manoeuvre Lisbon adjusted the backrest and pulled the pillows together to form a comfortable support. Then, with the help of the nurse, she slowly eased Patsy back.

'There we are. Wasn't too painful, was it?' She looked at her watch. 'I'm just going to give Nurse Brody a hand with her paraplegic. Buzz if you need any help. Back in a few minutes.' She turned to Patsy. 'We'll have those head bandages off tomorrow,' she said, and left the room. Patsy felt as if a whirlwind had just passed through.

'She's good at her job,' the nurse shrugged.

Patsy slowly raised her hand and pointed to a small notepad in the nurse's top pocket, and as if by telepathy the nurse knew exactly what she wanted. She held the pad in front of her and placed a pencil in Patsy's hand. With difficulty she scrawled the word *name* and then pointed to the nurse.

'Carol.' She looked overwhelmed. 'The doctor hoped you wouldn't be as damaged as they first thought. And you're not, are you? I'm really pleased for you, Patricia.'

She held her hand poised to write another word. *Bitch*. She pointed to the open doorway.

'No,' Nurse Carol laughed, 'she's all right really. Once you get used to her. You'll see.'

She wrote another word, *Bitch*, and pointed to the door again.

'Well maybe ... who knows?' She flopped into the chair. 'Well – all we have to do now is get you talking and walking. Not much to ask, is it?'

Letting the pencil drop from her hand, Patsy fell back on to her pillows and rested, hoping the sudden light buzzing in her head would stop. When the feeling of nausea had receded, she grabbed Nurse Carol's hand and gripped it.

'My God, you've gone as white as a sheet.' Her hand flew to the buzzer and within seconds Lisbon was back.

'What's wrong?' She flashed a look at Patsy and sat on the edge of the bed, reaching for her hand. 'It's to be expected. Take long deep breaths.'

She did as she was told and was more than relieved when it passed. She thought something had gone badly wrong.

'If you had been standing up you would have fainted. And that's the very reason why we've had you sitting up today. Your brain's got used to you lying flat. We have to inform it that Patricia Hemmingway is not going to remain immobilized.

'That was your first step, and since the colour is creeping back into your face, we can say that it was successful.' She looked at her watch. 'Two more minutes in the upright position and then it's back down again. OK?'

She rushed from the room again. 'Back in a minute.'

'See what I mean?' Carol beamed. 'She's good.'

*Yes*, Patsy thought, *she is good, but I still don't like her. But then I don't have to.* Moving in slow motion, she picked up the pencil again and looked into Carol's face. The pad was there in a flash. *Sleep.* She barely managed to finish the badly scrawled word.,

'Yes. I'll give you your medication while you're sitting up. Then you can rest until tea-time. How does that sound?'

Patsy was too exhausted to nod, even if she could. She

would like to have given herself that test, but she had not an ounce of energy. Writing that last word had finished her for the day.

'Now I'm going to write something, Patsy. Something that will stay with me for a long time. I'm going to write out your notes. "My patient wrote her first words since the accident."'

As Patsy closed her eyes, Jac's freckled face filled her mind. *Soon, Jac. Soon.*

Just a few days after Jack had promised Laura not to see Patsy without her, he changed his mind. *Just this once,* he told himself, *for Patsy's sake.*

'I'm just going round the Carpenters', Laura.' Jack rolled down his shirtsleeves. 'An unofficial meeting's been called.'

'Over the pay rise?' Laura feigned interest, hoping secretly that with the threat of mechanization at the docks decent redundancy offers would follow. One that Jack would be happy to accept.

'No. The employers 'ave scored on that point. We're bloody lucky to be squeezing a pound rise out of 'em. Tight bastards.' He pushed his chin up and struggled to fasten his top button. 'Some of us are worried what containerization is really gonna mean to dockers. It's pretty obvious that there'll be too many men for the work...' He slipped his tie under his collar and stood in front of Laura for her to tie the knot for him.

'What – even if they stop the governors employing casual labourers?'

He raised an eyebrow. 'You wait, once the full force of mechanization, containerization in particular, hits the docks, there'll be no stopping it. Manning levels will be cut – you wait and see.'

Laura chuckled quietly. 'Hop-picking all over again. Machines to take over from people...'

'Exactly. Anyway, that's what we'll be talking about. Not that we can do much to stop progress, but at least the men can let off a bit of steam, eh?'

'I was reading a bit in the paper the other day about the canals. How they should be used again, not for moving tree trunks and coal to the docks, the way the barges used to, but more for recreation. Pleasure trips.'

Jack grinned at her. 'Pleasure trips?'

'Yeah – boat trips, fishing, riverside walks...'

He shook his head and laughed. 'Riverside walks. Yeah, if you can get through the jungle of nettles and rusty old iron. The canal's a bloody junkyard now. Recreation?' He laughed louder. 'Boat trips? It bloody stinks down there. Who's gonna want to sit on a barge and sail up that sewer?'

'They're gonna clean it up, Jack – that's the whole point! Gonna make it a feature. A committee's being set up. I was thinking of going to the open meeting.'

'Oh yeah?' Jack's tone made it clear he didn't approve. 'They wanna clean up the streets first. How long's it been since the war ended? Twenty years – and some of the bomb-sites 'aven't been cleared.' He stood in the doorway. 'And what about the poor sods still living in prefabs – which were meant to be temporary 'omes?'

'I'll see if Kay wants to come with me. She'll think it's a nice idea.' Laura was determined not to let Jack put her down.

'Yeah – you do that,' he grinned and left.

254

Making his way towards the London Hospital, Jack's mind was full of memories of the waterways, how it used to be. As far as he was concerned the canal traffic should never have been allowed to decline. He could see the point of using the roads for speed where such things as newspapers and perishable fruits were concerned, that was obvious, but not for big imperishable cargoes.

If the Planning committee had any sense, they would forget pleasure trips and use the rivers to help ease the burden of congestion on the roads – if the one he was about to cross was anything to go by. Whitechapel was bad enough in the evenings and at weekends, let alone the rush hour.

As he walked into the hallway of the hospital, he quickly checked his surroundings and was relieved not to see any familiar faces. All he could hope now was that none of Patsy's relatives were visiting. The last thing he wanted was for it to get back to Laura that he had broken his promise.

No matter how Jack had tried to see things from her point of view, he couldn't bring himself to visit Patsy, after four years, with Laura hanging on his arm. It didn't seem right.

'Patricia...' Nurse Carol touched Patsy's shoulder. 'Are you asleep?'

'No one calls her Patricia you know. It's Patsy. Her mother should 'ave told you that.'

Jack's familiar voice shook Patsy. She hadn't heard it in a very long time but there was no mistaking it. *If I keep my eyes shut, will you stay, I wonder? Will you sit by my bed the way my parents do and talk to me as if you're trying to pull me back from the brink of death? Will you*

*speak as if you know I can hear everything one minute
and the next ask a nurse if I can?*

*I would like to open my eyes for you, Jack, see you
again, but...*

'I'm sure she's not asleep you know,' the nurse giggled
quietly. 'She never opens her eyes when there's a
visitor.'

'And at other times?'

'Oh yes.' She gave Jack a knowing smile. 'She can see
if she wants to.'

*You bitch. Just you wait until he's gone. I'll make your
life a misery. My finger will be on that buzzer every five
minutes.*

'Come on, Patricia ... or should I say Patsy? He's
worth making the effort for.' She gave Jack a flirta-
tious look. 'Very handsome. Lovely blue eyes, blonde
hair...'

Patsy could hear Jack chuckling. He was enjoying the
compliments. Same old Jack. If he imagined for one
minute that Patsy was going to open her eyes and fall
for his good looks and charm again, he was mistaken.

There was only one thing she wanted from him now –
a signature. She had failed in her first attempt to get her
son back and had no one to blame but herself. She had
played her hand very badly.

Being forced to lie back and think for hours on end in
that God-forsaken room had turned out to be a blessing
in disguise. She had worked out another plan to fight
the Armstrongs and win back her boy. She would get
public opinion on her side. She would engineer it so that
a journalist would interview her about the charge of
fraud which she had yet to face. She would tell the story

her way. That the Armstrongs had refused to tell Jac that he was adopted and wouldn't, under any circumstances, let Patsy see him.

She would tell the newspapers that she had been driven to crime. That she needed the money so she could take her son and begin a new life for both of them. She would blame Tom, who had made her give him up in the first place. She would say that Kay Armstrong bulldozed her way into the children's home one day and told Jac he had a sister.

Patsy had to stop herself smiling. It wouldn't do for Jack to see that she was feeling on top of things.

'She looks as if she's asleep,' Jack said. 'Maybe I should go and have a cup of tea, come back in twenty minutes or so?'

'Mmmm. Or I could leave you with her. You can sit here if you like, until she decides to open her eyes.'

'You really think she's having us on?'

'I know she is. And she knows I know. Ever since I discovered she could use her legs...'

Patsy found their conversation quite refreshing. The silly girl had a lot to learn about human nature. Maybe it was time to shock her into reality. Talk to her right out of the blue. Scolding herself for even thinking it, she settled for opening her eyes.

'Ah, you're awake,' nurse smiled. 'You've got a visitor.' She turned to Jack. 'I'll be in the ward should she need me.'

Jack nodded and sat on the chair next to the bed. 'Hello Patsy.' He waited patiently, hoping for a response.

Patsy stared up at the ceiling, leading him to believe she couldn't move a muscle. Her determination gave her

*Sally Worboyes*

the inner strength she needed. What a position to be in! She held the trump card.

Jack carefully lifted her hand into his. 'I'm sorry this has happened to someone like you, Patsy. You was always full of life.'

*Yes, Jack, and I shall be, once my batteries have been recharged. You're in for a fight – unless of course you join me?* That thought hadn't really occurred to her before. Maybe he would be happy to leave Laura, help Patsy to fight for their child. Move away with her to start again. It had been her goal once, when she first came back, when she was fighting fit and looking good, but now ... who knew what he would feel?

Maybe she should test him. After all, she had nothing to lose. Why not play on his sympathy? She moved her eyes as if it caused her pain to do so, and looked into his face.

'There're things I want to say.' He inhaled slowly and pushed his hand through his hair. 'They told me you still hadn't got your speech back.' He couldn't stop himself smiling. 'You always did talk too much anyway.' He stroked her hand. 'I'll tell you what. Let's work out a system. Close your eyes once for no and twice for yes.'

She dutifully closed her eyes twice for yes. It felt good taking the piss out of him.

'At least we can have a conversation – a one-sided one, but that's better than nothing.'

*I want my son back, Jack.*

'Your mum and dad 'ave been to see us. They want to see Jac. I don't think it's a good idea, Patsy, not yet. We haven't told him. We think he's a bit too young to cope

258

with knowing. But we will tell 'im, that's a promise. As soon as you're back to your old self. You wouldn't want him to see you like this, would yer?'

Patsy closed her eyes once, just to keep him talking. Best she knew everything now so she could execute her plan knowing exactly the way his mind was working.

'Once he's got used to the idea, you can visit him now and then.'

*Now and then? If only you knew.*

'And if he wanted to, I could get our Kay to bring him up to see you. Spend a Sunday together. You'd like that, wouldn't you?'

*Not good enough. I want more. Much more.*

'I'm thinking of leaving the East End.' He smiled his old little-boy smile. 'Running a small country pub in Kent. I've 'ad enough of the docks. It's changed, Patsy. I want out.'

She turned her face away and looked up at the ceiling.

'And it'll be good for Jac. All that country air.' He squeezed Patsy's hand. 'You wait till you see 'im. He's a smashing little kid. You turned out a good one there.

'You should have another kid, Patsy. Get yourself married. A lovely-looking woman like you.'

'I want my son back.' Her voice was a monotone.

'Fuck me!' Jack reached for the buzzer. He thought there had been a sudden breakthrough, brought on by him.

'No! Don't.' She glared at him. 'They don't know. Now listen. Jac knows who I am. And he loves me.'

Jack looked at her through puzzled eyes. His face was full of question and she lapped it up. The rug had been pulled from under his feet.

259

'My brain is fine. Any mother would want her son. You've got Kay. She'll give you grandchildren. If you don't give me Jac I'll take him, any way I have to.

'I'll use the press to get at you and Laura. I'll do everything to make your lives miserable – and that's bound to have a lasting effect on our son. If I have to I'll steal him the way I intended to and still get the sympathy of the public.'

'You can't be serious?'

'No? Try me.'

'Not if you've got your son's welfare at heart, Patsy.'

'It's my welfare that I'm looking out for now. Me. I'm the one who deserves a bit of happiness.'

'I won't deny that. But Jac's not gonna give you what you want. He'll tie you down. You won't be able to work with him to look after. You know how much you value your freedom. Well, you used to anyway.'

'Still the same old Jack. The talker. Well it won't work this time. Jac is my son and I will have him. Get that into your head and it'll make things easier all round.'

'What if he wants to stay with us?'

Patsy closed her eyes and smiled. 'Stop dreaming. I'm his mother. Of course he'll want to be with me. Especially when I start sending him one or two of his old soft toys I kept back.'

Patsy felt smug. She had taken the wind out of his sails and left him speechless. She waited a few moments and then opened her eyes. Anger filled her again as he disappeared through the doorway without saying goodbye.

'Fuck you too, Jack. Fuck you too.'

* * *

When Jack stormed into the front room in a thunderous mood, Laura thought something had gone wrong at the meeting. When he went straight to the sideboard and pulled out the half-bottle of whisky, she knew that it was much worse.

'Where's Jac?' he demanded.

'In bed. Why?' Laura watched as he poured two large whiskies.

'Here, drink this. You're gonna need it.' Jack swallowed his drink in one gulp. 'Right, I've got something to tell you and I don't want you to interrupt me. You can have your say later on. I've just come from the hospital, from seeing Patsy. She's not as ill as she's leading 'em to believe. Don't ask me why, cos I 'aven't worked that bit out yet.' He poured himself another whisky.

'She came to Stepney to steal Jac away from us. He *was* in her house that day and I'm sure he pushed her down the stairs. He probably thinks she's dead – that he killed her.'

Laura opened her mouth ready to speak but he stopped her. 'Now then, Jac – is he asleep yet?'

'No. He's reading Book Six.'

'Good. I'm getting 'im up. He's gonna learn the truth.'

'No, Jack!'

'Yes!'

Laura was so stunned she couldn't think. Her mind was a complete blank. Her world seemed to be collapsing around her and there was nothing she could do to stop it.

With the bewildered Jac in his arms, Jack strode back into the room. He sat the boy down on the settee. 'Now then son, I've got some good news for you. The first bit you already know about – you've got two mums instead of one, right?'

Jac gazed into his dad's face, narrowing his eyes beneath a deep frown.

'And the one you think you pushed down the stairs is alive and kicking. I've just been to see her. She sends her love.'

Jac's bottom lip curled. 'I thought she was dead.'

'I know. But she's not. She's in hospital, and they've made her head better. It was just a bad bump caused by an accident. Her fault – not yours.'

'But she didn't move ... she just laid there...' He wiped the tears from his cheeks and sniffed.

'She was knocked out for a little while but she's all right now. Do you wanna go and see for yourself? I'll take you now if you want me to.'

'No!' He looked across at Laura and did his best to speak normally, as if he wasn't on the verge of an outburst. 'Will you still be my mum?'

'Once she's out of hospital, she can come here and visit you, if you want her to,' Jack quickly said, covering for Laura who couldn't speak.

'I liked her at first until she scared me. She wanted to take me to Scotland. I thought she was just a dinner lady.'

Jack and Laura looked at each other and then the penny dropped. 'At your school you mean?'

Jac burst into a storm of tears, crying like he had never cried before.

Scooping him into his arms, Jack held him tight. 'It's all right son, it's all over now. She just wanted to take you home with her, that's all. She didn't realize how much we loved you.'

'Will she come back after me?' he said between sobs.

'No. She's sorry she scared you. She told me to say that. She's very, very sorry. She can't wait to go home. Away from Stepney. A long way away.'

'Can I sleep with you and Mummy tonight?'

''Course you can. You can lay on the settee till you fall asleep and when Mummy goes to bed, you can go with 'er. All right? I'll sleep in your bed—'

'No! I want you in bed wiv us!'

'Fine. That's good, if that's what you want.' He hugged Jac again and hid his face, composing himself. 'No more nightmares, OK? It's over.'

'What about Conker? Can he come in your bedroom as well?' Jac wiped his runny nose on the sleeve of his pyjamas.

'If you like, yeah. And tomorrow we'll go and see Patsy in the hospital. So you can see for yourself that she's OK.'

'Will she want to see me?' Jac's bottom lip began to tremble again as another lone sob escaped.

'I think so, yeah. We'll go together.' He looked over Jac's shoulder at Laura. 'All three of us.'

# Chapter Ten

As Patsy lay in her bed, she tried to think of ways round her new predicament. She couldn't trust Jack not to say anything about her state of health. She cursed herself for being weak and breaking her cover. Now she must plan her next move.

Certain that she could fool the hospital staff into believing that she had made a miraculous recovery, stimulated by her ex-lover, Patsy wondered if it was the right thing to do. Once she was out of the hospital she would be faced with charges of fraud and deception. Her thoughts flew back to gaining public sympathy through the newspapers, but would it work? *Today's news is tomorrow's fish and chip wrappings* was something she had heard somewhere and it had lodged in her mind.

Maybe she could try playing for sympathy. Get Laura Armstrong on her side. Patsy wouldn't get custody of Jac now that she was wanted by the police. She could even end up in prison if she didn't play her cards right.

The odds seemed heavily stacked against her but she felt defiant. After all, being in the position of having nothing, she had everything to gain. And if she had worked that out, it was a dead cert that Jack's mind would be running on the same track. He had more to lose, and that would increase the fight in him. How could she take him on and win?

*Jac's my son! My boy. I gave birth to him and I will get him back,* she told herself. *Even if it means dragging him halfway across the world to a country where the British authorities can't get their hands on him.* She would have to do some research. Find a safe haven. Then maybe she would attach herself to a man who had been born in her chosen country. Get him to help her. She could always drop the foreigner once she had reached her goal. Yes. That was the way. That would be her next move. Get out of that hospital and achieve her ambition.

'How are we this morning, then?' Nurse Carol was back on duty. 'You're looking a bit flushed.' She lifted Patsy's hand and took her pulse. Before she could pop the thermometer into her mouth, Patsy smiled at her.

'I'm feeling great.' And so she was. To see the shocked expression on the nurse's face was better than any medicine. 'It's a miracle, Carol. Did you light a special candle for me?' Patsy was determined to get as many people on her side as she could. 'I feel tired and heavy ... and my head hurts a little bit but other than that...' She half closed her eyes for effect. 'Did you? Did you light a candle for me?' she murmured.

'On Sunday, yes, but—'

'You're a saint. I think it first started when you gave me that massage ... I felt a warm tingling ... but it went away again once you'd stopped.' She squeezed Nurse Carol's hand. 'You are a healer...'

Dropping into the chair, the nurse looked into Patsy's face. 'I don't know what to say.'

'How about "Would you like something to eat, Patsy?" I'm starving.'

'Do you mind if I just sit here for a minute?'

'Of course not, Carol,' Patsy drawled. 'We'll ... share this very special moment.' She sighed sleepily. 'Just the two of us. The healed and the healer.' Patsy was having a field-day. Acting, she believed, had always been her forte. 'Let's just be quiet,' she said, her voice full of sincerity. 'I'll leave it to you to pass on this good news.'

Nurse Carol nodded, wiped her eyes and left the room, too choked to speak.

With her eyes closed Patsy took deep breaths. Her behaviour now would be of the utmost importance.

'Hello, Patsy,' Jack's voice shook her to the bone. 'I've brought Laura and Jac to see you. Shall I tell them to come in?'

'Yes, Jack.' Patsy allowed her eyelids to open slowly and then droop again. She spoke in a slow, tired voice. Her play-acting would have to be right up to scratch.

'Thank you for coming, Laura. Come and sit down.' She looked from her rival to Jac. 'I owe you an apology, little man.'

Pulling up a chair for himself and Laura, Jack nodded to his boy to sit in the one already by the bed. 'We won't stop long. Don't wanna tire you,' Jack said.

Taking a chair from Jack, Laura placed it as close to Jac's side as possible and sat down. 'Are you OK?'

'Not exactly my old self, Laura, but maybe that's as well. I've had plenty of time to think. I hope you can forgive me.' She stroked Jac's face. 'It's just that I'd been pining for...' She turned to Jack. 'I was being selfish. I was blinded by my own needs. And I'm really sorry for trying to take Jac from you. I've no rights... He might be my son, but you're his wards now, his guardians...'

'We're his parents.' Laura looked straight into Patsy's eyes. A no-nonsense look which dared her to behave badly.

Picking up on the tension, Jack added: 'We've told Jac that he's got two mothers, Patsy, and what a lucky boy he is—'

'Two mothers?' Patsy half smiled and looked up at the ceiling. 'Yes – I suppose that's one way of looking at it. You've been taking care of my child for me, Laura, being his mum when I couldn't be. You are a lucky boy, Jac. Your dad's right.'

'I 'ave to stop with my mum though.' Jac lowered his eyes.

'Of course you do. She can look after you better than I can. I've been very naughty. And I'm in a lot of trouble.' She grinned and shrugged, feeling confident that she would win him over.

'You're not in trouble with us – is she, Dad?' He looked pleadingly into Jack's face. 'You're not angry, are you?'

''Course not.'

'Ah – you're a good kid, Jac. But I'm afraid the police are not going to be as nice to me. You remember I told you that people were going to move into the house the next day, once we were in Scotland? Well, I said that more than one person could live there. And, so that we

could pay for train fares and food, I took money from
people when I shouldn't have done. They will be paid
back, of course...'

'So,' Laura cut in, 'you came out of your coma fighting
fit,' she said, trying to keep her cool. 'No brain damage
after all.'

'I've been very lucky. God has forgiven me.' Patsy
closed her eyes. 'All I can hope is that Jac will forgive me
too.'

'I do. Don't I, Dad?'

'Yeah. 'Course.' Jack looked on, bemused at the scene.
He didn't quite know how to handle it. Didn't know
whether to believe Patsy's sudden change of heart. It
was evident that Laura wasn't swallowing any of it. The
expression on her face made it clear what she was
thinking.

Opening her eyes, Patsy decided she must work on
Jack's wife. 'When I say I'm sorry, Laura, I mean – for
everything. Right back to the beginning.'

Laura raised an eyebrow but remained silent, unable
to muster even a glimpse of a smile.

'I'll get out of your life. As soon as I'm strong enough to
be discharged and face the music. I expect you'd like me
to go to the farthest corner of the world. And who could
blame you?'

'No she wouldn't.' Jac answered for his mum. 'Otherwise I'd never see you again.' He could feel himself
blushing. But Patsy knew exactly what he was about to
say and it was just what she wanted. He was accepting
the fact that she was his mother.

Closing her eyes again, Patsy made excuses that she
was tired and needed to sleep. She wanted them to go

before another round began, when she might lose a few points.

'We'll drop in again, Patsy,' Jack said, 'and fetch you some fruit and flowers.' He instantly regretted his words, realizing they would cut Laura deep.

Patsy slowly raised her hand to show her thanks, and then let it flop down as if exhausted.

As she stood in the doorway, Laura watched Jac as he gazed into Patsy's face. 'It's time to go, Jac.'

Surprising all three of them, Jac suddenly leaned over Patsy and brushed a kiss across her cheek. 'Get better soon,' he said and rushed out of the room.

As they walked along the corridor, Laura felt an urge to go back and talk to Patsy in private. She had been left with a tight feeling in her chest and a strong notion that something was wrong. She had felt threatened in that room, and the fear was still in her.

'You two go ahead, I'll catch you up. I've left something behind.' She threw a warning look at Jack – she didn't want him to stop her.

'All right. Don't get talking,' he said, hoping she would catch his double meaning. 'I know what you women are like when you get together,' he added, for the benefit of Jac.

'OK, Patsy – what's all the niceties about? And don't pretend you're asleep because I know you're not. I wasn't born yesterday.'

Keeping up the pretence, Patsy opened her eyes as if she were coming out of a light sleep. 'Laura? I thought you'd gone.'

'What are you up to?'

Patsy sighed and rolled her eyes. 'What can I get up to

now, eh? I'm not as well as I made out when Jac was in here. I didn't want to upset your son.'

'Oh ... you agree that he is mine now, then?'

'What's done is done. You surely can't blame me for wanting to see him? I love him as much as you do, Laura. I can't tell you how much pain I've suffered ... how many nights I've cried myself to sleep. Many's the time I've thought about chucking myself off a bridge...' Patsy was really enjoying herself now. She could tell by Laura's face that she had her listening – maybe believing.

'Try to put yourself in my place, Laura. How would you feel?'

'I have put myself in your place and yes, you must have suffered, I can see that, but—'

'Why don't you sit down? I'm not too ill to listen to you.' She feigned a weak smile. 'So long as you don't start shouting at me for the wrong I did all those years ago.'

'Of course I won't, that's all in the past.' Laura sat down. Her feelings were softening. 'Is that all you're worrying about? In case I'm here to get some kind of revenge?'

'I wouldn't blame you. No one would. I've had a long time to think about things. I've messed things up, haven't I? Couldn't keep Jack; lost Tom; lost my son. Then there's my parents – what I've put them through.' She sighed and shed a crocodile tear. 'I deserve what's coming to me.'

'And what's that?'

'Prison, I shouldn't wonder. Fraud? The law doesn't take kindly to that.'

'It was the way you did it, Patsy. Old Mrs Simons had been living in that house for a very long time.'

'I never threw her out, Laura.' She pulled herself up as if she were in pain. 'Could you prop those pillows behind my back...?'

'You're not gonna tell me she went of her own free will?'

'That's exactly what did happen. She came up to see me one night, full of tears and trembling. I asked what the matter was and she began to reel out this incredible story of how she had been taking rent for years, under false pretences. I couldn't believe it at first. She seemed such a nice old lady.'

Having made Patsy comfortable, Laura sat down again. 'I must say, I did think it odd that she left without a fight.'

'I told her to stay with her brother for a few weeks while I sorted it all out for her. It was only once she'd gone that the idea of doing the same came to me. It seemed like a good idea at the time. Ideas are a bit like that, aren't they? Great when you first think of them.'

'So what now? What are your plans?'

Patsy flopped her head back and sighed. 'I don't have any. Of course I'd like to stay in the area, see you and Jac now and then.' She shed another tear. 'I think if we had started on a different footing we could have become good friends. We did have something in common.' She looked at Laura and shrugged. 'Jack?'

'Yeah ... he's got something to answer for I suppose.'

'I think it's best for everyone if I just go away. God knows where to. But far enough so I don't interfere with your lives again. Especially not Jac's. It's not fair on the poor little devil.

'You know what I need? What I've needed for a long time? Someone to talk to. Daft, isn't it? How does the song go? "The best things in life are free" ... It's true, but the best things are very hard to come by. You have to earn them.' She sighed convincingly. 'I've got a long way to go before I can start again.'

'I've been a bit selfish, Patsy,' Laura suddenly put in. 'Only thinking of my side of things. Of course you can see Jac. He's your son. Just keep in touch as to when you'll be discharged from hospital and where you'll be living. Let's hope it's not Holloway,' she smiled. 'OK? Then we'll start making arrangements. And you don't 'ave to move out of the area. Why should you?'

'Thanks, Laura.'

'I can't really help you out over the fraud, but I'm sure they'll be lenient with you – under the circumstances.'

'We'll see. And Laura, just in case it's in your mind – I'm not after your husband. It's water under the bridge as far as I'm concerned, and from what I picked up yesterday, he feels the same.

'He never stopped loving you, you know, Laura. Never. And the sod openly admitted it to me as well. No, all I want is to see my boy now and then.

'I've got a new life to start – and to be honest, there is someone ... my parents won't like it ...' She raised her eyebrows. 'He's a foreigner – Cypriot. Born and bred over here, but he's dark-skinned and they're so old-fashioned. I was going to give him up, but I'm not now. I

realized, lying here night after night, how much we care
for each other. It could be love even. Who knows?'

Once Laura had gone, Patsy had to stop herself
laughing out loud at the silly cow. She had taken it all in
– even the last lie which had only just come to her while
they were talking. A Cypriot boyfriend? Well – it was a
flash of inspiration all right. Now she would have to find
one to fit the bill – and then use everything she had to
persuade him to take her back to his homeland – with
her little boy.

Peeling herself an orange, Patsy's mind turned to
Kay. She was the only one left to be manipulated. They
had got on quite well when they first met back in 1962.
Providing Patsy handled her with care she might not be
a threat. She made a mental note to ask Laura on her
next visit if Kay might come, so that she could apologize
to her too.


A week had passed since Kay and Steve had broken
up, and she decided it was time to face her parents and
tell them what had happened. Her face was still
bruised, but at least the swelling had gone down and
she could probably get away with saying she had
slipped down the stairs. She knew Jac hadn't said
anything or her dad would surely have been round by
now to fetch her home.

Pulling her dressing-gown around her, she was taken
aback when the telephone rang early on a Sunday
morning. She wondered if it was Steve, phoning to say
he was sorry.

She picked up the receiver cautiously and waited for
the caller to speak first.

'Hello Kay, it's Zacchi.'

'Zacchi?' Her voice sounded hollow. 'Where are you phoning from?'

'My flat. The cleaner scribbled a note by the phone to say you'd called.'

'But I thought you were letting the flat, and that you weren't coming back for six months?'

'I changed my plans. I want to see you. I think we should talk.'

'What about?'

'Us.'

'What if Steve had answered the phone, Zacchi? What do you think he would have thought, you phoning me this early?' Kay was irritated by his casual manner. She was, after all, a married woman, as far as he knew.

'I don't really care what he would have thought. I need to see you. I've hardly slept for thinking about us. Can you get away for an hour?'

'I can get away for a lot longer than that. Steve's not here. We've split up. But I'm not going to see you, Zacchi. You'll only confuse me again. I'm going away – for longer than six months. I'm going to the Bahamas to work. Pamela's taking care of the arrangements.'

Hearing Zacchi laugh made her angry. 'What's so funny?'

'You are. There's no way you could have planned something like that in such a short time. But that's not why I'm laughing. Steve's out of your life – now that *is* believable.'

'I know you'll find this difficult to understand, but so are you. You weren't there when I needed you, so you know what you can do now!' She slammed the receiver down and then took it off the hook. Fuck him.

Sweeping her long hair into a topknot and securing it with pins, she decided to cook herself some breakfast before soaking in the bath. She fancied a good fry-up. The works.

After putting on a long-playing record of the Beatles, she went into the kitchen and peered into the fridge. Bacon, eggs, tomatoes and a few mushrooms were the order of the day. Some fried bread too. Her weight had dropped a bit over the past week so she didn't care about the calories. It would take no time to put back the few pounds she had lost and get up to her proper weight of nine stone ten.

She ate her delicious breakfast with relish, left the dishes and went into the bathroom, turned on the taps and selected her favourite foam bath – Je Reviens. Checking her face in the mirror she was pleased that, apart from the bruises, she was looking like her old self again. It had been a nightmare of a week and the loneliness had at times been unbearable, but she had done it. She had stayed put and seen it through. Surely the worst was over now, and she could look forward to a new life with a bit of joy in it.

Lowering herself into the soft foam she felt wonderfully relaxed, and she blew soap bubbles off the palm of her hand. Then changing position slightly so that her foam-covered breasts were above the water, she closed her eyes and drew a finger across a nipple, bringing first Steve's face into her mind and then Zacchi's, visualizing his dark-blue eyes looking into her face.

The sound of the doorbell brought her sharply back to the present. She lay very still, listening to make sure the ringing had been real and not her imagination.

The shrill sound broke through again. She pushed both hands down her body to remove the foam and stepped out of the bath, pulling her light blue towelling robe around her. She had a feeling it might be Pam, here to persuade her out of the house. At least she would get a lift to her parents'.

'What did you mean – I wasn't there when you needed me?' Zacchi said, leaning on the wall with his arms folded. She tried to close the door but he stopped her.

'This isn't funny! I was in the bath!'

'So I see.' He walked past her and took the stairs two at a time. 'You can get back in it. I'll make myself some coffee while I'm waiting!'

Following him into the living room, she shut the door and pushed her wet feet into her slippers. 'What do you want, Zacchi?'

He spun round, grabbed her round the waist and pulled her against him. 'You.' He leaned down, his mouth searching for hers, then she heard his sharply indrawn breath as he took in her bruised face.

'How did this happen? Did he hit you?'

Quietly, she told him about the row with Steve. He heard her out and she felt the relief of unburdening herself. Then the memory of what it had felt like to ring him and find he had gone away resurfaced, and she pushed him away. He pulled her back, kissed her neck, slipped one hand inside her robe and squeezed her bottom. 'Stop playing silly games, Kay. You know I love you.'

Her resistance rapidly melting away, she gave him a friendly thump on the arm. 'Well, why did you *go* then, you sod?' She allowed him to untie the cord of her bathrobe.

'Because I was angry. I couldn't stand to be in this country knowing you were still sleeping with *him*.' He pulled her robe apart and glanced at her moist body. 'You don't need this on. It's hot in here.'

'Yes I do!' she said feebly, making no attempt to close her robe.

Getting down on one knee he looked up at her. 'Will you jump over the broomstick with me?' he joked. Then pressing his head against her stomach he murmured, 'I love you, Kay.'

Unable to stop him, her legs relaxed and she felt like screaming as he began to kiss her. 'You bastard . . .' she murmured, 'you know I can't resist you when you do that.'

Easing her down on to the floor with him, he pushed the robe off her shoulders. 'No, don't, Zac. Leave it on.' She kissed him lightly on the mouth.

'Why?' His voice had taken on that familiar deep husky tone which she loved.

'Because it's nice like this.' Her hands pulled at his leather belt and her body trembled with desire as she unbuckled it. 'Straight in, Zac. No messing. I want you now.'

She didn't have to ask twice. He pushed himself inside her and within seconds they were writhing in ecstasy, crashing against each other until together they reached a climax and their cries of arousal faded.

As they lay still, hugging each other, enjoying the

pulsating in their veins, the only sound their breathing, Kay knew that her love for Zacchi would never go away. He was part of her. Leaving him for another life was going to prove painful for both of them. She was going to have to be strong. Stronger than she had been in the past.

Curled up on the sofa, with Zacchi stretched out, his head resting on Kay's breasts, she stroked the side of his face. 'Zac?'

'Mmmmm?'

'You do realize how much it means to me, taking this job in Nassau?'

'You're not going to Nassau and you know it.' Zacchi opened his eyes and looked at her. 'You're staying right here, in London, and so am I.'

'No, Zac. I have to go.' She turned her head away, searching for the right words. 'I know I've been ... well, at least I've pretended to be OK about me and Steve breaking up but, well, it's been a nightmare. I'm fine by day, especially if the sun's shining, but at night, when I go to bed, I feel so miserable ... so *ashamed*.'

'He did the thumping, not you. He was the one who'd been deceiving you all this time. He's the one who walked out, not you.'

'I know all that. But I can't help it. I feel like a total failure. Don't ask me why. Perhaps it's because I had my own secret too, our secret.'

'I can understand that. But why run away to the Bahamas? What difference will that make, except that I won't be there to pick up the pieces when you fall apart again?'

'I don't know why. I just know I have to go. And I'm not being dramatic. Or playing silly games.'

'Are you saying this is it?'

She kissed him lightly on the forehead. 'Yes.'

'No more to say then, is there?'

'You can visit me. I'll come home after three months for a visit. And if it doesn't work out—'

'Zacchi will always be there.'

'No, that's *not* what I meant. You say you love me, right? And I know I love you. Well if it is love, one hundred per cent, then it should survive us being apart for a year or two.'

'That's rubbish and you know it. What you're asking is for me to wait. You go, and I'm back out there and into a relationship, if one happens my way.'

'I realize that.'

He jerked away from her and jumped off the sofa. 'What *is* this? Some kind of sick deal you want to set up? We each have relationships, as many as it takes, and then if we both happen to be footloose at the same time, sometime, our love's been tried and tested? Is that what you're saying?'

'No! God, you're bloody *impossible*. I'm saying it's *my* risk. I might lose you, I know that! But it's a risk I've got to take!' She clenched her fists and yelled at him. 'I've *got* to go! And I'm not going out there looking for an affair! I'm still hurting...'

'Steve meant so much to you that you're prepared to throw away what we've got – which is, and always was, more than the pair of you ever had, and you know it.'

'I can't explain it, but all I know is that I can't commit

myself yet. I can't be anything more to you than a soul mate. I just can't.'

Zacchi found that amusing. 'Soul mates don't usually do what we just did. Maybe you see me as a lover, a part-time lover?'

'No...'

'Perhaps it's me you're running away from?'

'I don't know.' She smiled and slowly shook her head. 'Or it might be that I've got wanderlust and I simply want to go to the Bahamas, to the sunshine.'

'OK. Fine. Call me when you get back.' His temper was beginning to calm now, but he was still annoyed with her.

'Of course I will. Just try not to get involved with someone else, for a while at least. Surely that's not asking for too much?'

His silence as he got up and went to the bathroom said more than any words could, and Kay knew she *was* taking a big risk by leaving him to the temptations that lay 'out there'.

Pulling up outside the block of flats, Zacchi wondered whether he might just drop Kay off and drive away without another word, or have a final crack at making her see sense. One thing he did know was that if she flew away, he had a very painful time ahead of him. A day didn't pass when he didn't think about her.

'I could do with some moral support, Zac, but it might backfire. You know what Dad's like. He needs someone to blame, and you would be first in line.'

Moral support? What did she take him for? When he saw the expression on her face, the strain and the misery, he softened. 'Tell me what you want me to do, Kay.'

'I don't suppose...' she avoided his eyes. 'It would be a bit much, really ... can I ask you to wait here until I come down and let you know if it's OK to come up, once I've told them?'

'I've got nothing better to do.'

He looked at his watch. 'Right, it's half past twelve. I'll give you until one o'clock. I'll be back then, and if you're not down here waiting, I'll go.'

'Where've you been, Kay? I've had Conker for ages and you haven't been to see us!'

Kay put her arms around her brother and gave him a kiss. 'Hug me then.'

Wrapping his arms around her neck he whispered in her ear, 'I've got two mums but I love ours the best.'

'Is that right?'

'Well, I don't *love* the other one ... but she's all right.'

'Well, well, well. Look who the wind's blown in!' Jack pulled his son out of Kay's embrace and swung him by the arms, landing him on his feet. Then, smiling broadly, he drew his daughter to him. 'We thought you'd forgotten all about us.'

'No, Dad.' She spoke in a quiet voice. 'I've had a few problems. I didn't want you to see me...' She turned the bruised side of her face away from him.

'All right ... all right. Come and sit down.'

'I'm going to say it all quickly, right? I don't want you to react, Dad, against Steve I mean, OK? If you do, I'll run out of this flat, I promise you.' She swallowed and wiped at her tears.

'Steve's left me. He's got someone else. We had a big fight when I found out about her and he hit me. He hit me very hard and more than once. He was seeing her all through our courtship. She was married then but now her divorce is through. It's my own fault, I should have read the signs. I should have known. And before you rant on about him, Steve I mean, you may as well know that I did sleep with Zacchi that night when you hit the roof. So I'm not so innocent, am I?'

Shocked by the revelation, Laura and Jack gazed speechless at their tearful daughter; at her drawn, bruised face. Laura drew a deep breath, composing herself, but Jack sat rigid, as if turned to stone. There was no sign of anger on his face — just a blank look. Several seconds passed without him breathing.

It was Laura who broke the silence. 'I can't believe it,' was all she could manage.

'I smelt perfume on his jacket and found a receipt for a single red rose he sent her on Valentine's Day – this year. He said he should never have married me. But I'm OK now. I've had plenty of time to think. I'm going back to work, but not in this country. I'm going with Pam to the Bahamas, to Nassau. Secretarial with good pay.'

Looking from her mother to Jack, Kay became alarmed. Jack's face was pinched and pale, and his entire body was rigid.

'Dad? You all right?'

He tried to say something but couldn't get the words out. He tried again: 'I can't take any more,' he said, clenching his hands. 'I can't take it.'

Holding an arm each, the two women helped Jack on

to the sofa. 'Ease his legs up, Kay. He should be lying flat.'

'I'm sorry,' Jack managed to say as more colour drained from his face.

'Don't try to speak, Jack. Just lie quietly for a minute.'

'Shall I get Zacchi? He's waiting in the car,' Kay said.

'Yes.' Laura looked earnestly at Kay. 'Don't be long.'

'Oh damn, I forgot. He said he'd be back in half an hour. He's gone to the pub.' She dashed on to the back balcony and saw to her relief that he was still there, leaning against the car, enjoying a quiet cigarette.

'Zacchi!' she yelled to him. 'Zacchi, quick! Come up!' He caught the urgency in her voice and vaulted over the brick wall on to the grass area which led to the block of flats.

'Sit with your dad for a minute, Kay,' Laura instructed, 'while I get him a glass of water. I'll open the door for Zacchi while I'm at it.'

Kneeling by Jack's side, Kay pushed her hand through her dad's hair. 'I'm sorry for causing you all this grief, Dad.'

He shook his head. 'It's not you ... it's everything ... it's ... it's everything.'

'We'll be all right, Dad. You'll see. Things have built up, that's all. Come to a head. It's all been happening around us but we didn't know. It might feel as if the world's collapsing around us but it isn't. It's just come to a head – that's all.' She was trying to convince herself as much as anything.

Taking the glass of water from Laura, Kay met

Zacchi's eyes and smiled at him. 'Thanks for staying around.'

She put the glass to Jack's lips, and held a hand to the back of his head. 'Can you get a couple of pillows, Mum?'

Looking from Jack to Kay, Zacchi was puzzled. 'What's happened, Kay?'

'I blurted it all out in one go and it was a bit much.' She smiled at Jack and was pleased that he could manage to smile back and nod in agreement.

'I'm gonna phone the doctor.'

Jack raised his hand in protest. He took pride in the fact that he never went to the doctor. That he was a fit man.

'It won't be a problem. He'll check you over, that's all.'

'I'll take over now, Kay. You go and tell Jac everything's all right. He's in his room.'

Kay glanced up at Zacchi and felt sorry for him. He looked lonely. As if he was soaking up the sadness, but wasn't part of the family scene.

'Me and Zac are getting back together again. We should never have broken up in the first place.' Zacchi turned his face away from her.

As she passed him on her way out of the room, Kay stood on tiptoe and kissed him on the cheek. 'I love you.'

Grabbing her hand, Zacchi stopped her. 'And the Bahamas?'

'Bananas to the Bahamas.' She squeezed his arm. 'Why don't you spend some time with Dad?'

Sitting down in an armchair, Zacchi reached across to Jack and offered his hand. 'No hard feelings?'

'About what?'

'Me and your daughter.'

'Tch . . . I'm the one who should apologize, Zac. What a life, eh? I hope you know what you're letting yourself in for.' Jack closed his eyes and sighed. 'Kay's a stubborn little cow, you know.'

'But we can't help loving her.'

'I'm gonna 'ave to doze off, Zacchi. I feel as if all the life's drained out of me.'

'That's all right. I could do with a bit of shut-eye myself.' He stretched out his long legs and sank his head into a cushion.

Laura finished giving the emergency doctor her address when she saw Eileen and Albert Hemmingway pass by the kitchen window. Replacing the receiver, she rushed to the street door to catch them before they rang the bell.

'I'm sorry, Laura, but we had to come and see you,' Albert said. 'Can we come in?'

Thinking quickly, Laura ushered them into the kitchen, whispering that they must be quiet. The last thing she wanted now was to have to explain to Jac who they were.

'Just sit down and don't say a word, OK? I'm gonna get Kay to take Jac to the park.'

Pulling Kay out of Jac's bedroom, Laura explained who had arrived and why she wanted Jac out of the way. 'Just you go, Kay. Leave Zacchi with your dad. I think a bit of male company will do him good.'

'Fair enough. But what do they want, Mum? Why are they here? I don't understand.'

'No, I don't suppose you do. I'll explain it all later – once they've gone.' She looked scoldingly at Kay. 'You

shouldn't have taken your phone off the hook. I tried
ringing you, more than once.'

'Have things been happening then?'

'You could say that.'

'It's not just my blurting out my troubles that's made
Dad ill then?'

'No. We've had a bucketful this past week or two.'

Carefully opening the door to the living room, Laura
was relieved to see that Jack was asleep and Zacchi
looking as if he was about to nod off. She closed the door
and went into the kitchen.

'Right,' she said, quietly shutting the door. 'What's
happened?'

'You'd best sit down, Laura,' Eileen said. 'This isn't
going to be easy for any of us.'

*Oh Jesus, what now?* Laura thought. 'Go on then. I'm
listening.'

'We've just come from seeing Patsy. And, well, me and
Albert are a bit worried. Well, more than a bit. I know
you've been in to see her and I think that was really good
of you. That's why we've come round. To tell you what
we ... well, what our fears are.

'We've seen a change in our daughter over the past
couple of years. She seems to have got gradually more
bitter – hard. The way she speaks to us at times—'

'Look. I don't want to push you, but Jack's not very
well and I'm expecting the doctor any minute.'

'I'm sorry to hear that,' Albert said, shaking his
head. 'Let me tell Laura, Eileen. It'll be easier for me.

'Patsy has changed, it's true. Grown older, grown
bitter, call it what you like, but she's turned into a
compulsive liar. We never know when she's telling the

truth. And we don't believe that she won't come out of that hospital not fighting to get Jac back.'

'She's too full of herself,' Eileen added. 'I know I shouldn't say it about my own daughter, but she's only thinking of number one.'

'She'll take Jac, Laura, more for spite than anything else. She hates losing. Always has done. I suppose, being the only child, we spoiled her.'

'No suppose about it – we did. And we've got to face that fact. It's our fault as much as hers, the way she's turned out.'

'What are you trying to tell me? That she's gonna have another go at kidnapping Jac? Is that it?' Laura said.

'We think she'll attempt to take him whichever way she can. And we all know the courts won't look favourably at her now. So there'll only be one course she can take – and she will take it, believe me.'

'No ... I think you've just got yourselves all stewed up. I saw her yesterday and she apologized. Said she would get out of our lives if it was what we wanted. She looked genuine enough.' Laura shrugged. 'Unless I'm a complete fool and she's taken me in.'

'She's up against the wall, Laura. She'll say anything. And she can be convincing.' Albert lowered his eyes. 'Very persuasive.'

'So what are you saying? That I should alert the police, or what?'

'No. We're warning you to be very careful, that's all.'

'Oh well, I'm sorry ...' Laura stood up, 'I can't live my life worrying that she might take him when I'm not looking. I'll go round the bloody bend!'

'Please don't tell the police what we've said, Laura!
She's in enough trouble as it is.' Eileen twisted her
handkerchief into a knot. 'Just don't listen to her lies,
that's all.'

'I won't go to the police, it's not my style. I'll see Patsy.
I can handle her.' Laura looked at her watch. 'I would
offer you a cup of tea, but I don't want Jac to...'

'I didn't hear the street door. They couldn't have gone
out.'

'No, possibly not. Jac is probably firing questions
at Kay and refusing to go to the park.' She was getting impatient with them. She wanted them out of the
flat.

'I'm sorry, but I would really like you to leave now,
before the doctor arrives or Jac barges in here and...'
She pushed her hand through her hair. 'Please...? Just
go.'

'It's not serious is it, Laura?' Albert said.

'No.' Laura felt like screaming at them but she didn't
dare raise her voice.

Albert looked at Laura and shrugged. 'I'm sorry, I just
thought—'

'I'm very pleased you came. I appreciate it. You did
the right thing. Now just leave it with me. Please.'

Once she had finally closed the street door behind
them, Laura heaved a long sigh of relief. 'Dear God,' she
murmured, leaning on the door, 'help me get through
this bloody nightmare.'


'Well, Mr Armstrong, it would seem that you've been
putting a brave face on it.' The Asian doctor smiled at
Jack. 'From what you have been telling me you have

had quite a lot to think about. And worry can be the cause of so many ailments. What you must do now is rest. And maybe have a friend around, a good friend. One with whom you can talk things over. Is there someone...?'

Jack thought about it. He thought about his mates down at the docks and there really wasn't anyone he could think of that he was close to. Apart from Liz and Billy, Laura and Kay, there wasn't anyone whom he could call a close friend.

'Bert...' He nodded slowly. 'Bert.' He swallowed and sucked on his bottom lip. 'He was my best friend.' Jack pulled his handkerchief from his pocket and blew his nose. 'He died a few years ago. It was all very sudden. Here one minute – gone the next.'

'And did you grieve for him?'

'Of course I did!'

'Let me put it another way. Did you cry as much as you wanted to at the time?'

'Cry? Do me a favour. I was too bloody busy to cry, doctor, fighting the management at the docks. We joined the unofficial strike, and you know why? Because Bert's job was given to a non-union man. A casual labourer.' Jack shook his head. 'That would 'ave killed Bert if he was alive.'

'You threw yourself into the cause, eh?' The doctor smiled and snapped his bag shut. 'Anything so that you wouldn't have to face up to your grief. Losing a close friend, a best friend, can be the worst loss of all.'

'You don't have to tell me that,' Jack said. 'But what was I supposed to do? I had to keep a smile on it for the sake of my sister, my Lizzie.'

'Your sister?'

'She was Bert's wife. They'd bin married for years.'

'Well, then it's even worse than I first thought. You not only lost a friend but a brother too.'

'Doctor.' Jack pushed both hands over his face. 'What are you trying to do? Make me feel worse, or what?'

'I'm trying to make you cry, Mr Armstrong. What you need is a bloody good cry!'

Jack widened his eyes. 'I know, but I won't. What good would it do?'

'You won't cry?' Again the doctor smiled.

'No, I won't.'

'But you are, Mr Armstrong. You are crying. Those tears are yours, not mine. And I think there are a lot more where they came from, don't you?

'Now then – I'm going to leave you a bottle of tonic and a prescription for some mild tranquillizers. They won't affect your ability to work. Although my advice to you is to take a few days off. Rest. Enjoy your daughter and your little boy. Enjoy the beautiful rays of the sun instead of craning your neck to see what's behind it.'

'Yeah, OK, I think I know what you're saying . . .' Jack narrowed his eyes. 'You're a clever man, Doctor,' he grinned.

'For an Asian.'

'Now I never said that—'

'It was my joke, Mr Armstrong. As an Asian I am allowed to make fun of our race. It's when other people make fun of us that we can be insulted. Who is the young man?'

'Zacchi? Now there's another story! Ah well, at least she's got him to help her get over her husband.'

291

'Mmm. He looks like a Romany.'

'Yeah, he is.'

'And you've known him for a long time?'

'Seven years, maybe more.'

'Yet when I asked about a friend you didn't put his name forward.'

'It takes time to make a friendship. A proper friendship,' Jack said, annoyed that this man was so astute.

The doctor laughed at Jack. 'Seven years? How long do you need?'

'Point taken. When should I see you again then?'

'When you are taken ill again – if I am on call. I'll see myself out.'

Once the doctor had left, Jack's family filed in to see him as if he were in hospital. 'Did he give you some medicine?' Jac asked.

'Yeah. Why? Do you want some of it?'

'No I don't. What's the matter with you then? Why can't you get up off the settee?'

'I can, Jac. But I don't want to. I like it 'ere, it's nice and comfortable.' He looked down at Conker who seemed to know that something was wrong. He was lying quietly, not moving a muscle, and looking dolefully at Jack.

'Come on, Conker boy, up you come!' Jack slapped his own leg. 'Come on then.' Yapping and wagging his tail, the puppy leapt on to Jack's makeshift bed.

'Where's Zacchi?' Jack asked. 'Not gone has he?'

'No, I'm still here,' Zacchi said, keeping in the background.

'Oh right. Good. Fancy coming round the Carpenter's for a pint?'

Laughing, Zacchi threw his head back and held up his hands. 'Ask Laura, Mr Armstrong – I don't want to get into any more hot water.'

'What's with the Mr Armstrong bit? It's Jack. And I don't have to ask my wife's permission to go to the pub. Never have done, never will. Down you get, Conker!' Lifting his leg too quickly, Jack caught the puppy and caused him to roll over and drop to the floor.

'Dad!' Jac swept his pet into his arms. 'That was cruel!'

'It was an accident, for Christ's sake.' Pulling himself to his feet Jack stood for a few seconds to check that he was all right. It wouldn't do for him to pass out in front of everyone.

'Come on Zacchi, let's get out of here. I could murder a pint of Guinness.'

'Can I come, Dad? Me and Conker'll wait outside. I like sitting on the step and as long as I've got my crisps and cream soda ... I won't keep opening the pub door – honest.'

'Come on then.' Jack turned and looked at his wife and daughter who were obviously not pleased. 'Coming?' he said, as if nothing had happened. As if he were one hundred per cent fit.

'No, you go. I'll put *my* feet up,' Laura said.

''Kay?'

'No, that's all right, Dad. You go. I'll see you later, Zac.'

Once they had slammed the street door behind them, Laura picked up the pillow which had slipped off the settee. 'I don't know whether I'm relieved or angry.'

'I think it's a mixture of both, Mum.'

'Yeah. You could be right,' Laura said, walking from

the room. 'I suppose I had better put the joint in the oven or we'll be having dinner at midnight. What a bloody morning.'

Opening the hatch door Kay looked into the kitchen from the front room. 'Do you want to hear all the details then? About Steve and everything?'

'If you like.' Laura tipped potatoes from a shopping bag into the sink ready for peeling.

'I don't want to bore you,' Kay said jokingly.

'I won't be bored.' Laura began to peel a potato, relieved that she had a reason to keep her back to Kay. She could feel herself sinking and she didn't want her depression to spread to her daughter. In truth, she had had enough too. What she really wanted was to fly away to an uninhabited island where she wouldn't have to see or deal with people.

She was glad that Patsy's parents had put her in the picture about Patsy, but here was another ordeal she was going to have to get through. And she would have to take it on by herself. There wasn't anyone she could share this with. Not Jack – he obviously wasn't as tough as he made out. Not Kay, she had too many problems of her own. Not Liz ... and certainly not her dad, whose senility alone was enough to worry the life out of his daughter.

'Just try to imagine what it was like, Mum, when I found that receipt for a single rose in Steve's pocket.'

'I can imagine.' Laura could do more than that. She could go right back to the time when she had first found the letter in Jack's pocket, four years ago. The letter from Patsy telling him how their two-year-old son was getting on.

'I mean, for Christ's sake! Hanging one of *her* paintings on *our* wall in *our* flat! What kind of a person would do that?'

Kay was talking six to the dozen and most of it was going in one ear and out the other. At least her daughter sounded happy, in a strange kind of way. Happy. The word floated through her head. *Happy. That would be nice, to feel happy again. To have no worries.* She cut the potatoes in half and dropped them into a saucepan.

'Zacchi will stop for a bit of dinner, won't he?' Laura said.

'If there's enough.'

'Oh yeah, there's enough. It's roast pork.'

'You told me that already. Anyway – so much for the Bahamas; sun, sand and sea...'

*Sun, sand and sea and my island for one.* Maybe it would happen one day. Not an island to herself, no, that would be asking for too much. But somewhere ... away from the crowds.

'So I suppose the next thing I have to do is contact a solicitor, start divorce proceedings. What do you think, Mum? Do you think I should take Steve to the cleaner's? He's making a bomb, you know. I don't see why I shouldn't have some of it.'

'That's why I went through your dad's jacket. I was going to take it to the cleaner's...'

'Dad's jacket?' Kay chuckled. 'What's that got to do with anything?'

*It's got just about everything to do with everything. If I hadn't found that note back then, I wouldn't have gone to Leicester to see Patsy. I wouldn't have Jac in my care. And I wouldn't have to go in and confront his real mother. Tell her she couldn't have her son. Tell her to go away.*

'I wonder how long Patsy Hemmingway will get?' Kay's voice broke into Laura's thoughts.

'What d'yer mean, Kay?'

'For fraud and deception. And it's seven years, you know, for kidnapping. Never mind the fraud.'

Laura turned to Kay. 'She'll go to prison?'

'Of course she will! What she did was serious! Once she's fit and well—'

'And you think she knows that?'

'Depends how badly her brain is damaged. If she comes out sound of mind, she'll be expecting it.'

'She hasn't got a lot to lose then, has she?' Laura fell silent. She felt increasingly uneasy. The threat of Patsy Hemmingway taking her Jac away hung over her still.

Later that day, after the family had enjoyed their Sunday roast, Kay and Zacchi went hand in hand for a long walk – to talk about their future.

'The one thing I don't want, Kay, is to tie myself down with a mortgage – not yet anyway. I'd rather rent than buy.'

'Me too.' She squeezed his hand, feeling happier than she had in a very long time. It was the same magical sensation she had experienced when they were first in love.

'I thought you wanted a house in the country?' He smiled into her face. 'Grow vegetables out the back and flowers in the front.'

Kay tossed her hair out of her eyes and laughed. 'You've got a good memory. I said that when I was fifteen.'

'I know. It's what worried me then. I'm a travelling man, don't forget.'

'Nothing wrong with that, Zac – for the time being. But what about when you've ... when we've, got children?'

'We'll walk over that bridge when we get there.' He put his arm around her waist and pulled her close, pleased that they had left the lazy scene in the Armstrongs' sitting room – Laura dozing on the sofa, Jack with his son on his knee, watching football.

'What's that word, Dad? I've forgot. The one that means you've bin given away?' asked Jac, suddenly.

'Not given away, Jac. Adopted. It's different.' Jack poured himself a beer and braced himself for what was to come.

Laura in her half-awake state pulled herself to. She also knew they were in for a session of non-stop questions, but this time it was what she wanted. At last they could talk openly about the secret which she had been carrying for too long.

''Ave we got any Cherryade?' Jac said, screwing up his face.

'No, you drank it all.'

'So why did Hem' adopt me then?'

'She didn't adopt you – we did.' Jack would have loved to sit his son down and explain everything from the beginning, but he knew better. Jac liked to ask questions.

'I thought she gave me to you?'

'That's right. She had you adopted. We adopted you. She gave you to us. Right?'

'Why?'

'Because I'm your dad. And I wanted you.'

'Didn't she want me?'

'Yes. But she couldn't look after you because the man she was gonna marry didn't want a ready-made family.'

'Who made me then? I thought you had to lie next to someone to make a baby.'

'That's right.' Jack pushed his hand through his hair. 'Why don't you go and have a lie-down, Laura?'

'No, that's all right, Jack. I would rather be in here so I can answer any questions Jac might want to ask me.' She was secretly enjoying Jack having to be direct with his answers for a change.

'Who laid next to Hem' then?'

'I did. She's a pretty lady and I liked her.'

'Don't you like her any more then?'

'Yeah – but I like your mum better.'

'Thanks!' Laura threw him a look to kill. 'I wouldn't mind a glass of that beer now.'

'You see, Jac,' Jack said, pouring Laura's drink, 'sometimes grown-ups are a bit naughty. I shouldn't really have laid next to Patsy 'cos I was already married – to your mum. You're not really supposed to do that. But I did.'

'And that's when you made me?'

'That's right. So you see it caused a bit of a problem. I wanted you once you were born, but so did Patsy. But I belonged here, with your mum and Kay. So Patsy kept you and I popped up to Leicester now and then to see how you was doing.'

Laura was amazed at the way he was explaining it away as if it was something which was an everyday occurrence. 'Your dad shouldn't have laid next to Patsy, Jac. It was wrong. But I never told him off because you were the result of it, and we love you. So a naughty thing turned out to be good in the end.' She could feel her temper rising but managed to keep it in check.

'What about Kay? Who laid next to Dad to get her?'

'I did,' Laura said, suppressing a smile. 'And if your dad hadn't gone off with Patsy, I might 'ave been the one who laid next to him to get you.'

'She was your girlfriend.' Jac sipped some of his lemonade and giggled. 'Dad's got a girlfriend.'

'*Had*,' Jack said.

'And I've got two mums. One I live with and one who'll come and see me.'

'That's it. Right. Now then, what's on the telly?' Jack picked up his Sunday paper, hoping that was the end of it.

'There's a girl in our class who's getting adopted. Her mum's got six kids and can't afford her as well so they're selling 'er. Did you 'ave to buy me from Patsy, Mum?'

'No, Jac. Children don't get sold. You give them to people who want another child...'

'So we're not worth any money then?' Jac frowned and thought about it. 'I remember Dad saying I was worth a million pound.'

'You are,' Laura said, 'but you're not allowed to buy or sell children. Otherwise I would sell you tomorrow,' she grinned and tousled his sandy hair.

'Would yer?'

'Tch, I was kidding, Jac. 'Course we wouldn't.' Laura could have kicked herself for possibly starting up another stream of questions.

''Ave I missed my programmes?' Jac peered at the television page of Jack's newspaper.

'Football's finished in ten minutes. Don't you wanna see the end of the match?'

'No. Can I take Conker round Grandfather's? I wanna tell him about my other mum.'

Jack looked sheepishly at Laura. 'You'd best ask your mum about that.'

'Yeah,' Laura chuckled, 'come on. We may as well get that bit over with. Go and put his lead on. If they're not in we'll take a walk down the Park and look for 'em. That's where they'll be.'

'He's gonna buy some chicks next week, down the animal market. I'm going with 'im.'

Laura sighed. 'Let's hope he comes back with chicks this time and not another surprise pet!'

Sitting in his favourite armchair, Billy sipped his mug of tea and enjoyed the late afternoon sun as it streamed in through the living-room window.

'Billy?'

''Ello?' He looked up and grinned at Liz. 'What's up?'

Pressing her hand against her mouth, Liz failed to stop herself laughing. 'You've...' She couldn't finish the sentence. 'Your teeth...'

'What about 'em?'

She cleared her throat. 'They're in upside down.' Her willpower to the fore, Liz managed to hold her deadpan expression. 'You've put your bottom set into your top gum.'

''Ave I?'

'Yeah.'

Billy ran his forefinger across his false teeth. 'You sure?' He stood up and peered at himself in the round wall mirror. 'Gawd 'elp us, so I 'ave!' He rubbed his chin. He couldn't understand it. 'That's why I couldn't get my bottom row in then.'

'I should think so, yeah.' Liz slowly shook her head. 'And why're you wearing that tea cosy on your 'ead?'

Taking out the false teeth, he pushed his face closer to the mirror. 'That'sh not a tea coshy, you daft fing. It'sh Beatie'sh old hat. She knitted thish hershelf.'

'Put your teeth in Billy, for gawd's sake,' Liz started to laugh, 'and take that bloody thing off.'

'It'sh keeping me head warm, gal.'

'Scorching hot bloody day! You don't need that!' She pulled it from his head and went into the kitchen.

Leaning on the sink, Liz wondered what she was going to do about Billy. His mind was deteriorating, there was no doubt about it. And yet he was so bright most of the time. And since there wasn't any medication for absent-mindedness, there seemed little point in dragging him off to a doctor. Billy had no idea how forgetful and mixed up he had become. As far as Billy was concerned, he was in tiptop order. So who was Liz to smash his little world to bits? *Best forget it, Liz, and enjoy some of the things he gets up to*, she told herself, *you wouldn't miss the laughs for the world – you know you wouldn't. Forget the sad side*. The sound of Jac banging on the street door brought Liz out of her rush of concern. So long as Billy caused no harm to himself, she would leave well alone. Let things take their natural course.

'I'll get it, Liz!'

'Have you put your teeth in?'

''Course I 'ave!'

He was speaking properly so Liz could only hope that when Billy opened the door she wouldn't hear laughter from the caller – whoever it was.

The sound of Conker yapping pleased Liz. Billy loved that puppy and the puppy loved him.

'Put that kettle on, Lizzie,' Jack yelled, 'we've all turned up!'

'No Kay again? Must be weeks since I've seen 'er,' Billy said.

'Don't exaggerate, Dad.' Laura kissed him on the cheek. 'Jac tells us you're gonna buy some chicks after all.'

'Am I?'

'Well *he* thinks you are. Reckons you're taking him down the animal market again.'

'That'll be nice. Yeah. I wouldn't mind that.' He held his arms out to Jac. 'Hello, sonny boy!'

Hugging his grandfather, Jac looked up and grinned. 'Guess what I've got?'

'What's that then?'

'*Two* mums!'

A hush fell upon the room as they all looked from one to another. 'That's lucky, innit?' Billy didn't know what else to say.

'Jac's got quite a story to tell.'

'I can tell you now, Aunt Liz – about when I went out and didn't say where I was going.' Jac sat on a chair and pulled Conker on to his lap. 'I was nearly taken off to Scotland!' he said, intent on getting as much out of the drama as possible.

'Make the tea will you, Billy,' Liz said as she pulled her pillbox from her pocket. 'I think I need to sit down.' She slipped one of her tablets under her tongue.

'OK, Liz?' Jack asked, not looking directly at her.

'Give me a minute.'

'My other mum tried to take me back. But I got away,' Jac said proudly.

'And that's why he shook like a leaf that day – he'd been scared stiff,' Laura said.

'I wasn't scared!' He hunched his shoulders and splayed his hands. 'I was out of breath!'

''Course you weren't scared! He was being a brave soldier,' Billy called from the kitchen.

'Everything's all right now though, Aunt Liz. She's not dead. Just banged 'er 'ead, that's all. She'll be out soon. I'll fetch 'er to see you.' Full of confidence now, Jac stretched his legs and stroked his dog. 'She's Dad's old girlfriend.'

'How the pigeons come home to roost, eh?' Liz slowly shook her head, looking at her brother Jack. She sometimes felt like strangling him.

'Grandfather 'asn't bought pigeons, 'as he?'

'No I bloody well haven't! What d'yer think I am – a circus?' Billy placed the tea tray on the table. 'You can help yerselves once that's brewed.' He looked at Liz. 'Where've you put the Bourbon biscuits? I've searched the bloody fridge, I can't find 'em.'

'In the biscuit tin – in the cupboard,' Liz said patiently.

'Oh right.' Billy shielded his eyes from the sunshine as he pulled the curtain across one side of the window for shade. Then, staring out thoughtfully he said, 'So what you're saying, Jack, is that I own everything out there. Everything that I can see and more.'

Jack raised his eyes and looked into Liz's drawn face. 'Did I hear right?'

Liz put one finger to her lips and then mouthed the words to Jack: 'Just go along with him.' The expression on her face conveyed that this was no joke.

'That's right Billy, yeah. Everything you can see. The brewery, the houses, the lot.' Jack shrugged his shoulders at Laura, wondering what was coming next.

'Ah well...' Billy said, keeping his back to them. 'Not much good to me now. You have it, Jack. Not the Tower, though. I don't own that. That belongs to the Crown.'

'You can't see the Tower of London from that window, can you?' Jac said.

'No, that's right sonny boy, I can't. But if you walked to the line where my land ends you could see it. I don't suppose my valet's turned up yet, Liz?'

'No Billy. I think he's buggered off.'

'Liz?' Jack nodded towards Billy.

'Leave it,' she whispered. 'I'll tell you later.'

Turning to face four bemused expressions, Billy looked a little surprised to see them all sitting there. 'Well, pour the tea out, Beattie,' he said, looking at Laura.

'So,' Liz said, moving the focus of attention away from Billy, 'it's all turned out OK then? And you're gonna tell us all about this new mum that's turned up?'

'If you want,' Jac said, cuddling Conker. 'It's up to you.'

'Come over 'ere then and sit on Aunt Liz's lap.'

'I was thinking about Billy Graham earlier on,' Billy said, staring at nothing, a glazed look in his eyes. 'How comes one man can attract all that attention? There must be something in it. Must 'ave bin thousands in Victoria Park that day. All sorts of people. All mingling together ... Catholics, Methodists, Christians, Jews ... all drawn together to listen to one man.'

'The man's a performer, Billy – looking for a stage,' Jack said. 'A natural. Could do with him to speak out for the dockers.'

'Nar ... sorry, Jack mate, it's more than that. Stage? The man was talking to us from the back of a bloody coal lorry!' He slowly shook his head. 'And he made a lot of sense, going over all the terrible things that are going on in this world. I remember reading once – can't for the life of me think where I saw it – a little sign next to a work of art: *The gifted create – the foolish destroy*. That's what Billy Graham was saying really ... God created all the trees and flowers and the sea, and what are we doing? Destroying it. Slowly but surely. We create things like the hydrogen bomb—'

'What did the evangelist 'ave to say about evil, Billy? How come God allows all that to happen, eh? Rape, murder, violence ... disease.'

'Never mentioned that ... well, not in that way. Said we're sinners who could save our own souls.'

'I've never 'eard such a load of rot.'

'Well it's all in the Bible, Jack.'

Pushing his shoulders back in agitation, Jack lit himself a roll-up. 'He's a good crowd-puller, that's all. Got magnetism, and a bloody good backing group – all

good-looking. All with good voices. Everyone likes a
singsong – he knows that. That's why people go. Not to
find God on the back of a bloody coal lorry.'

'He frightened me,' Billy murmured. 'Kept shouting
and pointing his finger.

'Well we'll find out, won't we, Jack? Once we get up
there. We can ask all the bloody questions we like.
Who knows – perhaps there is a need for sin?' Billy
murmured.

'Up where?' Jac asked.

'Heaven, sonny boy.'

'You reckon there is one then?' Jack pulled out his
tobacco tin and grinned at Liz. She threw him a filthy
look. One that told him to shut up.

''Course there's a heaven,' Billy said. 'I'll be very
disappointed if not, I'll tell you that much. If this *is* all
there is!'

'I wish I had gone with you now,' Laura said, handing
her dad a cup of tea. 'A month ago, wasn't it? A lot's
happened in that short time.'

'Well you've missed your chance! He ain't gonna come
back to the East End again – not for years anyway. We
should 'ave *all* gone!'

Billy sipped his tea and seemed to be in a world of his
own. Liz recognized the look. She was used to it. He
could sit like that for an hour or more. Then he would
come out with something so unexpected it would make
her laugh.

'Do you wanna 'ear about my other mum or not, Aunt
Liz?'

'Yeah, go on then Jac, fire away.'

'Now then ... which bit shall I tell you first?' Jac

mimicked his grandfather and stared ahead thought-fully. 'Oh yeah – when I first saw her, when she was a dinner lady at my school...'

'What was that all about then, Laura? Your dad going on about owning land and having a valet? Bit much, wasn't it?'

'Liz told me he was getting forgetful and a bit muddled at times, but I didn't realize it was that bad. She reckons it's senile dementia.'

'Yeah well, I can't say the thought hasn't crossed my mind before now. He is getting forgetful, I'll give you that. But all that talk about Billy Graham and the next world—'

'Yeah, all right Jack. Don't go over it.' Laura didn't want to think about it. 'We'll keep our eye on him and if it gets worse, I suppose we'll march him off to see someone.'

'You must be kidding! Billy, go to a specialist? That *would* finish 'im off.'

'Well what then? What're we supposed to do? Bury our heads in the sand? Pretend it's not happening?'

'Not much else you can do, Laura. It's old age. We'll just 'ave to hope that Liz can cope. She'll soon tell us if she can't.'

The living-room door slowly opened and Jac's face appeared. 'Dad, if Grandad owns the brewery – why d'yer 'ave to buy beer from the pub?'

# Chapter Eleven

Taking Kay an early-morning cup of tea felt like old times for Laura. As much as she was sorry that her daughter's marriage had broken up, she was pleased to have her back in the fold, if only for a few days.

'I'm leaving for work now love – shall I drop Jac off at Billy's, or will you be stopping here today?'

'He can stay with me,' Kay said sleepily. 'I might go back to the flat and pack some of my clothes, but if I do he can come with me. He loves a train ride.'

'Good. That's a weight off my mind.'

'Why? He's usually all right with Grandfather, isn't he?' Kay sipped her tea.

'Billy's not getting any younger, Kay, I don't like to take liberties with him and you know how draining Jac can be.' Laura didn't want to tell Kay what was really eating away at her. The threat of Patsy lurking in the background.

'Is he up yet?'

'Playing with Conker, in his room.'

'Oh right. Let's hope he stays in there for a while,' Kay

joked, 'so I can drink my tea in peace and wake up properly.'

On her way to work, Laura decided that she would go to the hospital first – she had told her boss about some of the family problems, so he would understand why she was late. No matter how hard she tried, she couldn't push the worry, instilled by Patsy's parents, from her mind. Three times she had woken during the night and always with the same thought. What had they seen in their daughter to cause them to visit Laura and warn her to take care? Their own flesh and blood: their only child. Had Laura not been so worried about Jack, and upset about Kay's bruised face, she would have asked more questions instead of pushing the Hemmingways out of the flat.

As she arrived at the door to Patsy's room Laura clenched her fists, willing herself to remain calm. She had to find out the truth.

Nothing could have surprised her more than the sight of Patsy out of bed with her hair freshly washed and her make-up on. She was still in her nightdress but a set of clothes was laid out on the bed and she was putting her toiletries into a bag.

'Packing ready to leave? It's a bit sudden, isn't it?' Laura said, trying to keep the suspicious tone out of her voice.

'Oh! You made me jump, Laura. I wasn't expecting visitors this early.' Patsy blushed but kept her composure.

'I'm discharging myself. I've spent nearly two days showing the doctors how clever I am. I think I've earned my right to leave.'

'And they know you're going, do they?'

'Not exactly. I'll tell them when I'm ready to vacate. Someone more needy should have my bed. It's only fair: enough time's been wasted on me.' She drew a deep breath. 'I don't deserve all the kindness.'

Carefully folding her nightgown, she laid it in her overnight case. 'Once I've sorted myself out, it's back to Leicester to settle down to a nice job again. All I want is a quiet life now.'

'And where will you stay until then?'

'Jubilee Street. I got my mother to phone Esther Simons and ask if I could stop for a week or two, until I was ready to go. She said yes. All thanks to my parents – she likes them. They get on very well.'

How she could tell Laura had no idea, but she had never been more sure in her life: Patsy was lying.

'What about the police? Won't they want to see you? Before you go back?'

'I'm hoping they won't be informed that I'm discharging myself yet, Laura. All I want is a bit of time before I have to face them.' She ran a hand through her hair. 'I can't take all those questions, not yet.'

'And you won't wanna see Jac during this ... convalescing period?'

'No,' Patsy said resolutely. 'I'm going to stay out of your way. I'll leave it to you to decide when he should see me. If you want him to see me, that is.'

'I don't believe you.'

Patsy looked up, 'Laura, how could you say a thing like that, after we got on so well...'

'Your parents came to see me. They're not so sure that you won't try to steal my boy away again.'

311

'*Your* boy?' Patsy spoke without thinking.

'Yes. *My* boy.'

'God, Jack said you were hard, but—'

'I'm going to make sure that when you leave here you'll board a train to Leicester – the same day!'

'I don't think so.' Patsy smirked. 'You're letting your imagination run away with you, Laura. What will you do – put a gun to my head?'

'No.'

'Look at yourself for God's sake. Who do you think you are? Making threats—'

'It's not a threat. I mean to see you off.'

'By force?' Patsy looked into Laura's eyes. 'Just you try. I'll scream blue murder.' She folded her arms defiantly and waited. But Laura was not going to be goaded into action.

'Actually, it would be in my interest if you did try to manhandle me,' Patsy chuckled. 'It'd add to the story that I'm thinking of relating to the press, about you. About your not telling my son that he's been adopted. And how you've stopped me from seeing him. How I had to go to such lengths to try and get my baby back.'

She stuck out her chin triumphantly. 'The journalists will love it – and so will the readers. Your name will be mud, and the authorities will make you give me my son back – in time. All in good time.'

'So your parents were right. You had no intention of giving up.'

'I suppose they must know best,' Patsy shrugged.

'The nurse told me that you're not supposed to leave here until tomorrow. What's the rush?' Laura had to will herself not to smack Patsy's smug face.

'I'm bored,' she said conceitedly. 'These surroundings don't suit me.'

'I think there's another reason. I think you're worried in case the police are waiting to hear that you're ready to be interviewed, and since you've got through Saturday and Sunday without them coming you daren't risk another day.'

'Think what you want. There's nothing you can do about it. Unless you want me to phone the local newspaper and tell them to get here pronto!' She closed her case. 'They could take a photograph of us. I can just see the headlines: "Local woman threatens mother of her adopted child as she crawls from her sick bed!"'

'OK Patsy – on the bed.' Staff nurse Lisbon appeared in the doorway. 'Well now – don't you look a pretty patient! Taken a shine to one of the doctors, have we?' she joked.

'I just thought I would make an effort,' Patsy sighed and climbed on to the bed. 'I don't have to have physio this morning, do I?' she said, childishly, amusing the staff nurse.

'It's for your own good.'

Leaving Patsy to her play-acting, Laura walked quickly along the corridor, determined to carry through her resolution to phone the police once she was at work. Eileen and Albert's visit had confirmed that they were just as sure Patsy was in fact dangerous.

Passing a small café off the Whitechapel Road, Laura felt the need of a few minutes by herself with a strong cup of tea and a cigarette. She wanted a little time to sort out her mind. Maybe she was over-dramatizing things – maybe Patsy would go away and never show her face again. Maybe her family life would soon be back to the way it was just a few months ago, normal and quiet, with her and Jack just getting on with life. Ordinary, simple, boring life. She smiled at the thought of it.

Tucking into their breakfast of smoked haddock and poached eggs, Liz and Billy listened to the news. 'This is lovely, Liz. You're a bloody good cook, you know that?'

'I've made a fruit cake for tea an' all,' she said proudly.

'Followed by a bit of the other if I'm lucky,' Billy said, keeping a straight face.

'You'd like that, would you?'

''Course I would. Who wouldn't?'

'And you reckon you're up to it, do you?'

'Dunno, but we'd soon find out, wouldn't we?' he grinned.

Ending the conversation there, Liz tried to imagine her and Billy making love. It would be a laugh if nothing else.

'I was up the hospital the other day, you know. They reckon I'm a bloody marvel for my age.' He forked a piece of haddock and dipped it into his soft poached egg. 'Fit as a bloody fiddle, apart from one thing.'

'Oh yeah?' Liz didn't bother to ask why he hadn't told her about the hospital appointment. He would tell her in his own time.

'I smoked strong tobacco, that was my mistake.'

'You haven't smoked for nearly a year now, Billy. I'm

surprised you managed to give it up. All credit to you. Will-power, eh?'

'Bit too late giving it up – that's my trouble. Should 'ave stopped years ago before it had gone too far.'

'Before what had gone too far?' A feeling of dread was creeping over Liz. What was he trying to tell her?

'When I think of all that money I've chucked down the drain, spending it on tobacco as if it grew on trees. Still, can't turn the clock back, can I? No. It's my own fault. If I had have given it up this would never have 'appened. And my savings would look healthier too.'

Liz refrained from asking him what would never have happened. She had a horrid feeling that she might already know the answer. Billy's rasping cough in the mornings, the pains in his chest, his slow weight loss. Maybe she had been wrong about the senile dementia: perhaps he was trying too hard, worried that his memory had been letting him down. But then Liz remembered his sudden speech the day before about owning half of London and having his own valet. Surely fate hadn't delivered him two cruel blows?

'That's why you regret not giving it up sooner, is it?' Liz could feel her heart thumping – dreading what it might mean. She didn't want to be having this conversation, but it would be unfair of her to change the subject.

'Nar ... that's not the reason.'

'Go on then, Billy – spit it out.'

'Cancer. On the lungs. Both lungs.' He pursed his lips and stared at the window. 'That's what tobacco's done for me.'

Pushing her plate away from her, Liz locked her fingers and took a deep breath. 'Who told you that?'

'Never mind who told me – I've seen the X-rays. It's bad news, gal, make no mistake.'

'What did the hospital say?'

'I just told you.'

'You know what I mean, Billy. What are they gonna do for you? What sort of treatment?'

'There won't be any treatment. They've given me three months.'

'That's a wicked joke! You should be ashamed of yourself!'

'Three months, Lizzie – that's all I've got left.'

'No love, don't. Don't say a thing like that to me, it's not fair. You know how sensitive I am. Don't joke about things like that, not to me. Take it back, eh? There's a good chap.' She looked pleadingly into his face, but she could tell by his fixed expression that he had delivered the truth, and that it was just as painful for him as it was for her.

She reached out and gave him her hand. 'How long have you known?'

'Officially? A couple of days – I think. Or was it last week? Anyway, what difference does it make? I've known for a lot longer than that. Didn't wanna face it. I put off going to the doctor's for as long as I could. He made an appointment at the hospital there and then.'

'So what they gonna do for yer?' She dried her eyes and blew her nose.

'Medicine.'

'Medicine? Is that it?' She sighed with relief. 'Billy, Billy, Billy! If they've only given you medicine it can't

316

be cancer, you daft old fool! There ain't no medicine for cancer.' She shook her head at him and laughed. 'You silly bugger.'

Billy squeezed her hand and tried to smile. 'Morphine.'

'No, you've got it wrong. Not morphine. You're getting all mixed up again.'

'Am I?' he murmured, a puzzled expression on his face. 'Shall I show you the bottle then?'

'Are you telling me . . .' She squeezed her lips together. 'Are you telling me there's morphine in this house?' She tried not to cry for his sake, but she couldn't help it. 'No . . . please, Billy, say it's not true . . . just for me, yeah?'

'I wish I could, Liz. I wish I could.'

'I knew I should 'ave made you eat your dinners,' she cried. 'You've not bin eating much, 'ave yer, not lately.' The tears were flowing now. 'I've noticed but I just thought you weren't keen on my cooking, that you'd become bored with it!'

Billy patted her hand. 'Come on, Liz. It's not as if I'm a young man. Seventy-seven next birthday – I've done bloody well for myself.' He slowly pulled his hand from hers and picked up his glass of stout. 'I shan't go out crying.'

'No, I don't suppose you will.' She took out her pill box and slipped a tablet under her tongue. 'You'll be the bloody death of me!'

'Now don't talk like that!'

Liz leant her head back and placed one hand on her chest. 'I'm sorry, Billy.'

'You OK?' He looked at her, worried. 'You usually are after a pill and that . . .'

''Course I'm all right. It'll ease in a minute.'

'Shall I get you a cup of tea?'

'Yes please. Make it weak though.'

Standing in the doorway, Billy looked back at her. 'All right, innit? I'm the one who's dying and you're the one who gets waited on 'and and foot!'

'Go and make the tea!'

Hearing him pottering around in the kitchen, her thoughts were in a whirl. She tried to imagine life once he was gone. Once she was alone. *First Bert, and now Billy. And I suppose I'll be next. What is it all about? What is the point?* Then she remembered her son David and the letter she had received the previous morning, telling her that his Australian wife had at last decided that she did want to start a family. *And that's what it's about, Lizzie. Birth. Life. And then death. We start at one post and we finish at another and somewhere in between we live ... the best we can.*

'I've put an extra sugar in for shock. All right?'

'Yeah. Ta, love.'

'Now then,' he said, as if he was addressing a meeting. 'I've got a proposition to put to you.' He sat down and looked into her eyes. 'How about us sharing the same bed? Not every night. Just a couple of nights a week. Cuddle up and be friendly. What d'yer say to that?'

Feeling herself blush, Liz shook her head. 'I don't know, Billy. You are a funny man. You sound as if you're proposing to me.'

'Well I am. But there's no point in bloody marrying yer if I'm gonna be in my box in three months' time. And you're already getting a widow's pension, so there's nothing to be gained there.'

His words sent another pain through her chest but since he was putting such a brave face on it, who was she to put him down? As he said, he was the one who was dying.

'My bed's a bit small . . .' She didn't know quite how to answer him.

''Course it is! It's a single, you dozy cow.'

'And yours *is* more comfortable. I did enjoy that one night when it was cold in the winter.'

'So did I. And what a pair of fools we've been to let it go this long before broaching the subject.' He leaned back and enjoyed the rest of his beer.

'I think I would still 'ave to keep my stays on though.'

'And your knickers?' He didn't think much of that.

'No – I never wear knickers in bed, Billy!'

'That's all right then. I noticed there was a nice gap just under the bottom eyelets. My hand'll slip under there all right.'

'Billy!' She laughed at him through her tears.

'And then when you're asleep I might just untie the pink laces and 'ave yer.'

'You sodding won't – dirty bleeder!'

'No?'

'No!'

'We'll see! It's that medicine. Eases the pain in me chest and makes me feel nice and relaxed and horny.'

'I can't believe I'm hearing this.' She hid her feelings well, for in truth, Billy was beginning to arouse her, talking about untying her stays like that.

'Well, you're in for a few surprises, gal, I can tell you. I might only 'ave three months in this world but as far as

I'm concerned, that's ninety-three days and ninety-three nights. Two thousand two 'undred and thirty-two hours.' He picked up his notepad and flicked through it until he found the page he was looking for. 'And ... one hundred and thirty-three thousand, nine hundred and twenty minutes! I haven't worked out the seconds yet.'

'You've worked all that out...?' Liz was amazed at the way he was handling the news he had only just been given – that in three months he would be dead. And there he was, working out how many minutes he had left. And he looked happy. It was a different Billy she was looking at. As if he was relieved to know that it was nearly over. Had he been in that much pain and not told her?

'Billy – there's something I want to say. And it's not because you're ill. It's crossed my mind a few times.'

'Go on then. You can say anything you like to me now, Lizzie,' he grinned. 'And I can say what I like to you – and to the whole bloody world!'

'I love you – d'yer know that? I bloody well love you. Don't ask me why.'

'Well you would do, wouldn't you? How could you resist me?'

She shook her head, in a world of her own. 'And I'll tell you something else. I feel like having sex with you, and that's the truth. You've been honest with me – I've been honest with you.' She dried her face and grinned cheekily. 'What d'yer say we go upstairs now?'

'See,' he laughed and splayed his hands, 'even at my age I know how to get a woman going. Come on.'

'I'd like to have a bath first.'

'Go on then, but just jump in and out again and leave

your water in for me. I'll 'ave a shave an' all. Put a bit of that aftershave on that Kay gave me last Christmas.'

'All right. And I'll use that talcum she gave me, and dab a bit of the perfume behind my ears – Coty Laymont,' she said in her mock-posh voice as she made for the door.

''Course, if you're gonna have a bath, you won't wanna get dressed again will yer? Won't wanna put your stays on?'

'That's true. I'll slip into that new apricot petticoat that Laura gave me last birthday. It's never been out of its wrapper.'

'Go on then. Before I change me mind.'

Lying in the bath, Liz wondered why she wasn't feeling more depressed about Billy's bad news. *Perhaps it's because he looks so well and sounds so happy. Maybe something happens once you know it's all coming to an end. Maybe the fight goes out of yer and you can relax and enjoy what's left.*

'You haven't fell asleep up there, 'ave you!' Billy called from the living room.

'No! I'm just gonna get out!'

While Billy soaped himself in Liz's bathwater, she took her best white cotton sheets out of the linen cupboard and found her favourite pillowcases with the forget-me-nots embroidered in one corner. If she had on more than just her petticoat she would have gone into the back garden and picked a few flowers for Billy's bedroom.

After tucking the top sheet tightly under the mattress and making perfect hospital corners, she stood back and admired her work. *Nice and fresh. Lovely.* She threw the

blue candlewick bedspread on top and smoothed it out
as Billy's voice suddenly boomed from the bathroom,
singing:

> *Take one fresh and ten-der kiss,*
> *Add one stol-en night of bliss,*
> *One girl, one boy, some grief, some joy,*
> *Mem-o-ries are made of this.*
>
> *Your lips – and mine, Two sips – of wine,*
> *Mem-o-ries are made of this...*
>
> *Then add the wed-ding bells!*
> *One house where lov-ers dwell...*

Chuckling to herself, Liz slipped in between the sheets
and waited for Billy, feeling younger than she had in
years. His mood seemed contagious. All she could think
about was that they had three whole months to enjoy
this new-found happiness. *I wonder if it would 'ave been
easier for me if I'd known in advance that Bert was gonna
die, instead of having him snatched away out of the blue?*
she asked herself.

'That was all right, wasn't it?' Billy said, sitting up in
bed, sipping his tea.

'It was lovely, Billy. I'd forgotten what it was like.'
Liz plumped her pillow. 'Very nice.'

'Shall we do it again?'

'What, *now*?'

'No, 'course not. It'd kill me off. In about an hour or
so.'

'No, I've got to be at work by ten.' She looked at his bedside clock. 'When's your next lot of medicine due?'

'Medicine? What medicine?'

'Your morphine.' Liz eyed him with suspicion.

'Morphine? Not me, gal. Penicillium. It's in my medicine cupboard, I think ... I'll take some when I get up. Don't wanna mix it with this tea.'

'Billy, you told me you was taking morphine – that you only 'ad three months—'

'I 'ave only got three months, according to the hospital. My lungs are full of cancer. Tobacco's done that.'

Liz shook her head and decided to forget it. She couldn't fathom Billy most times, so why try now? 'D'yer fancy another cup of tea?'

'Just the job. Bring some biscuits up as well.'

'I'm not fetching the tea up here! What d'yer take me for? I'm gonna get ready for work.'

'I've gotta get up then, 'ave I?' Billy said sulkily.

'If you want another cup of tea, yeah.'

Leaving him to bathe in his happiness and pride at scoring at his age, Liz went into the bathroom. She wondered when she should tell Laura and Jack about Billy's cancer. She would have to choose her moment very carefully. They loved the old boy as much as she did.

'That bit of the other's done me the world of good, you know that, Liz?' Billy dipped a biscuit into his piping hot tea. 'I'm not sure that I can manage it again tonight, though. Not twice in one day. But if you wanna raise me early in the morning ... if you know what I mean.' He winked.

'Yeah, all right Billy – I'll see how I feel.'

'Pretty good, I'd say,' he chuckled.

As she cut through the backstreets on her way to Hammond's, Laura met up with their family doctor. 'Hello, Mrs Armstrong. How is Jac?'

'Much better thanks. His grandfather bought him a puppy – that did the trick. Put the smile back on his face.' She hoped he wouldn't ask if they had found out if he had been through a traumatic experience. It was the last thing she wanted to discuss.

The doctor looked at his watch. 'I don't suppose you can spare a minute?'

'Of course I can, Doctor.'

'I was going to contact you today, funnily enough. About your father. I was going to ask you to call in at the surgery, but—'

'About his failing memory?'

'No, I'm not too worried about that. It's not unusual at his age. It's this business of him believing he's seriously ill. I expect he's told you.'

'No...? He hasn't said a word to me.'

'I've tried to tell him otherwise, but he truly believes he has cancer.'

'Cancer? Dad?'

The doctor put up a hand. 'No, no. He doesn't have it. That's the whole point. But neither I nor the hospital can convince him. He has some phlegm on the chest but that's all. They even let him see the X-ray at the hospital to ease his mind, but when he saw the slight shadow on the outside of his left lung, which was no more than a little fluid, he made up his mind it was cancer.' The doctor sighed. 'When he came back to see me afterwards, I told him to take his medication and come back in three months.'

'Tch – poor Dad, he must have been worried. He never said a word about it.'

'He doesn't seem that concerned, quite honestly.' Doctor Brynberg shook his head and smiled. 'He seemed more upset that he wouldn't see his chicks grow to be laying hens – after he had spent "good money" on wire mesh for their run! He asked me if I knew anyone who kept chickens in case they would like to buy it. I couldn't help smiling.'

'I wouldn't mind,' Laura said, 'he hasn't even bought the chicks yet. Just the mesh, so he could fix up his old chicken-run.'

'Well ... I should encourage him to buy his chicks. Take his mind off cancer. And please tell him you bumped into me and we had this discussion.' Doctor Brynberg shrugged. 'Maybe you can convince him he is very fit for his age.'

'Oh, don't you worry, Doctor – I know how to handle Billy-boy. I'm probably the only one who does. I'll get it into his thick skull all right, rest assured. To be honest with you, I have been worried about his memory and the way he gets things muddled.'

He shrugged. 'It happens. At least he doesn't live alone. Many have to.' The doctor tipped his hat, bade Laura good morning and walked away.

Once inside Hammond's, Laura made straight for the canteen. She wanted to ask Liz if Billy had mentioned his fears to her. Even though he hadn't got the disease, worrying about having it must be as bad.

'Have you got a minute, Liz?'

'Hello Laura, 'course I 'ave. Go and sit down and I'll fetch us both a cup of tea. D'yer wanna doughnut?'

'Too early for me. You have one though.'

'No – I'm watching my figure.'

Laura stood back and admired Liz. 'You look nice, Liz. Is that a new frock?'

'Yeah ... it's been hanging in the wardrobe since I bought it months ago. I thought the yellow flowers would cheer me up on a cloudy day.'

'But the sun's out in full ...?' Laura gave her a cheeky wink. 'Who's the lucky man then? Who's the lipstick for?'

'Wouldn't you like to know,' Liz said. 'Now go and sit down and let me get on. I'll 'ave the workers streaming in for their morning cuppa any minute.'

Settling herself, Laura mused on what the doctor had told her. She imagined Billy in the hospital, telling the doctor his job. She could just see him insisting on seeing his X-rays. *He must have driven the X-ray chap mad*, she told herself.

'Right then – what's on your mind?' Liz sat opposite Laura and brushed away some crumbs from the light blue Formica table. 'If it's bad news I don't want it,' she smiled.

'Billy!' Laura raised an eyebrow and sipped her tea.

'Oh,' Liz lowered her eyes. 'You've heard, then?'

'Heard what?'

'You wouldn't mention it if it wasn't the...' She pulled her little blue snuff tin from her apron pocket.

'Liz! Not in here!'

'Why not? The men smoke their pipes, don't they? Anyway, spit it out.'

'I would rather *you* told *me*,' Laura said, treading lightly, just in case Liz did know something she didn't.

'All right, Laura. I just hope we're talking about the same thing, that's all, because if we aren't, you're in for a bit of a shock. I was gonna come round and tell you tonight. I didn't wanna upset you at work.'

'Go on then.'

'You're dad's ... Billy...' She raised her eyes to meet Laura's. 'He's got cancer, Laura. In the lung.'

Laura shook her head and smiled. Seeing Liz's shocked face she quickly said, 'No he hasn't. He *thinks* he's got it. I bumped into Doctor Brynberg on my way to work. He filled me in. Dad's got a slight chest infection, that's all.'

'But he went on about only having three months to live! He wouldn't make up a thing like that!'

'Billy hasn't made anything up, Liz. He's just confused things a bit. Brynberg told him to go back and *see* him in three months, for a check-up.'

'Well I never!' Liz leaned back in her chair. 'And you're sure about this?'

'You gonna go and argue with the doctors as well, are you? The X-rays have shown he has some fluid on his lungs – and not much at that!'

'Well I'll be...' Liz said. 'Well that is good news, Laura, I can't tell yer. What a relief.'

'There's still the problem of his dementia, but the doctor didn't seem concerned about that. It's old age creeping on.' Laura stared down into the teacup in her hand. 'Or rushing on, more like...'

'I shouldn't worry too much about that, Mog!' Liz laughed. 'It's more funny than sad. Things he comes out with — I'll tell yer.'

'So he's not depressed and worried about himself then?'

Liz smiled to herself: *Hardly*, she thought. 'He was whistling like a mating-bird this morning when I left,' she said, full of herself.

'Oh yeah?' Laura picked up on her sister-in-law's confident mood. 'And why was that then?'

'You know what, Laura,' Liz said, leaning back in her chair, 'I think me and Billy should get married. Make it legal.'

'You what?'

'It's not godly, is it, people of our age having an affair? Yeah...' she said thoughtfully, a sparkle in her eye, 'a nice little wedding like our Kay 'ad.'

'Good God — you're serious!' Laura laughed.

''Course I am. I can see me in a long white dress, can't you?'

'Does Dad know about this yet?'

'Not yet, no.'

'*Liz* — when did all this come about?'

'That's my business,' she grinned.

'So the new look's for Billy. You pair of dark horses! You've lightened my day, you know that? But now I have to deal with one more problem. A telephone call is required.'

'Laura!' Smiling broadly, Liz called after her and showed a thumb. 'It was 'andsome!' Laura walked away shaking her head and smiling.

\* \* \*

*Fucking bitch cow!* Patsy fumed to herself as she hurriedly pulled on her skirt. She would leave anything she hadn't packed so far and escape from the hospital via the back exit, while the nurses were busy elsewhere. She would have to be quick, they were in and out like yo-yos.

She planned to get on a train, but not for Leicester. She would go where no one knew her name and she would buy a wig on the way. Then she would lie low for a while and work out a plan.

Once the corridor outside was clear of any nursing staff who might recognize her, Patsy stepped out of her room and wove her way between visitors, staff and patients who were taking a casual stroll between wards.

Stepping quickly down the stone staircase, Patsy heard the familiar voice of Nurse Carol on the flight below. Turning around she ran up the few stairs to the first floor and walked as fast as as she could while trying to look casual. Arriving at a door from which the cries of babies could be heard, she stopped in her tracks. A new thought came to her. If the police did act quickly and put out a description of her, no one would think to look out for a woman with a newborn baby.

She looked through the windows into the nursery and saw the row of cradles. *A baby*, she thought. *A baby to bring up as my own.* A smile crossed her face. Laura Armstrong could keep the six-year-old-Jac, who by now had probably grown to be just like the family he lived with. Seeing no staff around, she pushed open the door, picked up the first sleeping baby she came to, wrapped a blanket around it and walked out smiling proudly – as if she were the mother.

Strolling casually and remaining cool, she walked out of the main entrance and made her way to Whitechapel railway station. She remembered a hairdresser's along the Waste where they sold wigs. Quickly scanning the window, she spotted a long straight blonde one. Perfect.

Pointing at the hairpiece, she made her purchase efficiently and with a poised charm. It was a present for her sister who had been ill, she told the assistant.

With the baby on her lap, Patsy sat on a lavatory in the ladies' public convenience and pulled on the wig. She would check it in the mirror in the washroom and rearrange it if necessary. *Good baby*, she whispered to the sleeping infant. *We'll soon be as snug as a bug in a room somewhere far from here.*

Her next stop was Boots the chemist, where she purchased a dummy, a baby's bottle and some Cow & Gate powdered milk. Until she had found a room, the baby would have to make do with cow's milk in a carton from the vending machine in the station.

The cow, Laura Armstrong, had been right in her assumptions. The police had been waiting for a call from the hospital management. Patsy had succeeded in drawing the information from Nurse Carol. She was to be questioned once she was well enough. The hospital authorities had been aware of it, but because of the suddenness of Patsy's so-called remarkable recovery, they hadn't got round to making the call, and now she had slipped through their net.

While Patsy sat comforting the tiny baby in her arms, doing her best to act like the adoring mother, she tried to imagine what might be going on in the hospital. She smiled at the thought of Laura arriving with the police to find that Patsy had already made her escape. She imagined the pandemonium. The panic of the hospital staff and the distraught mother, when the horror of her baby missing was discovered. She felt the old surge of excitement shoot through her. It reminded her of the day she arrived at King's Cross with one purpose in mind – to win back her son. She had come a long way since then and there was not a shred of doubt in her mind as to where Jac's heart lay. She had won him over completely during his visit to the hospital. When the time was right, he would be putty in her hands.

Walking out of Barkingside Underground station, Patsy stepped up her pace. The baby had woken, and although the short outbursts of crying hadn't attracted any attention so far, she knew it wouldn't be long before hungry screams would promote unwanted interest from nosy bastards who had nothing better to do with their time.

She walked quickly along the streets from the station until she found a terraced Victorian residence with a sign in the window – *B & B Vacancies*. Patsy could only hope that the people who owned the house would not be averse to taking in a woman with such a small baby in her arms. If they were taking paying guests, the last thing they would want was a baby screaming at night, disturbing everyone. And who could blame them?

Picking up her suitcase Patsy took a deep breath, preparing her short speech, and climbed the scrubbed steps leading up to the large white door with gleaming brass letter-box and knocker.

'Ohhh,' crooned the middle-aged woman, 'what a little darling.' She carefully pulled back the blue blanket with one finger. 'Oh ... bless him.' She lifted her eyes and met Patsy's. 'Did you want a room, dear?'

'Just for one night. I'm moving on tomorrow, to my parents in Leicester.' This wasn't what Patsy had meant to say but she had been caught off guard by the drippy woman and had had to think quickly. The name of the town where she was known slipped out before she could stop herself.

'He's a very good baby and sleeps most of the time – especially at night,' she said, doing her best to sound maternal.

The woman stood aside and waved Patsy in. 'It's seventeen shillings for the room and full breakfast.'

'That's fine. Thank you very much. We won't be any trouble, I promise.'

'I'm Mrs Jones. I'll put you on the first floor. It's a lovely little room next to the bathroom.' She looked back over her shoulder at Patsy as she climbed the stairs. 'I expect you'd like some boiled water for his bottle? You don't look like you're a breast-feeder.'

'No; I couldn't,' Patsy lied. 'Milk fever.'

'Shame. Never you mind, dear. I brought up my third on the bottle and he's none the worse for it.' She unlocked the bedroom door and showed Patsy in. 'The sheets have been aired, and as you can see the room is very clean.' She stood back and admired mother and baby. 'Now then – you'll need a cot. It's pink I'm afraid, but I don't suppose the little mite will care about that. You settle yourself in and I'll put the kettle on. I expect you'll be ready for a nice cup of tea.'

'You're being very kind – thank you.'

'No trouble. It's nice to have a baby around the house again. Mine are all this high now.' She raised her hand above her head. 'I'll tell you what, why don't I make up the bottles for you?'

'I've, er, I've only got the one bottle...' Patsy shrugged. 'He's my first,' she smiled innocently. 'I'm not married...' she lowered her head in shame.

'I had a feeling you weren't. Men eh? Don't you worry – if your parents are behind you, that's more than enough.' She stopped in the doorway. 'Let me have his dirty nappy – I'll rinse it through for you. It'll be dry by the morning.'

'Thank you. I'll change him while you're making the bottle, shall I?'

'I should. Don't want him to be uncomfortable while he's having his feed, do we?'

Once Mrs Jones had closed the door, Patsy sighed with relief. All she had to do now was find something to replace the soiled nappy. Looking around the room she saw a small white towel on the rail next to the tiny bedroom sink. She would use that, and somehow keep the landlady out of the room so she wouldn't notice it was gone. But what preoccupied her more was a new thought which had only just hit her. The police would be looking for a missing baby as well as a patient from the hospital. They were sure to step up their search. She cursed herself for not having thought ahead. She would now have to make her second escape of the day.

Quickly removing the dirty napkin, she replaced it
with the clean guest towel and decided there and then
that she would not spend the night in this house. The
baby would – but not Patsy. She could easily make the
excuse that she needed to buy something from the
chemist's. She would have to forfeit her overnight case
and its contents. Her two favourite nightdresses were
in there, but that was a small loss by comparison. If
there should be anything reported about her, the
stupid cow downstairs might catch on and contact the
police.

Carrying the baby downstairs, Patsy stopped herself
from looking into its face. It wouldn't do for her to feel
remorse now, or, worse still, to grow fond of it.

'Excuse me . . .' she said in her little-girl voice, hovering outside the kitchen door as if she were too polite to
go in.

'Come in! Tch, I haven't even asked your name, have
I? Silly me.'

'Sarah . . . Sarah Jackson.'

'Oh, there! I called my first child Sarah. How funny.
Now if you'd like to sit down on that chair—'

'Mrs Jones, I hate to impose on you, but . . .'

'Yes dear, what is it?'

'I need to go to the chemist's . . . get some sanitary
towels,' she whispered.

'Ah. And you want me to feed Baby for you?'

'Would you mind?'

''Course not. I'm flattered to think you trust me. But
have a cup of tea first, eh?' The music playing on the
radio faded and six bleeps sounded – the news was about
to be announced, much to Patsy's horror.

Clasping her hand to her head, Patsy quietly groaned. 'Oh dear ... this headache ... would you mind awfully if we turned that off? It's very cheeky of me to ask but –'

Flicking the switch, Mrs Jones showed a hand. 'I only keep it on for company, since my husband passed away. Most of my guests keep themselves to themselves nowadays. People aren't as friendly as they used to be are they?' She opened a small cupboard and took out a bottle of aspirin.

'Oh no, that's OK, I've just taken something,' Patsy said.

'Oh well, I expect they'll start working soon.'

'Yes, especially when I take a walk to the shop. Walking always helps.'

'Does it? Well, well, well. I've not heard that before.'

'In fact, if you don't mind, I would rather go now and have my tea afterwards – if that's all right.'

'Of course it is, dear.' She held out her arms for the baby.

'There isn't a florist near by, is there? The nurses were so kind to me in the maternity ward, I would like to send some flowers.' Patsy needed a reason to be out longer than it would take to go to just one shop. She didn't want this woman becoming suspicious too soon.

'Ah, how thoughtful. Which hospital was it? The London?'

'No...' Patsy rubbed her forehead as if in pain. She couldn't think quickly enough. Couldn't remember the names of other hospitals in the area. 'Stepney,' she lied, hoping to keep Mrs Jones off track, should anything have been on the news.

'Oh, you mean the Bancroft!'

'Yes. That's it. Bancroft hospital.'

'Well now, let me think ... yes. Yes, there is a florist, but it's a good fifteen-minute walk, dear—'

'Oh, I don't mind that! I love walking.' She brushed her fingers across her forehead. 'And as I said, it will help my headache.'

'Well then, you go! And don't worry about...?' She looked questioningly at Patsy.

'David—' she said quickly. 'David John.'

'Ah ... that's nice. Yes, he looks like a David. Got plenty of hair, hasn't he? Bless him.'

Closing the door behind Patsy, Mrs Jones gripped the baby firmly in one arm, picked up the telephone receiver with her free hand and dialled 999.

Once outside, Patsy ran through the backstreet to the main road and hailed a taxi. 'King's Cross please!'

'King's Cross? That'll cost you a few bob, love.'

'Do I look like I'm down on my luck?' she said, half joking.

'No, as it 'appens. Sorry. It was out before I could stop it.'

'No harm done. But if you could step on it, I've got a train to catch.' Her tone made it clear she wanted no further conversation.

Leaning back in the seat, Patsy thanked her lucky stars that this driver was not a chatterbox but a good, fast driver who concentrated on the road. She would soon be free of London, the rent money from the duped tenants would see her comfortably through until she found herself a job.

She hoped that there would be a hairdresser's at King's Cross where she could buy another wig. She pulled a pair of glasses from her handbag and put them on. *A mousey-brown one this time, Patsy. To blend in with the dull mass of people.*

Her ticket clutched in her hand, she made her way towards the platform where she would board the train to Norwich. Catching sight of her reflection in a large window, she was satisfied with her disguise. She had removed all traces of make-up and with the boring, old-fashioned wig and the plain glasses, she looked almost middle-aged.

Settling herself in a seat by the window, Patsy rested her head as the train pulled out of the station. The headache hadn't entirely been a lie. There was a dull ache and it was worsening. She had taken some aspirin before boarding the train but they didn't seem to be working.

Feeling exhausted, she closed her eyes. Headache or not, she was ready for sleep. Once again her mind filled with Jac. She imagined the two of them running through fields sprinkled with poppies, laughing and holding hands. When the Armstrong family would be no more than a faded memory.

Leaning her head back, she began to drift into a light sleep.

'Your tickets please!' The voice of the ticket inspector broke into her thoughts, as he made his way through the train. She tried wishing him away, but his smell consumed her as he stood close by. A stale smell of cooked food and body odour.

Averting her eyes from his flushed face, she unclasped

her handbag and handed him her ticket without looking up.

'Patsy Hemmingway?' The voice of authority shot waves like an electric current through her entire body.

She stared up and peered at the two detectives standing behind the ticket inspector. 'I beg your pardon?'

The detective's face broke into a smile as he reached out and carefully lifted her wig. 'We'd like a few words...'

As Jack, Laura and Kay watched the evening news on the television, the reader was handed a piece of paper. 'News has just come in that the missing baby, taken from the London Hospital, has been found safe and well following information from a landlady in Barkingside who became suspicious when a woman registered at her boarding house carrying a newborn infant. The woman, who was a patient at the hospital, has been detained for questioning. There will be an update as soon as we have more information.'

'Jesus...' Laura murmured. 'It must be Patsy. She's finally flipped.' She slowly shook her head. 'I feel terrible, Jack. Maybe if I hadn't interfered and phoned the police, she would have just disappeared from the hospital and not taken that baby.' She stared out of the window. 'She's really done it this time.'

'Don't start feeling sorry for her, Laura. Can you imagine what the baby's family must 'ave been going through? When I think of all she's done – what she's put people through. Apart from the nightmare she's given Jac. Turning out poor old Esther Simons like that ... and now this.'

'How on earth are we going to explain this one to Jac? That his other mum is going to prison – or a secure hospital?'

'I suppose we have to don't we?' Jack said weakly, wishing to avoid more upset.

'Yes, Jack, we do. You know he'll ask questions.'

'I'll tell him,' said Kay. 'I'll tell him she's going to Holloway to be a dinner lady.'

'He'd probably believe that.'

'You're right, Jack – he would.'

'I'll spin him a yarn for you, on one condition.' Kay looked at Laura from the corner of her eye. 'That you come with me tomorrow when I meet Steve for lunch.'

'When you *what*?' Sometimes Laura could strangle her daughter. Surely she hadn't changed her mind again?

'He wants us to sort out divorce proceedings. He needs to be free to marry his *artist*.'

'No. It's not your mother's place to go with you, Kay. Zacchi's the one. Ask him.'

'You are joking, Dad?'

'You're gonna end up marrying him, ain't yer?'

'Yes, but—'

'Well, there you are then. The three of you should sort it out now. You should all lay your cards on the table. Make sure there'll be no repercussions later on.'

By the look on his face, both Kay and Laura could tell that he was referring to the mess he had made of his own life. And Kay knew that he was right. She wanted nothing from Steve but her freedom to be with the one she loved, Zacchi.

'And tomorrow I'll make inquiries about redundancy money. Then we'll find out if there are any nice little pubs available – in Dorset, not Kent.'

'Sounds good to me.' Laura smiled and winked at Kay. 'Let's get out of London – once the wedding's over.'

'Don't jump the gun, Mum! We don't intend rushing into anything. Anyway, the divorce'll take ages—'

'I wasn't talking about you and Zacchi. I was talking about Liz and your grandfather.' She rested her feet on the pouffe, pleased that she knew something they didn't. 'I think I'll wear red and navy with a nice big hat and—'

A sudden loud crashing shook the flat as Jac tried out his new drum set for the first time bringing Conker, running for his life, into the living room.

'Oh terrific!' Jack pushed his hand through his hair. 'Thanks a bundle, Kay. You couldn't 'ave bought him a better present. Oh well – there's no doubting his marvellous recovery now, is there?'

Travelling from the Old Bailey to Holloway Prison, Patsy ran her finger around the handcuffs on her wrist and smiled.

*You may have won this round, Laura – but I'll be out one day. And Jac will be that much older. Old enough maybe to make up his own mind as to which mother he would prefer to be with.*

Looking dolefully at the female officer to whom she was linked, Patsy managed a faint smile. 'I've caused so much trouble, haven't I? It's a hard lesson I've learned but I think I'll be a better person for it.'

The officer looked at Patsy, her face expressionless. It was hard to tell if she believed her or not. Lowering her head, Patsy managed to squeeze out a tear. 'A much better person,' she murmured. 'I owe it to my parents.'

As she glanced at the hardened face she thought she saw a hint of a smile. *You're a bloody marvel, Patsy. It won't be long before you'll have the entire prison staff wrapped around your finger.*

'You must despise people like me.'

'Shut it, Hemmingway! You're turning my stomach.'

'I'm sorry. I won't say another word.' *Bitch, cow, whore, dyke.*

'Just keep your mouth shut and you might survive in there.'

'Thanks for the tip.' *Slut.*

As the police car approached Holloway, Patsy's mind was filled with the face of her enemy, Laura Armstrong. Then she remembered the sickly Esther Simons with the tear dripping from her witch-like nose. Then it was the so perfect Kay who intruded. *Bitches, the lot of them.*

'Keep your hand still, Hemmingway.'

'Bollocks!'

The officer's robust laughter filled the police car. 'You won't last five minutes.'

*That's where you're wrong, vomit-face. I'll last till my time's up. Oh, and won't I be a star prisoner! One foot in each camp. Turning as many against each other as I can. Using the weak. Winning over the strong.*

As the car pulled into the prison grounds, the officer looked at Patsy and grinned. 'Face it, Hemmingway. This is another world, and—'

'I know that! And I can't wait.' She stuck out her chin defiantly. 'I've been trying to get in here for years.'

The look on the officer's face was the best tonic Patsy could have asked for. She had done it. She had got one over, and it felt good. She had a very strong feeling that she was going to enjoy her stay. She was feeling on top again.

SALLY WORBOYES

WILD HOPS

It is 1959 and emotions are running high in the Kent hop fields, where the harvest is traditionally picked by East Enders on their summer break. Picking by hand is becoming a thing of the past as mechanisation takes over. The Armstrong family – Jack, Laura and their daughter, Kay – are devastated by the news. Far from the bustle of Stepney, the hop fields offer hard work but fresh clean air and lively social gatherings around the campfires.

While Jack leads the protest against the machines, Laura Armstrong is otherwise preoccupied: will this mean the end of her seasonal love affair with the farm owner, Richard Wright? And what of Kay who, on the brink of womanhood, craves adventure and creates turmoil when she and the handsome gypsy lad, Zacchi, meet in secret?

As tensions grow between the East Enders and the local Romanies, it becomes clear that this summer will change lives for ever . . .

WILD HOPS is a vibrant tale of illicit love, firm friendships and the indomitable character of the East Enders.

'Sizzles with passion' *Guardian*

A Coronet Paperback

SALLY WORBOYES

BANISHED FROM BOW

Harriet was abandoned as a child in nineteenth-century London's East End. Ragged and terrified, she was forced to scavenge for her food. Mary Dean found her and took her to a smart house in Bow where she was brought up as a sister to Mary and her younger brother Arthur.

But 17 years later, Harriet and Arthur have fallen in love. Harriet soon becomes pregnant. Driven out of Bow by neighbours who spit at them and call them heathens, they seek refuge in two rented rooms in Stepney.

Eking out a meagre but free existence, they are happy – until Arthur, like so many others working as railway delivery-men, is caught pilfering and faces a prison sentence. This is soon to be the least of their worries. Harriet has kept a diary she stole as a child, the diary of the perpetrator of the Whitechapel killings. The Jack the Ripper murders. And now the owner of the diary has returned to the East End in search of Harriet and the diary – and will stop at nothing to get it back . . .

'Rich, vivid, gutsy and sexy – it will have you turning the pages into the early hours' *Eastern Daily Press*

A Coronet Paperback